CONTENTS

THE ADD CHRONICLES
Part One
Andrew David Dodge: The World's Worst Husband
(A Comedy, of sorts)

By Mike Legault

PREFACE

The ADD Chronicles and Film Fiction

This book is about an invention named Andrew David Dodge and his struggles as a husband, father, small business owner and, perhaps most significantly, a man in the landscape of 21st century America. It is written as a comedy; but, to paraphrase an adage, comedy and drama are flip sides of the same coin—the reason for the popularity of shows such as *Seinfeld* or *The Simpsons* isn't because they preclude the examination of sober topics, but because they put them in perspective, set within a world, dare we need reminding, of unremitting mortality. It's the same catharsis-at-a-distance provided by drama. If the assembled characters in this modest book shed some light on the limits and possibilities of life, and readers are entertained, and perhaps moved and delighted, then I've done my job and I rest my case.

I say this from the top, because I am keenly aware of the perils of serving up a book as an example of a "type" of thing; i.e. a genre, especially a new genre. The book, and the characters and actions comprising it, comes first, the classification, ideally, an irrelevant after-thought.

I did not set out to write a novel modeled on a three-act structure most typically, and tightly, embodied in traditional ("non-experimental") movies. It emerged, along with other "cinematic" elements, during the writing, naturally, almost without conscious reflection. Once I saw these cinematic aspects materializing, towards the end of the first draft, I realized it was the perfect vehicle for the story I wanted to tell. It also provided a ready-made mechanism for keeping the characters and action evolving, and a guide for where and when to place those action-turning events sometimes referred to as plot points.

The three-act structure is, of course, an ancient story-telling technique that was explicated, distilled and adapted for screenplays and movies by people in the film industry, most notably Syd Field. In this sense it is nothing new and my deployment of it to write this novel is just another example of the way it can be adopted, not as a formula, but as a basic form of organization, to give substance to an infinite variety of stories.

While tempted, I will defer at this time from delving into a detailed case for its unique adaptation to the novel, as represented by this book; as well as its role and future use as a flexible narrative device, encompassing all film *and* literary genres, to possibly cull back the dwindling and lost readership for fiction … Except to say, in a world dominated by the visual medium, perhaps it is time to return the visual to fiction? There may be a time and place for the bravado (and pretense) of a Film Fiction Manifesto. For now, I need to assume my proper role, disappear from these pages and allow the readers to read, and experience for themselves.

Enjoy, Mike

DEDICATION

To my daughters Kristen and Katherine, for whom I always attempt to be the best father

PROLOGUE:

Somewhere in Pakistan

Four bearded men in traditional Arab robes sit on the floor of a cave watching grainy, soundless video on a monitor: A smiling woman is kneeling next to shirtless toddler wearing diapers. The toddler is posing, holding a small baseball bat, evidently a birthday gift. The boy suddenly swings the bat into the side of a tall vase of flowers on the table, smashing it to pieces. The woman lunges for the boy, grabs the bat and whacks him hard on the diapers with her hand.

(In accented English)
"Home run!"

(Laughter)

A picture of an adolescent boy comes onto the screen. It is summer and the boy is wearing a bathing suit. The camera has trouble keeping the boy in view as he is constantly moving, darting back and forth, dancing a sort of spastic jig, then pretending to be a fish or monster with large teeth, then making a muscle and pointing to his arm. The camera pulls back and the viewers can see he is standing on top of a tall wooden platform next to a lake. The boy looks over the edge of the platform, then suddenly leaps spread eagled into the air, tumbling in a wild spin till he hits the water, sending up a spray of water as he lands full force on his face and chest. The camera stays on the boy, who appears to be unconscious, floating face down in the water. Then the picture jumbles, settling on a view of the lake's shore, as the body of another person flashes over the edge of the platform toward the water.

(In Arabic)
"Is that an oasis?"

"No, a lake. Rich American developers build them to sell homes on."

The close-up image of a young man flashes onto the screen. He is 19 or 20 and is wearing a shirt with three Greek letters on the front. The young man makes a goofy face, then kneels in front of what looks like a large slab of ice, tilted at an angle on top of a table, with a winding trough carved through it. The young man opens his mouth wide as another person standing at the top tilts a bottle and pours out a clear liquid onto the ice. The liquid runs along the icy trough and into the mouth of the young man. After a minute or two of drinking, the young man rises slowly to his feet, burps, wobbles, then falls flat on his back to the floor. The camera hovers over him, lying on the floor with his eyes closed. A foot nudges at his shoulder but he doesn't move.

(In Arabic)
"And this is the person with the secret?"

"Yes, the only one."

"Would it be hard to get it from him?"

The men look up at the monitor still showing the young man lying passed out on the floor.

(In accented English)
"Like taking candy from a baby."
(Laughter)

1 AN OFFER AND A COFFIN

Driving along a stretch of I-75 winding by the suburban office buildings, subdivisions and franchise restaurants north of Detroit, Andy Dodge's cell phone sprang to life, bleating a digital bass line, dum-dum-dum-da-da-dum-dum, the opening notes of *Under Pressure.*

"Dodge here."

"Mr. Nickel, let me guess, you're southbound."

"You got it."

"That means you're headed my way."

Andy paused. Shit! The lunch had slipped his mind.

"Yes, sir."

"You didn't forget about me, did you?"

"Absolutely not, Mr. Gloss."

Gloss chuckled, more at the officious "Mr." honorific than the lie. "That's good because it always lifts my spirits to see your sorry ass."

"The feeling's mutual."

"Besides, I've got something important to tell Mr. Nickel today."

"I'm there in 20."

It was a sun-splashed, late August day; a Friday at that. He was happy, as he usually was, and the prospect of the weekend and some much-needed down time buoyed his spirits into the realm of pure elation. The highway banked to the left with a sweeping view of a group of new 4,000-square-foot homes built in a faux English manor style with large-stoned, three-story turreted facades, crescent driveways and huge arched foyers. "Yeah baby!" Andy shouted pointing, channeling his salesman's instinct which informed him any sign of prosperity was in his best interest. He had already made two sales calls and was planning on hitting a bucket of balls before heading back to the office. Tonight, was his fantasy football league's draft and he still needed to research wide receivers, running backs and bench players. He'd open two windows on his computer and pretend to be working if Pearly walked into his office. Recalculating: Golf was now out. Gloss had thrown a monkey wrench into his plans but what was he going to do? The man was a pain in the ass, but also his meal ticket. It didn't matter the lunch hadn't been firmed. Gloss was an old-school, high-maintenance customer. If he missed the lunch Gloss would play on him like Clapton on a 12-string. But he wasn't going to miss the lunch. And nothing, not even Dick Gloss, was going to ruin his day.

Andy wove his car between an 18-wheeler and a jeep, swung to the outer lane, slammed the accelerator to the floor, but quickly ran into granny-traffic turbulence. He should have told Gloss 30 minutes. He shook his head as he passed the Golfatron complex with its large, white-domed driving range. He picked up an extra lane in Auburn Hills and swung free of traffic. He flew by a bank of boxy green-glass buildings he remembered as once being Ford offices, now hung with "For Lease" banners. He covered the distance from the Mextronics building past the swanky, curvilinear façade of S & M Fitness (nee Chrysler) headquarters to the cemetery that ran adjacent to the highway just north of Big Beaver—a stretch that usually took 15 minutes—in less than seven minutes. He was just about to ease his car into the middle lane when something flashed in his eye. He looked in his mirror and saw the cop trailing, still more than a quarter mile behind him. He might be able to make it, he thought. He pressed his foot full force on the accelerator and narrowly squeezed between two semi-tractors, then eased the car into the right lane, and in almost the same instant, sheared off at the 15 Mile Road exit at 90 miles an hour. He scarcely slowed at the bottom of the ramp and turned sharply around an embankment leading into a maze of streets coursing through an industrial park complex. He took a left, a right and another right and then, barely braking, turned hard and bounced the car up the drive of a low-rise, brown-brick shop, wheeling around behind the building to a secluded parking lot lined by tall juniper hedges. As he strolled into the small lobby of Gloss Industries, the *swoosh* of an angry-sounding cop car accelerated down the street.

"My," said Penny, getting up from her desk to peer out the window. "I wonder who the perp is?"

Andy pulled a Godiva chocolate bar from his satchel and put it on the receptionist's desk.

She snatched up the candy. "You sure know how to buy a lady's affection."

"I should. I'm married."

"Ha!" Penny chortled as she worked off the foil and took a chomp of the chocolate. At 50, she had given herself over to the freedoms of spinsterhood, which included liberation from the gym, dieting and having to feign an interest in anything other than soaps and Hollywood beefcakes. "If you were Bradley Pittman I'd kiss you, married or not."

Andy beamed the beam of a professional beamer, thinking how rare it was that cruel fate sometimes worked in one's favor, as the hulking figure of Dick Gloss emerged from the short hallway that led to his office.

"You're late."

He wasn't, but he apologized anyway. "Is Mac joining us?" He asked hopefully about the plant manager who often tagged along.

"No. We have business to talk."

Andy gulped, quickly rifling through the events of the recent past trying to recall if he had done anything to screw up. They walked out to Gloss's black Escalade SUV. An American flag on a small plastic pole was suctioned to the vehicle's left-rear window. As he climbed up and into the SUV, it occurred to Andy, in the ten years he had been selling to Gloss, the size of his vehicles had tracked nearly in concert with the man's steadily expanding girth. Naturally big at six foot four inches, Gloss's BMI had attracted the attention of his doctor, who had begun hectoring him to shed pounds. Gloss, typically, was fascinated by this latest development in his life, as if the red flags on his health were one more thing, like quarterly results, about which he was obliged to provide updates to the public. Andy had become as familiar with Gloss's medications, blood pressure and cholesterol numbers as he was with his wife's dress size. As he listened to the details of his latest doctor's visit, it occurred to him that Gloss might consider a more effective way to disseminate personal information the public so evidently craved: A podcast. The Universe According to Dick Gloss—All Gloss, All The Time, getting an inward chuckle from the subversive ping. Of course, the man was a million years behind the times in every conceivable way and wouldn't have a clue what a podcast was … but, it occurred to Andy, ruminations into realms of surreal and bizarre were, for some reason, naturally and spontaneously generated in his presence—go figure.

Gloss was in, for him, a cheerful, accommodating mood. He limited the choices to two restaurants but let Andy pick which one. Andy chose China Garden over Dos Diablos mainly because he did not want to eat a chicken Caesar salad with no croutons.

"Sweet and sour chicken, fried rice and an egg roll," Gloss intoned.

The waiter and Gloss waited expectantly for Andy to order. Holding the menu at the fold in one hand, Andy studied the selections, scratching his chin, drawing out the drama a few beats; then, with Gloss's glimmer mutating to a glower, he snapped the menu closed and cocked his head toward the waiter. "Ditto."

For months, maybe years, Gloss had riffed about an innovation he was in the process of qualifying and patenting. He held dozens of patents and Andy lumped them all together and tuned out whenever he started to talk about one of them. Making the art of polite attentiveness more problematic, these chats usually entailed digressions into arcane technical details. Then it happened:

"This ain't your father's autocatalytic electroless nickel reaction," he said, catching Andy's attention with the name of the material he, Mr. Nickel, sold to Gloss. Andy warmed inwardly knowing electroless nickel had the reputation of being the Cadillac of metal plating— super corrosion resistance combining a coating consistency with unheard-of tolerances, which also meant Cadillac, approaching Mercedes pricing. It was a chemical salesman's version of a perfect storm, the fabled Holy Grail, an endless, high-margin rainmaker.

"The damn thing about these tiny tumblers, I never thought I'd be anodizing. Anodizing! That's like a 6000-series, high-purity alloy processed with a multi-mixed acid electrolyte using fully automated process control of like, 62 operating parameters! It's the complete opposite of electroplating. Think about it—the part IS the freaking anode!" Here Gloss paused with his mouth open and starred at Andy, apparently expecting a reaction. Andy began to muster a gesture. "And a titanium-niobium coating to boot! Who ever heard of that shit!!?" Gloss thundered as heads turned around the restaurant.

"The hard part is controlling the microstructure which is determined by the relation between anodizing current and voltage."

"Dick ..."

"See, high current density can produce a thicker, more porous stage-four anodic film, which is shitsky, cause then you have to scrap the whole freakin' batch. That's a hundred grand down the Motor City sewer."

"Dick ..."

"On the other hand, the applied voltage can affect the total charge distribution in a bath of tertiary ions with a dynamic viscosity of 1.005 centipoise, which, according to Diefenbaker's law, can lead to a confluence of charge at sinusoidal points around the part resulting in a non-Newtonian distribution in the film, sort like an asymmetric, three-peat fart on steroids, which anyone can tell you is not a barrel of laughs."

"Dick!"

Gloss looked up nonchalantly. "Questions, Dodge?"

"What the hell is a tiny tumbler?"

Gloss leaned forward with gravity. "What I'm about to tell you is confidential."

"Okay, forget it. I don't ..."

"You have to."

"Why?"

"I'm coming to that."

"Look Dick ..."

"Shut up and listen ... Tiny tumblers are centrifuges, a very special kind of centrifuge used to separate fissile U-235 from non-fissile U-238. You know what fissile uranium 235 is?

Andy threw his hands up. "Jesus Christ, Dick. Ya think I'm some kind of featherweight jackass?"

"No featherweight at all, pal."

Gloss continued, catching his breath after a span of convulsive laughter. "But here's what makes the tiny tumblers different. They separate the good uranium from the bad uranium—50 percent more efficiently!!"

Andy looked blankly at Gloss.

"Wow, that's fantastic."

Gloss stared at him. "Do I detect sarcasm?"

"Break it down for me, big guy."

Gloss rolled his eyes and shook his head slowly. "There's a U-235 shortage for peaceful uses like nuclear-powered electricity, aircraft carriers and submarines. No new sources BUT the main reason is uranium separation efficiency has only been improving at a rate of a few percent—every 10 years! Overnight we're 50 percent ahead of the rest of the world."

"O … K?"

"Which means we can now extract U-235 from low grade types of ore that were once impractical to use."

"Now I'm feeling it."

"But there's a catch."

"Always is, except for the advantages of electroless nickel."

"Most of that low-grade uranium is in Elbonia."

"Oh, shit."

"Yeah—Pakistan, Afghanistan et al. All the "Say-*Stans*" of the world."

"Bin Laden land!"

"He's dead, nincompoop."

"No, I mean …"

"The world's a safer place?"

"No, I mean …"

"Yeah right!" Gloss cast a dubious glance at Andy.

The waiter set steaming plates of sweet and sour chicken in

front of them.

"Look at that beautiful red glaze," Gloss said. "Almost like someone nuked a whole bunch of commies."

Gloss said he had discovered the secret, after much trial and error, of the signature oriental condiment before them, sweet and sour sauce. The riddle was in the ratio of ketchup to vinegar. Andy listened attentively to the reveal, understanding he was not allowed to have opinions or interests himself. It was the salesman's burden, but in the presence of Gloss it was a highly distilled edict. Indeed, Andy knew there was nothing he *could* say that would be of interest to Gloss. Unbeknownst to Andy, this insight, and his strict adherence to its code of conduct, ingratiated him to his client and lay at the core of his professional relationship with the man. In the Glossonian *weltanschauung* there were two types of people: those who wanted to learn, and those who wanted to argue, debate. Gloss had no use for intellectuals, his term for the latter group. That's why he had written a four-volume set of company procedures, bound in large-ring, black-covered binders, laying out explicit directions for everything from writing a shipping order to cleaning the toilets. He even had a procedure for writing a procedure. Initiative yes, debate no. Andy wanted to learn, and, Gloss thought, he had a certain amount of, not necessarily initiative, but raw stamina, untapped energy. He wasn't a coach potato was the best thing he had going. But this facility would require massive amounts of schooling in the ways of the world to ever become focused and useful. From this highwater point, Gloss's character assessment of this vendor's representative plunged precipitously: He suspected if Andy weren't married, he'd probably be a crack-snorting, surfing ho-dad, a homosexual prostitute, or both.

"So, tell me, Mr. Nickel, I've always wondered. What does a smart, deserving, successful and sophisticated woman like your wife see in pond scum like you, no offense of course."

Andy considered the question as Gloss shook with laughter. He was so familiar with his insults posing, as it were, behind a veneer of frat-house, smack talk it no longer registered as anything other than prattle he had to endure. First, above all else, do no anger. Gloss was a paycheck, a retainer fee, not a living, breathing person one would try to empathize with or understand. Through naturalization, Andy's brain automatically concocted neutral, disingenuous ripostes to these slights and slanders, a point he took pride in.

"You know seaweed? That's a type of pond scum but some cultures consider it a delicacy. I guess Marcia's taste runs to the … ahh, what you might call, the exotic."

Gloss laughed louder. "Exotic. That's good. Next time I see some roadkill along the highway I'll bring it home and tell my wife to cook something exotic."

Andy drifted. The mention of Marcia had caused something in his brain to turn over. Like an engine on a cold morning, a consciousness slowly rumbled to life, vibrating and throwing out an exhaust of mental details connected to another, parallel life of his—family, children, wife. These details—partial to-do lists, doctor's appointments, vacation plans, little league and soccer game dates—floated haphazardly into his brain. He began to tense up in his shoulders and neck as these bits and bytes, once let out of the tight psychic space they were stored in, seemed to expand like a balloon on the nipple of a helium tank. The detritus of this other dimension ejected the moment, erased clarity and caused him anxiety of some unknown source. Andy sifted through it, knowing and sensing there must be some hidden meaning. Yes, meaning. But what? He gazed across at Gloss talking, his mouth moving in silence. What was it he had said about Marcia? Smart … desirous … deserving. Marcia was deserving. Yes, that was it. Of what? A hot bath, takeout, a movie? Suddenly it hit him. He had made a mental note about it the night before. He had to remember something important about today and now he had remembered it. He *was* the man. It was a special day. A day for a husband to be grateful, show appreciation. Now he had it. It had come into his thoughts and he had it pinned to the cork board of his Superego. Or was it his Id? He could relax now. All those details could go back into their cerebral footlocker. He was, as he regularly assured his boss Pearly, "on top of it."

Andy was snapped back into the present at the sound of the word "sell." The sibilance of the word acted on his auditory sense in the same way the metallic tang of blood acted on the senses of a shark. It pumped adrenaline into his system. He became focused, aroused. He, a vegetative nuisance thriving under oxygen-depleted conditions in small inland bodies of water? Oh, hell, he was all of that and more if it would give Dick Gloss some twisted, sadistic pleasure. He was a dog-breathed, donkey-eared, slithering tapeworm; a simpleton distilled and redistilled and trained to wait for the wisdom of Gloss to breathe life into him, to correct him, enlighten him, give him marching orders. Now, how many drums of muriatic acid did you say you wanted to buy?

"Earth to Andy. You did one of your brown-outs."

"Not at all. Let me write down your order."

"Take some Strattera, will you. I don't need to buy anything right now."

"You want me to do an inventory?"

"Look, I'm winding this down."

"You're what!?"

"As I said, it's going to be tough to *sell* this company, but that's what I've decided to do."

"Come again?"

"What part of this don't you understand, Mr. Nickel?"

Andy blinked, his mouth agape, trying to absorb this news. In some way Gloss was the existential underpinning of his professional being. He could doubt the motivations, the health, the very sanity of Dick Gloss, but he could not doubt that Gloss paid $100,000 a month to Tartan Chemical under the account number of Tartan Chemical salesman Andrew David Dodge. He grasped the disquieting implications immediately. A sale of the company put the entire account in jeopardy. A new owner usually brought in his own suppliers.

"Whew, I mean, gosh, Dick. Have you thought this through?"

"I have and it boils down to this—I made myself an offer I can't refuse." He chuckled dryly. Gloss was moderately well-off but the only thing he really enjoyed flaunting was the panache associated with being a self-made man.

"So, we'll see you on the reservation playing the slots? Get real man. That's not you."

"Travel ... for the wife ... Look—I'm a living fossil. The

world's changed. Technology and the internet rule. It'll take someone younger to grow this company.

"Look Dick, come to …

"And there's something else. There are forces out there, Andy. Dark Forces."

"Yeah, like when Dr. Octavius's mechanical tentacles became fused to his spine and he tried to take over the world—that was so cool."

"No! Foreign interests, with a lot of help from Wall Street and Washington, are out to steal, cheat and lie in order to break the backbone of the American dream—making things and selling them for a 20 percent markup. If it keeps going this way the two-car garage will soon become the two-bicycle shed."

"So, you're throwing in the towel? *That's* un-American, Dick."

Gloss's face quickly twisted with anger. "I could sell this company to a Chinese outfit in two minutes and make a bundle. You could chrome plate my johnson before I'd do that."

"Sorry, I didn't mean …"

"Listen. I'm going to be up front with you," Gloss said, lowering his voice to a conspiratorial level. "Crossbow Chemical is interested."

Andy suddenly felt a queasy tingle in his stomach. Crossbow, through its reptilian and omnipresent sales agent, Brad Jurasic, was the only other company in the region that sold the special nickel and titanium formulas that Gloss used to manufacture the parts he sold to bigger fish around the world. If Crossbow were serious, someone could start spreading margarine on him right now.

"Why didn't you tell me first?"

"Jurasic stopped by. Hard-working young man. How many rounds of golf did you play this week?"

Gloss bit off half an egg roll in a single bite. "Look, it will all work out big guy," he said, demonstrating his talent of enunciating, chewing, breathing and swallowing all at the same time.

"Not if Crossbow buys you out it won't."

"Screw Crossbow."

"Say what?"

"Screw 'em."

"You?"

"No, you. Pull the rug from under 'em."

"Okay. How?"

"Make me an offer."

Andy blinked, hearing for the first time the sound of the tinny, oriental music, some sort of flute and a ukulele, in the background. Where did they come up with that shit? "Very funny, Dick."

"I'm not joking. Do I joke?"

"Never."

"Ten million will do it."

"Where the hell am I going to get ..."

"Think! Mr. Wannabe. Has it ever occurred to you that you have a head for a reason?"

"How's my head going to help me?" Gloss apparently took him literally.

"Dumb fuck! Raise the goddamn money. Use your connections."

Andy stared at the convulsions of Gloss's huge, rubbery face as he devoured his meal, the words sinking in.

"Look, if you mean Marcia ..."

Gloss slapped the side of his head.

"A vice-president of a bank and heiress to some very old money. That's a slam dunk."

Andy laughed. "Do you want the money in small or large bills? Look, Marcia's not a real vice president. She's in HR, the bank ..."

"I think someone's being sensitive."

Andy glared at Gloss. "Why do you want to sell to *me*, Dick?"

"I'll tell you something I shouldn't," Gloss glanced behind him, then leaned over the table. "For one thing, I don't want to sell to Crossbow. I don't trust them. I built this company from scratch and I want it run the right way. Second, you believe in the American Dream, like I do. You'd fight the competition and keep the technology, wealth and jobs WE created here, where it belongs. I know you would."

Andy dabbed his fork around the red stuff. "This is all very nice of you, Dick, but I don't know anything about your business."

"This is perfect set-up for you. The shop runs itself. It's a god-damn cash cow. How old are you?"

"Thirty-nine."

"About the same age as I was when I went into business. In five years, you'll have the loan paid off and be on the first tee every day by noon."

Andy stared at Gloss as he shoveled three forkfuls of fried rice into his muzzle and fitfully chewed, practically working up a sweat while he ate. He gave Gloss a befuddled look and slowly shook his head.

Gloss gazed sternly across the table, then threw up his hands as if surrendering. "Okay, I'll tell you the truth." He looked flustered, struggling in an odd way Andy had never seen before. "There's an-other reason. It's because … I mean … I know I don't show it but … but … you're the son I never had to teach how to be like me so I could be proud of him," he blurted out quickly. Then he straightened, pushed back his chair, stood up and cleared his throat. "Don't ever tell anyone I said that." He sat down and plowed back into his plate of food as if nothing had happened.

When Andy returned to his car there was a message on his cell from Nathan Pearly. "Dodge, umm, when you get this give me a call. I expected you, umm, in the office a couple of hours ago."

Pearly liked to play the tough guy, but a John Gambino he was not. Black Bakelite-framed glasses, Brylcream-slicked hair, hollow-chested, he walked with a sort of swaying motion, arms swinging like pendulums out to the side, head tilted back, as if at any moment he might attempt to shimmy under a waist-high limbo stick. A graduate of one of the best engineering schools in the country back in the 80s, Pearly had never once looked for or considered a job offer from an-other company—and he bragged about it. As a reward for his loyalty the company had given him the official kiss of death: a permanent job as a middle manager. His job, de facto, was to keep tabs on the accounts and whereabouts of Andy and half a dozen other sales representatives, zigging and zagging around the Midwest, supposedly watching over their clients and accounts like border collies tending to their flock. In practice, the frequency of "calls" on golf courses, bars and strip clubs, far outnumbered contacts with customers. With cell phones, texting and email, the Tartan Chemical sales force played a digital game of Where's Waldo with Pearly, pulling the wool over his eyes with ever more elaborate guises. From June to August, Joe Gemelli, a colleague of Andy's, was usually never more than 30 feet from the tiki bar on his pool patio, emailing story lines, the more far-fetched as the day, and beer, progressed: *Cold-called three shops in Chicago and demonstrated the superiority of our TC 3084 degreaser over the competition. Ask Donna to email Material Safety Data sheets.* And so, with everything under control, Pearly had time on his hands. He walked up and down the hall, munching windmill cookies, drinking Tang from a coffee cup, and sticking his head into offices. It was Andy's bad luck to have a territory near enough to company headquarters to be assigned an office, which then created an obligation to be in the office, which meant an undue amount of face time with Pearly.

As he drove, Andy thought about the lunch with Gloss. The more he thought the more he resented it. Not his bullying, patronizing manner or the barrage of insults—all of which he was accustomed to and sloughed off as the price he paid for, well, being in sales. He was offended, pissed really, by the absolute certainty with which Gloss assumed he, Andy Dodge, was muddling along, biding his time until he was lucky enough to be given the chance to be the next Dick Gloss, at which point, beyond a shadow of a doubt, he would fall to his knees and send hosannas arcing heavenward … But why would he? Being Andy was fun. On the other hand, he was quite sure, being Dick Gloss was not. And Gloss Industries was part and parcel, really one and the same, as the human being and psychopath Dick Gloss. You couldn't separate the two.

"Umm, yes, Andy, I'm glad you finally got back to me—hee hee hee. Someone has, umm, to get over to umm, umm, Mega Screw and Fastener. They, umm, say they're having a big problem and need us there—hee hee."

"Can't you send Ian?"

"Umm, he's out already, umm, putting out the fires. Isn't that your customer, hee hee?"

Mega was on the far side of the county, making it certain he'd get stuck in rush hour traffic on the way back. When he got there, it was the usual muddle into which he was often dropped: parts were breaking in a Hobbs machine and there were 15 different theories being floated for the reason. Andy spent the next three hours shuffling samples of a machining coolant Tartan sold between the shop floor and the lab in the back of the plant. Lenny, the lab technician, ran tests on the coolant and found it met specifications.

"You leev to see annota deh, bhas," said Lenny.

A man in overalls burst through the lab door holding a plastic bag. "We found the problem," grinning, he reached into the bag and grabbed the tail of a dead rat the size of a small dog. "Damn thing got up into the hydraulic lines and threw the whole machine out of whack."

He decided to get off the highway and take two-lane roads back to the office. It would take longer but at least he'd be moving. Something about motion calmed him. Meetings, the antithesis of motion, he dreaded most. Hey, he wondered, maybe someday a shrink convention will invent a new disability — "barredegressphobia"— so he, like half of the freakin' country, could punch a ticket on the government dole … Nah, never happen. How could they ever build a guilt-trip poster campaign around a bunch of guys like him? It was hilarious to even ponder.

It was after six when he reached his office. Pearly was long gone. He logged on to his Fantasy Football league's website and began browsing players' statistics. His team, the Bodacious Ballerinas, had finished third out of 12 teams last year but this year he had already trash-talked up his boast to win it all and bag the top prize of one grand.

Ian Hunt popped his head into Andy's office. "Bleeding green for the company again, are you, mate?"

Andy nodded. "The team, the team, the team!"

"Okay. Stocks, football or porn?"

"Plotting sales strategy."

"That's an oxymoron."

"Hey there, careful what you call me, I'm sensitive."

Talk you into a pint?"

Half an hour later they were sitting in the Mountainback Grille and Sports Bar, a cavernous facility with a rustic, knotty pine interior anointed by the area's working stiffs as the mail-it-in joint of after-work congregation. People crowded two-deep around the mammoth, kidney-shaped bar that ran through the middle of a multi-tiered eating area. Flat screens beamed sporting events around the world from every angle.

"Have you ever heard the drumbeat of destiny?" Andy asked.

"Hear what?"

"Destiny, you know, like a higher calling."

"Good God, lad, no. I'm just an old bloke from the Midlands who found his way out of musty old England."

Ian worked on the R & D side. He had a long, pale creased face and a voice made raspy from a lifetime of Rothmans. He simultaneously looked much older than 50 and acted much younger.

"That's destiny."

"I suppose."

"Why did you leave?"

"I got tired of sitting around pubs listening to everyone pretend they're droll and witty."

"But the English are witty."

"It's all a game you learn from a very young age."

"What about Americans?"

"Americans are hard boiled. I like that."

"That's a game, too."

"Yeah but at the end of the day you get more than a pasty complexion and bad liver from it."

They ordered another pint. Andy told Ian about his lunch with Gloss. Ian called it "extraordinarily fascinating shit."

"There's no way I'm taking him up," Andy said.

"Why not?"

"I like what I do and I'm good at it."

Ian shrugged. "You work exactly as hard as you have to."

"Another reason—I'm lazy."

"Oh, we're all lazy, lad. You, however, are a sneaky, reckless, son of a bitch."

"You mean like playing fantasy football at work."

"Like playing eighteen holes on company time, like driving 90 in a 55 zone, like blowing off staff meetings."

"I didn't know you were up for meritorious behavior."

"I'm not, but this is about you."

"This is not the real me about which .... you are referring to."

Ian smirked. "Dodge, you're a rebel whose only cause is yourself. You think you're above the rules."

"What's so bad about that?"

"You're going to get whacked."

"I get whacked, I get whacked. My call."

"Fair enough. But at least you could be grateful on occasion."

"Grateful?"

"Yeah. All the times I've covered your ass in 10 years and I've never once heard the two simple words that keep on giving."

Andy felt a twinge of remorse. "Geez, you're right. Sorry for being a creep, man."

"You're not a creep—you're just ... out of it."

"Okay, I'll change."

"The hell you will, but maybe you'll have to anyway."

"What?"

"Haven't you heard the rumor—Pearly's leaving."

"No flipping way! Pearly?"

"Golden parachute."

"Damn ... He's annoying as hell but at least ..."

"You can ignore him?"

"Yeah. First Gloss and now Pearly. What a day."

"Makes you grateful for what you got, right?"

"Yeah ... Look, Ian, thanks for keeping my jewels out of the fryer."

"Don't mention it."

They drank to Pearly. They drank to Gloss. They drank to all the nubile young women they suddenly noticed standing around the bar. "Ah, women, the essence of life," said Ian. "Get laid as often as you can because, sure as the river rises, the body wastes away, and you begin to look and feel like a sun-shriveled piece of shit."

At Ian's observation, something clicked in Andy's thoughts. He put down his glass, a beaded line of sweat suddenly forming on his upper lip. He felt a sharp shooting cramp in the lower pit of his stomach. He stared blankly ahead, the banks of television monitors blurring into a prism of color, a look of abject fear rising into his face.

"What's a' matter, mate?" Ian asked.

"Speaking of shit, I just remembered … It's my anniversary."

2 CONSEQUENCES AND A CAUSE

The crowd inside the darkened theater listened raptly as the famed Amazonian ethnographer and conservationist, Georges Furdanko, brought his presentation to a close.

"And so, in answer to the question, can the remaining uncontacted, indigenous tribes of the Western Amazon River basin survive contact with the white man? In my view, unfortunately, they cannot. Contact with the West inevitably leads to decline, decay and decadence."

Applause. A young man near the front raised his hand and stood. "Like, has anyone ever been killed by an anaconda on one of your trips?"

Professor Furdanko furrowed his brow and scratched his chin. "Hmm, oh yes, yes, one time one of my guides was attacked while bathing and swallowed whole. But that was an isolated incident and normally the giant snakes are quite content feeding on the babies abandoned by the tribes that live along the river."

A group of women walked out of the auditorium into the breezy afternoon and down the street toward the college town's commercial district of shops and restaurants. Two of the women, Millie Ketchum and Marcia Riker-Dodge, strolled together a bit behind the main group. They covered a short block and took up the rear of the ordering line at the Fleetwood Deli, a quaint, cramped, campus institution. Millie ordered a tuna salad and fries, and Marcia went for The Mean Green: avocado, cucumber, tomatoes, dill and lettuce in a pita. The sandwiches came with a freshly baked madeleine—a delicious little treat that, like cucumber sandwiches and shortbreads, reminded her of her family and home "back East" when each weekend day culminated in high tea, which, after a brief interlude (often very brief), segued seamlessly into cocktails and long, multi-course dinners.

They found the only open table on the enclosed veranda at the rear, which suited them now.

"Have you thought of telling him to see a psychiatrist?" asked Millie.

"No, but I've thought of seeing one myself."

Millie sent an exuberant, staccato cackle through the restaurant. Marcia raised her eyebrows and unfurled her napkin, a grin creasing the corner of her mouth. It was a type of laugh one might hear in a bowling alley lounge bar: bombastic and ballsy and mildly annoying if you heard it enough, but one so thoroughly and naturally Millie it charmed people.

She and Millie had met at college and become roommates in their final two years, renting the upper floor of a large, old house with a mansard roof and fire-escape stairway off the kitchenette that served as a private, upper-floor entry. They were an odd match, it occurred to her and just about everyone else, but then—the connection just struck her—so were she and her husband. It affirmed the platitude, "opposites attract," which she never truly believed, and yet, at the same time, it also nixed the more substantiated theory of relationships based on rapport—people are innately attracted, even if at a superficial level, to people like themselves. But maybe it was neither. Maybe her choices in life could best be explained by the checkbox marked "other," or "not applicable." True, Millie and her personalities, backgrounds and outlook on life were dissimilar. Yet—and here the incorrigibility of life to conform to the "hissing of the spent lie" (one her favorite lines) truly asserted itself full force—Millie was also her muse, her MO and embodiment of her life philosophy: Get out of your comfort zone, lively up yourself, and "now for something completely different." Kaboom! She wasn't as outgoing as Millie, but she was independent, took risks, and was modestly proud of it. There were some qualifications to that philosophy approaching mid-life, but she still clung to the ideal of it. She was glad the bi-monthly Tri-County Women's Business Association meetings allowed them to stay in touch. Millie had risen to become a senior sales director at a large temporary hiring firm. She was tough, no-nonsense and into her career for the long haul, traits Marcia admired. And she would always be grateful to Millie for befriending her when, as a young woman accustomed to east coast private schools and summers on Martha's Vineyard, she arrived on campus in Ann Arbor, quaintly cosmopolitan, yet, nonetheless, situated in the middle of the rivet-popping, brat-scarfing, beer-swilling Midwest. Millie had been her mentor and guide in this untamed interior, a part of the country few people she knew back home had visited and many feared—the dreaded fly-over territory, a bottomland, they assured themselves, populated by assorted camo-garbed, toothpick-chewing gun freaks, religious zealots and bored insurance agents who wanted to murder their frigid wives. A time-warp where bikram yoga, kimchi, chickpea flour and yuzu marmalade had yet to be discovered. A larger, eerier Area 51 where businessmen still wore creepy, high-gloss polyester suits, pregnant women smoked, and 'diversity' in the workplace meant accentuated neutral tones in office wall treatments. A locale so bereft of modern sensibility and culture that people still drank water from the tap, thought an Ionic column a witty op-ed piece, and mistook the Bilbao for latest Disney Pixar release. She had walked of her own volition into this breach, and it was a frequently commented upon point of amazement with her family that she had not only survived but chose to settle there. What was next? The Sudan? The tribal regions of Pakistan?

"There's a pattern here."

"Yeah, the pattern of a train wreck."

"Now, Marcia."

"He forgets to put gas in the car when I ask him. He forgets to call when he's working late—once he forgot to pick up Jessica from her soccer game—and he was there!"

Millie cackled, and Marcia glowered into the middle distance. "I'm sorry, it's just so ..."

"Weird?"

"Well, yeah, now that you mention it. Maybe it's the stress of being in sales?"

Marcia shot Millie a chastising glance, then took a bite of her sandwich.

"Buck up, son, and get the job done, my dad would say." Millie pumped her arm in a vaguely lewd way. "Have you tried giving him a swift kick in the ass?"

Marcia sighed. Millie was wearing a string of pearls over a lime chintz top.

"Are those pearls cultured?"

Millie fingered the necklace. "These? Jerry gave them to me for my birthday. Gee, I hope they didn't cost too much."

"Look, you have to be realistic girl," she said between chews. Then Marcia watched transfixed as Millie leaned over the table, eyes dilating in real time, and morphed majestically into her leash-yanking, alter-ego conditioned by years of real-world exposure to all flavors of numbskull antics and pathetic dissimulation and the culling, by necessity, of the luxuries of empathy and compassion. "We're talking men here—boys! Creatures from never-never land who never, really, ever grow up. Oh, yes, we hear the advocates for the sensitive man, the new-age man, the men-can-cry-too society. We see them out with baby backpacks and diaper bags, we hear the tales of stay-at-home dads and Mr. Moms and when this propaganda machine is humming on all cylinders we become overwhelmed and disoriented and start thinking, hey, maybe we can raise the bar on our men and welcome them with open arms as full-fledged members of the species—human beings endowed with a sense of family and civic responsibility who put others before work and themselves, possess a soul, feel, empathize and communicate. And you know what? It's all bullshit. Why? Because men have a deformed little piece of DNA called the Y chromosome, and that little piece of DNA is the yada in the clamato, the mayo in the mayhem, the hay in your chardonnay."

Marcia stared at her friend in glum silence.

"Fly."

"Huh?"

"My God, Millie, that is so depressingly cliché-ridden, daytime, talk-show crap. Men are little boys? We should just accept that God made the male species to be permanently psychologically and intellectually arrested?"

Millie slapped her hand on the table. "You hit the proverbial nail on the goddamn head, sister."

"That's … just … fucked, excuse my English."

"It's a cliché because it's supported by a couple of thousand years of evidence."

Just then, the ladies noticed a man standing at the side of their table. "Bonjour. Do the madams mind if I join you?" Professor Furdanko, smiled and bowed slightly holding a tray of food.

He wore a neatly trimmed goatee, flecked with some gray, and his dark hair was gelled and combed straight back from a high, imposing forehead. The professor had an olive complexion, with eyes, steeped in years of introspection, deep set and sad. "You must forgive my intrusion, ladies, but sitting with you is a much more inviting prospect than having to lunch with some of my students."

The professor asked the women what they thought of his presentation.

"It was sooo interesting. To meet androgynous people like that."

"Indigenous," the professor smiled.

"Yeah, those tribes," Millie said. "Who knew there were still people running around buck-naked chucking spears."

"Ahem, well yes, I suppose it is a small miracle."

A brief pause allowed Marcia to glance puzzlingly at her friend, then interject. "Their society seems very peaceful and egalitarian."

"For the most part that is true," he looked appreciatively at Marcia. "Women and men share power and in some tribes' women make the decisions. But even in those tribes the men are still the hunters, the providers."

"Sort of like the 1950s in America."

"Actually, one of the things that fascinates me is the similarity between their society and ours. There's quite a bit of consistency."

"Really? Now you're losing me … may I call you George?"

"Of course." The professor took a deep breath, then smiled. "You have to see beyond the obvious.

"Yes," Marcia jumped in. "That's true. I'm always telling people in financial planning that same thing."

"Have you ever heard of the totem and taboo?"

The women glanced at one another.

"It doesn't matter. The point is that anthropologists have discovered that there are universal stories, myths that underlie all cultures. These myths give cultures certain differences, but they also mean there's a great deal of sameness to human beliefs and values around the world."

"Isn't that just the cat's pajamas."

"For instance, there's a creation myth everywhere and it explains a lot about society today," the professor continued. "I think it's pretty clear that men have psychoanalytically interpreted that myth to mean the world is a male creation."

"Really?"

"Of course. It's obvious."

"So, you think that somehow this is why we are the way we are, I mean, like at a society level?"

"I not only think it, I know it, madam. Womb envy accounts for our entire male-dominated power structure and our competitive, dare I say mad, consumerist, materialistic society bent on destroying the planet."

Marcia and Millie sat in polite silence as the professor stabbed his fork into his Caesar salad for emphasis.

Just then Millie's cell phone rang. She stood and strolled away from the table to take the call.

Marcia finished her sandwich and cleared her throat.

"Where in France are you from originally, professor?"

"Up until four years ago I had lived my entire life in the 8th Arrondissement of Paris."

"What brought you to the States?"

"Money."

"Really? What do you miss most?"

The professor stopped eating and looked into her eyes. "Good food, stimulating conversation and intelligent people."

"Oh." Marcia looked away, placing her napkin on her plate. When she glanced again at the professor, he was holding his hand over his face, ostensibly weeping.

"I am sorry, madam. I did not mean to insult. It's just that ... *Vichyssoise*. I miss zee *Vichyssoise*," he said, wiping his eyes with a handkerchief.

The women walked out of the restaurant and headed toward the parking structure around the block.

"He's a condescending little shit sucker."

"Millie! He's European—they're more comfortable with, ah, uncomfortable conversations. "

"He can vichyssoise my ass."

Millie steered her SUV through the side streets crowded with students in the direction of the highway. Marcia took out her cell and checked her voice mail. There was a message from Jim Jenson, the bank's lawyer, updating her on the case of a branch manager they were firing for sexual harassment, another from her yoga instructor giving her the time and date of a make-up session, and a message from her sister Beatrice asking for advice on the arrangements for her parent's upcoming 50th anniversary celebration. There was also a long, rambling mushy message from Andrew. Since he had stood her up on their anniversary last week, he had been calling her at work three or four times a day. She let him go into voicemail and, only later in the day, listened to the messages. Fortunately, he didn't try to explain or justify what had happened. There was no explanation. Sometimes she would replay a message, listening carefully for any signs that his contriteness might be a harbinger of genuine change in their relationship. Usually, she concluded, it wasn't but his persistence, along with a deft, touching ability to admit his flaws and failures, at least pointed to a vague possibility of ... hope and some form of reconciliation. That in light of the misconduct, however, was several marital novenas and many dozens of prostrations away.

"Andrew wants to take me out to dinner."

"And?"

"I'm working late."

"Perfect. With a tin cup of water in solitary confinement."

"In the basement."

"Marcia, I don't mean to be nosy but is Andrew the philanthroping type?"

"Philandering?"

"Yeah, you know, a pig."

"No. At least I think not."

"Good. So, it's not hopeless."

"Yes, I suppose it's not hopeless."

"But then, what are you going to do?"

"What do you mean?"

"Marcia, it's going to happen again."

"Oh, I'll make him promise it won't."

"There has to be a mechanism, or it will."

"Mechanism?"

"Yes, a mechanism, in this case, for inducing behavioral change."

Marcia gazed blankly at her friend. "So, what, we're back to a swift kick in the ass?"

"I'm glad you asked," and Marcia saw a strange, demonic grin come into Millie's face; the grin of a person who looked after her interests, relished a good fight, and understood that a woman never, ever had to play fair.

He could smell the sweet, earthy aroma of the grass in the cool night air as he walked onto the field under the lights. The team looked sharp in its dark blue jerseys and white pants as it lined up for calisthenics. He took a place in the front row and one of the boys, a captain, his lips protruding over his rubber mouth guard, came up and slapped him on the side of the helmet. The team counted in cadence, the words ONE, TWO, booming into the chill, long trails of vapor rising out of the boys' mouths as they shouted. He could see the other team in their scarlet and gold uniforms gathered at the far end of the field. They looked huge, the size of full-grown men. He glanced away. Coaches wearing school wind breakers walked between the players. One coach, who appeared extremely young, stopped and gave him a fierce stare inches from his facemask. He felt butterflies in his stomach. Then the game began. One of the opposing team's players ran up the sideline dragging three tacklers. "You guys suck," he yelled at their team bench. Then the coach was shouting, "Dodge, get in there." He ran onto the field not knowing where to line up. He dropped back. The play was starting and tall players in scarlet and gold were sprinting down the field. He ran backward and the ball was in the air, coming toward him. He reached up, tipped the ball and watched as it came spinning down into his arms. He was running, two huge players closing ground. Then, as he was about to be crushed, he saw a man typing. The man was dressed in a suit and sitting behind a desk in front of an old-fashioned type-writer. Sounds of cars honking and police sirens came through a win-dow. He heard some words … big bull … tough ride … third place. A bluish light flickered faintly. The TV was on. He opened his eyes and gazed at the ceiling, then raised his head. He was lying half-covered by a blanket on the sofa. He rubbed his eyes then, with a jolt, sat upright. It was Saturday morning, he recalled. He looked at his watch. Shit! He had fifteen minutes to get dressed and make it to make it to the golf course for his tee time.

He bought a cup of coffee at a drive-thru and began driving the side roads toward Sylvan Meadows Country Club. A sign at the entrance of a high school said, "New School Year: Welcome Class of 2014." Wow, had it really been 20 years since he graduated? There was that time thing again—scary shit. He got behind a pick-up truck with the words, "No Fear," monogrammed on the back window next to a drawing of a pistol-wielding cartoon character. Hmm, he thought. He had a lot of fears—paperwork, traffic jams, awkward or boring so-cial situations from which there was no ready escape, and, now that she was marinating him in a brew comprising equal parts indiffer-ence, derision and contempt, his wife.

Indeed, it had been a long, wretched week. It would be great to be out in the elements, in clear air and sunshine, with the guys. Jurgenson, the general manager of sales, had a nifty word he threw around quite a bit. Transparent. Let's make sure all our dealings are transparent, he'd say, whatever the hell that meant in the inherently murky, asterisks-impinged endeavor known as sales. But transparency, the idea that the world was knowable, that you could trust what you heard and saw, truly was a beautiful idea.

Sylvan Meadows was a 7000-plus-yard course with water, lots of sand traps, and multitudes of trees and hills. He stood at the side of the first tee taking practice swings with his GoBig Blueline driver, the "big mutha," as he called it, feeling the tingle in his stomach he always felt before playing. The driver felt good in his grip, the V-groove between his left thumb and knuckles pointing at his right shoulder, his arms, legs and hips all moving in unison. He was going to pound it today; he could feel it.

"Boomchakalaka, baby, are you ready for some golf ball?" his partner Vince Delray shouted, miming the well-known Monday night mantra. Vince was dressed in yellow knickers, baby-blue golf shoes, tartan cardigan vest and cap emblazoned with a Royal St. Andrews insignia.

"Personally, I'm going to enjoy every fucking minute playing golf with a guy resembling a gay Scottish peacock," said George Sollacio, dragging on a cigarette in a golf cart next to the first tee box.

"George, I am happy to do my part to enhance the entertainment value of the day for you. Anything I can do to increase the pleasure, let me know."

"Okay, lose."

Andy stepped up to the ball, squared his stance and lined up his shot. The tee was elevated, and the long, emerald fairway curved slightly to the right, around a line of trees. What a beautiful sight. Eyes frozen on the front edge of the ball, he rocked back on his right foot, swung the big mutha up and over his head, and smoothly wheeled the club down, through and up in an arc that ended with the club behind his left shoulder. The ball curved up and over the front edge of the tee box, then nosedived into the turf, rolling down the slope and coming into view as it bounced along the cart path and settled into the rough about 100 yards down the fairway.

Nick Lever, George's partner, had managed the best tee shot of the group, a low line drive in the middle of the fairway that left him, nonetheless, with a hefty fairway wood to the green. George was in the trees to the right and Vince had hit what would have been a spectacular drive if the fairway were rotated about 45 degrees to the left; his ball had landed in the middle of a group playing on the adjacent fairway of the 18th hole.

Andy climbed into the cart and Vince drove. Vince, his fraternity brother and roommate at college, had set up the foursome. He had driven up from Chicago, where he helped run his family's chain of up-scale home furnishing stores. He came to the Detroit area three, four times a year on business. Usually Andy invited him to stay at their house but this time, as he had hinted, it did not seem like a particularly good idea.

"So, how's the gulag?" Vince said with a crooked grin, an expression that conveyed more scorn than sympathy.

"Oh. Yeah."

Andy, with some misgivings, told Vince the story.

Vince shook with sarcastic-tinged laughter, and the cart nearly veered off the path into the ditch. "Oh, shit, that's good," Vince said, switching to the voice of a TV interviewer, "Can you tell us in your own words, Mr. Dodge, what were your first thoughts at that precise moment when you realized you had forgotten a date with your wife on your anniversary?"

"Don't joke about this man."

"You do something this stupid YOU are a joke."

In the clubhouse bar, George shredded his scorecard and was about to set the pile of scraps on fire when the manager stopped him. The clubhouse manager sent a free round to the table. Yes, George shouted, he could be bought.

It came out that George, a general contractor, via some complicated and, it seemed to Andy, somewhat shady arrangement, bought bathtubs, spas, kitchen cabinets and other supplies wholesale through Vince and Nick.

"It's all about price, price, price, Vince."

"If you'd like I can get you some bargains on 'damaged goods,'" Vince said, his tone signifying a more metaphorical meaning.

George held up his finger. "The only thing I won't buy is damaged goods." The remark elicited a droll chuckle from both Vince and

Nick.

"Whadaya do?" George asked Andy.

"Chemicals."

George raised his bushy eyebrows and nodded his head, impressed. "Good business, but not what it used to be. Too many God damn tree huggers."

George, Andy had figured as soon as they met, was a certain type of sensitive person's re-incarnation of the anti-Christ; a brawny, cantankerous, intimidating Neanderthal of a man with an ego the size of a battleship; a species that many tens of millions of humans had hoped or presumed was extinct. Come to think of it, Andy thought, George was a lot like Gloss, but despite that, or more precisely because he didn't work for him, he had taken an immediate liking to him. Damn, life was weird.

"Oh, we're not hurting," Andy said casually. "I do some seven-figure accounts."

"Who do you sell to?"

"Ah, you know—owners, guys who buy stuff, those types," he said, not sure how to best describe the rogue's gallery with which he had to deal.

"I mean companies."

The first company that came to mind was Gloss Industries.

"You know Dick Gloss?"

Andy grinned and looked George in the eye. "Sweet and sour chicken, fried rice, egg roll."

"Son of a ..."

"He's my top customers."

"Dick and I played football together at McComb High. He's on the Chamber but I haven't seen him for, hmm, maybe a year. What's he up to?" Andy was pleased to pull George into his confidence.

"Don't tell anyone this. He's selling."

"Selling? Gloss? Dick Gloss *is* metal plating. He's a giant in the business."

"You're telling me."

"Well, I can't say that I blame him."

"How come?"

George looked away and let out a nervous chuckle. "Oh, well, you know. Small business. It's tough out there."

"Dick's business is pretty steady. I don't see that changing."

"Nah, you're right. He probably just got tired of all the bullshit. You guys want some food?"

After they ate, George and Nick left together. Vince talked Andy into another beer.

"So how you feeling?" Vince asked.

"Scared."

"Ya got to go home."

"Yeah."

"Have you had 'the talk' yet."

"No. She won't talk."

"That's bad."

 "Cruel."

"Well, I'm afraid it means one thing, pal."

Andy made a pistol with his hand and pointed it at his head.

"Nah, she would have already done that by now."

"Then what?"

"So, you've groveled, right?"

"I'm unworthy, you're beautiful, I love you, please forgive me, I'll change."

"Hmm, that's bush-league groveling in my book."

"Best I've got, brother."

"Then there's nothing to do but wait."

"Wait?"

"Wait."

"What?"

"Her bullet points."

"For?"

"The change part you promised."

"I wish she would hurry up."

"Careful what you wish."

"Why?"

"Dumb shit! Stiffing your wife on your anniversary is a high marital crime. As far as annals or any historical record goes, it could be unprecedented."

Andy hung his head.

"It's barely a hair below bigamy."

He sat up and stared into the distance.

"It's going to be *mucho* painful, buddy."

"I'm such a fucking idiot."

"Now we're getting somewhere."

Andy shook his head, letting the words sink in.

"It's going to require that sustained level of sincerely pathetic soul searching and pleading for her to even care enough to pick you up and whack you."

"Wow!"

"Yeah, wow."

"Ok … I get it."

The two men sat in silence for several minutes, Vince checking texts on his cell.

"Can I tell you the truth?" Andy said.

"Sure."

"I don't really want to change."

Vince blinked, his mouth agape.

"Okay, okay, I do."

Vince ran his hand through his mane of brownish-red hair. "Look, you know what the Greeks said—not the Kappa Sigma's, the real Greeks, you know, Plato and company? Change is constant. You can't step in the same stream twice. That's the way of the world. Change is not all bad … Not better necessarily, but not all bad either. Just different."

"Different."

He grinned, leaned closer to Andy and lowered his voice. "Hey, you want to know the secret to a good marriage," letting a dramatic pause linger and heighten the poignancy of the moment … "You need a freakin' mission."

"Huh?"

"A cause. You know, something bigger than yourself. Some all-consuming passion. She gets pulled in, becomes your ally, your partner, your buddy."

"Marcia would never take up golf."

"No. That's just a pastime, a hobby. Think big. I mean, really big. Think saving-the-world, building-an-empire big."

"This is complicated."

"No more complicated than keeping a hundred demanding customers happy. You can do it. After all, you are the person who got the university to fund our fraternity's wet-tee-shirt-for-charity contest. Such an achievement speaks of a brilliance not yet fully realized."

"Yeah, well, I was motivated."

"That's it, motivation."

"I never thought being married required motivation."

"I'm going to pretend … you're smarter than that."

They finished their beers and left money on the table for the tip. As they strolled out of the clubhouse along the winding brick walk lined with begonias to the parking lot, Vince could be seen with his arm around Andy's shoulder, talking quietly into his ear.

3 BOBBLEHEAD BOOM

A tall, ragged-looking pine tree grew in the far corner of Andy and Marcia's backyard. The tree was wedged into a triangular space formed by a wood-plank fence, an unruly lilac bush, a junction of power lines above and the square frame of a kids' playhouse on the ground in front. Andy had learned that the tree was a variety of evergreen commonly known as the red pine, a botanical tag which suggested the obvious correlation to dead pine. For clearly, as he liked to point out to anyone who would listen, the tree had none of the redeeming features one commonly associated with living things, plants or otherwise. It grew no flowers, fruit or leaves. It provided no shade during summer hot spells. Every branch oozed sap which, once it contacted human skin, was inert to ordinary soap. It annually produced a bumper crop of hand-grenade-sized pinecones, which required time (his) to pick up and discard. Lastly, it regularly shed two-inch long, syringe-like needles which, in accordance with the third law of thermodynamics, were distributed with maximum disorder to all quadrants of the lawn. In five years, by Andy's estimate, the tree had meted out more pain than a quack dentist in a lifetime. An excruciating cry of grief, emitted when one of the slivers lodged in a toe or heel, had ceased to elicit alarm or empathy, merely registering a derisive scoff for being dumb enough to walk across the grass in bare feet.

The tree, like a car or pool imagined by novelist Steven Bling, was evil. Andy had long wanted to vaporize it. Chopping would be much too messy and time-consuming. A controlled explosion of, say, one well-placed stick of dynamite bored into its trunk might do the trick. To his wife, however, the thought of culling a living tree on their property, even a miscreant one, was unacceptable. End of discussion. What part of his iron-clad logic for eradicating this blight on humanity did she not understand? Not even a promise to replant a stately hardwood, such as a birch or chestnut, in the exact location, could convince. Perhaps, giving her an unwarranted benefit of the doubt, the tree, like the ugly duckling, had won her over. Now, as he maneuvered under the dank, squalid canopy of branches trying to remove a vine that had worked its way up into the tree's bowels, he realized he was resigned to coexistence with this tree. Still, this was not something he wanted to be doing. He leaned back and yanked on a tendril of the plant with his full weight when the vine gave, and he flipped on his back into a bed of needles.

"Aaeeeeeiiii, shiiiiittt!" He tried to avoid moving. A more effective and feared form of torture could not have been devised by the keepers of the Tower. Who the hell said suicide was ##%!!? painless. Anesthesia, he needed anesthesia. He quickly tried to calculate the quantity of bourbon he had in the house. Then he heard the screen door on the patio slide open.

"Dad, Mom's on the phone. She wants to talk with you."

Marcia had not spoken a direct word to him since that night, which, Andy mused for ironic escape, had been anticipated by FDR long ago as "a day that would live on in infamy." He had a sudden, chilling recollection of a blue-glass dolphin figurine whistling just past his left cheek and exploding against the wall as he ran for cover. Since then, he had been on his best behavior. He woke each morning before his wife and made coffee, prepared the kids' lunches and tidied up the kitchen. He had fixed a dozen little problems around the house, such as leaky faucets, squeaky hinges and dysfunctional doorknobs, the type of minor, nagging glitches that bugged Marcia. He had washed, waxed, buffed and vacuumed Marcia's van till it shone, he thought proudly, like a Park Avenue pimp's. For dinner he eschewed the grille and Hamburger Helper and fussed to cook fare along the lines of couscous, organic ratatouille and salmon soufflé. Still, he had received nothing but cold silence, communication through voice mail, email and hostile body language; in his solitude he had begun to become resigned, inclined to think it hopeless. Now, lying on the ground as a meme for a pin cushion, he felt an adrenaline rush and a subsiding of pain, sensing instinctively that, at last, the other shoe was going to drop. He bit his lip and in one swift movement lifted his back off the ground, the pain of puncture wounds blunted by a mixture of hope and fear, that strange concoction of emotions he knew all too well.

He ran to the patio door and snatched the phone from his son.

"Hey, honey."

"When do you leave for your golf league?"

Andy looked at his watch. "In a couple of hours."

"I'll be home before then. We'll talk."

"Sure, hon …" The phone went dead before he could reply.

Andy's banishment—going on week three—to the basement, technically solitary confinement, fell short of hard labor. Since buying the house five years before, he had parlayed the room into the quintessential man cave. It was a home within a home, a place where he could not only chill, muse (i.e., daydream), play, and entertain, but also comfortably ride out the tempests that inevitably kicked up when a man and woman cohabitated. If he had had one small genius as a husband, he allowed himself, it was that he had anticipated the vital necessity of such a room to the well-being of a marriage. If, during these moments of excommunication, he had been booted into the garage or shunted into the spare bedroom and forced to make do with a dozen satin-covered, pastel throw-pillows and back issues of Home and Garden, he had instinctively known he probably would have felt less penitent than he should. His man cave (although he tactfully eschewed from flaunting it as such) was THAT place, designed, in part, to quarantine these hiccups and outbreaks before escalation. Within this sanctuary, with its cushy, carpeted comfort that deadened both sound and angst, minor flare-ups and major marital solar storms consumed themselves through the miracle of "Newton's Arrow," i.e. the movement of time, that substance of the universe that was both our undoing and our salvation; in this particular case, the latter—the indelible constant and healer; the only universal healer, for all that ails the human soul.

This was hallowed ground, the inner sanctum, a space in which not one spore of drama-inducing retrovirus could ever take root. The over-arching theme was "Life is a party." Hey, why reinvent the wheel? The centerpiece, an oversized sofa festooned with a Boston

Red Sox stadium blanket, a gift from Marcia's parents, sat at the room's far end in front of a 100-inch flat-panel HD television. A moose head with antlers decorated with a various team ball caps, hung on the opposite wall behind the cherry-wood wet bar, equipped with a baseball-bat shaped tap for draft beer, a rotating drink dispenser loaded with liquor bottles and a carved-wood display cupboard holding an array of stainless-steel bar-tending utensils. Filling in the space between the two walls was a felt-lined poker table, a wall-to-wall hand shuffle board, a small alcove with a desk and computer, several shelf sets displaying autographed baseballs and photos taken at sports venues, and, in a nod to the whimsical, a framed wall poster of Luigi V. Brugnatelli, the inventor of electroplating, a gift from Dick Gloss. In leftover niches were an original, vintage Pac-Man console, a dartboard, a hanging punching bag, a matted area with a medicine ball and set of barbells and several sets of recliners, bar stools and tables for lounging around the flat-panel. Andy was sitting at one of these stools as Dylan dabbed cotton balls soaked with rubbing alcohol at the red welts on his back.

"Ouch. Careful there, Bubba."

Once his wounds were attended to, Andy began to get dressed for his Wednesday night golf league. He pulled on a teal polo shirt, a pair of khakis and walked to the closet off the utility room where he stored his golf clubs. He opened the door, walked to the back of the closet, and froze, his lips involuntarily mouthing, "WHAT THE FUH … " In the corner at the back of the closet where his clubs usually leaned was an empty space. His pulse began to race. His head suddenly felt as if it had been thrust into a furnace. He struggled for a breath, gazing intently at the spot where he always placed his clubs, as if, knowing the clubs were there, he simply needed to wait for his eyes to adjust to the light. He closed and opened his eyes, turning to examine every inch of the tiny, enclosed space. No clubs. There had to be a mistake. Maybe he had carelessly misplaced them while distracted. He was sure he hadn't, but he ran downstairs to look anyway. No clubs. He walked back to the closet, opened the door and stared in again. As clear as day, his clubs were MIA. Panic began to grip him. He shouted to Jessica and Dylan to come down from their bedrooms.

He asked if either of them had seen his bag. They both shrugged. He ran wildly out the door into the garage. With all the stress he'd been under, perhaps he'd placed them in the storage shed. He ripped open the doors of the shed and saw the usual chaotic jumble of never-used tools and forgotten toys. Not one sign of a swank, burgundy leather golf bag with 14 gleaming golf clubs. He popped the trunk on his sedan and peered into the compartment, praying for a miracle and the sight of his clubs resting, like a missing child, securely on the floor. Nada. Kaput. He slammed the lid down and stood motionless, hit by the sickening certainty of the unfolding disaster—his clubs had been stolen. It was obvious. The kids had gone out after school to play and forgotten to lock up the house. He had dropped by in the middle of the day and found the house unlocked more than once. He had scolded and lectured them about it, apparently to no avail. He stomped into the house, calling their names. He was just about to lay into them when Marcia walked in.

"Mom, Dad's golf clubs were stolen."

Marcia set her shoulder bag on the kitchen counter. "Is that right," she said coolly.

"If I've told these kids once, I've told them a million times to lock the door when they go out."

"Kids, you can go to your rooms. Your dad and I need to talk."

Alone, Andy paced in front of her.

"Andrew, your clubs are not stolen," Marcia said, emitting a sigh.

He looked at her warily. "You've taken my clubs?"

"Sequestered. They're stashed away in a nice, safe place."

"But honey, I have a tee time in 45 minutes."

Marcia threw up her hands. "Do you want a golf game, or a marriage? It's your choice."

"Marcia, you're being unreasonable."

"Am I?"

Oh, no. It hit him immediately. Delete, delete, delete.

"It would be one thing if you had just forgotten our anniversary. Can you imagine how humiliating it is to have a waiter apologizing to you because your husband has stood you up for dinner? Oh, I suppose I should be asked to forgive the human propensity for err, in this case squashing the equivalent of a pie in his wife's face. But this didn't start yesterday. We've been married 13 years—I'm sure the number's just a coincidence—and in that time I have tolerated your thoughtlessness, your recklessness, your self-centeredness, your indifference, your 'benign' neglect nearly the entire time. Andrew, even when you're here you're not here. You always have something on the go, some project. Fiddly diddly, fiddly diddly," She made some strange, contorted gestures with her face and hands suggesting she was on the brink of going berserk.

Andrew gazed in the air. He still wanted to buy 100 shares of Snapple on E-Stock and needed to call Critter-Ridders about the raccoon nest behind the shed.

"Andrew! Are you listening?"

"Yes, of course."

"No, you aren't, you're daydreaming. It's hopeless."

"No, it's not. I was thinking ... I realize I sometimes get distracted, and I know I need to change. I will change ... I want to be a better person ... a better person for you."

She sighed. "I think we just want different things."

He took her hand. "We want the same things; we just have different ways of expressing it."

She gave him a funny look. "It can't go on like this."

"I know," he moved his hand to her waist. "Marcia, for the last three weeks I have felt nothing but shame for the way I hurt you that night.

Marcia blinked. She drew back and stared at him; her mouth open in wonder. Ten, fifteen seconds passed in silence. Astutely, Andy resisted the temptation to add another superfluous word.

Fifteen more seconds elapsed, and Marcia shook her head, looked away and then, as if summoning some inner strength took a deep breath and slowly, cautiously turned her gaze back to his.

"Andrew you just said something thoughtful ... and sincere. I'm trying to process it."

"That's because it was sincere."

The top corner of her lip quivered. She bit at it, beginning to tear. "You care?"

He put his arms lightly around her waist. "Of course, I care, I love you."

She fought off the tears, breathed deeply and sighed. "I want to be happy, Andrew."

"I want you to be happy."

"Really?"

"Yes, really. I'll do anything."

"Anything?"

"Anything."

Marcia straightened and looked him in the eye. "Okay then, this is what it's going to take. You and I need to have a Reee—laaaay—shunnn—ship. Can you read my lips, Andrew?"

He nodded.

"Do you know what that is?"

He nodded again.

"No, you don't, so let me remind you. That's when two people talk. That's when two people share what's inside of them. That's when two people do things together."

He swallowed and hung his head, but within he felt a wave of relief go through his body. The conflict had peaked, and, thankfully, resolution beach was in sight. "I know," he said, holding her hand. "Let's work on it."

"Yeah, let's work on it. Starting now."

He didn't hesitate. As Marcia watched he pulled his cell out of his pocket and speed-dialed his golf partner.

"Hey, Ben, it's Andy. I'm not going to be able to make it to-night. I have a date—with my wife.

Andy took her hand. Marcia looked up and let out a sigh.

"You want an iced tea?"

"Yes, that would be nice."

"Let's go sit on the deck. We have some catching up to so."

"Yes, we do."

The reconciliation had taken place, perhaps not coincidentally, only a few days before the celebration of the 50th wedding anniversary of Marcia's parents, planned for the Labor Day weekend. It would have been difficult surviving the occasion embroiled in a marital snit. There was the drive out to Massachusetts, for one thing, which took 12 hours. More important, Marcia was incapable of faking anything. If she were upset with him, it would show; even worse, the friction would be more prominently highlighted by the sedate, intimate way his in-laws customarily socialized. These were not people, as Andy had once summarized upon years of reflection, inclined to bouts of extemporary bacchanalia.

The morning of their departure Marcia and Andy made the bed together. Marcia, still in her negligee, walked around the end of the bed, put her arms around his waist and smiled. "You see, being with your wife isn't so bad." It was one of the most mind-boggling things about marriage, Andy thought. One moment it could be unrelenting hell, sort of like being seasick on a ship rolling through an endless storm in the middle of the ocean, then the next moment the skies had cleared, and you were bobbing along a palm-fringed lagoon in a state of bliss.

They made the drive out to Massachusetts several times a year. From Michigan the shortest route to New England took them through Canada. Andy exchanged $100 at the border and got back $160 in Canadian dollars.

"Dad, how come you get more Canadian money when you exchange?"

"Because America keeps the world safe. It's like thanking us for coming over."

"That's not true," Marcia laughed. "It's determined by what are called 'exchange rates,' Dylan."

"Okay, check that kids. Whoa, would you look at all the trucks. Maybe they're bringing in the game-show hosts."

Andy felt better than he had in a long time. He was with his family, driving, seeing the sights. Ahead lay the prospect of an obligation-free weekend. After all, it was the Riker's family wingding.

All he had to do was look pretty. Marcia was on edge, as usual, whenever her family convened. He did what he could to calm her but the clan's inter-personal history, with its stomach-churning mix of guilt and complex moral and intellectual one-upmanship was far too convoluted for him to sort out. He had ceased pretending to have any understanding of it and happily assumed the role of spectator. He had one rule for himself: Do not under any circumstances become emotionally involved or invested in anything said or done. His strategy for survival among the Rikers was one of astute, adroit, determined ingenuousness. He thought of it as his bobblehead deployment. If you wanted the head to say yes, you pushed it from the top; if you wanted it to say no, you pushed it from the side.

They arrived at the Peace Bridge to cross back into the U.S. at Buffalo. Andy paid the toll and had driven only halfway across the bridge when their vehicle was stopped by the line-up of cars queued to get through customs.

"This is insane." He slapped the steering wheel with his hand.

"Just relax," Marcia said. "We're in no hurry."

Andy rolled his eyes. Despite her intelligence, which he admired, Marcia sometimes had a knack for making well-intentioned but absurd statements. Was it possible, in some existential sense, time did not matter? Sure. Everyone's going to die. But there was another, more pressing truth. It was now noon and he had at least another nine hours of driving in front of him. He accepted that. Nine hours was dictated by the laws of physics. It was rational. Anything over nine hours meant something was intervening to screw things up. In the present case, the thing doing the intervening, he suspected, was a petty little person doing a petty little job in a petty little customs booth at the end of the line-up of idling cars.

Every minute or two the line-up would move forward a few inches and stop. It took 45 minutes to get over the crest of the bridge, and another half an hour to reach the lines of traffic that fanned off to separate booths. There were eight lanes and Andy steered the car into one in the middle. Five, then ten minutes passed and still their car had not moved. The cars in the lanes on either side of his moved steadily past him. He opened the window and poked his head out trying to peer around the van in front of him. In the lane on his left, a young blonde woman in a yellow convertible waved and giggled as she and her much older sugar daddy drove ahead. Finally, after another 35 minutes had passed, his car was idling in front of a sign that announced, "Do not pull ahead until the car in front has cleared." When the car had been waved through, he punched the accelerator and drove up to the window.

The window remained closed for more than a minute. Finally, it opened and a heavy-set woman with dark, brush-cut hair turned slowly away from a monitor to look at him.

"Was that rubber?"

"Cramp in my foot, ma'am. Sorry about that."

The woman gave a thin, malevolent smile and stood, evidently wishing Andy to apprehend that she possessed the physique of a small linebacker. She asked about a dozen questions, pausing after each of his answers, as if pondering which file every new tidbit of information he provided should go into, slime or idiot? She slowly inspected their passports, turning every page, sliding them through a scanner, typing on her keypad. She made him turn off the ignition and open all the doors. She sauntered to the rear of the van, un-zipped each suitcase, patted down each item of folded clothing, felt inside each shoe and opened every night kit and toiletry bag. As she waddled by the car to the booth, she waved them through, pausing at driver window to give Andy a demonic-looking smirk. They had been detained at the bridge over two hours.

The rest of the drive passed uneventfully. Andy thought about work and his upcoming week. Fall was the busiest time of year for him. Budgets were due, and he was pressed to make his sales tar-gets. He had another meeting scheduled with Dick Gloss to discuss the sale of his company. Gloss had been leaving him messages. He had purposefully waffled with Gloss on the premise it was good sales PR to let him think he was seriously considering buying his company. Now he would have to be blunt with him. Not blunt exactly. He'd say something to the effect that he would love to own his wonderful company but couldn't hope to run it as astutely and profitably as the metal-plating guru Gloss. And he didn't have the money. He had come to some resolution about it. The sale of Gloss Industries, and the potential loss of business, worried him, but the world did not begin and end with Dick Gloss. Life would go on with or without big Dick. There were other Dicks to fry.

Marcia's parents lived in a small town about 45 minutes west of Boston. The town of Stanbury was an epicenter of colonial history but the first thing a newcomer or visitor to the area usually learned was the average price of a house was a million-plus dollars. The Riker estate, which had been in the family for ten generations, was worth considerably more than this. Within the circle of immediate family and close friends, it was considered poor taste to even mention the possible monetary value of the property.

It was approaching midnight when they drove into the semicircular driveway that fronted the main hall of the sprawling, brick, colonial-style Georgian house. Over the years the house had been added on to; wings to the right and left of the original house, including a bronze-framed, green-glass window conservatory-solarium, as well as an enlarged front portico, and the extension of a great hall and observatory in the rear, now technically gave the house a "neo-Palladian" look. Parked along the other side of the drive Andy could see an Audi, a BMW and a gleaming, long, low stylish sedan that seemed taken off a set on *Masterpiece Theater*. A young man in a short white jacket strode up to the window of their minivan.

"Just pull ahead to unload, sir. We'll park it."

Mr. and Mrs. Riker greeted them as they stepped into the spacious foyer lit by a large chandelier.

"Hello, Andrew," Mr. Riker grabbed his hand firmly. "You are keeping well, I can see."

"Trying my best, sir."

"How's the golf game these days?"

Andy blanked for a moment, thinking of his sequestered clubs.

"Tiger does not yet have to worry."

"Ha! Good show. Can I interest you in a scotch?"

The kids disappeared with various cousins. Marcia, walking with her mother, and Andy, strolling slightly behind the tall, grayhaired, listing figure of Mr. Riker, were led into the large front drawing room where a small party of people was gathered. He said hello to Marcia's aunt and uncle, Sylvia and Donald, and was introduced to an old business associate of Mr. Riker's, Nolan Roswell, and his wife. Also present were her younger sister, Claire, and her boyfriend, Barrie, a close acquaintance of theirs, Sean, and his fiancée, Marcia's older sister, Beatrice, and her husband, Eastman Finch.

Mr. Riker brought Andy a scotch and Finch came over and wrapped an arm around his shoulder.

"Mr. Andrew Dodge. How ya doing', big fella?"

A strong scent of cologne, a nutty, slightly leathery aroma, enveloped Andrew as he wheeled around and took in Finch, whom he had not seen in over a year. He was tan and freshly shaven; his facial features preternaturally smooth and wrinkle-free, almost synthetic. A lemon cardigan was draped over his shoulders and knotted under his neck and his thick, jet, gelled coif reminded Andy of the song about a werewolf—it was perfect.

"Same old, same old."

"Come on, a go-getter like you?"

"Yep, still moving chemicals."

Finch aped shock. "Andrewwww, that's a commodity business. You can do better than that."

"It pays for the chicken feed, as we like to say back on the farm."

"Well, I guess if there weren't wage slaves in the world, it would be necessary for God to invent them— heh-heh-heh."

"Yeah, he'd probably have to belch us into existence."

Finch slapped him on the shoulder. "You are funny."

"Still doing the hedge fund?"

"That's history, mi amigo. I've branched out, started a new business. I help international clients achieve their business objectives, which, believe it or not, is not always access to venture capital, HAHAHA! The IPO on my firm has, well, let's just say it's gone out with a bullet."

"If anyone's fast, it's you."

"I get bored," Finch said, pulling his cell from his pocket and quickly scanning his messages. "BTW, did you see my new toy when you drove up?"

"The Audi?"

"Dude! I drove an Audi when I was in college. The Bentley. Nineteen sixty-three, S3 Continental drophead coupe convertible. Bea thought I had paid too much until she found out how good she looks in it."

They were joined by Barrie and Sean, who began to pay homage to the Bentley. Finch relished the attention of the young bucks.

"Listen," he said in a whisper. "It's better than Viagra. I have to beat the babes off."

After another scotch, and detailed descriptions of Finch's recent purchases of real estate in Malibu and Naples, Andy began to feel drowsy.

"Have a good rest, old boy," Finch said as Andy excused himself. "And remember— enunciate, do not use contractions and, whatever you do, do not sling-slang. Nothing makes the old windbag crankier than the vernacular."

They were staying in the upstairs "blue" bedroom, one of seven in the residence, not counting the guest house. The bedroom had a bathroom equipped with a marble inlaid Jacuzzi, as well as a fieldstone fireplace and small, wrought iron-railed balcony. Andy walked out the French doors and stood on the balcony while Marcia prepared for bed. A large white tent had been erected in the yard between the terraced patio and the walkway that led to the lake. Even now, past midnight, uniformed people were scurrying about arranging flowers and spreading linens over tables in anticipation of tomorrow's party. Moonlight shone on the lake in the distance.

A copy of the *MIT Technology Review* lay on the small table between two chairs, the imprint of Mr. Riker's wide-ranging interests, dispersed throughout the estate. He picked it up and glanced at the cover. *New Insights about the Brain—and how to get the most out of yours.* "Hmm," Andy's nonverbal utterance hinting at intrigue. He was jolted out of his momentary revelry, however, by the recollection of his encounter with Eastman Finch.

"Wage slave." He muttered.

◆ ◆ ◆

Sunlight slanted into the room through the cracks of the curtains. Andy rolled over to kiss Marcia, but she was already out of bed. He could hear the shower running and it all came back to him: When visiting here there was something akin to competition between Marcia and her sister Beatrice as to who would be the first awake and be in the kitchen helping their mother with breakfast.

The Riker's retained a domestic staff that included housemaids, gardeners and valets, but Martha Riker allowed no one to cook but herself. The impulse of the naive outsider was to applaud her gumption and self-reliance; however, nothing was so simple around the Riker's little *pied-à-terre*. The chore of preparing three meals a day inevitably caused Mrs. Riker's sciatica to flare up at some point and turned the simple act of eating into an endless source of anxiety. When Andy arrived in the spacious sunroom off the kitchen that was used for breakfast, Marcia and Beatrice were already fussing to get their mother off her feet and resting.

Mr. Riker seemed to be the only person in the household immune to the tension produced by his wife's essentially unnecessary exertion. He was engrossed in a crossword when he caught a glimpse of Andy.

"Aha, there's Andrew. Take a seat here," he said, pointing to the chair next to him. For some reason, which eluded Andy, Mr. Riker had an obvious fondness for his son-in-law. Andy suspected it was some aspect of his bobblehead dimension, which created a rapport between himself and Mr. Riker—that being a deaf ear to noisome emotional and psychic static—but he could not be sure.

"These blasted *Boston Globe* crosswords. There are too many pop cultural references. What's an '*Everybody Loves Raymond surname*'?"

"It's a television show, papa," said Claire, who was the only other person at the table.

"A television show?"

"Yes. A rerun."

"Who watches it?"

"I believe the answer is Barone, sir," Andy interjected.

"Barone? Yes, that would work. Good show, Andrew."

Mrs. Riker came in carrying a plate of sliced cantaloupe, grapefruit, pineapple and strawberries. "You'll have to excuse the strawberries: imports," she said, wincing as she put the plate on the table. "They are not as ripe as I would like."

"Do you know what the French word is for grapefruit, Andrew?" Mr. Riker asked. "Pamplemousse. Isn't that a fantastic word? Pamplemousse."

One of Robert Treat Riker's many pet peeves was the decline of language.

"The way people talk today, Andrew, is a disease," he discoursed as they munched on fruit. "When I was in law school you had to know grammar," he brought his fist down hard on the table and made the plates rattle. "All this like this, and like that. Where did it come from?"

"Valley girls," Andy offered. "California."

Mr. Riker stared open-mouthed at him. "Oh, my, we are all becoming valley girls. God help us."

After breakfast Marcia and her sisters went for a bicycle ride and Mr. Riker took Andy for a tour of his rebuilt solarium.

"People assume we're filthy rich but most of the money is tied up in this estate, which can never be sold." Mr. Riker talked as they strolled down a long hallway hung with landscape paintings and old photographs of Boston landmarks and neighborhoods. "I haven't worked in over 20 years. In a sense we're all a bunch of free-loading deadbeats living off the money of our ancestors. Luckily they're all dead so they can't criticize."

The solarium was a two-story, domed, rectangular glass-and-steel room situated at the far west, front wing of the house. The structure, which replaced a small, greenhouse at the side of the house, had been a work-in-progress for as long as Andy could remember, and had only been recently completed. The octogenarian guided Andrew through the room with visible pride. "This," he said, waving his hand as they walked into the surprisingly cool interior, "is the culmination of everything I believe in."

The back or "posterior" of the room, as Mr. Riker put it, was devoted to growing rare and exotic plants, which he cultivated from seeds. Hundreds of small clay pots with color-coded labels were arrayed on benches under tubes of fluorescent lighting. The colored labels designated the plant family, and, inscribed in meticulous handwriting, with the species name. Andy gazed intently at the label on one of the larger pots, "Hipp…ay…as…troom…."

"Hippeastrum Mandonii," Mr. Riker broke in. "Beautiful, showy flowers—already bloomed. I'm preparing my winter batch of plants," Mr. Riker said, pausing in front of a section of plants sprouting with broad, flat leaves. "These are bromeliads, a family of about 2,400 species native mainly to the tropics."

They walked into the middle of the solarium where a spiral staircase led up to an enclosed platform with a telescope. Mr. Riker pushed a button and a large glass panel on the ceiling began to retract sideways. "Meade 16-inch refracting LX-400 with robotic control. I can pick out the pimples on a Martian's arse. Bang-up view of the Perseids last month."

"The meteors? I heard something about it on the news."

"Yes, did you catch it?"

"Er, no … it was cloudy that night."

Mr. Riker led him past a desk and shelves stacked with the electronics of a ham radio station, into a room partially walled off from the rest of the solarium. The room housed a collection of antique, period scientific instruments, a small bench laboratory with an elaborate, multi-stage glass-tube, distillation set-up rigged with various clamps and tripods, a large drying oven, a new gas-liquid chromatography machine and a functional fume hood.

"People today are all idiots, Andrew," he said after a brief dissertation about an oscilloscope in a bank of electronics analyzing a signal's amplitude, frequency and distortion. "It won't be long before chimpanzees will be filing discrimination suits. No one makes anything! Everyone earns their living today staring like zombies into a computer monitor all day or, in the case of my high-rolling son-in-law, Eastman, helping unscrupulous parties in their pursuit of greed.

No one knows what pewter, brass, or ceramic is made from, what the Archimedes principle is, or how a battery works. That's why I admire you. You're out there dealing with acids and bases and all kinds of toxic substances. You have your hand on the pulse of the real world, Andrew!"

Mr. Riker, standing in front of the odd-ball array of old tools and instruments, gave Andy brief lectures about a sextant, an oscillating steam engine valve gear, an antique, double-beam apothecary's balance scale, a cork-making machine, an iron mandrel for making leather boot and shoe uppers, a device for measuring the hardness of materials and an exact period replica of the first reflecting telescope built by Sir Isaac Newton.

"Here's something the grandchildren like," he said, tapping a gadget set on a long bench running along the set of windows facing south with a view of the front grounds and circular driveway. It was a more sophisticated variation of a simple spy glass used to focus sunlight to a hot point, he explained. One lens collected the light, another directed it and a third focused it. Mr. Riker fiddled with the knobs and a bright point of light appeared on a metal sheet at the end of the bench. After about 30 seconds the metal was smoldering with an orange glow at the point of light.

"It's 1500 degrees where the light touches," he said in slightly diabolical tone. "I could burn a hole through every wall straight through to the kitchen, and with any luck, put Martha out of her misery once and for all… Ho ha! Just kidding, of course."

Andy strolled around the grounds for a while then spent the rest of the morning in their bedroom watching the pre-game shows for the first full weekend of college football. The party was technically a late brunch, scheduled to start shortly after noon. He opened the doors to the balcony. It was a dazzlingly bright, late summer day. The groomed grounds and terrace below were a hive of activity, as people rushed about attending to final details. To the side of the main powder-blue tent, a smaller white tent had been erected from which, it appeared, the dinner would be served. An ice sculpture of a sailing schooner, an icon in the Riker's family crest, was placed in the middle of the patio, around which had been laid red carpeting leading down the terrace and into the tent. Best of all, Andy observed, copious, linen-topped serving bars were arrayed around the grounds so that the intrepid guests could work their way from the very front to the very rear of the congregation and never be out of hailing distance (and a credible excuse for weaseling away from excruciatingly dull small talk) of the next round.

Marcia returned. Their bike ride had not gone well. Beatrice and she had wanted to treat themselves to a caramel mocha latte at the Starbucks in town, but Claire objected on grounds Starbucks exploits labor in third world countries. They ended up getting lukewarm, watered-down Nescafé from a gas station minimart.

"Why didn't you two just go to Starbucks by yourselves?"

"You wouldn't understand. Everything is not as simple as the Andy brain conceives it," she said, tapping him on top of the noggin.

Marcia had toiletry prep work to do before the party, so Andy put on his sport coat and went down to the patio to wait for her. He ordered an old fashioned at the bar and turned, intending to stroll the grounds when Eastman Finch strolled up.

"Starting early, are we?"

"Yep, and with any luck I'll be smashed by the time you give your speech. That way I'll find you amusing."

"Oh, I'll be amusing, old boy, you don't have to worry about that. Where were you all morning. The boys and I took a cruise in the Bent and were looking for you."

"Daddy Riker took me around the hacienda. Good bonding time."

Finch ordered a Corona and shook his head. "I don't know how you do it."

"Do what?"

"Let him patronize you."

"He likes me, and I rather like the man myself."

"Pshaww. He's using you. Can't you see that, dude?"

"No, I can't … dude."

"You're his pet project. Someone he can pour his ideas into. An empty vessel."

"Really?"

Finch took a swig of beer. "Yep. When you married into this family, they bought you. It'd be different if you had your own money, like me, but as an heir to their estate they got you by the short hairs and old man Riker has carte blanch to brainwash you with all the clan lore. I'm not saying *I* see you that way, pal."

Andy felt a sort of rigor mortis infiltrating his calm, bobble-head demeanor.

"Well, *old boy*, I was going to keep this quiet, but I might as well let you and the world in on the news, so no one gets me panties for Christmas. I'm buying a company."

Finch raised his perfectly trimmed eyebrows and smirked. "Tell me *more*, big guy."

"Seven figure revenues."

"Seven figures!?" Finch closed his eyes and swallowed a laugh, his face, in the next instant composed in earnest sincerity. "Andrew, that's a windfall that's going to get you on the radar of the government—you'd better hire a lawyer. What's the gig?"

"Plating operation."

"Plating?"

"Yeah, metal plating. Electroless nickel, chromium, and some other technology that's too proprietary to talk about."

"You mean like a factory?"

Andy and Finch were separated by a two-foot space of silvery summer light. He gazed at Finch's creaseless, carved mahogany face etched in a mirthfully mocking expression, and took a step closer. "Yeah, you know, like one of those dirty, filthy places with underpaid, overworked peons that make your Bentley and polo mallets." Andy reached out and grasped the collar of Finch's shirt with his fist and twisted, causing him to scuffle to keep his balance.

"How … incredibly …retro. Congratulations! Need to go over my notes."

Finch backed warily away, then turned and walked briskly to-ward the house. Guests were beginning to arrive for the party, which would begin formally with a gift presentation by the children in less than an hour. Marcia still hadn't appeared, so Andy wandered past the ice sculpture and down the side of the terrace on to a path that led to the rear of the house's west wing. He walked a short distance, daydreaming, and when he looked up he realized he was standing next to the solarium. He walked toward a door that came out on a small concrete landing, opened it and went inside.

It was quiet and peaceful inside and he breathed in the fresh aroma of plants. No wonder old man Riker had gone to such lengths to build this. Here was a bona fide haven for tinkering. A man could while away the hours here in pursuit of sundry diversions. There was a soft gurgle of water somewhere. He walked between the rows of plants touching the shiny leaves. He turned and toddled toward the front of the room and came to the bench holding all Riker's instruments. He swirled a flask that had some green solution in it. He picked up a silver weight from a felt-lined box and held it in his hand. He rested his hand on top of Riker's light-focusing contraption. Bright sunshine slanted through the glass into the room. Outside along the semi-circular drive he could see Finch's Bentley gleaming in the sun, parked aside from the other cars. He must have ordered the valets to keep their hands off it. "Empty vessel!" Andy thought. He twisted one of the knobs on the device and a light beam shot out the front. He paused, turning his gaze back to the Bentley. Andy pulled on a lever and the device rotated, pointing through a window to the outside, in the direction of the Bentley. He looked through a scope on top of the tube holding the lenses and saw the beam darting across the car's fender. He moved the tube slightly, so the beam came to rest on the right rear tire. He reached out and turned another knob until the beam became a small, bright point of light. The tire began to smolder. In an instant there was a loud pop, followed by a hiss as the car's bumper settled on the curb along the drive. Andy closed the lens and swung the instrument around.

"Disabled vessel," he chuckled, and strode out of the solarium back to the party.

On the patio, the crowd was being herded for the gift presentation. A small stage had been erected at the foot of the patio in front of the tent. He caught the eye of Marcia who, along with her siblings, was seated on the stage beside their parents: Mrs. Riker, in a full-length silver and black dress, and Mr. Riker in a tuxedo. The Riker's had requested that any gifts be given in their name to the Cape Mary Historical Society, of which they were one of the founding families. The children were presenting them with a seascape painting by the famous marine artist Fitz Bergamot Langdon. Marcia and Beatrice were going to unveil the painting, which sat shrouded behind them, but Eastman Finch had been appointed to first warm up the crowd.

"I'd like to welcome everyone to our humble *soirée.* As you can see, when Martha and Robert Riker decide to do something, they do not know the meaning of the phrase 'to slum'— ha-ha-ha."

Martha and Robert both shifted uncomfortably in their seats.

"Lest anyone think this is just an expensive little chichi bash, I want to assure everyone that Martha and Robert have, as usual, found a way to make an event commemorating 50 years of marital bliss, deeply meaningful."

A soft chuckle spread through parts of the crowd.

"But before going into the formal details of the presentation, I'd like to pay homage to a few of our distinguished guests."

Finch pulled out some index cards and recited the names of Congressman Trent Kelly and his wife, state Supreme Court justice Rosalyn Babson, partners of various law firms, CEOs and Board members at a half-dozen Fortune 500 companies, and a world-famous surgeon who spent half of every year working for free in Africa.

"Last but not least, I would be horribly remiss if I did not mention a very special person, one who I love as my own brother, my brother-in-law and Marcia's husband, Andy Freaking THE MAN Dodge —Andy, where are you?"

The crowd of guests murmured and searched, and with several people nearby recognizing him, Andy lifted a finger a few inches into the air.

"Andy has just informed me he is trading in his job as a chemical sales representative to become owner of his own company!"

Andy forced a half smile and waved at a quiver of polite applause. On the stage he could see Marcia looking at Finch with an open mouth.

"Way to go, Andy!" someone shouted.

"Yes indeed, you heard it here first. And wrap your head

around this. Andy has decided to do his part to keep American jobs in America and help the middle-class by becoming owner and president of, are you ready for this? A metal plating factory! Let's hear it for him!"

There was silence before a few scattered claps began to crescendo into a facsimile of applause. Just then a thunderous boom shook the air. Guests shrieked, and glass shattered on the patio as people dropped their drinks in fright. A woman from the kitchen staff came running out of the house toward the stage.

"Hurry! There's been an explosion on the front lawn."

A group of people led by Andy and Finch raced across the patio, through the house and out the foyer. Down the drive a huge plume of black smoke rose into the air. On the ground, barely visible through the smoke, orange flames danced around the crumbling shell of a vehicle. It was Finch's Bentley.

Finch was livid. "Call the fire department! Call the police!"

"Stand back," Andy yelled. "It may go off again. These things were made before halogenated flame retardants."

Finch pulled his cell out of his pocket and looked fiercely at Andy. "I'll get to the bottom of this, Dodge."

An instant later, Robert Riker walked up and stood calmly between them, gazing at the burning wreckage. "Looks like we have some fireworks with our party. Oh, well, it was an over-rated, tarted-up clunker anyway. Come along, Andrew, let's have a drink. I want you to tell me more about that company of yours."

4 UP AND OVER

The following Tuesday, Andy, along with the rest of the Tartan Chemical sales force, sat restively in the company's main conference room awaiting the start of a meeting. The assembly had been hastily called by general manager Dean Jurgenson and deemed "mandatory" in the emails he had sent out over the holiday weekend. Andy was seated between Joe Gemelli and Flip Davis, based out of Chicago and St. Louis respectively, both of whom had flown in that morning. Andy had not seen either since the annual company golf outing in June. Gemelli was finishing a long rendition of 'what I did on my summer vacation' when Jurgenson walked in.

"Good morning, gentlemen," Jurgenson, nattily dressed in a navy suit and red tie, said cheerfully, his greeting calling attention to the fact that his sales force was indeed a non-coed platoon. "I trust everyone has had an enjoyable, relaxing summer … My, my Joseph," he said, looking in the direction of Gemelli. "What a healthy bronze glow! I hope you're not forgetting to use sunscreen."

Gemelli smiled apprehensively, a soft chuckle suffusing the room.

"I've asked you here today to deliver some important news. As I'm sure you are all aware, our sales for the last, oh, six or seven years, has been as flat as a breadboard. This means, of course, that we're not making enough bread to keep certain, important people you'll never know happy," Jurgenson's expression striking an artful balance between the sincere and facetious.

"No doubt you are all familiar with—vicariously of course— the saying, 'if it doesn't kill you it will make you stronger?'" Jurgenson gazed out at twelve blank faces. "Well gentlemen, I've concluded if it does kill us, I'd rather it be you than me." A fit tennis junkie, their ostensible "big boss" had the lean, focused demeanor of a tiger stalking prey as he paced nimbly back and forth in front of the room, seeming to make eye contact with everyone in the room simultaneously.

"To that end I think you'll all agree some changes are in order. I've accepted the resignation of Nathan Pearly, effective immediately. Actually, I fired his ass but that doesn't get out of this room."

A nervous murmur rippled through the room. Jurgenson raised his hand.

"It is obvious that for all of Nathan's, ah, skills, he couldn't find the cheese if someone dropped it in his trousers. We'll be holding a retirement party for him in a few weeks at the Braywood Mall food court. You're all invited, of course."

The men sat in silence. Pearly was more than just their manager. He was a symbol of company stability; the embodiment of an ideal, cherished as sacrosanct by every man in the room—that company loyalty trumped the dehumanizing, profit-driven, dog-eat-dog tactics and dictates of the world.

"Yes, I'm afraid we need to change, gentlemen. But let's be honest, we need help to get there. And I think I've found just the person to help us. Will you please show Sondra in," Jurgensen said to an assistant standing by the door.

The door eased open and a young woman wearing a short red-and-white checked blazer and black mini-skirt strode quickly into the room and took a position close to Jurgenson's side. She stood gazing up at him with a 1000-watt smile that somehow seemed to convey a tad more than merely a professionally cheerful decorum.

"Gentlemen, I'd like you to meet your new boss, Sondra Cleaver." With the introduction, she turned her eyes, with some effort it seemed, away from Jurgenson and looked around the room, her smile slowly fading, as she took in the group of men with bored expressions slouched in their chairs around the table.

"Sondra's background is, well, unique. She has no experience in the chemical industry. Actually, she has no experience in sales, either. I see that as a strength, not a weakness. What Sondra excels at, I've discovered firsthand, is running a tight ship. As manager of the Grosse Point Tennis Club concessions stand, Sondra has raised prices three times and virtually eliminated double parking. So, with that,

I'm going to turn things over to the dynamic Ms. Cleaver, who I believe is eager to get to know you on a more personal basis."

Jurgenson walked out of the room and, as the door fell back and latched, a vacuum denoted by the first moment of stillness instantly filled with dread, communally felt, for the absolute power the woman standing before them now wielded over their lives, once a domain of contented, hassle-free employment. Sondra Cleaver, hands clasped at her waist, paced slowly off to the side, then back again. Yet even as they braced for the worst, their new boss's appearance —skirt edging into the realm of surreal in paucity of materials skirts are usually made of, with lush, shoulder-length brunette hair she flipped to the side smiling, it seemed, mischievously as she pondered her control over the cadre of characters before her—registered in the consciousness of each man in the room as "hot." The men understood a cough from the back of the room as a sort of relief from the collective over-stimulation happening involuntarily deep within the most primal gland of their brains.

"Guys, let's be honest," Sondra Cleaver at last spoke. "You probably think I'm unqualified. You think I got this job because I'm a young, attractive female. You think I'm standing here because Dean, I mean Mr. Jurgenson and me, are closely acquainted. You know what? You're right. No doubt you're all familiar with the figure of speech, 'take it like a man.' I suggest each one of you virile, strapping hunks of male sales flesh do just that and we'll be fine."

What unfolded that day was every Tartan Chemical salesman's version of the inner circle of hell: meetings. Sondra Cleaver initiated her sales force to the new management style with an hour-and-a-half PowerPoint presentation. The slide show delved deeply into the sales history of every salesperson for the edification of everyone in the room. Bar graphs proved indisputably that the accounts of every salesman peaked in their first year of employment with Tartan, then went into steady decline. The sole exception to the trend was Andy's account, which, thanks largely to Gloss, showed a slight rise over a ten-year period. Andy was beginning to involuntarily glow with a small measure of pride when Ms. Cleaver put up another slide subtracting the sales of Gloss Industries from his overall account. The slide depicted a jagged line tracking precipitously downward.

"Mr. Dodge, correct me if I am wrong, but I believe this is called a 'one-trick pony'," she said, raising her glasses slightly to look at him. "Lose that pony and the show is over."

The afternoon was devoted to "breakout sessions," one-on-one meetings with Sondra Cleaver in which performance was appraised, objectives established and timelines to meet those objectives set in spreadsheets. More ominous for the men walking out of those meetings was the sickening realization that this was only the tip of the iceberg. There were to be follow-up meetings, tons of new paperwork and heavy doses of "professional development." By the end of the day most of the Tartan sales staff had managed to update their resumes, search the internet and send out several applications. Gord Simkowski, who had over 30 years with the company, was the exception. He grabbed Sondra Cleaver's appraisals and objectives and ripped them to shreds. Walking out of the Tartan Chemical headquarters for the final time, he suddenly paused and peeled back on an impromptu vamp. "Alexa," he said in front of the handful of somber salesmen lounging in the foyer waiting for their meeting with Sondra, "turn on the air conditioning at my condo in Sarasota." Then, in a fairly laudable digital-assist*anteese* … "Okay AC turned on …. And cueing 401 K—5, 4, 3, 2, 1 BOOM!", he sidestepped out the door, dancing a spastic jig across the parking lot to his car.

After his meeting, Andy sat at his desk in mental and physical paralysis. He had begun to click on the link to his fantasy football league but canceled it. Ian Hunt popped his head into Andy's cubicle.

"I hear Ms. Cleaver rather enjoys slicing and dicing." Being in R & D, Hunt essentially worked unsupervised; his was one head safely out of range of the new boss.

"If Pearly were here I'd kiss his squeaky-ass Sponge-Bob shoes."

"Ah, our revels are now ended, are they?"

Andy pushed back in his swivel chair to look at Ian. "How philosophical would you be in my shoes?"

"I'd be resigned. I'm too old to give a shit about anything other than a shortage of 12-year-old reserve Glenlivet."

"She's going to 'sit in' with me on my sales calls next week. One day on the job and she's mother-henning me to death. Gloss will never let me forget this one."

"Well, ole Dicky is not long for this work-a-day world now any-way, is he?"

It was as if someone had just snapped his ass with a towel. Leaning back in his chair, Andy stared at and through Ian, his thoughts suddenly many miles away.

The drive home from Massachusetts had not been favorable to thought googling, a type of aimless, transportive daydreaming Andy enjoyed when left in peace and solitude with time on his hands. He was fascinated by memory; how, for instance, he could recreate a virtual past-reality, in precise detail: the high school gym on a cold Saturday morning in January before practice—the woody-waxy aroma, the pale yellowish light, the leathery thud of balls bouncing against the shiny wood floor—or recall that he bought a box of ban-dages, now in the medicine cabinet at home, during a trip to Florida and paid a clerk with conjunctivitis in one of her eyes. No time for lost-time recollections on this drive. Instead, because of his own silli-ness, he admitted, because he had allowed himself to be baited out of bobblehead dimension, he was paying the price with a lead role in drama.

Marcia claimed to be not so much angry as "hurt and em-barrassed" by his covert announcement of plans to buy a company. Nonetheless, fury seemed to be gaining the upper hand. How in God's name, she sliced her hands in the air as the kids tuned out with their cell phones in the back, could someone approach him with an offer to buy a company and it not occur to him to tell his wife? Wouldn't he feel like sharing this little tidbit of information with her? Wouldn't there exist the inkling of an urge to confide, to tell her something interesting that had happened to him? Wouldn't he want to fill her in on the details? Wouldn't he want her feedback?

She had a point, he had to admit. Why hadn't he mentioned it to her? The implication, he gathered, was that he was either un-thoughtful, secretive or both. Yet, as far-fetched and inexplicable as it may have seemed to her, he protested, the error, if that was what it could be called, was really one of omission rather than commission. He did not *decide* not to tell her. It simply had not occurred to him to tell her. And the reason it had not occurred to him to tell her is that he had not taken the offer seriously. He had changed his mind at the party on the spur of the moment. (He had too much pride to tell her Finch had incited him into it.)

The notion of him owning a company injected a much-needed dose of humor into the drive. Marcia threw her head back against the headrest and laughed as if she were viewing the best of *America's Funniest Home Videos*. "Andy Dodge, owner and president," she enunciated the words slowly, then observed, "Sort of like oil and water." She then enumerated the reasons why the combination was, "a formula for Armageddon." Andy the president would have to be patient, Andy the person was impatient, Andy the president would have to be organized, Andy the person was disorganized, Andy the president would have to supervise people, Andy the person enjoyed as little responsibility as possible … She rattled off another six or so of these insights in a lighthearted, sing-song kind of voice, as if she were picking petals from a daisy. He listened with detachment at his wife's rendition of "I'm married to a nincompoop." The truth was that when he had confided to Finch, he hadn't really been sincere. Por-traying the plan as a done deal had merely provided psychic relief from the compulsion to remove several of Finch's blindingly white front teeth via a head butt ala *WrestleMania*. He couldn't tell her this, of course. That was one of the fundamental conundrums of marriage. Women could be totally above board, and men, well, they had to be on their utmost guard to avoid giving in to the temptation that the right thing to do was to tell the truth on all matters, big and small. It was WAY more complicated than that, and any man who succumbed to this pablum was a level above an idiot, that being a jackass, even, perhaps, crossing into the realm of lunatic. Would she be less angry if she knew he was merely trying to save the family from a messy scene? Somehow, he was sure, she would focus on the seediness, not the nobility, of the gesture.

Sure, becoming an entrepreneur intrigued him "on paper," as something he could pursue, if he wanted. And he had even vowed that he would never again allow Finch to insinuate he was a company man or a kept man or any other variation of eunuch he could concoct and truly go into business for himself—someday. But, to that minute, the only iota of energy he had devoted to the ambition was to picture himself, feet propped on his desk, the odds for the first race at Pimlico on one computer monitor, and a game of *Destiny-of-Duty* on another.

Now, everything had changed. The arrival of Sondra Cleaver, and the imminent sale of Gloss Industries, were like two walls in a horror movie slowly closing in on him. The only way out was up. There was no doubt about it. Whether he really desired to do this, whether he was prepared to do this, whether he was even capable of pulling it off, didn't matter. He was now in the hands of higher powers.

It was early evening when he arrived home from the office. Ian had asked him out for a pint to settle his nerves, but he declined. He had business to take care of, he informed him. As he was driving home, a large passenger jet swooped low over the highway coming in for a landing at Detroit Metro. Flying and jets fascinated him, and becoming a pilot was the only thing he had ever really wanted to do since he was a kid. Then why hadn't he done it? That door had probably closed forever because he had failed to act. That wasn't going to happen again, he vowed.

Dylan was in the kitchen casing the refrigerator when he walked into the house.

"Where's your mom?"

"Upstairs. She just got home."

"Good. You and Jessica get dinner for yourselves and veg-out.

We'll be a while."

Marcia was standing in front of the dresser in their bedroom pulling her arms out her blouse. Andy closed the door. She had a great body still, toned from some type of yoga called "Nia" and 15 miles of jogging a week. He walked over, put his arm around her bare waist, and pulled her against his chest.

"How was your day honey?" he asked.

She drew her head back slightly to look at him. "Have you been drinking?"

"No, thinking."

She chuckled dryly. "Okay, Einstein, you hunk, what's up?"

He kissed her. "I'm not sure I'm ready for this," she said.

"You'd better be. We're talking the Big R and the Big S."

"Huh?"

"Relationship and sex, I mean spontaneity— it's in all the magazines."

"Since when do you read about relationships in magazines?"

"Okay, it's on the cover of magazines."

"Ha, ha, thanks for the context."

"This is the new me."

Marcia gave a quizzical look. "But it's a bit weird, Andrew, right after work ..."

"Sometimes weird is good."

She cocked her head and smirked. "Now that's something you know about."

He picked her up and tossed her gently onto the bed. An hour later they were lying eye-to-eye on their sides, enjoying a kinkier version of a blissed-out serotonin buzz. For a moment, Marcia was taken back to their first days together, after meeting on a holiday in Jamaica. He had been charming and hilarious, and they had exchanged phone numbers before leaving. Then she'd taken the leap and allowed him to visit her at her apartment in Boston.

"Remember that first weekend?"

"Yeah, you burned the flank steak but I like my meat well done. I took it as a sign."

The phone beside the bed rang and they let it go into voice

mail. "Hey, Andy. It's Ben. Just wondering if your bowels are functioning normally this week or if I should look for another partner. Let me know, buddy."

"What timing."

"You want your clubs back?"

"Someday. I'm playing like crap anyway."

The next morning Andy arrived at the office and found an email titled "Fair Warning" in his inbox. It was addressed to all sales staff from Sondra Cleaver: "It has come to my attention that a number of Tartan Chemical employees indulge in extra-curricular internet-related activities while at work. This is to announce a new policy, effective immediately—namely zero tolerance of all and any such internet-based activities, including on-line gaming, fantasy sports leagues, dating services, shopping online, stock-trading, gambling, discount liquor sites and all non-work-related email, including wives, ex-wives, current girlfriends and escort services. I have asked our tech-support department to provide me with a weekly summary of all staff internet activity filtered by every individual's IP address. The penalty for a first offense is dismissal. If anyone would like to discuss this or any other matter, make an appointment on my calendar, and allow at least one hour." The memo, as always, was affixed with her personalized signature slogan, in Gothic font "**Freedom is Slavery**."

A short while later, Andy put out the equivalent of an all-points bulletin for Dick Gloss.

"Where is he?" He asked Penny.

"I think he's with that nice young man from Crossbow—what's his name?"

"Jurasic."

"Yeah, him."

"Damn. Can you contact him?"

"I can call him on his cell."

For the first time Andy was peeved that Dick Gloss was

unreachable. The only person who knew his cell number was Penny, who was forbidden to give it out. Andy had taken to calling these and his other peculiarities, "Glossian," and the unknown cell number was a letter-perfect demonstration of the term. It created a layer of bureaucracy that ceded to Gloss an extra measure of leverage, control, the very essence of the man. If you left a message on a person's cell that meant the person, by common courtesy or professional ethics, would be required to respond to the message within a few hours or a day at most. If you left a message with a staff person, who knew when or even if you would hear back?

It was late afternoon when Gloss returned his call. Fortunately, Sondra Cleaver had just left after stopping by to suggest he tidy up his desk and cubicle. Gloss agreed to meet him after work.

"Let me guess, Mr. Nickel has had a change in heart," Gloss bobbed in his swivel chair behind his desk.

"Dick, I'd be thrilled to buy your company."

"You're too late. Crossbow's made me an offer."

"Is it final?"

"Nothing's final till it's final, but how do I know you're for real."

"I'm for real, trust me."

"You got the money?"

"No, not yet."

"Then you're not for real."

"Damn!"

Gloss detected a pang of anxiety previously missing.

"Okay, let me guess, you need some help with that lovely, sophisticated but understandably dubious wife of yours?"

"Uh huh."

"Let me think this through. This can't be any more difficult than back titrating the pH in tank 3 with a 0.50 molar solution of potassium hydroxide.

Marcia had dabbled in drama and theater in college, taking

courses on playwrights, great plays and staging and the bug had stayed with her. There was nothing to compare, she would say, to a live performance. She still occasionally took in a play with a friend; her husband having been granted a lifelong dispensation after he fell asleep and began snoring during a performance of *The Cherry Orchard.* She was therefore mildly flabbergasted when Andy brought home two tickets to The Royal Shakespeare Company's performance of *The Tempest.*

"Are you sure about this, Andrew?" She asked, gazing at the tickets with a look of joyful shock.

"Don't worry. I shan't snooze."

She threw her arms around his neck and hugged him. "I love you, Andrew David Dodge."

Certainly, it had come to her attention that his behavior had more recently been odd, that is, normal. For one thing he talked to her. Not a lot, by any means, but some. After dinner, instead of rushing outside or into the basement to pick up on the threads of one of his umpteen on-going projects or activities, he lingered a bit at the table. True, he fidgeted a great deal and she suspected he was only half listening, but he was there. One night, when she told him the story (long, she realized, by his standards) of a problem the bank was having with employees surfing the internet on company time, he proffered some sound advice—send out a memo counseling Internet discretion. The old Andy, she confided with amazement to her neighbor and jogging buddy Tera Talbot, would have sided with the deadbeats goofing off on company time.

She couldn't figure it, but she decided to relax and enjoy the "new" Andrew. The play was being staged in an auditorium on the campus of the University of Michigan. They decided to make an evening of it and eat a late dinner after the play. It was a balmy, autumn evening and as they strolled to the theater after parking, she glanced at him in his smart-looking sport coat and slipped her hand under his arm. He hadn't aged a day since they met but maybe he was finally starting to grow up, she thought.

They took their seats near the front of the mezzanine and were flipping through their programs when Marcia nudged him.

"Andrew, Patrick Newman is playing the lead role of Prospero," she exclaimed.

"Who?"

"You know, Captain Renoir of *Galaxy Trek*."

"No shit!" he said, Marcia nudging him as several people turned around to stare. "Didn't know he went in for this type of thing—can't pay as much as television."

"Andrew, actors don't always act for pay. They act for roles. It says here he got his start doing Shakespeare."

"Really? I guess Renoir is sort of the cerebral type."

"This is so exciting!" She leaned over and kissed him on the cheek.

After an announcement to turn off cell phones, the lights dimmed. The silhouette of an old radio shone through the stage curtain and the whistling noise of a heightening storm grew louder. The curtain opened and a group of men wearing heavy rain gear ran chaotically in and out of the inside of a ship. The first five minutes was all shouting, of which Andy did not understand a word.

The scene ended, and the curtain opened on a bald man in ragged clothing sitting at a rickety table. The crowd gave a quiet "ahh" of approval, recognizing the actor of *Galaxy Trek* fame.

Marcia whispered. "That's Prospero. His kingdom has been taken away from him and he's used magic to make the ship crash on this island."

The *Galaxy Trek* actor moved restlessly around the stage.

"I have done nothing but in care of thee, thee, my dear one, thee, my daughter, who art ignorant of what thou art, naught knowing of whence I am, or that I am more better than Prospero, master of a full poor cell, and thy no greater father."

"I thought he was Prospero," Andy hushed.

"He is, but not the Prospero his daughter knows."

Andy decided he wouldn't try too hard to figure out what was going on and instead just watch the actors, as if he were at a movie. Miranda, Prospero's daughter, was pretty. The guy called Caliban was a brutal-looking wretch and Prospero seemed to enjoy kicking and whipping him every chance he could get. Ariel was a smart-aleck and did not appear to enjoy working for the *Galaxy Trek* dude very much. In fact, Andy thought, for a guy whose kingdom had been stolen from him, Prospero did not seem to have much of a fan club.

At intermission Andy suggested they get a refreshment in the lobby. They wandered over a short, elevated walkway leading to the stairs and down into the atrium, crowded with people trying to pretend they were not gawking at one another. Suddenly, Andy felt a sharp slap on his shoulder and lurched forward.

"Dick!" he said, turning around. "What the …"

Gloss turned. His eyes slowly widening, and a slightly exaggerated look of surprise on his face. "Well, well, well, Mr. Nickel, this is the last place I'd expect to find you."

"Have you ever met my wife?"

"No, but with all the time Andy spends talking about you I feel I have." Gloss extended his hand.

Marcia, with an expression of surprise, glanced at Andy, then back at Gloss. "I've heard a lot about you … too."

"This is my wife, Angie," Gloss moved aside and a short, stout woman with a beehive of hair the color of antique brass stepped forward.

"My pleasure," she said with a graceful, delicate southern drawl.

They chatted as the line moved forward. Gloss said he was a huge *Galaxy Trek* fan and when his wife told him Patrick Newman was coming to town he bought tickets the next day.

"It's so like him," Angie waved her hand. "A connoisseur of the arts."

They reached the bar and ordered. Gloss insisted on buying. The group shuffled through the throng with their drinks to an open space along the atrium windows. Marcia and Angie conversed amicably. You could stick two women who had never met in a cell together and within ten minutes each would know more about the other than two male buddies knew about one another in a lifetime, Andy thought. Gloss raised his eyebrows and nodded in the women's direction. Andy forced a grin, feeling Gloss might be acting goofy; not wanting to attract the attention of Marcia's incredibly well-honed, sixth sense for the out-of-whack. He asked him if he got his email about the new reporting requirements for Class 4 hazardous substances, and Gloss went off on a riff about government over-regulation. Andy relaxed, sensing they were back on their natural footing: The world according to Gloss.

A chime began ringing to signal the start of the next act.

Gloss blocked the group from proceeding, Pavlov-like, inside. "Angie and I are planning on getting a bite to eat after the play. We'd love it if you could join us."

Marcia deferred to Andy. "Honey, that's an order not an invitation." Gloss's booming laugh could be heard through the atrium.

The second half of the play zipped along, as Andy drifted in and out of the proceedings. Prospero continued to flog and thrash Caliban, Miranda appeared to fall in love with a fellow named Ferdinand and everything turned out just right at the end with Prospero getting back his kingdom and Ariel ecstatic he no longer had to work for him. The *Galaxy Trek* dude got a huge ovation at the curtain call. Andy had even come away with a line he vowed to remember: "Misery acquaints a man with strange bedfellows." He was in disbelief he clearly heard the line, yet alone grasping its meaning. Man, in seven words, it occurred to him, old Shakespeare summarized a truth of the human condition. Note to self—words equal …. something … really cool when used correctly? Yeah, that was it.

They met up with Gloss and his wife and fell in with the flow of the crowd moving toward the exit. The night was cooler, but still pleasant. Andy had cautioned his wife to allow Gloss to pick the restaurant, but as nothing grabbed him, he threw the decision open to the group, saying he was "easy to please." Marcia had wanted to try a place called The Mongolian Grille, but Angie gently lobbied for a generic-looking Italian restaurant with an oval neon sign in the window advertising Miller Lite. It was mostly deserted at this hour and they took an oversized booth near the front window and the neon sign.

The waitress brought menus, large laminated sheets. Gloss declined his, saying he already knew what he was going to order— lasagna, garlic bread and a salad. Everyone else studied the sheet and Angie chided her husband. "Why don't you try something different, Dick? Every time we eat Italian it's the same thing."

Marcia gushed about the play. "The acting was superb of course, and the set was really done well—sparse but original."

Angie, a former English teacher, quizzed Marcia about her interest in theater.

"I love, LOVE *Macbeth*. I think it's the best play of all time."

"Ah, a tale of ambition and duplicity," Angie said in a low, brooding tone.

"I played Lady Macbeth in our high school drama club's play. 'Screw your courage to the sticking place and we'll not fail.'"

"Fascinating how people have these interests and sides to them you wouldn't guess."

The simple décor of the restaurant was pleasantly subdued downscale and collegiate. Angie ordered a carafe of wine. She was a child of the antebellum south, she said, raised in Savannah, where Gloss had met her while stationed at the Fort McCasey army base. After Gloss returned from Vietnam, they married, and Angie taught high school for 20 years before retiring to "become her husband's cook, accountant and psychologist." She hadn't traveled nearly as much as she had hoped, but now that Dick was selling his business, she was planning to trot the globe, with or without him in tow.

Andy saw Dick's eyes light up at the mention of the sale. He took a quaff from his beer, set it down and leaned his hefty torso over the table toward Marcia, across from whom he was directly seated. He raised a finger and waved it in the direction of Andy, who he referred to in distant terms as "your husband." Did she know that "your husband" had extraordinary people and leadership skills? "'Your husband' as in one Andy David Dodge?" She enquired skeptically. The Andrew Dodge she knew was—how could she put this delicately as he was sitting here and had been so wonderful to arrange this evening— detached, at times? Oh, yes, this was indeed the homo erectus to which he was referring and as far as that perceived flaw in "your husband," Gloss said, that was a shortcoming even thoughtful, considerate people occasionally suffered from, a result of extraordinary powers of concentration and the compulsion to "lose one's self in the task at hand." He had known Andy had had this knack with people for quite some time and here was the proof: Most remarkably, "your husband" was liked by all of Gloss Industry's employees, a group of people who, as a rule, took the Hells' Angels as role models and would find fault with the Mona Lisa if he had it been hung in the company cafeteria. Did she know "your husband" was the only person, other than his wife, to whom he could confide personal, business and trade secrets and that the reason he could do this was not because, as it might be assumed, it would go in one of his ears and out the other, but rather that he could trust him. A person's trustworthiness was an indicator of good business sense and acumen, Gloss told Marcia. And did she know that "your husband's" knowledge of the fundamentals of electroless nickel plating was second, a distant second, true, only to his own knowledge of the exceedingly intricate batch-chemical process, but that said, with a little application, a little diligence, he would have a very good chance of becoming a "rising star" in industrial metal plating. Oh, yes, this person was a straight shooter, a good listener and an all-around nice guy. Moreover, he had a gut feeling about "your husband" formerly known as Mr. Nickel, the salesman Dodge. He sensed he was ready for a challenge; that, like the warrior and seeker, he was ready to break with his past, set off on a lifelong journey of learning, continuous improvement and a prolonged, dog-eat-dog fight with the foreign companies that were attempting to undermine and steal our manufacturing base, the bedrock of our standard of living and national security. Marcia squinted in askance at this last digression, but Gloss was on a roll. He sensed —no, he much more than sensed—he KNEW, even as he knew that Captain Jean Luc Renoir would somehow find a way to vanquish the Croataics (even as his last phaser burst was deflected, his auxiliary power fizzled and the Croataic king teleported his entire army into the bridge of the Enterprise) in episode 89, that "your husband" was destined for big things, even, dare he say, heroic things as the next owner and president, exclusive of patents and some licensing agreements, of Gloss Industries.

Angie was sipping a wine, still gazing at the menu and seemed not to have heard a word of her husband's verbose panegyric. Marcia emitted an indistinguishable guttural sound that may have been the autonomic nervous system's version of a cross between a groan and a "whew." Andy, who had never been out with Gloss in a non-work social setting, had something of a flash or an insight that all reality, at least the human social part of it, was fabricated by people such as Gloss, who had a gift or a will to create out of thin air the dramatic terms by which others were forced to react, take sides, think things they wouldn't ordinarily think, and make decisions. The world *was* a stage, but it was the Glosses of the world who were the directors.

The waitress came with garlic bread and salads. Gloss quickly peeled open the red-and-white checked cloth in the basket and plucked out a long, extra-thick roll of bread. He opened his mouth wide and bit into the bread once, twice, three times, chewed, and seemingly defying the laws of physics, again began to dissertate. He was just beginning to say how fortunate it was they had run into one another when he fell abruptly silent. Gloss looked up, fear in his face, eyes bulging and mouth open, then bent low over the table stretching and holding his neck with his hand. His arm flailed, knocking his beer mug onto the floor and he half rolled out of the booth, staggering into the empty table next to them. Angie screamed; Marcia put her hands to her mouth. Andy stood, put one foot on the booth's bench seat and leaped over Marcia. Gloss was wobbling, his hands clasped at his throat, face turning a deep reddish-blue. Andy shoved Gloss at the shoulder, grabbed him around the waist and squeezed hard. Gloss spasmed backward with his full weight and Andy would have fallen with Gloss on top of him if the cook hadn't run out of the kitchen, come up from behind and braced him. "Too low," the cook shouted. "Squeeze him higher." Andy, panting heavily, scrambled to keep hold of him. Gloss was dragging him around like a rag doll. Andy suddenly felt rage swell up at this man who enjoyed bossing him, belittling him, tutoring him, patronizing him, and who was now doing his best to make him look like a bumbling fool trying to save his life. A millisecond of a vision of Prospero happily flogging Caliban flashed into his brain. He planted his feet in a spread-eagled position, locked his hands under Gloss's sternum, let him roll forward a bit, then, under the influence of adrenaline and anger, grunted and jerked his arms up as hard as he could, pulling Gloss off the floor, his legs dangling as he balanced against the ballast of Andy's chest. Gloss retched, and, with a sort of a pop, a pinkish-white blob flew across the space of 10 feet and splattered on the window just below the oval, neon Miller Lite sign.

Gloss stood hunched over, hands on a table, trying to catch his breath. Andy was drenched in sweat. Angie ran up to Andy and threw her arms around him. "God bless you," she said, sobbing. "Bless you, bless you, bless you." She planted a kiss on each of his cheeks.

Marcia sat frozen in the booth, hands still covering her mouth. Finally, she stood, put her hand on Andy's shoulder, and gazed up at him with a look of amazement. Gloss slowly turned around, wiping his face with a towel the cook had handed him. Still hunched, he raised his hand and pointed at Andy. "Someday," he said, panting, "you're going to thank me for thanking you for saving my life."

5 OUT OF THE FRYER

Robert Treat Riker was sitting in a padded wicker chair on the lanai overlooking the turquoise water of the Intracoastal Waterway when the phone rang. He overlaid an issue of *Yankee* on his thigh and picked up the handset from the patio table.

"Hello, Father."

"Marcia, dear! I was just thinking of you."

"And me, you … obviously. How's the weather?"

"Another frightfully sunny warm day I'm afraid. We'll have to make a difficult decision soon on whether to take *Balboa* up to Marco Island or capitulate to the Henson's invitation for cocktails."

"And Mother?"

"She's out gardening now and I imagine she'll collapse soon—oh yes, I can see her, she's wincing badly."

"You should be more sympathetic, Father."

"You're right—oh, shoot, she's wincing badly."

"Father!"

"I know, my new year's resolution and I've already broken it. But enough about martyrdom. Today is the big day, is it not?"

"Yes, Andrew officially took over the company this morning. It's his first day as president of Gloss Industries."

"That's the only thing I objected to. It should rightfully be called Dodge Enterprises or Dodge Metal Parts or Dodge something-or-other anyway."

"We didn't have a choice really. Some legal sticking points related to patents. The name's grandfathered. After three years we can change to Andrew David Dodge's Chocolate Factory if we like."

"And how is president Andrew doing?"

"Gloss is orientating him for the day before casting off to Thailand and parts unknown."

"That seems awfully short. I trust he's reachable if Andrew

gets in a pickle."

"He says the place runs itself. Besides, Father, Andrew is a big boy now."

"Oh, yes, I know. I'm so glad you came around to him. He needs you behind him. I've been studying him for a time, and I think he's ready for this."

"He'd better be."

"He'll do famously. You've invested your share of the estate wisely."

"Don't mention that papa ... it makes me a bit nervous."

"Nonsense. And he's making real things with real workers for real people. None of this hedge-fund credit swap default derivative's mumbo jumbo. This country was built by the Edison's and Ford's of the world, not by financial carpet baggers like my well-heeled son-in-law Eastman Finch."

"Eastman has done very well for himself and his family, Father. I'm sure you're happy for Beatrice."

"Oh, yes, I suppose he knows what he's doing, whatever it is."

"Yes, he does. By the way, Beatrice mentioned something odd. Seems Eastman suspects Andrew had something to do with his Bentley blowing up. I can't imagine why he would think that, can you?"

"That's ... ridiculous. Where did he get that idea from?"

"He said one of the gardeners saw Andrew in the solarium shortly before the explosion."

"So?"

"The car was in front of the solarium."

"Rank delusional paranoia, dear. Those old cars are all rattle-traps and safety hazards. Probably a leaky gas tank."

"Investigators say the fire started on the tire."

"Now look, for the pocket change it put him out, give the poor boy my condolences and tell him to back off. I won't have this amateur conspiracy speculation getting into the open. Andrew has his hands full and doesn't need to be accused by someone in the family of something he didn't do. Besides, I rather enjoyed seeing that over-priced pimp-mobile burn. Highlight of the day."

"Father—I'm going to pretend I didn't hear that."

Andy woke that morning, the first day after New Year's, with a jolt. Normally, he rose slowly, drifting in and out of a dreamy sleep until the clock-radio alarm clicked on, slapping it quiet with his hand, then almost falling asleep again before the wake-up mode kicked in and the annoyingly cheerful voices of the radio DJs who were hell-bent to make it clear that, yes, the universe was putting another day at his disposal, and rested, ready or not he had to get up and do something. Today, however, the first inkling of consciousness threw on the flood lights inside his brain. He not only had to get up, he *had* to get up. He slid his legs out from under the covers and groggily sat up on the edge of the bed in the dark. There, it occurred to him, it was probably the first time he had ever gotten out of bed, with the exception of when his wife had gone into labor, without having second thoughts about it and wishing he could crawl under the warm covers and snatch a few more moments of deep, renewing, dream-filled REM sleep.

But then everything had changed, and he, not someone or something else, had directed it to be so. He groped his way through the dark into the bathroom, shielded his eyes and flipped the light switch. Through half-closed lids he reached inside the shower stall and pulled the water tap on full blast. Half an hour later he was showered, shaved and dressed in a charcoal suit, white shirt and red paisley-patterned tie—a slam-dunk power ensemble for his first day of a new life.

"Andrew," Marcia called in the dark from the bed as he walked out of the bathroom. He felt his way around the edge of the bed until he touched the warmth of her hand. It closed tight and pulled him down.

"Best of luck, honey," she said as he leaned his face over and kissed her. "And remember, ask questions, take notes. No one expects you to know everything. It's your first day on the job."

"Marcia," he said, nestled against the silky warmth of her

cheek, "I own the company. I'm supposed to know everything."

"I just think you have to be realistic, that's all. Don't do or say anything rash. Admit ignorance."

"How about if I just walk in with an orange Bozo wig."

"Don't be defensive. You know what I mean."

It had snowed overnight and when Andy arrived at the plant Gloss was clearing the walkway with a snow blower in the semi-darkness. Gloss directed him to the first parking spot in front of the building. Gloss had deferentially moved his truck one spot over.

"Perfect timing," Gloss yelled, wearing a Detroit Red Wings varsity-style jacket, waving Andy over as he got out of his car. Gloss pushed the blower into a drift sending a plume of snow skyward where it swirled in all directions and blew back down on Andy.

Andy stooped and walked up to Gloss. "Can't you get one of your guys to do this?" He shouted over the din.

"This is non-value-added work, which means it's mine, I mean your, job." Gloss laughed heartily, his cheeks a flushed red. He let go of the handle and the machine stopped. Gloss removed his glove and held out his hand. "Welcome to your company, President Dodge."

"Thanks," Andy gazed dismally at the snow blower.

"Let me show you how this antique works. One quart of oil for every five gallons of gas. Push the prime for a cold start. Pull the choke up and let her rip." Gloss yanked the start cord and the machine roared to life. "Have a go, Mr. Prez. Best way to earn the respect of the employees first day. I'll be inside making coffee."

The cold easily penetrated Andy's lightweight overcoat. He tried pointing the blower chute in every direction. It didn't matter: A stiff wind roared unimpeded down the street blowing snow back into his face. After five minutes his teeth began to chatter. After ten minutes the tops of his ears began to sting and he began to lose feeling in his feet and toes, which were soggy from snow penetrating the sides of his loafers. Once he had finished the sidewalk, he trudged stiffly into the tiny office foyer wiping ice from his eyelashes.

"Look what the cat dragged in!" He heard a howl of laughter and turned. Penny was sitting, a rotund, cashmere-pink object de blasé, at her desk behind the wood-paneled counter marking the boundary of the front office. "Not a bad job but you need to clear around the overhead door in case we get a delivery."

Andy felt water dripping down his forehead. He reached up his hand and brushed back his hair. It was crusted with ice. "Sure. I'll take care of it once I thaw out."

A blonde, thin, haggard middle-aged woman in a blue lab coat standing near Penny walked out from behind the counter. "You might want to consider toweling off before you drip all over the floor and create a safety hazard … boss," she said, before vanishing through the door into the plant.

"What's her name again?" Andy asked Penny.

"Luann. She's your quality control department."

"She's a smart-mouthed little …"

"Andy," Penny interrupted. "May I call you Andy?"

"Yes, of course."

"Luann don't mean no harm. She had a bad marriage and hates men."

"Is that so?"

"Humor her. You need her more than she needs you."

Gloss came out of a room adjacent to the office holding some papers. "I was just making some copies for you. Let's get your coat hung up and I'll show you how to make coffee."

"I'm fine, thanks."

Gloss chuckled, leading him down the hall into the small lunchroom. "It's not for you dingbat," slapping him with the papers in his hand. "It's for Penny, Luann and the crew."

"You're the president and you make the coffee?"

"Times have changed, Mr. Nickel." Gloss lowered his voice to a whisper. "You remember what happened when the proletariat got upset in France and Russia?"

Andy gave Gloss a bewildered look and Gloss winked.

"The filters are in the cupboard. The procedure is taped to the wall. One scoop for every two cups of water. This is Penny's cup here. She likes it double-double."

"Well?" Gloss admonished as he turned to go out.

Andy shuffled back to the counter and lifted Penny's Garfieldemblazoned mug from the rack, poured out a double-double, and deposited it dutifully on Penny's desk.

"Not there, here," Penny said, pointing to a sideboard by her computer.

He dutifully moved the cup to the correct spot. "Sorry."

Andy's sarcasm failed to register with Penny. "Don't worry, first day on the job, you'll get the hang."

He walked a short distance down the hall to Gloss's large rectangular office situated at the far end of the building's front wing. Andy had been in the office many times, and immediately noticed the bare walls, stripped of plaques, certificates and photos. A huge framed picture of Gloss standing next to a sailfish he caught in the Keys sat propped against the wall on the floor. The blinds on the large pane of glass behind his desk, usually closed, were pulled fully open. A stack of legal-sized manila folders was piled on the desk.

"Pull up a chair."

Gloss took a swig from a bottle of Coke.

"Why don't we start with an RFQ."

Andy vaguely recognized the term.

"Rib-fry-quota," Gloss beamed mischievously.

He took a request-for-quote form for a pinion gear out of a file and began to go over the various sections. Take notes, Andy remembered.

"I need to get something from my bag."

"Sure."

Andy took out a small electronic device and laid it on the desk in front of Gloss.

"What's that?"

"A digital voice recorder. I can get up to 100 hours on this doodad."

Gloss laughed and looked at his watch. "You're going to be able to sing karaoke for about 92 of those because I've got a plane to catch at four this aft."

Gloss spent the next few hours extemporizing about customers, purchase orders, acid baths, degreasing, chromium plating, copper plating, the lost art of tin-nickel plating, sand blasting, capital equipment write-downs, health and safety training, environmental compliance reporting, QC/QA, ISO 9000, employee wages and records, payroll, company server and software systems, plant and office security, supplier contracts, hazardous material handling, waste disposal, taxes, plant blueprints, shipping procedures, invoicing, with digressions and mini-lectures on the periodic table of elements, atomic absorption spectroscopy, Michael Faraday, the large hadron collider, the best deli in the area to buy kielbasa, his medication-induced constipation, his golf game, the ruination of the country by Hollywood commies and liberal media, and a long-time thwarted desire to assassinate the head of the Detroit Water and Sewer Department.

Andy, accustomed to waiting out Gloss's long-windedness, now sat transfixed and utterly overwhelmed.

"I started this company with a Koroseal-lined chrome tank, vapor degreaser, filter and a bus bar," Gloss said. "Used a garden hose for the main water line. I'm handing you over a well-oiled machine. All you got to do is keep it humming."

Andy swallowed, and nodded weakly. Just then Luann poked her head into the room. "Power kicked out on the six-tank, boss. We're down on the number one line."

Gloss stood up. "Come on, prez. Let's get you some action."

They put on safety glasses and walked through the door that led from the offices into the lab. A young man in jeans and a white lab coat turned as they walked in. Gloss walked up to him.

"Whatcha doing, Donny?"

"Back-titrating hydrochloric acid from line 2, tank 4 with sodium hydroxide. Mac needs the pH."

"Good. When you're done, I want you to show Mr. Dodge here around the lab. He's your new boss."

Andy held out his hand. "Nice to meet you."

Donny shrugged and took it. "You from these parts?"

"Yep, Sterling Heights."

"Cool, you know Melissa Bodine?"

"Not off the top of my head."

Donny laughed, "Top of my *head*, ha ha, that's great! You're funny, man."

They walked out the back door of the lab into the plant. A pungent, sour chemical aroma washed up Andy's nose, nearly causing him to choke. He knew the smell, but this morning it somehow seemed stronger. He grabbed a paper towel as his eyes began to water.

Gloss took a deep breath. "I love the smell of sulfuro-chloro-benzene in the morning. Cleans your system right out. Don't worry, in a week it will smell like fresh linen to you," Gloss chuckled.

The plant, about the size of a couple of side-by-side football fields, was laid out on a grid demarked by three plating lines, one for plating nickel, one for plating chromium and a "utility" line that could be used for a mix of operations. Each plating line consisted of about 12 open, 500-gallon tanks, divided into two rows of six, with an elevated catwalk between them. It took three people to operate each line—one person to rack parts, another to operate the overhead hoist that moved parts up the front side of the line, and another person to move parts in and out of the tanks on the back side of the line. Most of the tanks were heated, and plumes of steam swirled up from the plant floor into the girded steel rafters, making an orangish haze around the banks of fluorescent lighting hanging in the beams. Even though it was winter, Andy felt a discomforting, tropical-like heat press through his clothes, and reached up to loosen his tie. The heat, smell and hazy light caused him to be nominally less aware of the unidentified, loud din—a sort of amplified humming, that permeated the air and mandated the use of elevated voice levels, or shouting, during plant-floor conversation, such as it was.

Gloss marched to the far corner of the plant, Andy trailing in his wake, and stationed himself before a garage-door sized, metal-clad box, divided on the front into yard-square panels. Gloss yanked open one of the panels.

"This here is the switch gear box," Gloss yelled. "When we get a voltage surge it blows out circuits. Goddamn power company uses outdated equipment—you'll get to know this panel like your medicine cabinet."

Gloss grabbed a cardboard box and a pair of oversized tongs

from a nearby shelf. He walked back to the panel, opened the box and pulled out three, shot-gun-shell-like red tubes. "Plant runs on a 3-kilowatt power system and 383AF circuit breakers. These here," Gloss said, holding up one of the red tubes, "are 1200-amp fuses."

He opened another smaller panel, pulled on black, rubber gloves, grabbed the tongs, yanked out the bad fuses, and installed the new ones, all in less than 30 seconds.

"Got it?" he said, turning to face Andy.

"How do you know which ones are bad?"

"It says right here, above the door: 15 aught, 32 five-000, 12A. That's the six tank, line one."

"Oh."

"Simple, huh?"

"Sure, but that's pretty dangerous stuff, you know—high voltage and all that. Shouldn't a qualified electrician be handling it?"

Gloss assumed the sort of benign, kindly expression one uses when talking to infants and the infirm. "Oh sure, I could hire an electrician, a pipe fitter, a fork truck driver, maybe even a health and safety director. That's $300,000 out of my, I mean your, pocket. Or let me put it in terms you can appreciate. That's ten years-worth of table dances at The Glass Slipper."

Andy gulped.

"Yeh-eh-eh-eh, dude. Get it? It's not rocket science."

"Couldn't Mac take care of it?"

Gloss stared at him. "Look, just between you and me, Mac dropped out of school in ninth grade. In fact, in this entire company, there's only one person who has a high school diploma—Penny. And she missed magna cum laude, if you know what I mean."

Gloss started to stroll away but suddenly turned. "You aren't having any doubts about this, are you?"

Andy stared into Gloss's voluble face, hypnotized by both its sheer, fleshy immensity and the waves of expression that seemed to flow across it, forcing out a laugh at last. "It's a bit too late for that."

"No, Mr. Nickel, it's way too late for that."

"Mr. Gloss, I mean Mr. Dodge, I mean probably both of you, you are needed in the front office," Penny intoned through the plant loudspeaker.

When they reached the office, a man with a neatly trimmed salt-and-pepper beard, trench coat and wire-rimmed spectacles was standing stiffly in the office foyer.

"Darren Tilsdale," Gloss boomed. "OSHA inspector region five. Where in the hell have you been keeping yourself?"

The man's long, peaked face remained completely immobile. "Not at the country club, Gloss."

"That makes two of us," Gloss said, holding out his hand. "How long has it been, a month?"

"Two weeks, actually," he said, keeping one hand attached to his briefcase and the other in the pocket of his fastidiously pressed London Fog.

"Right. Can I get you a coffee?"

"We've received an anonymous report you might be in violation."

"No!" Gloss aped surprise. "The same anonymous person as last time?"

The smallest of smirks creased the corner of Tilsdale's mouth. "I'll need to review your recordable injury logs, of course."

"We don't have injuries."

"That's what bothers me?"

"It bothers you that no one gets injured?"

"It bothers me that you never have a report of an injury."

"So, let me get this straight—we're bad for being good?"

"I'll also be doing a complete plant inspection."

"Be careful out there, Tilsdale—those part racks weigh a ton each. I wouldn't want one of them to accidentally fall on you."

"Gloss, I've been inside blast furnaces and sheet metal presses as big as your building."

"Tilsdale, I'll admit, you are a person who lives dangerously. But let me introduce you to the new person who's responsible for seeing you make it out of our filthy, job-creating operation alive: Andy Dodge."

Tilsdale turned and looked at Andy.

"Mr. Dodge, have you ever read the Occupational Safety and

Health Act?"

Andy's eyes darted from Tilsdale to Gloss back to Tilsdale, re-calling, in a moment of clarity, that the only books he had read cover-to-cover were *The Secret to the Short Game* and *101 Killer Cocktails.* "It's on my list."

Tilsdale smiled, glancing at Gloss. "This is going to be fun."

Back in the office, Gloss noticed the look of concern in Andy's face. "Don't worry too much about Tilsdale. His bark is worse than his bite."

Gloss paged Mac and the three of them headed out for lunch. On the way to the restaurant Gloss made a stop at a plumbing supply store. A burly man with a clean-shaven head and a drooping Fu Manchu mustache greeted Gloss in Spanish as he walked in. The store consisted of a single long counter situated in front of an open warehouse of supplies stocked on ceiling-high, gray metal shelving. A short sidewall behind the counter was hung with racks of clips attached to yellow slips of paper. Several glossy, decades-old magazine playmate foldouts were pinned randomly in spare areas along the wall.

"You got that order of PVC fittings?" Gloss asked.

"Sheeet, I thought you wanted CPVC."

"That'll do."

The man threw a square cardboard box on the counter.

"Ricky, this is Prez Dodge, the new owner of Gloss Industries."

"You can call me Andy," he said, holding out his hand.

The man took Andy's hand. "Deek and I served in the same platoon in Nam. Deeky carried me three miles through the jungle with shrapnel in my leg."

"Under fire."

"Sheeet, rockets wheezing over our fucking heads."

"Place crawling with Cong."

"You need anything man, jeez, let me know."

Andy nodded and smiled, trying not to cringe as Ricky clenched down on his hand with each rocket and bomb.

"Anything, usted comprende?" the man said, looking fiercely into his eyes.

"Yes, sir, I mean sure, Ricky."

"Eeet's a dangerous, dangerous world out there, amigo."

"It is? … Oh yeah right. It's friggin' scary."

"Ricky helped me with a couple of my inventions," Gloss said, winking at Andy.

It was chicken-Ceasar-salad-no-croutons day for lunch. Mac dutifully ordered the greens, following Gloss's lead, but Andy wavered. He studied the menu while the waitress repeated the specials. He could feel Gloss staring him down. It was a breach of manly etiquette not to know exactly what you wanted when you walked into a restaurant. Andy finally ordered the steak fajitas, then glanced sheepishly in Gloss's direction. It was an instinctive reaction, and he chided himself for it. Fuck him, he thought, straightening up in his seat. He gazed nonchalantly at the lunch crowd along the bar, asserting his independence from this maniac who, as a living, breathing anachronism in modern, victim culture, could probably be charged with bullying and dozen other 'hate' crimes, such as his standing reference to Madonna as a dumb bitch.

"Thwack!"

Andy leaped in his seat at the sound. Gloss had brought his hand down hard on the acrylic-coated wood table.

"We need to have a toast, Mr. Nickel."

The waitress had brought a round of Coors Light, and the three men clinked the necks of the bottles.

"May prosperity rain down on you like free radicals in the acid bath of life."

"A hero of our time," Mac saluted Andy with his bottle.

"That's very poetic, Mac."

"Straight out of Lermontov's novel of the same name."

"Oh."

"It's about this dude who is powerless and doesn't fit in—reminds me of Mr. Dodge here," Mac chuckled wryly.

Andy hooked his free arm around the back of the booth and took Mac in. He had a wide brow, sunken cheeks and dark, slightly oriental eyes. His hair, a faded russet, was pulled back in a short ponytail. He had become acquainted with him while selling the

Tartan wares. Mac ran the plant's inventory, as well as carried out assorted odd jobs in his role as "plant manager," which was really Gloss, of course. Andy had to get the chemical inventory numbers from Mac whenever he called on Gloss, and their conversations, while brief, always covered a lot of unusual terrain. Andy had casually sized up Mac as a good ole boy, an image in keeping with Mac's battered blue Ford pick-up equipped with a gun rack and a bumper tattooed with a confederate flag—a source of continual, open-wound-like angst and paranoia for Ja-Coby, the company's sole African-American employee. Only now did Andy recall that there was always a magazine rolled up in the back pocket of Mac's jeans.

Mac had been married three times and had six children from four different women, only two of which were his wives. During his wild years, which he claimed were over, he'd been chain-whipped in a bar brawl that had started when he accidentally crushed the toes of a biker babe with his hog at a Hell's Angels' rally. One particularly nasty blow to the head was a source of headaches and dizziness to this day. He had done time in two states for "various misdemeanors," been through rehab, filed for bankruptcy, recovered from cancer and chemotherapy, had a daughter addicted to pain killers, an autistic son and a mother with dementia. The court had issued restraining orders on one of his ex-wives who had buried a paring knife in his shoulder. "Guess it was a sign things weren't working out," Mac drawled. He had lived and worked in 42 of the 50 states and three countries doing "anything that required liftin', haulin' or diggin'.'" And he had yet to turn 40.

"You don't sleep much after 40, you know that?" Gloss broke in.

"Man, I can't cotton that," said Mac. "I like my zee's."

"It's an hour here, get up and pee, repeat."

"Shoot the dog, dude."

"Look at it this way—you bought the company at the right moment in your life, Mr. Nickel."

Andy was digesting this remark when Gloss launched into a panegyric about his own vitality and work ethic, which somehow digressed into analytical lament about the high cost of energy and the effect it was having on the bottom line.

"That is a problem you are going to have to apply your keen mind to, Mr. Nickel."

"Yeah but don't forget the trouble in the Caucasus," Mac spoke. "If the Russians keep advancin' into South Ossetia it could cause a whole heap of trouble with the Baku-Tbilisi-Ceyhan pipeline. You take a couple of million barrels of crude offline and watch what happens to the price of green beans."

"You read a lot, Mac?" Andy asked.

"Picked it up my first time in Folsom. Nothing like a little time in the pokey to turn you into a *feelasopher.* Now it's the only hobby I got—other than trappin' coon."

Gloss let out three distinct "ha's", which resounded above the din of the restaurant. "Correct me if I'm wrong but wasn't it Socrates who got burned at the stake?"

Mac drew off his beer. "No, they just gave him something like 20 or 30 Quaaludes."

"Well, see what happens to *feelasophs?*"

Andy's eyes glazed, looking through Gloss. For a moment he went blank. He saw himself rising, walking around the rim of the table, and standing in front of Gloss, who looked up at him with a goofy, befuddled expression. Andy slammed his fist hard into the side of Gloss's jaw, making his head ricochet into the back of the booth. Andy watched in delight as Gloss's head wobbled back and forth, as if tethered to a spring. Every now and then Andy reached out and slapped it to keep it wobbling, like a bobblehead doll.

"Sir. Sir?"

Andy felt a nudge and leaned aside for the waitress carrying a tray of food. He looked at Gloss who was talking cheerfully to Mac. He blinked, shook his head, and feeling a sudden need to splash some water on his face, stood and walked toward the back of the restaurant, in the direction of the restrooms.

"Don't forget to wash your hands dude," he heard Gloss call out behind him.

Tilsdale was sitting at a table in the small cafeteria filling out paperwork when they returned from lunch. "You've got hydraulic oil on the floor, two improperly stored drums of sulfuric acid and three people not wearing hearing protection," he informed Gloss.

"Not me—him," Gloss said, pointing at Andy.

"Okay, I'll get on it," Andy informed Tilsdale. His tone of dismissive authority gave him a twinge of satisfaction.

"Mr. Dodge, are you aware that there is a dangerous accumulation of fumes in your plant?" Tilsdale asked without bothering to look at Andy.

"Those aren't fumes, they're just smells."

"I've taken some readings. There is two-tenths part per million of ammonia nitrate, one-tenth part per million of hydrogen sulfide and point zero eight micrograms residual acidic nitrate, all exceeding allowable limits."

"We've always been in code," Gloss protested.

"The code's changed," Tilsdale said dryly, still writing. "It's gotten *stricter.*"

"I'll put some fans out there, blow the stuff around," Andy said.

"Mr. Dodge, I could shut your filthy little operation down this very moment if I wanted to. As I always try to give new, ahem, customers the benefit of the doubt, I'll grant you 30 days to come up with an action plan to get in compliance with federal law."

Just then, a worker in coveralls burst through the cafeteria door. "I … I can't breathe," he said, slumping into a chair.

Gloss looked at Andy and rolled his eyes. "Okay, Duberg, we'll send you to medical."

"Where's that?" Andy asked.

"Penny. She's also shipping, receiving and accounts receivable."

Tilsdale rose and packed his briefcase. "I'll be honest with you, Mr. Dodge, I don't like companies like yours. See what you do to the employees?"

"Pay them?"

"Put them in harm's way and subject them to a life of cease-less drudgery."

"Kiss my keester, you donkey-eared Swabian transvestite."

Gloss yanked Andy by the arm into the hallway.

Back in the office, Gloss threw three black, six-inch-thick bound volumes of procedures on the desk. "If you get in any trouble consult these. Covers everything from recharging the ion exchange columns to changing the toilet paper. The ISO 9000 auditor nearly came in his pants inspecting these."

Gloss began to get noticeably antsy, pacing as he spewed out a cavalcade of final instructions about the minutia of the business, checking his Garmin watch with GPS navigation as he talked. He and his wife had to be at the airport in an hour for their flight to Bangkok.

"Now, Mr. Nickel, this way, please," Gloss said, curling his finger for Andy to follow him. "I've been saving the best for last."

Andy took out his recorder.

"What I'm about to show you is top secret, and this isn't mentioned anywhere, even in the procedure manuals. Just shut up, turn the damn thing on and listen."

He led Andy to the far back corner of the office, reached into his pocket and took out a small, egg-shaped remote-entry key fob. He clicked it and a square panel on the office floor, hidden by the weave of the carpet, slid open revealing a metal platform. "Get on." Gloss clicked another button and the platform descended, the panel closing above them. They were in, what first looked like to Andy, a recording or broadcast studio. The room was lit by several standing tripod lamps and the walls and ceiling were entirely covered with dark blue indoor-outdoor carpeting. At one end was another small room with large glass window. Gloss opened a door next to the window and walked inside.

"This is the control room."

"Dick, control room for what?"

"The plating of niobium-titanium, uranium enrichment tubes —the tiny tumblers."

"Say what?"

"Patent 18367428-DG. Came up with a way to enrich uranium 50 percent faster."

"I didn't know you did this."

"I've told you a hundred times."

"I forgot."

"Well, now you know—again. But no one else does, and the U.S. government wants to keep it that way, verstehen sie?"

"Mum?"

"Can't even tell your wife."

"Someone has to know about this, right?"

"The U.S. government pays $1000 for each tube. You will make 100 tubes a week in that plating tank over there. The procedure is on the computer under the file big backslash mother backslash bazookas. Your contact is a guy named Calvin Clancey, a super-sized, super-heavy, in-your-face black dude. Clancey works for the Pentagon. I've already sent him your biometric data. Each week Clancey will contact you with different drop-off instructions for the tubes and pay you $100,000 in cash. You are to deposit that cash immediately into the account indicated on the computer. Sixty percent will be forwarded to Gloss Industries, i.e. you, and as the patent holder, I get the rest. Got it?"

"Man, sounds complicated."

"Piece of cake."

"What if something goes wrong?"

"Not allowed. If it does, however, push the red button on this key fob," Gloss slapped the fob into Andy's hand.

"What happens then?"

"Don't know, never had to use it."

"This is crazy, man."

"Mr. Nickel, welcome to reality. Have to run."

After Gloss had left, Andy sat in the office gazing at the spot in the floor with the hidden hatch. The shift was over, and all the workers had left for the day, leaving the building composed in tranquility. A contract janitor popped his head through the door.

"Sir, when would you like your office cleaned?"

"A bit later."

Andy leaned back in his swivel chair and propped his feet on the desk, thinking of Sondra Cleaver, and letting out a soft chuckle. This was all his, he thought, gazing around the office. He reached over and grabbed the computer mouse. Several quick clicks later he was on Santa Anita Park checking the post time and picking his horses for the day's daily double. No Sondra, he thought, freedom is damn cool.

6 OPERATION COTTON CANDY

From his office on the 60th floor of the south tower of the CNT Center, Eastman Finch had a clear view of the Upper West Side, Midtown and all the way down to the Bowery, signaled now, like the Phoenix, by the rebuilt, freshly-finished, 104-story, One World Trade Center. What a city! No one, no entity, no concomitant of pure evil, however well-funded or acutely conceived, could ever bring this city down, he mused. On this Tuesday in late January, Finch was sitting at his desk talking on his cell, as he was 90 percent of the time, what entailed, loosely speaking, a verbal exercise in some dimension of dissimulation, with a multi-tasking element added in—an acute, hyper-appreciation of the view spread out before him. Even in mid-winter the panorama that presented itself was spectacular, with the gaggle of midtown buildings, like some crazy, urban, glass and steel, crenelated recreation of the Badlands, sweeping away to his left, and the Hudson, a wide, deep blue chasm between the north and south of life, between the Perrier-Jouet Brut and the brute, between Movado and mendicant, between apogee and almost. Finch loved the apo-gee, but he had his sights set on an even higher trajectory: Gin Lane, South Hampton.

True, he had enough assets right now to cash out and easily clear the ticket on the Georgian, ocean-front estate he'd been ogling. But circumstances, mainly petty tax reasons that could turn non-petty in a hurry, required him to keep these assets on the bench and under the radar. The great recession, after all, even six years later, had changed America, and Finch knew full well the serfs and finger-waggers of the world woke up every morning with the face of people like him hand-painted on their bocce balls. What he required to acquire, and at last give him upper footing on his wife Beatrice's patronizing, old-money family, was a fresh, stockpile of cold, hard cash. And all he needed to do that, really, was pull one magic rabbit out of his hat—the Street Holy Grail also known as an over-the-topper, uber-deal or unmentionable. Fortunately, something with all the telltale features of it appeared to be falling into his lap this very moment.

"I'm down for that Bambino," Finch broke into the multi-party conversation. "I'll have Tiffany do a patent search and get back to you *tout suite*."

Finch checked the three new calls that had come in on his cell. One was from his masseuse, another from his racket ball partner and a final call from Brianna. The last had come in on his burner cell, a phone registered officially in his secretary, Tiffany's, name and used only for designated "unofficial" business. He left Hank Berlinski a voice mail canceling their match at the West-Side Story Racket Club, then dialed Brianna on the burner.

"Hey, baby."

"Fuck you."

"Baaabeee!"

"I'm tired of this shit. This is the second time you've stood me up in a week. I'm not your fucking rent-a-mistress."

"Okay, okay. Listen, just give me till eight; there's a big deal going down. I'm doing this for you, sugarpop."

The implication of a large sum of money immediately calmed the nerves of the young lady. "Purple Rose?"

"Just tell Ricardo to give us our usual booth with a view of the park."

This complicated things. He had originally canceled their dinner not because of the impending deal, but because Beatrice had harangued him the previous evening to promise to keep their appointment with the marriage counselor. Now it was back to plan A. He figured he might as well deal with this sooner rather than later.

"Hey, Sweetie, how's your day?"

"Fuck you."

"Honeee!"

"I'm tired of this shit. You're calling to cancel, right?"

"The deal of the century is coming down, baby. I'm doing this for us."

After he got off the phone with his wife he walked into the adjacent office and planted a kiss on the cheek of Tiffany. Blonde and perpetually tan, Tiffany had the body and looks of an exotic dancer, which she had once been. Finch had offered her the secretary job after meeting her on a trip to Las Vegas. He paid for her apartment on Second Avenue and picked up the tab on most of her expenses, including a usually hefty monthly Visa bill, but restricted his relationship with her to "contact flirting," and an occasional dalliance with no semblance of deeper meaning going into it, nor going out it, so to speak. Common sense dictated that one never had a serious affair with one's own secretary; besides, Tiffany filled one of the most indispensable roles at any New York financial firm—testosterone magnet and de facto rainmaker. He knew of at least three deep-pocket clients who were blubbering over her. Now, admiring her violet mascara, white teeth and warm smile, he regretted—not seriously of course—taking up with Brianna instead of Tiffany. Tiffany was really a simple girl and easy to please—she just wanted stuff. Brianna on the other hand was educated and dangerous. He had made a major blunder in that sense and the only strategy he knew to pursue at this point was to concoct ways to delay the consequences of that mistake, as long as possible.

"I need you to look up a patent registered to a guy by the name of Dick Gloss. It's for some kind of titanium coating. Can't imagine why that would be valuable."

"Let me write this down. D … I … C … K. What did you say the last name was?"

"Gloss, as in lip gloss."

"Oh, why didn't you say?"

"Find out everything you can. I'll see if I can locate where this shit is made."

The arc of Eastman Finch's lucrative career had coursed from day trader, to mutual fund manager, to hedge fund manager to, at present, owner and CEO of his own private equity firm, Bluestone Carver. Technically, as he liked to say, his job was to put money in contact with other money. The ways and means of doing this, however, were multi-faceted, and his work occasionally required him to take on "special projects," such as the one he was presently entertaining. Some of these projects involved overseeing or executing tasks not traditionally associated with a financial services firm. Realist that he was, Finch had no problem providing clients with "value added" and stretching the boundaries of what a firm such as his was and wasn't supposed to do. As a result, his company was quickly getting a reputation, even in international circles, for its uncanny, indeed some suggested, strangely supernatural, ability to make things happen—literally.

Though he had yet to learn all the details, the project proposed to him earlier in the day excited him for numerous reasons. First, no one else would do it. No competition meant a higher fee, almost like a government job. Second, it was clear that this was not your ordinary, small-time take-over bid. Someone or something wanted something bad, and this enhanced the propensity to waylay common sense and adopt a "money is no object" stance. As well, the source of funding, he was told, would remain anonymous. Finch knew a desire for investor anonymity, from the government's perspective, was a "red flag," because of the implication that a portion, or all, of the money would be neither traceable nor taxable, which, from his perspective, merely imbued the project with another level of merit. Lastly, the deal, from his initial perusal, appeared to have perfectly legitimate firewall protection of three to four front companies, sort of like a set of nested Russian dolls which, with correct engineering, rested inside each other but never touched.

Finch opened his browser and typed "Dick Gloss" into the search box. The search returned about 60,000 results, including several on the first page that were X-rated. He clicked on the first "official site" link and opened the home page of Gloss Industries. Under "About Us" Finch read:

> *Gloss Industries is a state-of-the-art nickel and chromium plating operation serving the automotive, transportation and aerospace industries. Founded by Dick Gloss, Congressional Medal of Honor–winner and holder of more than 50 patents, the company has been at the cutting edge of commercializing*

innovative technology in the metal plating industry. As of January 1, the company is now being managed by new owner and President Andrew Dodge. Mr. Dodge, who has over 15 years' experience in the industrial chemicals industry, has vowed to continue the company's tradition of innovation, quality and customer-driven service. Please feel free to contact Andy directly and ask him about the "take out specials" and new customer appreciation nights, this month featuring mojitos and a live mariachi band.

Finch pushed back in his chair. Son of a Somalian pirate if it isn't Granddaddy Riker's favorite auto arsonist himself, Andy Unabomber. He grinned. Never will be executing an offer of non-refusal be easier, more enjoyable or more satisfying. Gin Lane, here I come.

Beatrice Riker-Finch watched as her 16-year-old son, Sullivan, drove out the driveway and down the tree-lined street of their Greenwich home on his Vespa Ciao. She lamented that it had been a mild winter, allowing him to drive the damn thing even more. It was her husband's idea to give him the moped for his birthday and she fretted every time he went out on it, from the moment he left until the moment he arrived safely back home. Indeed, it seemed to her, she now spent most of her time in modes of anxiety. Perhaps, she mused, sixteen years of being married to Eastman was beginning to take its toll. The realization that a case could be made (as her sister, Marcia, had once suggested) that she was turning into her mother, appalled her. She was, by hook or crook, determined not to let that happen.

She walked to the rear of the house, let their Akita, Totoro, in through the French doors of the sunroom and tidied up a pile of magazines on one of the antique oak end tables. A Tiffany glass window covering in the design of a cupola caught the angling rays of the low winter sun, scattering red and blue light into the room. Daisy Higgins of the Greenwich Decorative Art's Society was coming over for tea and Beatrice still hadn't decided if she should serve scones or shortbreads, both of which were store bought, or home-made pumpkin bread. Still another decision looming was whether to use the porcelain Japanese tea service or the cabbage-rose patterned Wedgewood china—the dilemma being iconoclastic versus traditional.

Ten minutes later, Daisy, who bore a striking resemblance to a younger version of former First Lady Jocelyn Barker, walked breezily into the front hall.

"I just love your house, darling, every time I lay eyes on it."

"I'm beginning to hate it."

Daisy blinked and shook her head, "Girl, what on earth is wrong?"

The two women retired to the sunroom; tea served in Wedgewood, with scones.

"You've been acting erratically for some time, Beatrice."

"Eastman's cheating on me."

"Oh dear, I'm so sorry," Daisy said placing her hand on Beatrice's knee. "No wonder you've been out of sorts."

"Actually, I could give two, maybe three shits."

Daisy looked at her with mouth agape. "You *have* changed, Beatrice."

"It's all about location, location, location. And kids."

"But what about *your* life?"

"In what dimension would that be?"

"Here, of course," Daisy said, noticing Beatrice's hands shaking as she raised her teacup to her mouth.

"Well, I plan on living in a parallel universe from now on."

"Ah-ha, ah-ha," Daisy forced a laugh.

"As Sartre said, if you are lonely when you are alone, you are in bad company."

"Ah, yes, hmm."

"Besides, I think a Soul Cycling Class would be fun."

"Oh, yes, Ava Goldman took one of those and said it cleaned her out."

"Literally?"

"No, metaphorically, at least I think that's what she meant."

"I wouldn't think Ava could handle something like that."

"Really. I mean the woman bruises like a Georgia peach."

"I want to be a bruiser. I want to bruise."

"Have you heard from your sister?"

"Oh, she's got it made in the shade. Great job, wonderful, down-to-earth, normal husband."

"What does he do?"

"Chemist or something."

"Must be highly intelligent."

"Oh yes, he can light it up."

"He can, can he?"

"And pound the rock."

"Shoot from the hip?"

"Even better, shoot on the fly."

"I see. Now what about that property in the Hamptons Eastman's been eyeing?"

"He shan't buy me."

"Is he putting in an offer?"

"I believe this will be done."

"I hear Mort Feinstein is going to jail on securities fraud."

"Another one bites the dust."

"The world has changed."

"Only the strong survive."

"So true."

"The bruisers, and the bruised."

"My, that's a gorgeous porcelain fishbowl planter. Is that *Effete de Burgundy?*"

"Parisian-brothel rococo."

"Where did you get it?"

"I think Totoro dug it up."

"Hmm, really? Well, it's been nice visiting with you, Beatrice, but I just have to get my rugs out of the dryer." Daisy reached into her Gucci bag. "Why don't you give this man a call when you have a moment; he's done wonders for me," she held out a business card.

"Dr. Leonard Berlioz? You think I need to see a shrink?"

"Darling, we all need to talk things out once in a while."

"I am NOT going fucking crazy!" Beatrice clasped her teacup, stood up and hurled it at the brick wall above the fireplace mantle, the exploding shards of ceramic raining in tinkling arpeggios to every corner of the room. "There, is that the act of a crazy woman?"

Daisy drained the last of her tea. "I know exactly how you feel, dear." Then she stood and rifled her cup across the room with a swift flick of her wrist.

The two women stood in silence gazing down at the broken remains of their afternoon tea. After a moment they embraced in a hug, each not sure if the other was laughing or crying.

Oprah was on the television, which, being a chunky old analog, sat on an elevated platform in the corner of a sparsely furnished room, in the top floor of a three-story building overlooking a deep, wooded valley in Northwest Pakistan. Oprah was interviewing a former crack addict, who, with the help of a gay policeman, had turned his life around and was now building for Habitats for Humanity and playing harpsichord in a baroque-music orchestra for formerly homeless people.

"I just find your story so intriguing," Oprah beamed at the man, leaning toward him with her legs crossed. "How did you learn to play the harpsichord?"

"I have an addictive personality. I traded my coke addiction for a harpsichord jones. Practiced 12, 14 hours a day."

"Fascinating. And where did you find a harpsichord? I mean it's not exactly something you can pick up at a garage sale."

(laughter)

"My partner, Frank, had one in his basement. When I was at my rock-bottom lowest, Frank took me in off the street, fed me and took away my crack pipes."

"Is Frank here? He is? Let's bring him on. May I present Montell's partner, Frank."

(shouts of glee, hugs, creepy convulsive sobbing)

"Ladies and gentlemen, let's take a break here and we'll come right back to tell you the rest of this amazing story."

A turban-topped man in a white robe rose from one of the sofas arranged against the walls and clicked the mute button on the remote.

"Allah Akbar."

"Allah Akbar," droned the 12 or so men sitting in the room.

"We have DVR so we can watch the show later," the man standing said. "Malak has to get back to his flock, so we need to click-start the meeting."

"Kick-start," said one of the seated men. "I think you mean kick start."

"Yes," said the man whose full name was Abdul Afzal Jabbar Khan Lala but who went by moniker A.J. "I believe we have a quorum."

A.J. reported that the planned torching of the ski resort north of the Swat river had been successful, thus eliminating a potential incubator of Western tastes and values.

"Allah Akbar," the group intoned.

He then reviewed the names of new people receiving the group's death fatwa, asking for any recommendations.

A man raised his hand. "George Bush."

A.J. threw up his hands and moaned. "Zubair, you do this every meeting. George Bush is already on the list."

"So, I make point, you got problem with that?"

"And what is your point."

"That George Bush should die a thousand deaths and his ashes buried in monkey shit."

A.J. slapped his forehead with his palm. "Okay. Let it be noted in the meeting minutes that Zubair has moved George Bush die a horrible death over and over and his remains fed to a pack of hyenas—are we go to good now?'

"Good to go."

"Right."

A.J then reported that the umbrella group for pirates hijacking cargo and cruise ships around the Horn of Africa had requested funding for five Miami Vice-style speed boats.

"If we supply the boats we get a 25 percent take of the ransom," said one man who was sitting.

A man with a long, thin face and beard, a face seen often on Western television, and presumed dead, raised his finger. Everyone fell silent in anticipation of his words. "No, 50 percent."

"Fifty percent," the group repeated. "Allah Akbar."

"It is done," said A.J. "Now, I want to report some exciting news. Our long search for a way to enrich our own uranium ore has brought fruit. We have found a company in the States that makes just what we need."

"Ha!" said Zubair. "That's best one I hear all day. So, we just call them up and put in order."

A.J.'s eyes narrowed. "Have you ever heard the saying, where there's wool there's a way."

"You mean where there's a will there's a way."

The man with the thin face seen often on Western television and presumed dead raised his finger again. "God will be on our side."

"Allah Akbar."

A.J.'s cell phone rang. He reached for the phone clipped under his robe. "This I expect will explain things better to the doubting nattering nabobs and ho-hos in the room." He pushed the speaker-phone button on his cell.

"Hello, is this Abdul Afzal Jabbar Khan Lala?"

"It is me."

"This is Graham, your contact in London. Allah Akbar."

"Allah Akbar, my friend. I hope you are talking on a non-traceable phone."

"Yes, the signal is scrambled through an enigma box three times before sent."

"You are wise."

"Anything to help the overthrow of decadent, corrupt Western civilization and at last establish a utopia based on the teachings of Mohammed, Zoroaster and Balthazar."

"Ah, certainly," A.J. said, making the coocoo sign with his finger. "Now, what can you tell me."

"We have located the rumored technology the U.S. government is using to make the once slow, exceedingly complex task of producing bomb fuel as easy as making cotton candy."

"Yes, but how are we going to get our hands on this cotton candy making equipment?"

"Through an international deal broker in New York."

"He can make a deal?"

"Yes, he assures me he can. In the U.S. they call it an offer of non-refusal."

"Is it safe?"

"They tell me the man who now owns the company is apparently a lazy nitwit who only cares about golf, partying and fantasy football."

"And what is this dealmaker's price to execute an offer of non-refusal?"

"Twenty million up front, twenty million on delivery." All in the group turned their eyes on the man with the thin face often seen on television and presumed dead. The man raised and waved his hand. "Chicken feed."

"We will have the money delivered to the dealmaker electronically from a number of private, non-traceable accounts and currencies. Half upfront, the other half on delivery of the bomb-making equipment."

"Allah Akbar. But my friend, what can you do to compensate me?"

A.J. shrugged, pushed the mute button, then spoke. "Do you prefer death by machete, épée or Swiss Army knife?"

Laughter echoed out of the room and across the valley to the hills where Malak's sheep were peacefully grazing.

Fifteen minutes before he was to meet Brianna at the Purple Rose, Eastman Finch received the call confirming that the terms of the deal had been accepted. Elated, he immediately phoned his accountant in the Caymans to provide contact information required to initiate transfer of the funds and operation Cotton Candy.

"Any problem keeping that amount of cash under the radar?"

"It's using non-cloud algorithms, almost like digital chits. Even the U.S. government can't keep pace with a million 30-year-old gamer-hacks still living at home with nothing but time on their hands to wreak digital antic hay. We'll bleed it in a few million at a time, over various investments."

When he got off the call, he rifled through his contacts and scrolled through the names, finding the information for Melinda Chow, publicist.

Finch chuckled dryly touching the number. "Publicist, right."

"Hello?"

"Melinda, Eastman Finch. I've got a job for you."

"I'll only take it if it will make the world a better place."

"God, I love working with people of high integrity."

"As the Joker once said, whatever doesn't kill you only makes you want more. What's up?"

"An unmentionable, project code 'Cotton Candy.' Here's the deal ..."

Half an hour later Finch walked into the Purple Rose, not a hair out place and freshly scented with the Pierre Cardin fragrance Brianna liked.

"I was about to leave," Brianna said when Finch slid into the booth beside her kissing her neck.

"No, you weren't," Finch laughed.

"Damn if I wasn't."

"Well, I'll make you happy—bottle of Cristal," he told the waiter who had arrived at the table. "We're celebrating."

"You're always celebrating, Eastman. You're the most celebratory person I know."

"That only means I always have a lot to celebrate. You're lucky."

"What is it this time?"

Finch related, in very vague terms, project Cotton Candy, emphasizing the monetary terms.

"Sounds suspicious to me," Brianna said. "Who would pay that kind of money for what amounts to a take-over of a job shop."

Finch, who had one facial expression, a sort of smirking grin accented by glint-filled eyes, as if he were perpetually amused by himself, gazed with this look into Brianna's flawless olive, Mediterranean complexion.

"Proprietary technology, baby. PT."

"For what?"

"For what, for what? For what does it matter?"

Brianna stared solemnly at him for a long moment. "Okay, I'm done asking questions."

"Good. Sammy," he told the waiter who was now serving the champagne, "could you bring us an order of tuna wasabi crisps and the watercress and shrimp *salade.* We're splitting."

Finch lifted the fluted glass and looked through the low lighting, across the marble floors and out the glass walls overlooking Central Park, the tops of bare trees dimly lit by the unseen streetlamps below. "Here's to us, baby. To faster horses—me, and younger women—you."

Brianna put down her glass.

"I'm afraid I can't drink, Eastman. I must tell you something … I'm pregnant."

7 ENTANGLEMENT

At Christmas, just before Andy took over the reins of Gloss Industries, Marcia had given her husband a couple of business books. One book, *Empowering Employees—Whether They're Ready or Not*, was on the best-seller list, and another, *Get the Lead Out —Leadership Principles for Clowns, Misfits and Curmudgeons* was getting talked about as part of the fresh, kick-in-the-pants, business "anti-matter" movement, with catchy, counter-intuitive, motivational mantras such as "Loveable Losers are Still Losers." After he had taken off the silver and gold wrapping to find the books, Andy gazed at them in a speechless stupor, as if he had just been handed the clay tablets of the palace archives at Knossos written in Linear B.

Marcia nudged up against him on the sofa, wreathing her arm under his. "You promise you'll read them?"

"Sure thing, honey. They're so ... big."

"Andrew, you are now in charge of an entire company. You need to expand your horizons and learn some new things."

"I think I've got it wired, honey. I'm the boss; they do what I say."

Marcia smiled dismissively. "Okay, okay, I will," Andy demurred.

So it was that each night in bed, he spent 15 minutes, usually with much fidgeting, reading and picking up what he could. He had a strong, visceral aversion to pages full of unbroken text; instead located and browsed pages with diagrams, bulleted points and lists of things to do and don't.

"They could save a few hundred trees if they just printed a damn summary of the key points," Andy remarked one night.

"There are case studies in there. That way you get to see how good managers solve difficult problems."

Their marriage, it occurred to Andy, had never been on firmer footing. Marcia, with nominally more experience in managing, became something of his confidant and mentor. She nit-picked less and seemed to forgive his inevitable lapse or foible more readily. It was playing out just as Vince had foretold—a marriage needed a higher cause, a mission, a crusade—who knew? From Marcia's perspective, Andy carried himself differently. It wasn't a complete makeover by any means; there were still some potholes, serrated edges. But there was potential. What had once required blind faith now merely demanded a bit of imagination. All steady as she goes, hold the course, and the way looked to be generally moving forward, some bad, some ugly, but more, increasingly good. Even though it was still early days, he seemed to be becoming more cognizant, when working with people, of the nuance required, in one's expression, words and tone of voice, to achieve a desired outcome. He didn't always make the right choice, but she could tell he was clearly trying, rather than resorting to the one-size-fits-all response (the one entailing the least complication for himself) that used to be his default setting. Marcia had no way of knowing just how profound a change this was, striking, as it did, at the core of his bobblehead philosophy of life-coping skills. Nor could she quite put her finger on other subtle transformations suggesting growth, industriousness, and, dare she say, maturity. One Saturday morning, several weeks after he had taken over the company, they planned to stop for breakfast en-route to Jessica's volleyball game. When they arrived at the selected restaurant there was a 30-minute wait for a table. Andy looked at his cellphone and quickly came up with an alternative. "That's cutting it close to the start of Jesse's game—there's construction on John R. and no easy way around it. I know a little place up the road that does breakfast tacos to go." It was nothing more than a line item in the books of most wives, but it was Marcia's fate to be on the outside looking in on most wives. Instead, Marcia found herself admiring the quick mental arithmetic and unexpected decisiveness on display. The Andy she once knew would have dawdled, sought consensus and ended up "going with the flow," no doubt risking missing the start of Jessica's game.

The back-story to Andy's noble strides in the realms of leadership and time management was this: Gloss's much-hyped selling point, the promising prospect of well-oiled, hassle-free operation that, like some miracle perpetual-motion machine, ran itself, was shattered in about a half a day. Shortly before noon on his first full day in the office after Gloss's departure, Luann poked her head into his office.

"Heat's down on tank three, boss. Got four racks of parts and nowhere to put them."

Andy was sitting with his feet propped on the desk, laptop balanced on his stomach, typing a Facebook message to a high school classmate. He gazed up at Luann. "Tell Mac to fix it."

Luann laughed. "Mac don't know how."

"How about Donny or Duberg?"

"You must be kidding. Those nimrods couldn't spell cat if you spotted them the c and the a."

"So, who's going to fix it?"

"That be you ... Mr. President," she said sarcastically, flapping her hands in the pockets of her blue lab coat as she walked briskly out of his office.

Andy sat in the silence, a warm sinking feeling coming into his chest and stomach. He lifted the laptop off his belly, placed it on the desk and sat up in his chair. Damn Gloss, he thought. His instincts told him something was off with this operation his first day and that the obsessive-compulsive core of the man, even in absentia, was behind it.

"Call holding on line one," Penny spoke through the intercom.

Andy snatched the phone, vaguely hoping it might be someone who knew how to fix tank three.

"Mr. Dodge, I presume?" The man spoke with a thick, snooty British accent, which sounded more weird than real.

"It is. How can I help you?"

"HAHA, GOT YA!" Andy jumped and pulled the receiver away from his ear. "Yo, this is Calvin Clancey," he said, executing a seamless glissando into south-side Chicago patois. "I'm your eye in the sky, your superfly, the man with the cash, if you got the stash. How is the newly minted C-E-O doing on God's graciously green and fecund ga-ry-a-ry-a-sphere this fine morning?"

"Ah, so-so?"

"Mmm-mmm, supercaladocious-extra-copacetic. Mr. Dodge, I am calling to arrange the 3 p.m. pick up of 100 whoopee widgets otherwise known as tiny tumblers used to make the fuel to keep the world safe from dangerous demons, despots, dictators and other dastardly mother stabbers and father rapers. Y'all got my package?"

"Oh yeah, right, look Calvin we're going to have to put that off. I've got a prob…"

"Whoa, whoa, hold it right there, Yankee Doodle Andy. Didn't Big Daddy Shiny Schlong inform you—100 tiny tumblers every Wednesday? This is not an option. See, this ain't the lazy hazy crazy $10,000 screwdriver days anymore over at the five-sided anus. We got rules and the rules must be followed. Let me bring you in on something. This little project, of which you are now a part, is being followed by a man with Greco-Roman style pied-à-terre over on Pennsylvania Avenue. Oh, you don't need to know the reason why, all you need to know is this: If I don't come back with the tubes, the boys over at DoD will be packing junk up my trunk like a mob of rear rangers on crack. We haven't met yet, but let me assure you, I don't like junk in my trunk, and you want to keep me happy."

"They're not made yet."

"Well then, don't think and do. I'll be waiting at Tubby's Small Appliance Repair Shop and Wiener Bistro on Nine Mile."

"Shit!" Andy slammed the phone down and began rifling through the drawer of his desk. He found the key fob to the enrichment tube plating room, clicked it and went down the shaft on the small platform below the floor. He was at the bottom when he remembered he needed the procedure. He clicked the fob again, rose out of the shaft, scurried to lock the door of the office and scrambled back to his desk.

"The freakin' president," he muttered as he searched his computer for the file Gloss had mentioned.

"City water department is here," Penny said over the intercom. "They want a sample of our discharge."

"Tell Mac to handle it."

"Dick always did that."

"Screw Dick, get Mac."

"Okay, but I don't think he knows how."

"What can go wrong? Oh, and hold all calls, I'm busy."

"But what about ..."

"Hold all calls!"

"Yes sir, geez ... grouch."

After 15 minutes, Andy located the procedure, printed it and rode the platform down into the room with floor-to-ceiling carpeting. He walked into the control room and read to himself aloud, "Load 100 blank tubes into the fixture located inside the plating tank." The plating tank was a plastic tub, about the size of two washing machines, with a lid. He opened the lid and saw a circular, plate-like device into which 100 perfectly symmetrical holes had been machined. The device was attached at the middle to a spindle, the base of which was sealed and mated to a motor below the tank. Andy peered around the room. A double column of pale green boxes was stacked under the table below the small window. He grabbed one of the boxes, opened it and found dozens of five-inch long, pewter-colored tubes, each about an inch wide, divided into three bulb-like sections. Andy loaded 100 tubes into the fixture, then read to himself. "Pour 5,352 milliliters of 'Solution A' and 3,767.25 milliliters of 'Solution B' into the plating tank. Turn on heater and mixing motor and close lid. NOTE: THE REACTION PRODUCED IN THIS TANK IS POTENTIALLY EXPLOSIVE. TEMPERATURE MUST BE MONITORED AND PRECISELY CONTROLLED. KEEP FUME HOOD ON AT ALL TIMES. TUBES WILL BE FULLY PLATED IN 14 HOURS."

"What the ...? Explosive? Fourteen hours?" Andy mixed the liquids into the tanks, set the temperature controller to 186 degrees and turned on the motor. A high-pitched whirring sound, almost like a siren, began as the motor picked up speed. He put his hands over his ears and closed his eyes. After a minute the sound leveled into a sort of dull drone, suggesting nothing more dangerous than a running dishwasher. Andy let out a sigh and checked his watch: It was 12 noon. The tubes would be ready at 2 o'clock in the morning.

Back at his desk, he gave Clancey a call and explained the

situation. Clancey started in on him, but Andy kept his cool. Nothing more than a little glitch owing to the passing of the baton, Andy explained. If only government ran so smoothly. Clancey bitched, strafing him with threats and innuendos, but ultimately could do nothing but agree to wait at Tubby's till 2 a.m. for the package. "I'm putting this on you if they come after me, Yankee Doodle, so you might want to look into picking up some boxers with a drop drawer." Andy was about to log back on to Facebook when he remembered the problem with tank three.

When he walked through the laboratory door and into the plant, Luann, Duberg, Mac and Donny were talking on the catwalk that ran between the two plating lines. Andy strolled warily up to the group. Immediately all four people fell silent, rearranging themselves to form a tight semicircle facing him.

"How's it going?" Andy asked after a moment of tense silence.

As they stared Andy gazed nonchalantly around the plant, noticing two racks of parts dangling from hoists above their heads.

"Isn't that dangerous?" Andy said, pointing to the two tons of potential energy above them.

The four employees stood still, almost at attention. Finally, Mac, taking a tentative glance at the others, spoke up. "Whaddaya want us to do?"

Andy blinked. "What do you mean?"

"Ya see, boss, we're used to Dick tellin' us what he wants done."

Andy cleared his throat. "I want you to do your jobs."

Mac looked dubiously at the three other workers. "Ah, ya see, I don't think you understand. We didn't know what to do unteel Dick spelled it out for us."

Andy rubbed his chin, as his dad had always rubbed his chin when contemplating a sticky problem. It was a posture forever engraved in his mind and closely associated with fear generated by gravitas and authority. "Hmm, I see. Well, Mac, what do you normally do then?"

"I find the parts Dick tells me to run."

"And, Duberg, what do you do?"

"I rack the parts that Mac tells me to rack."

"Donny, how about you?"

He shrugged as if being interrogated. "I run the parts Duberg racks for me."

"Luann?"

"I fill out the paperwork for the parts and make sure these deadbeats are doing their jobs, as well as a million other things no one gives me credit for."

"So, it all begins with Dick?"

"Well boss, you could say it begins *and* ends with Dick, but now you is Dick," Mac said with a crooked grin.

The day unraveled like the space shuttle with a pinhole in its wing; just as a disaster could be caused by something as trivial as a piece of flying foam, so too, it seemed to Andy, as he sat at his desk well past midnight wearing a coat, scarf and gloves, had the day's carnage been set off by niggling, unforeseeable events. Smoke from the flash fire in the plating bunker was gradually clearing through the open office windows. Around midnight, something like a small sonic boom shook the building. Luckily the fire had extinguished itself, doing nothing more than charring the wall-to-ceiling carpeting. When he was able to enter the control room, he found the lid to the tank had been blown off; the tubes, still in the fixture, a dull, unplated pewter, just as when he had put them in. No niobium-titanium coating on these babies. Andy peered at the barrels containing the plating solutions, trying to recall his actions: Had he dispensed 5,352 milliliters of Solution A and 3,767.25 milliliters of Solution B into the tank, or vice versa? He most definitely had neglected to turn on the fume fan. But it could have been worse, he consoled himself, even as he dialed Clancey to tell him there wouldn't be a delivery that night. Clancey went incendiary, accusing him of breaching his contract, compromising national security and causing his hemorrhoids to flare up. Terms of the contract, Clancey informed him, meant he would still supply 100 tubes, but forfeit 50 percent of the $100,000 payment. "It's a little late fee we built in to protect the taxpayers' backsides, if y'all know what I mean."

The heat on tank three, which functioned as a cleaner or degreaser, never did get started. He spent the afternoon trying to decipher Gloss's procedure for changing a fuse; shorting out two other tanks and nearly electrocuting himself. When an electrician arrived, he likened the plant's array of fuses, capacitors, rectifiers and switchboxes to "something out of a cheap science-fiction horror film" and advised him to gut and replace the building's entire electrical system. "You'd need to be a Dr. Frankenstein to keep this set-up running smoothly," he told Andy. All his employees had gone home by the time the tank was fixed. Hardly any parts had been run, nothing shipped and (because some auto parts were supplied just-in-time) his company had caused a shutdown of the assembly line at the Chrysler plant two blocks away. He didn't want to think about his meeting with the Chrysler plant manager which, Penny informed him, had been scheduled for him at 8 o'clock sharp the next morning.

The icing on the Limburger had been the news that the water sample Mac had given the city sewer department was 13,000 times over the federal discharge limits for nickel, cadmium and lead. It didn't require astrophysics to figure out Mac had given the department a sample *before* rather than after the wastewater had passed through the ion exchange treatment stack at the back of the plant. Nonetheless, Mac had signed off and certified the sample and that meant, the city's public works director informed Andy, an automatic $25,000 fine. Propping his feet on the desk, Andy leaned all the way back in his chair and stared at the speckles in the taupe ceiling tiles. He recalled an old Lennon song: *I'm just sitting here watching the wheels go round and round.* The grass was not always greener and change for change sake was often just pennies and nickels. He had never thought he would, but he missed Pearly, Ian, Joe Gemeli and the boys over at Tartan.

He exhaled, feeling his eyelids begin to grow heavy. Suddenly he was jolted upright. He ran his palm over his forehead and down the skin of his face, which had the texture of greasy diner-booth vinyl. Against his will, his mind began running the day's numbers: $50,000 lost on the tiny tumblers, plus $25,000 fine, plus a whole day's lost production, plus a $2000 invoice from the electrician.

"Holy freakin' shit. What the hell have I gotten myself into?"

As a young girl, Melinda Chow was the delight of her family. She took her first steps at six months, spoke in complete sentences at two and could beat her dad in Chinese checkers at age three. For her fifth birthday she memorized Lord Alfred Tennyson's poem *The Lady of Shallot* as a gift to her parents. By the age of ten she could play all of Chopin's 21 nocturnes; by 12 she was playing Ragtime and doing camp, vaudeville-type routines, complete with bow tie and straw boater, at school functions and family gatherings. Then, at 13, something snapped. She discovered Goth, punk rock and Mylie Cyrus. She dyed her hair magenta and tangerine and pierced her lip, tongue and navel. Where once she chose her friends selectively from a collection of Mensa-caliber high achievers, she now gravitated toward kids with no apparent interest or aptitude in anything, save for hating their teachers, parents and every other form of entrenched authority. This group, while it included a few artistic types, mostly comprised would-be street urchins on the road, if not already there, to petty crime and drugs. She didn't mince words or sugarcoat her brazen preference for her new-found life philosophy: "Being bad is more interesting and fun than being good." Her parents tried sending her to counseling, then ended up being the ones getting the therapy. When she graduated from high school, she turned down scholarship offers from Yale and M.I.T. and moved to Miami, ostensibly veering away from the more tawdry and destructive influences around her. She worked in a fashion boutique in Coconut Grove by day and clubbed on South Beach in the evening. She moved in with a wealthy fashion designer, Clem Orlando, had her boobs enlarged and at 21, started her own public relations and security firm, Chow-D (she laughed when people surmised the D stood for "down") Associates. Nevertheless, Chow-D offered its clients a palette of attack-dog style services for promoting and protecting their interests, haranguing or defaming people and harassing businesses or agencies that posed threats to their well-being, i.e., cash flow. Whatever wayward tendencies Melinda may have had as a teen, she now channeled into carrying out assorted, well-paying odd jobs that would forward the interests and protect the reputations of a select list of movers and shakers, many of whom were sent to her by her boyfriend, Orlando. Now 28, Melinda had built her firm into one of the fastest growing small businesses in the country, as cited in *Wealth* magazine. She loved a job with an element of risk, even danger; she was attracted by personas that wafted a certain unmistakable scent, *eau de avarice*, and the balls it took to go for it all. It was the process, not the prize that ultimately attracted her. Money, she confided to people in the inner circle with her and Orlando, was nice. But it was the hunt and the kill she really relished.

And, so it was, several years earlier, she had swung into the orbit of one Eastman Finch. She was at an arts fundraiser in Coral Gables when Orlando introduced her to him. "Eastman helped me with my first IPO," he said, as Finch took her hand and kissed it. "I've heard about your work with Ramforth Financial," Finch winked, referring to a rumored money-laundering firm based on the Caribbean island of Montserrat. "Not easy keeping the Feds at bay for that long. Very impressive."

Melinda winked back. "Those hounds can be turned into puppies if you know how to treat them. Besides, Mr. Ramforth is great guy. You don't believe everything you read, do you?"

"Baby, I don't read, I get even."

"No fucking shit? Chow-D Associates, at your service."

Within two weeks of receiving Finch's call from New York, Melinda had rented an office and incorporated Rent-a-Wonk, a temporary hiring agency, located in the suburban outskirts of Detroit. Attending her first chamber of commerce meeting at a Holiday Inn, she ordered a wine at the cash bar, skillfully deflecting, in less than five minutes, the come-ons of a car dealer, a dentist and a tortilla manufacturer, and steered her way toward a man with a boyishly styled mop of tousled brown hair, standing with a small group of people, sipping a beer and nodding his head, it seemed, incessantly.

"Do you have a tic?" She asked, injecting herself into the pod huddled around the evening's speaker, a man with a taxidermy franchise chain.

The group turned their eyes on Andy. "Yeah, I have an attic, what about it?"

"No, a tic. You know a nervous twitch. Your head keeps bobbing up and down."

"Ma'am, sometimes a nod is just a nod."

"And sometimes a cigar is just a cigar. My name is Melinda."

Two days later Penny ushered Melinda Chow into the foyer of Gloss Industries.

"You must be Penny; I've heard so much about you."

"What'd he tell you?" Penny asked suspiciously.

"Nothing but good, dear girl," Melinda said, setting a box of Ferrero Rocher hazelnut cream chocolates on her desk, along with the latest issues of half-dozen gossip magazines.

Penny's eyes widened.

"Bless his nut-filled noggin. Maybe I will get him something for Boss's Day after all."

"In the short time I have known Andrew, I have heard him call you his saving grace, his solar corona, his *Beata Beatrix*.

"Pervert. He may be into that kinky stuff, but I am NOT."

When Andy married, he ended his participation in the universal male national pastime—the cognition of female beauty, and the desire to, well, chase it. This made him, in this one way, an ideal husband. For Andy, the decision was moral and ethical of course, but also practical: He was now forbidden to be emotionally and physically involved with other women, so why bother gawking at every angelic feminine creature that fortuitously crossed your path. Besides, the time and energy he recouped by detaching himself from this biologically imposed inanity could now be re-invested in life's infinitely more gratifying pursuits: Golf, grilling, Q-box and the timeless quest to mix the perfect martini. Now sitting across from Melinda in Marcel's, a trendy, dimly lit bistro, he felt the rebooting of something which, if he had ever read Freud, can never be turned completely off. Melinda was wearing knee-high leather boots, a black mini-skirt and a long-sleeved, white blouse unbuttoned in front at least one button lower than the level required to *imagine* what her bosom looked like. She set her menu down, rotated slightly askew in her chair, and crossed her legs, flipping her long dark hair over her right shoulder with a graceful *glissade* of her head.

"Ah, so why are we here again?" Andy said with all the nonchalance he could muster, afraid to take his eyes off the menu.

Melinda laughed. "You're funny."

Feeling suddenly frisky and risqué, Andy broke into his Rodney Dangerfield routine. "My wife and I were happy for 20 years. Then we met."

Melinda slapped the table. "That is dead on."

"It's a gift, I guess. My dad was a funny."

"Really?"

"Oh yeah, life of the party."

"What did he do?"

"Car salesman. Damn good one, too. Once sold 53 cars in a single month—still a record with the National Car Dealer Association."

"Ah ha, so now I am beginning to see a glimmer of that fine stock from which rose the future entrepreneur, president and mover and shaker before me. Fascinating."

Melinda, who owned an apartment in the St. Germain de Pres and had once dined with the Maharaja of Jaipur, ordered the Coquilles St. Jacques. Andy said he was considering the steak tartare, but with a gentle nudge from Melinda (it's a bit undercooked here) switched to flank steak and *frites*. When their meals arrived, Melinda toasted. "Here's to the beginning of a long and successful relationship—professional of course," she added, giggling.

Andy felt strangely comfortable and at ease with this woman he had known for less than a week. He was trying to think of the word that described her but the best he could come up with was fun. "Drop-dead gorgeous," was merely stating the obvious, so for the time being he focused on the former. If he could put his finger on it, and this he avoided doing, she was less uptight and judgmental than a certain someone. Melinda was like a waft of tropical sea breeze. She seemed to genuinely like him for who he was. He told her about the customer appreciation night with mojitos and a Mariachi band

and Melinda hooted. "That is so rad!" Next up, he was planning a frat-party theme, featuring the music of Bif-Rock, and a beer pong tournament, he announced, winking at her.

All was not well however, Andy confided after another beer. His company had sprung some leaks. Operations seemed to be spinning out of control. He was going to implement an employee empowerment program as described in the book his wife had given him, but before his workers were empowered, he could be hoeing in Octopus's Garden.

"You know what, Andrew—you are wasting your talents on trivial bullshit."

"I am?"

"Yes. You need to upgrade your personnel. Off the top off my head I'd say you need a Sparky Anderson and an Al Gore, at a minimum."

"A Sparky?"

"An electrician and an environmental manager, if for nothing else than to keep you alive and out of jail."

"Sounds expensive."

"Look, doll, I specialize in temp help. Plus, I like you, so I'll cut you a good deal."

"Gonzo."

"Exactly. Usually an electrician would run about $100 or more an hour. I can probably get you one for, say, $10 an hour."

"Sounds like slave labor."

"You are so politically incorrect, Andrew," Melinda said, leaning over the table. "We are *so* on the same page."

Andy had errands to run after lunch and had followed Melinda to the restaurant. As they strolled out the rear door to the parking lot, Melinda walked gingerly in her heeled boots in the ice strewn parking lot, clinging to his arm. As they reached her BMW, Melinda said she would be in touch soon.

"Cool. Lunch was great," Andy said holding out his hand.

Melinda looked aghast.

"Where I'm from a handshake is an insult to a woman."

"Sorry, didn't mean … "

"I'm going to teach you the French way."

Andy gulped and felt his heart pounding as Melinda put her arms around his waist, pulled him close and kissed him on each cheek. After the kisses she cocked her head and smiled, still holding him around the waist.

"Are you going to remember, Andrew?"

As Andy considered his reply a white SUV pulled into the parking lot and steered slowly down the aisle. As it cruised by the clinging couple, Andy was in a state of oblivion, grinning inanely up into the pale sky.

"Oh, my God," said the woman driving. "That's Marcia's husband, Andy Dodge," she announced to her two female passengers. The woman driving the van was Marcia's friend, Millie Ketchum.

8 BREAK DANCING

Shortly before Valentine's Day, Marcia received a call at work from her sister. Marcia got up and closed the door to her office.

"Bea, you sound upset, what's wrong?"

"I need to see you."

It was a well-established pattern. In the 15 years Beatrice had been married, and the 13 years Marcia had been betrothed, the two sisters had frequently traded roles as marriage counselors. The weird, and perhaps fortunate, circumstance was that their marital meltdowns never coincided; instead the pattern, if it were traced on paper, looked something like superimposed sine waves, the peak of one's marriage often being the trough of the other's. To Marcia's chagrin, this was exactly the case now. Her marriage had been on the upswing, roughly coinciding with her and her husband's purchase of a smelly metal-plating factory. Marcia liked to think of it as the rekindling of a dormant, but fundamentally deep romance; although, at more skeptical moments, prompted by a sober recollection of history, it struck her that the uptick might not be anything more pro- found than the pragmatic need of two business co-owners to jell and get along. That was okay: She'd take practical and efficacious any day of the week at this point in her life.

Now Beatrice needed an infusion of sisterly wisdom. The tim- ing, though, couldn't have been worse. Marcia had been shackled at work for several weeks trying to finalize a report going to the bank's CEO and was certifiably whacked. Also lamentable, her husband had thoughtfully taken the initiative and planned a sort of semi-romantic Valentine's weekend, arranging for the kids to spend the night at his parents and purchasing a package deal for a basketball game that included—he had told her more than once—two free shooters of your choice at any of the arena's bars (you can have mine, she replied each time). It was Tuesday, and Marcia sighed as she listened to

Beatrice ramble about her husband's infidelity, but then something, a sharp veer away from her customary theme of hurt and anger and toward the hysterically incoherent, made her sit up in a panic.

"Bea, calm down. Make the arrangements—I'll meet you half-way … somewhere."

That was one of the ground rules for these therapy sessions: neutral site, away from kids and husband. The site chosen by her sister, the Adirondacks, was far more than halfway between Connecticut and Michigan for Marcia. When Marcia grumbled, Beatrice cited her fear of driving in the winter. Her sister had learned to drive only a few years ago, at the age of 38—another instance of what Andy called "cause for pause" about his in-laws' talent for highly interpretive history, that is deconstructing their foibles in a way that always cast them in forgiving, even admirable and heroic, terms, sometimes bonking his head with his hand when similar details came to light. Only with time had Andy learned to chuckle at the family's consistently inconsistent attitude toward truth; a disconnect between the naked facts and what they could only logically mean, with apparently no awareness of the dissimulation they employed without an iota of irony. A mature acceptance for this variety of human vanity nonetheless, Andy couldn't resist aping disbelief when Marcia informed him that Beatrice had gotten her license: "She gave in? I thought better of her." Marcia caught the sarcasm and responded drolly. "Her husband motivated her. Maybe you could call it 'Born to Run'."

On the Thursday before Valentine's weekend, Marcia, nearly comatose, drove to Detroit Metro airport after work, took two puddle jumpers to Albany, then a bus to the village of Courtney, where a van was waiting to take her to the Domain Belle de Bois. Beatrice never slummed, and with the Belle de Bois, her record remained perfect. From the moment she walked into the spacious, main lodge with its high, pine-beamed cathedral ceiling and majestic fireplace, Marcia felt as if she had been beamed to another kid-, work- and worry-free part of the universe. The place literally oozed with peace and tranquility. The manager, Jean Pierre, a tall, swarthy man with dark eyes and a charming smile, greeted her, arranged to have her bags taken up to her room and asked if she would like an aperitif or glass of wine. Beatrice, who had been waiting for her in the lodge, hugged her and they took a seat on a sofa near the cozy fire. Jean Pierre brought them wine. Her sister seemed composed, happy to see her and disinclined to talk about her troubles for the time being. Giant logs wheezed and sizzled in the huge, glowing brick fireplace. Marcia leaned back into the plush cushions of the sofa, feeling the wine work its way into her shoulders and neck and enjoying listening to the familiar, lilting voice of her sister.

Eastman Finch was driving down West Side Drive trying to make it across town to a meeting with his real estate agent on Long Island. The Woolcott estate on Further Lane in the East Hampton's had just come on the market, a delayed, but much anticipated consequence of hedge fund manager Bernie Baroni's indictment on embezzlement charges a few months earlier, and Finch was getting an exclusive showing. Further Lane and the Woolcott Estate wasn't Gin Lane—it was better. Not very often does life hand you something on a silver platter. Talk about a fox guarding the hen house. That dunce, Dodge, could literally be given a commendation by *the resistance*—as his man in London called the client. You didn't need an embassy *chargé d'affaires* to have an inkling for what *the resistance* was, but he had himself covered five ways till Sunday. All he was doing was putting money in contact with other money. Someone wanted to buy (technically steal) something, and he was helping them do it. As for the what, how and why of it all, he knew nothing. Middleman, clean and simple. It was the same reductive arrangement as a buyer and a real estate agent. If the buyer turned it into a crack house or brothel, that was someone else's problem.

Traffic ground to a halt. He wanted to make it down to the 42nd street exit but was only to 60th street. He looked in his rearview mirror and noticed a black Mercedes with darkly tinted windows behind him. Was it the same car that had come out behind him in the garage? He couldn't be sure. There were a million similar looking limos and pimpmobiles in this city.

His burner phone rang. It was Brianna.

"Where are you, Eastman?"

"Just going over the Queensboro Bridge."

"I thought we were going to meet before you left?"

"Got tied up, sugar."

"You coming back into the city?"

"Probably not. Beatrice went out of town in a snit. Kid duty."

"I know."

"You know?"

"Yes, we had a little chat."

"When?"

"Earlier today, before she left."

"Really? I thought she had a hair appointment."

"Eastman, I told her everything."

"Well, it was probably going to come out sooner or later," he said cheerily. "Hope it doesn't mean you're mad at me."

"You've been avoiding me ever since I told you I was pregnant."

"Baby, I'm in the middle of a big deal, that's all."

"There's a big deal cooking in my belly right now."

"How'd the conversation go?"

"You know what she told me?"

"Let me guess, she gave you her recipe for steak Diane?"

"She said, 'Go ahead and have that baby, sister. Need any tips on breast feeding, I'm there for you.'"

Finch, whose expression while he talked betrayed no more emotion than a man being read a line of code by a software developer, studied the car behind him in his rear-view mirror. In the stalled traffic an Arabic-looking man wearing a short-billed, black chauffer's cap was getting out of the driver's side. Just as he figured—an Iraqi taxi.

"Eastman, are you there? Eastman we need to talk!"

"Hold on, sugar."

Suddenly Finch heard a loud thump on the roof of his Beamer, then watched as the silver-black carcass of a rodent slid down his windshield.

"Whoa, hey, you're never going believe this. It's raining dead rats."

Without an iota of perceptible change in the mirthful, light-hazel plasticine of his features, Finch flicked the wiper switch and the blade swept the rat onto the pavement. "Gotta run. At the toll booth. Call soon," he said, all the while easing his car along the road's shoulder until he reached the 54th street exit.

The next morning, Marcia and her sister took breakfast in the bright, airy dining room of the lodge. Beatrice looked fresh and composed as she sat down at the table by one of the high, French windows, her brunette hair, which she had always worn straight and shoulder-length, newly cut and styled with an undercut in back and an inward curl that framed her porcelain neck, jaw line and chin.

"You look beautiful, Bea," Marcia said, with a slight but detectable note of wonder in her voice.

Beatrice reached across the table and squeezed Marcia's hand, thanking her with a wistful smile and glow in her eyes.

"Oh my, look at what a gorgeous day we have," Beatrice said, gazing out the window at the sun reflecting on the white expanse of freshly fallen snow. The main lodge was situated on a ridge overlooking an egg-shaped lake, surrounded by an unbroken vista of hillsides wooded with pine, spruce and bare-branched hardwoods. To the right of the lodge, along the edge of the ridge, a small skating rink set between a white picket fence was being shoveled by a workman. "We have to take a walk today," Beatrice gushed. "It will be so much fun."

Jean Pierre, who seemed to do a little of everything, came over to pour coffee. "Bonjour, mesdames. I trust you enjoyed a pleasant night's rest?"

"Oh my, I slept like a log in a log cabin," Beatrice said, smiling brilliantly at the Frenchman.

"Perhaps the setting has something to do with it," Jean Pierre said sweeping his hand toward the window.

Marcia looked curiously at her cheerful, unusually glib sister as Jean Pierre talked about the inn's history. Jean Pierre's father had purchased 5,000 acres, including the south shore of lower Lake Matatauk, over 50 years ago and built the lodge and outlying cabins himself using only trees and materials on the land. Jean Pierre, with help of his brother, Geatan, had cleared over 30 miles of ski trails, and the new spa facilities, including fitness room and men's and women's saunas and steam rooms, were completed last year. Their chef, who had been trained under master chef Alain Dubois of the New Orleans School of Cooking, created a new menu every night, emphasizing seasonal and local ingredients.

Jean Pierre took their orders to the kitchen and Beatrice let out a sigh.

"You know what I was thinking about last night? Remember when you and I took that tour of Napa Valley wineries a few years ago? We went to that one winery and there was that guy doing lines from *Sideways.* We were tasting a new varietal and this guy says to the owner, 'This tastes like the back of a fucking L.A. school bus,'" Beatrice began to shudder with laughs, covering her mouth. "That was so funny."

"Yes, it was," Marcia said, nodding, an 'am-I missing-something' wrinkle etched in her brow

"We should get away more often, sister."

After breakfast they shuffled across the lobby into the great room where Jean Pierre was giving the guests a rundown of the day's activities and a *précis* of the inn's facilities. Marcia and Beatrice discovered they had booked into a photographer's themed weekend, which accounted for all the shutterbugs they had seen traipsing around the place with bulky shoulder bags and tripods strapped to their bodies. The photography set, which seemed to be everyone except them, would be setting out to capture the art of winter wonderland all afternoon, and a world-renowned photographer would be making a pre-dinner presentation on her recent trip to Antarctica. Jean Pierre cautioned the guests against sundry indiscretions, including bear baiting and free climbing ice-encrusted rock ledges, warnings that, to a clientele more pre-disposed toward poetry readings and origami, only caused an eye-darting, collective consternation.

The two women opted to hit the much-touted ski trails, though neither of them had ever cross-country skied. How hard could it be? For four hours the sisters snowplowed, pancaked, belly-flopped and wish-boned over hill and dale. To make matters worse, they misjudged the downgrade on the outbound, which not only carried them farther than they realized, but made the journey back to the lodge a tale of terrain regained in tortuous, it seemed, dozens of feet per hour.

"Have fun?" Jean Pierre asked as the women straggled into the lodge with ice balls dangling from toques, hair and gloves.

They went directly to the spa, each getting a massage, a facial, and then immersing themselves in a scalding hot tub until they had lost nearly all willpower to move. As they lethargically dressed, it occurred to Marcia that maybe Beatrice was waiting for her to bring up her marriage and coax her troubles out of her. The Riker family, as a rule, did not openly discuss their feelings. It was considered trite and embarrassing. The relegation of baser, tawdry emotions to the realm of the fleeting and transcendent was considered the proper way to deal with such things. Stiff upper lip and all that. Their mother, with her penchant for blow-by-blow reporting of her every ache and pain, was the only family member granted dispensation for this rule. For everyone else, a certain stoic tolerance of discomfort was expected. Beatrice had obviously reached such a threshold but now seemed to be in denial. No, Marcia reconsidered: More likely, having been immersed in turmoil for so long, she was now getting a five-star respite from it and not inclined to dredge up and review the squalid mess her marriage had become, even though that is precisely why they were there.

She decided to let it slide for the time being. Beatrice's marriage to Eastman had taken a heavier toll on her than her marriage to Andrew had on herself. Andrew's miscues, antics and thoughtlessness caused her, at times, fits of maddening, hair-pulling exasperation, but ultimately, with time and penance on his part, they could be forgiven. They were the result of defective goods, charged back, unfortunately but fairly—as she had consciously chosen them—to the customer. Eastman deliberately and blithely tortured Beatrice. Over the years, Marcia had noticed a slight but subtle change in her sister, a hardening of her exterior, a cold emptiness in her eyes and face, and a growing, worrisome remoteness. It was now heartening, if not perplexing, to see her sister so happy, alive and alert this weekend. She deserved to be happy, poor girl. If she wanted to talk, she'd talk.

It was nearing dinner, they were both famished, and Marcia suggested they go directly from the spa to the lodge's great room to take in the renowned photographer's slide show on Antarctica.

After the 50th slide of icebergs, ice flows, ice islands and people and penguins standing on ice, Marcia's thoughts began to drift. She missed Andrew, she admitted to herself. Yes, he had his blemishes, but he was in principle a good person. Beatrice's predicament made her realize she had often unfairly given Andrew the short shrift, magnifying his misdemeanors while failing to appreciate his positive attributes. Enduring, often overlooked qualities such as … well, he was … kind, yes, kind—that was it. He got along well with people. Andrew was still boyishly handsome; certainly, it wasn't out of the question that a woman *might* be attracted to him. But she seriously doubted that Andrew could or would return the interest. God bless him and the few other men on earth whose eyes and hearts didn't stray with every sweet piece of ass that wiggled down the street. But there was another fail-safe: The Andrew she knew was incapable of the prolonged attentiveness and patience required to seduce a modern woman. What were the odds, she wondered, that Andrew would cancel a golf game or poker night to sneak out and see his concubine? She had taken one science class in college and the term "vanishingly small" had stuck in her mind. It was a mathematical term used when referring to remote possibilities. The odds were vanishingly small to approaching zero that Andrew would, one, notice another woman and, two, concoct a tangled scheme to deceive and cheat on her. Sitting on the sofa in the lodge, she chuckled at the mere proximity of the two words, Andrew and affair, in her thoughts. It was laughable, really. Try as she might, and she didn't try hard, she couldn't imagine it. Birnam Wood would visit Dunsinane, and she would pen a blockbuster Broadway musical before such a thing would conceivably occur.

The slide show concluded with a question-and-answer session that seemed to go on ad nauseum. A man with mutton-chop sideburns and long gray hair tied in a ponytail (they had met him the previous night sitting by the fire, discovering he had played the recorder solo on the sixties-group, the Droll's one-hit-wonder, *Wild Fling*) asked the photographer to return to slide 82 and explain her choice of focal settings and lenses. Marcia and Beatrice, now ravenous to the point of being ornery, walked across the lodge foyer to the dining room, where Jean Pierre was laying out service and directing dinner preparations.

"Bread, bread, please," Beatrice pleaded.

"Bien sûr, mesdames. And wine?"

"Oh, hell yes."

A recommendation was made, and accepted, for the 2006 St. Emilion Bordeaux. The two women, well ahead of the photographer's mob, had secured a quiet corner table. Small candles on the linen-covered tables flickered orange in the dimly lit room and Pachelbel's *Canon* played softly in the background. Jean Pierre brought, opened and poured the wine.

"You are spoiling us," Beatrice said. "We may not want to go back to the real world."

"Ah, but this is real, is it not?"

"Real, but temporary."

"Oh, so it is a question of time?"

"Yes, time."

"That I cannot help you with, although we do have week-long packages at an attractive discounted rate."

Beatrice began telling Marcia about her son Sullivan's upcoming Lacrosse season and her daughter Cody's riding lessons. The wine, as Jean Pierre had promised, was indeed robust, and under the influence of one glass, Marcia realized she could take it no longer.

"Bea," she interrupted. "You do remember the reason I came all the way here, 500 miles, two planes and a bus, after a grueling week of work, at your request?"

Beatrice gazed at sister for a second, as if trying to recollect a long-ago event. "Oh, that? That's all been resolved. Everything's fine."

"What!?"

Beatrice told her that shortly before she left to come to the inn, she had an epiphany. Oddly enough, it was a revelation set off by a call she received from Eastman's pregnant mistress—can you believe it? It was then, face-to-face, so to speak, with the hussy, that she felt her feathers ruffled and an overwhelming compulsion to drive out this intruder and defend her nest. She knew, of course, that Eastman loved money too much to ever marry this bitch, but what was wrong with that if it came out on her side? Life and love were sometimes more black and blue than black and white. In the strong, instinctive rush of emotions she was feeling, something snapped. She consciously realized, for the first time, that she was as shallow and unrepentantly greedy as her husband, and that it was the pretense that she wasn't—nothing but a big lie she had programmed herself to tell and act out—that drove Eastman into the arms of other women. In a nutshell, she had no one to blame for her husband's infidelities but herself.

"I can't tell you what an incredible sense of peace and relief came over me when I took responsibility for our problems and forgave myself," she said, looking at Marcia with a calm, reposed smile and gleaming eyes. "All those years I'd been in denial. Now I know who I really am—a grasping, want-it-all, self-centered shrew. Sigh."

Marcia folded her arms, blinked and stared at her sister in disbelief as she began to describe one of the estates in the Hamptons they were considering buying. "Eastman has pulled a rabbit out of his hat again. What a berated but brilliant man I have for a husband. Before, we were super, fabulously well-off. Now we're drop-dead, off-the-charts rich. Glory fucking Alleluia! Cheers!" she said, raising her glass of Bordeaux.

Stunned to silence, Marcia tore off a piece of bread, and chewed deliberately as Beatrice expounded on visions of Elysian Fields she foresaw for the rest of her life. She was going to take up painting again; Eastman knew several dealers in New York who would sell her work. She was going to redesign and redecorate large portions of whatever house they decided to buy, re-start writing an old novel and take up French provincial cooking, cabinet-making and maybe karate. They were taking the kids to St. Kitts for spring break where they were all going to learn to scuba dive. She was in the middle of a long dissertation about how Marcia needed to liberate herself from the Rikerian family folklore and its self-congratulatory sense of superiority, infected as it was with guilt and ridiculous premonitions about the judgment day, when Marcia's cell phone bleated in her handbag.

It was Millie Ketchum. She thought about letting it go into voicemail, but in need of a break from the surrealism of the moment, picked up the call.

"Millie?"

"Marcia, hi. Sorry to call at this hour. Are you alone?"

"No, but it's okay."

"Oh, Marcia. I don't know how to tell you this. I've been thinking about this for some time, wondering if I should or shouldn't, but reckoned I wouldn't be a very good friend if I didn't."

Marcia felt a light tingling in her stomach but managed a laugh. "Millie, we've been through a lot," a throw-away that caused her a moment of confusion because they hadn't. "Don't worry, I'm sure you are doing the right thing."

"Well then, uh, okay—Andy's cheating on you."

"Ha ha! How do you know?"

"I saw him in the parking lot of Marcel's hugging an attractive young woman."

"When?"

"Last week."

"Millie, I hug men at work sometimes. It's a professional _"

"No, Marcia, this was an embrace—I know the difference."

"Prolonged?"

"Gazing dreamily into each other's eyes prolonged."

Marcia took a deep breath and exhaled. The memory of a thousand little slights and transgressions, the things she had convinced herself an hour ago she needed to overlook, welled up into her thoughts. Her sister's sick, twisted white washing of her husband's behavior, was one of the most shameful, pathetic displays she had ever witnessed. There was no way she was going to play the happy, psycho-pussycat. Unlike her sister she knew who she was when maimed—Lady Macbeth: "Infirm of purpose! Give me the daggers."

"Marcia! You okay?"

"Yeah, yeah. Millie can you do me a favor?"

"Sure thing, roomie."

"Do you know the name of a private investigator?"

"Oh yeah, we use them all the time dealing with the scum we have to screen."

"Send it to me—now!"

The same day, Saturday afternoon, Andy was sitting at home alone watching a show on big game hunting in Alaska. The hunters were stalking the Dall Sheep, and the camera, framed as if the viewer were looking through a rifle scope, zeroed in on a large, spiral-antlered male as he gingerly picked his way across a jagged, knife-edged cliff in pursuit of females. Andy snorted and segued into documentary voiceover: "Oblivious to the dangers of sheer 5,000 ft. crevasse below him, the male Dall gamely pursues the female in order to pass on his genes to the next generation, sort of like the human male."

He glanced at his watch. He'd have to start getting ready to leave for the game soon. When Marcia informed him mid-week that she was going to have to spend the weekend in the Adirondacks playing marriage counselor, it left Andy in a lurch. He called his parents to cancel the kids' weekend sleepover, thinking he'd get a sitter for Jessica and take Dylan to the game. His mother however, insisted he bring the kids, complaining that they hardly ever saw them and informing him they had already purchased four tickets to the Saturday-night premiere of the *Phantom.* Andy spent Thursday calling up friends and golf buddies pitching his extra ticket— the Locomotion Girls and two free shooters! Everyone had iron-clad, unbreakable commitments with their wives or girlfriends for Valentine's Day. He was resigned to going alone when he remembered Ian Hunt over at Tartan Chemical. Hunt, the consummate confirmed bachelor, was usually up for any activity that could directly or indirectly involve alcohol. "Oh, you're a good bloke for remembering me, Andy, but I shan't be able to make it. World-cup cricket quarterfinals are on—Brits versus the Pakis."

Friday afternoon he was sitting at his desk staring at the tickets when Penny patched through a call from Melinda Chow.

"Hey, big guy, I've got you a Sparky and an Al. They can start next week."

"Perfect," Andy said, suddenly getting an idea. "Hey, Melinda, by any remote chance do you like basketball?"

Andy had arranged to meet her at Shanahan's, a bar and restaurant about equidistant between his house, her apartment and the arena, a few hours before the start of the game. A February thaw had melted much of the snow and the night had a warmish, spring feel and smell to it. On the drive over Andy began to have second thoughts about asking Melinda to the game. By no means did he consider it a date. Nevertheless, it was a little bit weird for him to be going out with an attractive, single young woman while his wife was hundreds of miles away and his kids were conveniently at a sleepover. But the world had changed, right? Women and men mingled professionally all the time. That's what it was. It was like him taking a customer to lunch for the greater cause of building rapport. As a former salesman, he knew how important personal relationships were in business. Of course, Melinda wasn't his customer, he was hers, but that was a technicality. Melinda was pro-actively helping him (boy, was she pro-active) to solve some dire human resource deficiencies that were hurting his business. In this sense, she was like a customer—someone who ultimately padded his bottom (hee hee, no pun intended) line. Who said a customer had to be someone who bought something from you? There were all kinds of ways sellers could be buyers and buyers could be sellers. Some people put way too much stock in labels.

Melinda was standing outside in front of the bar when he drove into the parking lot. He steered the car in front and rolled down the side window. Melinda leaned over. "Wanna go in for a quicky?"

Andy parked the car, laughing as he did. But how about that? A woman who suggested having a drink. Talk about a paradigm shift. This experience represented rich, and as far as he was concerned, pleasant new ground.

In the deep, unexplored regions of Andy's subconscious there resided a smidgen of conflicted hope that his senses, as sharp as they usually were on these matters, had betrayed him. Long before he was married, there was a precedent for this. He would meet a girl, think he was in love, only to discover in the follow-up rendezvous she had one permanently blood-shot eye and was on medication for early-on-set dementia. Maybe Melinda, on their first meeting, had merely cleverly made herself up to be a facsimile of the *Penthouse* poster-girls with which he had once papered the walls of his dorm room. Through the science of cosmetology, (which, if a man accidently meandered into the maze of a department store cosmetics department, he understood, was really a cosmos, extending far beyond the realm of mere physical sciences to delineate), which included silicone, hormones, tinting, tanning, vitamin and probiotic regimens, herbal infusions, synthetic injections, juice diets, spa retreats, Pilates, hatha yoga, hot yoga, yin yoga, the bar method, compression treatments, hydrations, exfoliations, stone massage, low-voltage currents, microdermabrasion, probiotics, prosthetics, meso-diuretics, meta-osmotic-ablation and subliminal phonetics, women had come up with more excellent ways to glaze over the most hideous effects of human warts than men had. Until, indeed, if, it revealed itself, there was no reliable, proven method to ascertain where the real ended and the bogus, in the extreme sense of the principle, began within any given woman's body, and after a time perhaps the person herself had no clear accounting of it any longer either. (*So tell me what I see, when I look in your eyes? Is that yooooou, baby, or just a brilliant disguise?*) And so it was, in this conflicted state, and to assuage his guilt as the moment neared, Andy held onto some meager, inane hope that Melinda, on this their third meeting, would out herself with some, heretofore undiscovered defect; perhaps the cleverly camouflaged physique of a Russian Olympic swimmer painted with a body tattoo of Satan, or even something as triv-ial, but femme-fatale bubble-bursting, as unshaven armpits, earwax buildup or a wayward, sprouting nasal hair. Forgivable foibles in per-spective, but ones he vowed to view as telltale flaws of a too-perfect persona , which he desired revealed as his heart began to race sitting in his car, contemplating the imminent omega moment of his covert rendezvous with Ms. Chow, if that was even her name.

Any chance for salvation from personal accountability by default was dashed when he strolled into the bar and saw Melinda looking as goddess. Smiling and waving to him near the hostess stand, she was wearing a beige sweater coat over a teal silk blouse; tourniquet-tight Calvin Klein's tucked into calf-length brown leather boots with four-inch heels. As he approached, Melinda flipped her entire length of brunette hair over her shoulder and threw her arms open. Andy, aghast at himself yet, at the same time, acutely aware that he had probably not, check that, never had been, within breath-ing distance of a woman as beautiful, went limp as he felt her pull him into a cloud of flowery feminine aromas and kiss him on both cheeks.

"Ah, good boy, you didn't forget," Melinda said with a giggle. "Come on, got us a table," she said, taking him by the hand.

Andy swallowed as they sat down at a high table with wooden stools. The waitress came immediately and Andy, suddenly feeling conservative, ordered a small beer.

"Oh, come on. I want to party with Mr. Mojito," Melinda said, winking. "I'll buy."

While the waitress was getting their drinks, Andy, with a vague sense of dread about the situation, fidgeted nervously, calcu-lating his options. Perhaps he could just slap the tickets on the table and run out the door. Or excuse himself to go to the john and never come back. A girl had once done that to him on a date and the damn thing was, he was relieved about it. Melinda certainly didn't need him; she could pick up any guy in this bar and the neighboring three states.

"You seem quiet, Andrew. Do your Rodney Dangerfield for me."

Andy declined, despite persistent needling from Melinda.

"In that case, here's to the success of Gloss Industries under the dynamic, visionary leadership of President, CEO, COO and CTO Dodge," Melinda toasted when the drinks came.

Andy threw down the mojito in a few gulps.

"Young man, you obviously worked up a thirst on the drive over. How about another round?"

After three rounds, they hopped in Andy's car and drove to the game. Andy was noticeably more relaxed; once again convinced of the unquestionable soundness of professionally bonding with a person who was providing him with the critical support and resources needed to get his business on track. Melinda teased him about wanting to order steak tartare and once working for a man named Dick Gloss, occasionally patting his knee or thigh for emphasis. Andy felt his world expanding. This was the difference between being the owner of a company and (with a nod to a sleaze ball named Finch) a wage slave. It conferred responsibilities, duties, but also required deeds that might be construed as perks that people, especially spouses, needed to accept with tolerance. In his position he needed the support of a partner who could rise above pettiness and the rush to judge or be jealous. One needed to be flexible and not see new ways of doing things as threats. That's what leadership was. He was there; others in his life had to follow.

They arrived at the arena just before tip-off, grabbed a couple of beers at the concession and took their seats. Despite the affirmation that his intentions were ethical and all above board, Andy thought it wise to issue a check down.

"Melinda, you know I'm married, right?"

Melinda, her shoulder snuggled against Andy, shrugged. "In that case, why have you never mentioned her name once?"

Andy pointed to the ring on his finger.

"I am sooo oblivious about those things. So, where is the little lady tonight?"

"Out of town."

"Sweet deal. Here it is Valentine's day and she leaves hubby all by his lonesome."

"Crisis."

"Ha yeah, right," Melinda said, raising her eyes in a gesture that conveyed he was a dupe to believe it.

The Pistons were getting blown out, and Melinda and Andy strolled into one of the arena's bars at halftime. Andy, finally able to redeem his ticket stubs for two shooters, ordered a Jager Bomb, while Melinda chose a Lemon Drop.

"That went down smoothly," Andy said. "Let's do another."

"Now that's the Mr. Mojito I've been waiting for."

Andy went for an Alabama Slammer, a concoction of sloe gin, amaretto and Southern Comfort, and Melinda settled on a Girl Scout Cookie—coffee liqueur, Irish Crème and peppermint schnapps.

"How do they fit all that in such a small glass," Andy said after throwing down the shot.

"It is a small miracle," Melinda affirmed.

Andy told Melinda he should thank his lucky stars she was on his team. It was a brilliant idea to bring in the people he needed to get the job done and he didn't know why he hadn't thought of it himself. Gloss was a fossil, 50 years behind industrial best practices. His employees had been brainwashed to think they couldn't think unless Gloss said they could think, and then been trained to think only what Gloss himself would think.

"Oh gweat, gwasshopper Gwoss, we ah awl helpwis, eegorwant, fawking jawkasses. Pwease teh us wha do befah we harm oursawf and otters," Andy said, channeling his inner itinerant Buddhist monk.

Melinda choked on sobs of laughter, clasping the arm of the chair to keep from falling to the floor. "You … missed … your … calling," she said in apparent sincerity. With the game on the television and access to a full-service bar, Andy didn't see anything to gain by returning to their seats. He ordered two Big Bamboos, comprising 151 rum, triple sec and orange juice. When the shooters came, Andy gargled the potion before swallowing. Melinda stared at him in wide-eyed amazement.

"Why are you so mysterious?" Andy asked, resting his arm along the back of her chair.

"Andrew, please! I'm just a working girl trying to stay out of the bread line."

"What do you do—really?"

Melinda rolled her eyes, smiled and nestled against Andy's shoulder. "Well, if you must know," she said, "this is a little thing I do on the side, just to stay on the up and up, if you know what I mean."

"Is that so?'

"Yes."

"So, what is your main line of work?"

Melinda put her mouth close to Andy's ear and whispered. "Effective discipline. I'm on a mission to turn all the world's naughty boys into good boys."

Andy's grin grew wider by the second. "Am I a naughty boy?"

"You are the naughtiest of the naughty, Mr. Mojito."

"Mr. Nickel. That's what Gloss used to call me."

"I like Mr. Mojito better. I'm the one calling the shots around here, remember," she said, blowing softly into his ear. Suddenly Andy's whole body went rigid as he felt a soft, silky wetness trace along his ear lobe and upward.

"Whoa, what kind of shooter is that?"

"That, Mr. Mojito, is a tongue twister."

Melinda asked the bartender to bring Andy a Firecracker, a little number consisting of tequila, Goldschläger and Rumple Minty. Andy chugged it and slammed the glass on the bar.

"Damn. I don't know who thinks of these things but I'm glad they do."

After the third shooter, Melinda had switched to Perrier and lemon, dedicating a concessionary speech with the bartender as witness, "Still undefeated and reigning heavyweight shooter champion of the world, Mr. MoooojiiiTO." Melinda counted to Andy's fifth shooter, then lost track. The game ended, and a large, raucous crowd swarmed into the bar. Andy high-fived, exchanged business cards and bought everyone at the bar a Jager Bomb. "Here's to the Pistons. They suck," was a toast which resonated perfectly with the crowd's mood, eliciting a huge roar of approval. Music throbbed and the throng adopted Andy as its de facto host for the night. "Hey, Andy," shouted a large man with a goatee and a vague resemblance to the legendary radio DJ Howlin' Jack, "Come over here. I want to introduce you to my chick." His chick, Howlin' informed Andy, was a cousin of *American Icon* winner Taylor Scone. Andy fell to his knees, took the young woman's hand, and brushed it against his cheek, breaking into a rendition of "You Are So Beautiful," the song Ms. Scone had sung to win the show. The crowd pulled back and Andy, sensing the energy, segued spontaneously into "stupid break dancing," a routine he had previously only performed, on command, for his kids. People clapped and whooped as Andy executed a rendition of the "mannequin" as an elderly person with a shaky arm and a twitch in his neck. "Here's something I call the meatloaf," he said. Lying flat on his back on the floor, Andy quickly rotated to his left side, then to his right, then back again, in time to the music; ending up on his stomach and going right into a series of lunging, serpentine movements that bore a resemblance to a charging sea lion. He bounced up, spun, struck a Travolta-esque *Saturday Night Fever* pose, then, with a skip, launched himself into a one-handed stationary handstand, the infamous "armchair" move. The crowd went nuts as Andy held the handstand for two, three, four seconds, then slowly, like a tree with its trunk chopped, flipped over landing flat on his back on the marble floor.

Safely stowed in the passenger seat, Andy assured Melinda he was fine and did not need to see a doctor.

"You were the man tonight, Mr. Mojito," Melinda said steering the car on to the expressway.

"Nah, it was nothing."

"No, it was definitely something."

"You know, I just like to give back to the people. To the people, man!"

"You left it all out there, big guy."

"Those are my people. My people! I love them!"

"You were oozing love tonight."

"You think they felt it?"

"They felt it; oh, I'm sure they felt it."

"Really?"

"Oh, yeah—can't wait to read the reviews."

Andy was still in good spirits, gabbing most of the drive home, keeping Melinda entertained with a bit of Dangerfield, dumb blonde jokes and X-rated limericks. He was surprised when they pulled into his driveway, even though he'd been giving Melinda directions to his house the whole time.

"Here already? Oh hell, don't be shy, come on in and have a night cap with me."

The last thing Andy remembered of that night was putting some popcorn in the microwave. The next morning, he lay in bed looking at the ceiling, contemplating which hurt worse, his back or his head. He decided the pain in his back was sharper, like a railroad spike hammered into his lower spine, but the pain in his head was more gruesome; a hot, humid, deep, vibrating throb that spread from the back of his skull to the front just behind his eyes. Compared to these two sensations, the queasy, churning feeling in his stomach was minor.

He turned and glanced at the beautiful, half-clothed woman lying beside him, then went back to gazing at the ceiling. He blinked, trying to recall where he was. He slowly pushed himself to sitting and looked around the room. There was his pine dresser. There was his walk-in closet. He was at home. Holy fucking shit. He was home!

It took him five minutes to shake Melinda fully awake. He soaked a towel in cold water and dabbed her face. He found her blouse in the living room. Luckily, she had not taken her jeans off—it would have been easier to pull the skin off a cat than to get that shrink-wrapped denim back on her. He looked at his watch: It was nearly noon. Marcia's plane was due in two hours and he was supposed to have picked up the kids an hour ago. He led Melinda down the stairs, through the garage and into the car.

"What's the rush?

"The ball's over, Cinderella."

Melinda chuckled and mumbled groggily. "Is your ass grass?"

Andy tapped his noggin. "For a lesser man than Mr. Mojito, maybe."

9 EMPOWERMENT AND MENDICANCY

In the nearly two months Dick Gloss had been on the lam, as he liked to say, he had lost 15 pounds, been hospitalized twice, detained by airport security in Ho Chi Minh City for making disparaging remarks about Ho Chi Minh, interrogated by customs in Singapore for failing to declare and pay duty on several jade-handled poniards, and nearly jailed for assaulting a rickshaw driver who had peddled them through the middle of a prostitute- and junkie-infested section of Kuala Lumpur.

The trip had been planned by his wife, Angie, and Gloss had agreed to it, not because he wanted to see new sights and cultures, but because he thought it necessary to be out of the way and even out of the country when Andy took over the company. To say Dick Gloss was not naturally disposed to travel was tantamount to a quip from Captain Obvious: The subject and the realities of the experience were plainly mutually exclusive. Thus, the problems posed by this disconnect were irresolvable and began almost as soon as he started the most basic and essential part of a journey, getting from point A to point B. Expecting him to graciously tolerate the hassles, drudgery and inconveniences of baggage check, security, airport ambience, transfers and inevitable delays was like expecting the family dog to be polite and unobtrusive around the dinner table. More maddening to him, very often, no one seemed to know anything. Flights were simply ”late” or “canceled”, no explanation given. The universe, to Gloss, was a causal place and the absence of cause was irrational. He instinctively grasped the problem—lack of leverage. The airlines could treat people with contempt because there was no alternative to travel over long distances. One airline could undercut the others by offering better service, but why would they when the bar was so low? Meaningfully improving service cut into one's profit. Better to peddle apocryphal marketing baubles—faster check-ins! (ha, not really), a free bag! (for a limited time on trips with more than three layovers), upgrade your seat for only $25 dollars! (since when is an aisle seat in row 37 an upgrade?). No LEVERAGE! The words were anathema to the ears of Dick Gloss. It meant you were powerless. We're in charge, whaddaya gonna do? Whine your way across the Pacific? Ha, that's what they thought. He was not one to take this insolence in silence. Once, when their plane had sat on the tarmac for a half an hour waiting for clearance to take off, he got out of his seat and banged on the door of the flight cabin demanding to know the reason for the hold up. This caused even further delay as flight crew deliberated whether to return to the gate and hand Gloss over to the authorities. He stayed only because a background check revealed he had received the Congressional Medal of Honor and had unusually high-level security clearance from the United States government.

Then there was the issue of his digestion. It had been fine-tuned, much like a heifer's or yak's, to require a consistent pulse of similar or identical chow, repeated in precise intervals through the day and week. Only in the narrowest interpretation of the word, considering the basic human food groups, was Gloss an "omnivore." At the base of the pyramid of his diet were the Five Staples: beef, chicken, gravy, pasta and pumpernickel. Kielbasa, cream cheese, deep-dish pizza, Ego-waffles, Cheerios, Oreo cookies and potatoes also figured prominently in his diet. Only at the behest of his doctor, as he had slid into his middle-age years with precipitously high LDL and triglycerides, had he ventured into dietary botanical realms, and to the amazement of his wife, took a fancy to iceberg and romaine ("I like crunchy") heavily dribbled with types of salad dressing. Fish, lobster or any shellfish were forbidden from entering his house, and even the smell of cooking seafood could nauseate him.

All this had been anticipated. Gloss had stuffed copious amounts of Maalox, Alka Seltzer, Ex-Lax and Milk of Magnesia into his luggage. He had also packed three boxes of soda crackers and a jar of peanut butter to thwart a possible worst-case scenario wrought by weird, inedible foods: starvation. What had not been foreseen was the prominent role fish played in the typical Southeast Asian diet. For the first four days in Thailand, Gloss had eaten nothing but plain rice, chicken kabobs, tapioca pudding and bananas covered in chocolate sauce. Then one night, at the urging of his wife, Gloss threw caution to the wind and ordered vegetarian Pad Thai ("It's just noodles with some seasoning, Dick."). He thought the dish tasted "strange" and "like crunchy peanut butter with some oregano or something in it" but nonetheless, in need of heft in his stomach, and having enough similarity to one of his staples, pasta, he devoured the entire plateful before his wife had finished her coconut soup. Unbeknownst to them, the Pad Thai was made the authentic way with a special little secret ingredient, the oriental mystery mojo, fish sauce.

Gloss was laid up in his hotel room for two days. Unable to walk, they took him by stretcher and ambulance to a Thai clinic, where he was given an IV for water loss and put on electrolytes.

Angie Gloss artfully endured the tribulations of traveling with her husband. She had developed a knack over the years of being sympathetic to her husband's foibles, rants and precarious health, while at the same time downplaying, mitigating and staying cheerfully detached. (When Gloss ripped the rickshaw driver out of the cab by the arm, Angie intoned calmly, "Be careful Dick, he's only 100 pounds soaking wet."). No mean feat being your own person with a partner as imperial as Gloss, but with her books, interest in the arts, quirky, adventurous sense of fashion and her southern-bred easygoing charm, she had, against long odds, pulled it off. When Gloss had gone belly-up post Pad Thai, she booked an excursion to the sacred Ayutthaya ruins with two women she had befriended on the trip. Given her husband's reluctant-tourist tendencies, she was adept at improvising and at ease fending for herself while traveling, having taken many trips with her sisters and friends over the years when Gloss was pre-occupied with his business.

By the time they had reached India, Gloss had settled into a state of mind broken by repeated exposure to the impositions of travel, much as one can build up a tolerance to poison in small doses. He still roiled inside, but now merely smirked or shook his head, muttering to himself at every newly revealed idiocy and inefficiency.

Gloss, with a deep fear of filth and vermin, had agreed to come to India on the condition they did not stay in any of the country's large, teeming cities. He had once seen a *Discovery* program on Bombay and his opinion was fixed: "I'm not going anywhere where they shit on the side of the street." Accordingly, this leg of the tour featured pastoral settings, with stays outside Agra, near the Taj Mahal, and Shimla, a remote city at the foot of the Himalayas in northern India. Not wanting to take any chances, Angie had booked rooms in five-star hotels. In Agra, the Oberon Udap, rated "the eighth best in the world," was immaculate and gleaming. Their room, the size of a bungalow, opened out onto a private terrace with a rose-pink marble floor inlaid with tiles tracing intricate arabesque geometric patterns. "Finally, some workmanship," Gloss remarked as they sat outside on the first morning, having coffee in the warming sun.

Since Thailand, Gloss had returned to his earlier regimen and strictly avoided all native food dishes and most meat. Still, no matter how much rice or how many bananas he consumed, it seemed he never could feel substantially full. Like a drip in a faucet that gets worse, this deficit of calories began to gnaw at him as a perpetual, low-grade sensation of hunger. He had been dreaming of a chicken—not overcooked, dried-out chunks on a stick, but a real chicken, with crispy brown skin and juicy dark meat falling off the bones for weeks. Now at this bastion of Americanized comfort and standards, relief appeared in sight.

"This chicken here," Gloss said, pointing to the menu. "How's it made?"

"Baked, sir," said the waiter.

"Baked?"

"Yes sir, in an oven."

"No spices?"

"If that is how you wish it prepared, certainly."

Gloss sat silently pondering. "It's not an Indian chicken, is it?"

The waiter did not even blink. "No, sir. Our chickens are imported from France. Bresse Chickens."

"No, I want a portion with the leg and thigh, too."

The chicken was delectable. Gloss savored each bite of the

succulent meat, which he could pick off the bones with his fork. To his sensitive palette, the potatoes had a slightly bitter, astringent taste but he was ravenous and found if he chewed them with a bite of chicken they went down fine. Later that night, however, he was awakened by a rumbling deep in his bowels. He spent the rest of the night hovered over the toilet. In the morning, the hotel manager accompanied them to the local hospital.

"I do not understand, we have the highest quality and sanitation standards," he said to Angie as Gloss lay on a bed dozing from the medication to bring his fever down.

"How do you make the potatoes?" She asked.

"Those? We fry them, in a large skillet."

"Do you ever fry fish in the same skillet?"

"Fish? No … I mean, can I say never?"

Two days later they were on a flight to Paris. Angie, who knew how to cajole and reason with her husband, also knew when an issue had been unilaterally decided. Unlike younger women, who thought they had to have input, or even the final say, on every decision, she didn't fight it. You choose your battles; her mother had schooled her. Besides, she thought it probably was a good idea to leave early and bypass planned visits to Sri Lanka and Egypt—they were just courting more disasters. Gloss had wanted to fly home directly, but as a bargaining chip for cutting the trip short, he agreed to a make a stop in the City of Light. "Dick, they have real Italian restaurants there. If nothing else, you can live on the bread."

Driving to their hotel from the airport along the Champs Elysees, Gloss's spirits were lifted. "French can't fight worth a lick, but they know how to make things pretty."

"They're lovers, Dick."

"That's an excuse."

The next afternoon, while Angie shopped, Gloss strolled into a bar called La Doobies. American sounding enough, he thought. He sat down at the bar near two men and ordered a beer. The two men were talking and Gloss, while not trying, could hear their conversation.

"Like, what was she thinking?"

"I don't know, like I was going bananas."

"Do they have like a concierge at her hotel?"

"Oh, my God. You would not believe this place. It is like soooo far out of the way."

This went on for several minutes. Finally, one of the men glanced over at Gloss. Gloss met his eyes and nodded.

"Where you from?" He asked Gloss after a brief exchange of pleasantries.

"Michigan."

"Like, I hear the economy is bad there."

Gloss took a swig of his beer, fixing a stare on the men, both of whom were sporting trimmed goatees. "Do you mind me asking how old you are?"

"I'm 36, he's 35. Why?"

Gloss downed the last of his beer, put money on the bar and stood. "You fellas talk like a couple of dingbat teenybopper girly girls."

Gloss turned to walk away when one of the men laughed.

"Every guy our age talks this way."

Gloss stopped and turned to look at them. "Then every guy your age wears panties."

He walked back to the Champs Elysees and sat down on a bench under some large trees. It was cloudy but not unpleasantly cold. His cell phone, which he had forgotten he had, began to ring. The ring tone, which sounded like someone playing extremely fast scales on a harpsichord, annoyed him but he didn't know how to change it. He slammed his hand into his coat pocket and yanked it out.

"Gloss."

"Where the hell you been, motherfucker, I've been trying to reach you for two weeks."

He smiled at the sound of Calvin Clancey's voice.

"Out of reach and out of commission. How's my favorite non-disabled, Afro-American male been hanging?"

"Nearly hung, man. We got ourselves a goddamn mother-fuckin' problem."

"We?"

"Hell yes, we. You still in this. You gettin' a kickback."

"A royalty."

"Don't mince words with me, Dicky. I may be your favorite nigger but you my main honky. We be joined at the junk."

"Lay it on me, Calvin."

"It's your man, Yankee Doodle Andy. He ain't up to the snuff, he ain't bringing the stuff, he don't have the buff, my man's a motherfuckin' cream puff."

"What do you want me to do?"

"Whaddaya want me to do? Yo' pretty boy missed three shipments already. May I remind Mr. Medal-of-Honor that Uncle Sam puttin' out a whole bunch of goddamn fires around the world. We runnin' a bit low on the U235 we need to keep those aircraft carriers hummin'. We don't get those tiny tumblers, The U.S.S. *Nimitz* might as well be the Good Ship Lollipop."

"What do you want me to do?"

"Get yo' fat white ass home and fix it."

"You know I can't risk contacting Andy."

"Listen, that shit off."

"What!?"

"It off, done. We pullin' out."

"You damn well … "

"Dickie, you talkin' mumbo-jumbo conspiracy trash you gotta have some facts to back that shit up."

"I told you, intelligence caught al Qaeda trolling the patent."

"So what? There's a lot of fucking trolls."

"Then chatter to steal it when I sell."

"How we know that wasn't a goddamn hoax?"

"Hoax?!"

"And how many years ago was that? We put dogs out sniffin' up the tree for every goddamn conspiracy rumor we hear, we got no G-men to make coffee."

"The DoD is supposed to have his back."

"What's the worst that could happen?"

"They steal the formula and equipment."

"You messing with me, shiny schlong? I thought you said there weren't no goddamn formula."

"There's a procedure; the formula's in my head."

"So those bad boys have to steal your head. You see why I gotta problem here?"

"They can easily figure the formula once they have procedure, and the equipment to make it."

"So maybe we bring the whole motherfuckin' thing in house."

"Fuck, no! Not yet."

"We can do that. It's all in that blood on the contract."

"Not without me, you can't."

"Y'all know what yo' problem is. Y'all think you're still in Nam fightin' the gooks. You a hero once and now you got a motherfucking hero jones."

"Don't go there, Clancey!"

"Oh, I'm going there. And I tell you one more thing. I'm givin' yo' boy one month to get his shit together. One month or we're pulling it all in house."

"There's too much at stake!"

"At stake? I'll tell you what's at stake, my motherfucking virgin ass is at stake. And I only got one rule about that. If I get it, you get it, you know, share the pleasure. Y'all hear what I'm sayin'?"

The employee conference/meeting room at Gloss Industries was a long, windowless room, with thick, hunter-green shag carpeting, dark-wood paneling and overhead track lighting that never seemed to provide enough light. In the center of the room was an oblong table around which a dozen vinyl upholstered, swivel chairs were haphazardly arranged. Various mismatched chairs were aligned against the back wall, and in the front of the room was an easel holding a white board on which was inscribed "Employee Empowerment Meeting" and below that, "Help yourself to a coffee and donut—relax, be happy." and below, scrawled in a noticeably different handwriting, "We'll be happy when it's time to go home."

A couple of employees loitered at the sideboard where the coffee and donuts were served.

"Are there any jelly-filled left?" asked Penny.

"Just some old-fashioned plain and a few glazed," said Donny.

"Geez, what a tight wad. Dick always used to get some Bavarian crème and even muffins and fritters," Penny said.

"If Dick were here we wouldn't be having this meeting."

"Ha, the only meeting this knucklehead should be having is with a shrink."

Just then a woman in a business suit bounced into the room. She had short auburn hair and carried a black leather shoulder bag.

"Good *morning*. How is everyone on this fine day?"

"Good morning, Mrs. Teacher," an employee in the back of the room intoned.

The woman smiled as she put her satchel on the table. "And who, may I ask, is this polite young man?"

"Duberg."

"Full name, please."

"His momma didn't give him no first name," Luann said. "Figured it wasn't worth wasting two words on a rock."

Raucous laughter shook the room, with Duberg laughing the loudest and longest.

"Well, *my* name is Colleen Stuart and I'll be your facilitator today. Mr. Dodge will be joining us a little later this morning."

"You mean Mr. Dumbo?" Duberg said.

Ms. Stuart continued serenely unpacking her satchel. "Since this meeting is about empowerment," she said when the laughter had subsided, "the first thing you should know is that I am empowered to kick any employee's ass out of this meeting and send them home, without pay, for being disruptive. Now as far as Mr. Dodge goes, I think he's pretty smart cookie for investing in training to make you empowered employees and let me tell you why."

All the best companies have empowered workforces, Ms. Stuart told them. She ticked off a list of *Fortune 500* companies, where employees, not managers, make decisions, solve day-to-day problems and think creatively. We live in a flat, digitally interconnected world that moves far too fast for a single person or several people at a company to direct and decide everything, she spoke, showing PowerPoint slides with workers in Chinese factories and Indian call centers. She put up another series of slides outlining the four keys of empowerment: objectives, resources, communication and trust. The previous owner, Mr. Gloss, was intelligent and well-meaning, but the reason he micro-managed you was because he didn't trust you, Ms. Stuart informed them. "Mr. Dodge, on the other hand, believes in your abilities to think on your feet, take charge and succeed. It's a win for you, and a win for the company. Any questions?"

Andy walked into the room as Ms. Stuart was explaining to Duberg that, no, being empowered did not mean you could take a smoke break whenever you felt like it.

Mac stood up saying he didn't want to be negative, but he had a few concerns. He understood that globalization will require U.S. workers to compete with workers in China and other places, but given high-frequency algorithmic trading, wondered if there was any real way to assess or compare capital and discretionary costs anymore. "When computers start to manipulatin' the stock market, everythin's virtual so the whole world-is-flat thing sort of becomes pawsay, as the Frenchies say." He also questioned whether empowerment was the right way to go. He had been reading an article in the *Harvard Business Review* saying maybe the great business "gooroo," Tom Bingly, had been right all along, and that leadership is more important than what any single employee may or may not do, and that maybe the practice of grossly overpaying top CEOs wasn't a bad idea after all. "You can't put the cart before the horse, as we like to say down on the Ponderosa."

There was a moment of awkward silence as everyone waited Andy's response. Andy tried to pull his ear thoughtfully but hit himself in the cheek with the splint cast around his middle two fingers. "Mac, I can assure you I am not overpaid, but if you have that issue of the *Harvard Business Journal,* bring it in— I'd like to see it. Overall, however, based on everything I've read, I believe there's a pretty strong consensus that empowerment, in the long run, yields better results than micromanaging."

Andy cleared his throat and glanced at Colleen Stuart, who, standing with arms folded in the front of the room, let a smile crease the corner of her mouth and gave a nod in his direction.

Ja-Coby raised his hand to speak. "Y'all know what I think. I think this is y'all's way of getting more work out of us for the same jack. I didn't mind Gloss telling us which way to get off the pot. I don't wanna *thang*. If I wanted to *thang* I'da gone up and got a damn diploma."

The night before, as he had nothing else to do, Andy had re-read parts of the book Marcia had given him and anticipated questions such as this one. It was under the section "pitfalls to watch for."

"Ja-Coby, you bring up, ah, a good point— but you're wrong. It's not like you're going to be asked to do rocket science. But if Mac gives you a schedule, you should be able to figure out which parts to rack and in what order to run them. What is so hard about that?"

"I think what Mr. Dodge is saying," Ms. Stuart added, "is that YOU are the best person he has who knows which parts to run in the most efficient, cost-effective manner. You know your job better than anyone else."

"The hell I is. Gloss take that damn sheet and come up with 17 ways to Sunday to make the quota. I couldn't do that if y'all sent me to me to study with that Einstein cat."

In the back of the room, Duberg, beginning to snigger uncontrollably, put his arms around his head on the table.

"I think the bigger point," Andy said, taking a deep breath after a moment passed, "is that GLOSS ISN'T HERE!" A dozen faces around the table looked at Andy in frozen, open-mouthed silence. Andy stared fiercely in silence before continuing. "You want to anoint Dick Gloss Jesus Christ and appoint me the village jackass, go ahead! But I do know one thing. If this company doesn't change and change FAST, this goddamn little gravy train of yours is going down the tubes! When the unemployment checks run out and you have to fend for yourselves in the real world, then you'll find out it's NOT thinking that's hard! Because you know what you'll be doing? You'll be changing sheets at the Hav-a-Nap Hotel or picking avocadoes in 150-degree heat or pumping shit out of Porta Potties or a thousand other wonderfully non-lucrative careers with no responsibility, no vacation days and no benefits! You think I'm an idiot, a nincompoop, a meat-head? Hell yes, I've made mistakes—way too many. But at least I take responsibility for my actions. Jesus fucking Christ people. Look at you. You're infants! Children! 'Okay, kiddies, open your books to page 25. Line up for recess. Straight line! Put your homework on my desk. Oops, Donny, you forgot to put your name on it.' Fuck that shit! What did Gloss feed you? Pablum? Grow up! This isn't a fucking day care facility! And I'm sure as shit not going to take care of you!"

Later that evening, after he had put another batch of tiny tumblers into the tank in the bunker, Andy strolled out of the building to his car parked in the reserved spot in front of the door. A wet, heavy snow was falling, making the asphalt shiny and slick. Wonder-ful—welcome to March in Michigan.

He tossed his gym bag and satchel into the back seat and was about to climb into the car when he noticed a large moving van backed into the loading dock at Eisner Industrial Lighting, a company located directly across the street from him. He'd become acquainted with the owner, Max, and had asked his advice on how to improve the track lighting in the conference room. As he pulled out of his build-ing's drive, he saw Max in his overcoat and fedora walking to his car, parked along the curb. Andy slowed and rolled down his window.

"What, did I piss you off already?"

Max peered in through the window. "Andy! Hello my friend."

"What's up?"

"Long story, but in a nutshell, a developer made me an offer I couldn't refuse. Says he's going get re-zoned and open a gentlemen's club."

"A strip joint?"

"I guess."

"Cool. Where you going?'

"Across town. Didn't want to sell really, but as my father used to tell me, if someone wants to pay over-market, let them."

As he drove in the darkness along the busy divided highway, the wipers making a monotonous swishing sound, he reviewed the day's events. He'd had some initial misgivings about his speech, but Colleen assured him it was "brilliant" and "necessary." He knew, too, it was a homily a longtime brewing, but at the same time wondered if he would have been so inclined to make it in the absence of financial duress. Thinking about the performance in front of his employees gave him a tingle of pride and pleasure; small consolation given the minefield he was presently negotiating, but he'd take anything at this point. Besides his son, he had never lectured or reprimanded anyone. His philosophy was live and let. But his role had changed. He had a stake in the behavior of other people. His employees had it coming, to be sure, but what about him? How had he adlibbed such a magnificent, finely wrought and sincere fury? Because he now had a stake in their behavior.

The tiny tumblers were another matter. The process of plating a proprietary niobium-titanium coating onto the intricately shaped tubes was far trickier than Gloss had let on. He had had to scrap at least half of the batches he had attempted to make so far, leaving Clancey in the lurch, costing him tens of thousands of dollars and making him the target of Clancey's unceasing barrage of insults and threats, which often stopped just shy of some form of implied torture. He had become so stumped by the problem, he had taken the dicey, and technically prohibited action of approaching Ian Hunt for advice. He figured he could trust Hunt—he was the quintessential under-the-radar guy, someone who would rather walk through a pen of Komodo dragons than do anything that might conceivably complicate his life. Plus, Andy still bought his bulk chemicals from Tartan, so it wasn't out of bounds for him to put a call into their senior technical service representative. Hunt said titanium niobium plating "was completely out of his fucking field," but advised Andy to check the temperature settings and recalibrate. "And if you have a rabbit's foot or a votive candle, you might try that as well," he told him.

Yet, in the grand scheme of things, deadbeat employees and tiny tumblers were the least of his worries. Steering his car into the fitness facility's parking lot, he looked forward to a grueling, gut-busting, sweat-drenched workout to induce a state of mental and physical exhaustion and thus become, like his employee Ja-Coby, disinclined to "thang."

Two hours later he was lying on a towel on the top bench of the sauna feeling like a slab, it seemed, of extruded thermoplastic rubber. The door of the sauna swung open and slammed shut.

"Mind if I throw some water on the rocks?"

Andy opened his eyes and turned his head. It was Brad Jurasic, his former nemesis over at Crossbow Chemical. With his pale, almost translucent skin, patches of stringy, matted hair pulled forward over his scalp, and pronounced overbite, Jurasic reminded Andy of a possum embryo freshly extracted from a jar of formaldehyde.

"How's the boardroom treating you?" Jurasic asked, taking a seat on the bottom bench.

"It has its perks, dude."

"Boffo," Jurasic said with a customary, snide tone, Andy recalled. "Then maybe, as prez, you should be the first to know—we're going into metal plating."

"What?"

"Geez, Mr. Dodge, I'd expect to at least hear a 'hip-hip-hooray' for another company creating jobs and wealth through free markets."

"Why would you start plating? It's not your core business."

"Close enough. Besides, Mr. Crossbow has been hankering to get into the plating business for a while. Now that Dick Gloss has retired, he sees an opportunity for some reason. I can't imagine what that would be."

Andy laid his head back on his rolled towel. "I have the best request-for-quote program in the business. Bring it on, Jurasic."

"Now that's a better attitude."

"That's just the start."

On the way back to his apartment, Andy stopped for some takeout.

"Dozen wings."

"Breaded, barbeque, ranch or teriyaki?"

"Barbeque."

He walked up the stairs to his second-floor apartment in a sixties-era multiplex called Ambassador Arms. When he closed the door to his room he could immediately hear a dull vibrato sound, voices, music, a laugh track from the television in the apartment above him—or maybe it was below him. Sounds seemed to emanate from all directions in this three-story building constructed, it seemed, of balsa, papier-mâché and thumbtacks. He had met the people in the unit above, Eddie and Corina, on the stairwell a few days before. "If I get too loud, dude, just pound on the wall a couple of times," Eddie had told him.

Andy dropped his gym bag on the floor, walked into the kitchen, set the wings on the counter and grabbed a beer from the fridge. He fell into the lone lounge chair in the apartment and flicked on the television. He hadn't set up cable service yet and received only two or three channels, on a good night, one of them with a fuzzy, intermittent picture. Then again, he wasn't sure he could afford cable. He was, in fact, technically broke; so broke his application in a swankier apartment complex, Glen Meadows, was rejected. He had taken out a loan against his business assets just to meet his day-to-day expenses.

Andy took a sip of his beer and thought of phoning Marcia, once again begging for forgiveness, but knew he would only get her voice mail. His case admittedly, on face, was weak. Pathetic, really. When she had received the report from the private investigator on her cell stating, "Brunette female, approximately 30 years old, observed exiting house with male subject Sunday morning," her first call had been to her lawyer. Upon arriving home Sunday afternoon, she gruffly brushed past Andy, issuing a chilling "don't touch me," stomped directly upstairs, threw two large suitcases on the bed, into which she began tossing Andy's clothes. Andy's innocuous, "What's up, sweetie?" was met with a string of expletives so foul it would have turned the stomach of a Chechen assassin. His "I can explain," provoked a flurry of furious jabs, clubbing karate chops and Tae kwon do-style kicks to all parts of his body. Andy survived the pummeling by adopting a version of Ali's famed rope-a-dope tactic, curling his arms over his head and midsection while gradually backing his way out the room. If not for a misstep at the top of the stairs, he would have come out of it with nothing worse than multiple contusions, a cauliflower ear and several deep gouges. Tumbling backward head over heels down the stairs, however, he cracked his hand against the hard wood balustrade, breaking the ring finger on his left hand in two places. He checked himself into the emergency room of the hospital later that night. As he rested on a roll-away in the hallway, a nurse, appreciating his stoical patience in face of complete medical disregard for his injuries, felt compelled to apologize. "No worries," Andy said, happy that he had a bed for the night. "Tell the doctors to attend to more urgent matters."

Since that moment, about two weeks ago, his only direct communication with Marcia had been through her lawyer, one Hillary Higgins. He had yet to retain a lawyer himself, holding to the dim hope that another night alone, and Andy's pleadings and protestations, filed, as they were, into the vacuum of voice mail, would bring Marcia to her senses. He was also superstitious that if he did bite the bullet and hire one of the creeps, it would mean that the likelihood of going over the brink was much more certain. He had always had a low, but still nominally rational and humor-tinged opinion of the legal profession. That view had now decayed into visceral loathing. To say lawyers were the bottom feeders and bacteria of human civilization was slandering whole classes of biologically important fauna. Bacteria did nothing worse than decompose and recycle what was already dead and rotting. Lawyers, however, orchestrated misfortune and disaster and used the proceeds from the carnage to fund their champagne and canapé-accompanied vacations retracing the steps of Alexander the Great; or to hold black tie charity balls to help all the homeless put out of work when their companies went belly-up from multi-million-dollar class-action settlements. Ms. Higgins perceived his insolence. "You need to get yourself an attorney, Mr. Dodge," she scolded him a day earlier on a call to tell him she was sending over a draft of the separation agreement. "This is serious."

Unable to communicate directly with Marcia, Andy, in desperation had phoned Millie.

"That woman was a business associate of mine. I got drunk, she drove me home, nothing happened," she told Millie.

"I saw you two hugging in the parking lot of Marcel's, buddy boy."

"For God's sake, Millie, that was a friendly good-bye hug."

"Looked to me like you were getting your nut right there in the great outdoors."

"Will you at least tell her I still love her? Think of the kids."

"I'll relay the message, but I wouldn't get my hopes up, Studebaker."

Andy felt a pang of hunger and remembered the wings. He grabbed some napkins and the box of wings and returned to his chair. He took a wing and bit into it, pausing with the first couple of chews. Ranch, not barbeque! He was about to fling the entire box across the room when he paused and took a deep breath. Maybe he could get the basketball game on TV. He flicked the remote repeatedly, then remarkably, the game came into view. After a couple of minutes, the picture on the television began to go awry, moving up the screen in wavy horizontal lines. Hey, he observed, I'm getting to relive my childhood, picturing his dad cursing and jumping off the living room couch to fiddle with one of the skinny plastic knobs at the bottom of their analog television set. He flicked the set off with the remote, already conditioned to listen for noises carrying through the walls from surrounding apartments. It was quiet for a few seconds and he relaxed. Suddenly some horns blared, and the loud baritone voice of an ad man reverberated through the walls. He heard Eddie bound off his chair and walk heavily across the floor above him. "I hate this commercial." A little farther away he could hear their baby crying. Andy reached over and pounded twice on the wall. Eddie jogged back to a spot approximately above him and thumped the wall twice quickly. "Got it, dude."

10 THE KILLING FIELD

About a week after Valentine's Day, Eastman Finch was relaxing on the balcony of his beachfront condo on Longboat Key. The sun had just set below a hazy shoal of clouds, sending an afterglow of golden tangerine and magenta into the pale sky above the dark blue Gulf. Gulls, pelicans and oyster catchers wheeled and swooped over the waves washing to shore with a steady, soothing *swoosh*. Farther offshore, several dolphins arced to the surface.

Finch rested his feet on the rail of the balcony and put his arms behind his head, taking in the view. Before coming down he had closed, with a $5 million down payment, on the Woolcott estate. The beachfront mansion was not only a prime piece of real estate, but came with a lineage, built by the founder of one of America's iconic department store chains. With the housing market booming again, he had brokered the price of the 19-acre domain below asking, "below" still being an unmentionable sum of money—unmentionable because these were the times we lived in. You didn't fly corporate jets, you didn't get outrageous bonuses and you didn't flaunt wealth. He could play the game whatever which way. It didn't matter how many rules, written or unwritten, the merry band of Beltway bandits dreamed up, people always found a way around or through them. Still, it went against his instincts and he had fond memories of the rollicking high-flying 90s. His first job had been as an analyst at one of the Street's established firms; he recalled the day he met the president, Ace Bloomberg, in the hallway for the first time. Someone introduced them, and Ace meticulously sized him up, then asked him if he knew anything about an IPO on a tech firm that had just come out. Finch didn't but began to blabber anyway. "Fuck you," Ace said, turning and walking away. Finch, despite the kick in the crotch, won points with his team for not even flinching from the blow; a few months later Ace was one of his racquetball partners.

Yet, even with the mob-rule edict, the Woolcott estate was too big a prize for people not to notice. This was New York after all. People judged you on what you did, not on what you intended to do. No, not exactly—people judged you on what you DO. There was no past tense in New York, only the now and the immediate next minute. You hit 40 home runs during the season, so, what are you going to do for us in the World Series? You climb Mount Everest, so what, you going to get a television show out of it or something? Word would get out. The estate represented not so much his arrival as his flourish, complete with bannered coronets and bunting fluttering in the breezes. He could now walk through any door of his choosing—a patron of the arts, corridors of power, even an ambassadorship was not out of the question (Ace had mentioned the latter, jokingly, but Finch had instantly appropriated the idea).

The purchase of the Woolcott estate did all this, and more: It put a checkmate on Brianna. Call it blood money if you will, but the likelihood of Beatrice divorcing and fleecing him for every centime he owned had, in a blink, become implausible on the heels of impossible. This was apparent from the glow in her eyes when their agent had first shown them the house. Baroni and his wife had sunk a mint into renovating, and everything, from the 1000-square-foot, natural-light, open-concept kitchen, furnished with a German-built, stainless steel, double cavity, gas-fired wall oven, multiple granite-top islands and a step-down wine cellar, to the original refurbished, hand-carved cherry and rosewood corbels, to sconce lighting, to 270-knot-per-square inch Sarouk Persian rugs, conformed with Beatrice's vision of a dream house. "This is much better than anything on First Neck or Lily Pond," she cooed. The clincher, if one was needed, was the breathtaking, unobstructed, panoramic view of Mecox Bay, created when Baroni had boldly bulldozed through the 2000-year-old protected sand dunes and wetlands in front. Her capitulation was formally announced a few days after her return from the Valentine's Day retreat, when they spent a long kiss-and-make-up evening together, replete with Chinese take-out and champagne in their bedroom. Beatrice apologized for "pushing him into the arms of other women," and Finch allowed, without an apparent trace of irony, "I'm not perfect." Beatrice, smitten by the prospect of becoming a Hamptonesse, seized on the remark to affirm, "Neither am I." "Cool," Finch replied, "Let's have another glass of champagne and screw."

Afterward, Beatrice had begged Finch to tell her more about the deal.

"It's a take-over. Some technology or something."

"Who's it for?"

"Not sure. My boy in London is in contact with the client. Some outfit in the middle east."

"Middle East? Ooo, someone must be up to no good to pay that amount of money."

Finch shrugged. "What's it my business? If I had wanted to change the world, I would have become an actor."

"Eastman, I just had an idea. Why don't we bulldoze the whole fucking dune? It's just blocking our view."

Finch walked into the condo, filled his glass with more wine and went back out to the balcony. Beatrice and the kids were shopping on St. Armand's and would return for dinner later. He was about to sit down when the burner phone in the pocket of his chinos vibrated.

"Eastman, this is Melinda."

"Hello, my beautiful Natasha. Tell me something GOOD."

"Wish I could."

"No, no, just do."

"Okay, my boobs are still 36 DD."

"That's what I'm talking about!"

"Listen, Dr. Strangelove, we have a teensy-weensy problem."

"Small problems I can handle."

"Dodge has fired me."

Finch, for a moment, was speechless. "No fucking way."

"Way, dude. His wife thinks he's having an affair with me."

"Shit, that was you? I heard she threw the nitwit out of the house."

"It all came down this week. I only had my guys in there two days."

"They find anything?"

"Rumor is he makes something in a bunker below his office. No one has ever seen it first-hand but that's got to be the enrichment tubes."

"Security?"

"Tight. Gloss put the system in. Passes and codes in and out. Laser-activated motion detectors at night. Cameras with 24-7 monitoring. Plus, Dodge has some sort of pocket device that puts him straight to the White House. At least that's what he claims. He showed it to me the night we went out. I searched him when he passed out but couldn't find it."

Finch thought for a moment. "Ha … ha …Ha ha ha ha."

"Why are you laughing?"

"Because, ha ha, the answer just hit me."

"And?"

"We whack him."

"Whack him?"

"We can't do a bag-job now. With that kind of security, it's the only option."

"I don't want to whack the guy."

"Why not? He's a fuck-up and a nuisance anyway. His wife would thank us."

"Yeah, but …"

"Someone told me you can blow an aspirin out of the air with a Remington at 50 yards."

"Purely a hobby."

"I hope my Natasha isn't getting soft. May I gently remind you I've already paid you ten percent upfront, $2 million, with another ten percent due upon completion of the job."

Melinda sighed, annoyed. "Okay, Finch, don't fuck with me."

"Good. Here's what we do. Find out who owns the building nearest him with the best view of his office. We need to confirm how he gets in and out of that bunker before we off him. Did your guys get the pass code?"

"No, the secretary let them in."

"Could we bribe her?"

"She'd probably do the job for us if we asked."

Abdul Afzal Jabbar Khan Lala (A.J.) was in a deep, dream-filled sleep when he felt someone jabbing his shoulder. It was his young son, Naib.

"Father, Dr. Prof. Abdul Qaden Khadami A. Q. Khan is here to begin his presentation," Naib informed him.

"Shukran, my child."

A.J. sat on the edge of his cot and groggily rubbed his eyes. He had spent the night directing the construction of a small landing strip. The airstrip, in a remote valley 20 miles north of his village, had been under construction for over a year and was behind schedule, in great measure because work could only be done at night, but also because the airstrip was one part construction, one part concealment. Before finishing every night, workers needed to cover each freshly graded and leveled section with uprooted shrubs, trees, boulders and other debris, to make it satellite proof. It was like trying to shear a lamb with a Monopoly token, he would tell his leader. Not that his fellow mujahedeen had one iota of sympathy for him. As he stood up to dress, he muttered sardonically to himself the phrases he heard so often: "It's gut check time. Step up to the plate. Suck it up. Just do it."

It was a short walk over to the community center, where the nuclear weapons expert and national hero, Dr. Kubla Khan, as he was fondly known, was to speak. As he neared the hall along the winding, narrow streets he passed guards stationed at every corner, their fingers tense on the triggers of their AK-47s and Uzis. He saw other men stationed on the tops of buildings with grenade launchers. If a Cruise missile comes in, I'll look for your body parts in Lahore, he chuckled to himself as one of the men looked down, waving at him. But God is great to have sent us the doctor and he chastised himself for his fondness of Western sarcasm and ironic commentary. It was a miracle and the brothers fighting the infidels and the war to end all wars must take every precaution. With the doctor on our side, victory was now certain.

A.J. took a seat on the last rug remaining. The great Dr. Khan stood on a small wooden platform placed in front of the room. He wore a mustache, which seemed to droop to one side, and a shabby, dark olive, wool, three-piece suit. A.J. stared up in amazement at a man whose picture he had seen many times.

The doctor held up a rock. "This is piece of uranium ore from a new mine that just opened in central Kyrgyzstan. It contains, oh, about one-tenth of one percent uranium, maybe a half a gram. Of that half a gram, 99.3 percent is uranium 238 or shit uranium. That means that in this entire rock there is less than a hundredth of a gram of good uranium 235, the enriched stuff that makes a nuclear bomb go boom-boom."

He threw the rock into the audience of a couple dozen men. "Now, gentlemen, seeing that about 100 pounds of enriched uranium is needed to make a Boom-Boom, it would take, using the ore produced in Kyrgyzstan and the old-fashioned method of separating uranium 238 from uranium 235, oh, about 10 years to make a bomb capable of turning New York City into a pile of rubble, by which time I suspect a laser-guided missile will have acquainted most of you with your virgin brides in the hereafter. With the new titanium-coated centrifuges created by the great American inventor and businessman Dick Gloss, however, you can get the amount of uranium 235 you need, with my help, in less than a year. Gentlemen, our only chance of defeating the infidels is to get our hands on the Gloss centrifuge. And there is one and only one person alive who can keep us from obtaining the technology to make the centrifuge, and his name is Andy Dodge."

At the mention of Andy's name the room broke into a raucous chatter. The man with the thin face well-known to Western television audiences and presumed dead, rose and raised his hands for quiet.

"Doctor, we are honored by your presence and the help you are so generously providing to the Jihad," the man said. "But what do you take us for, chopped liver? We have an operation in place to capture the bomb-making devices from Dodge."

Shouts of "Allah Akbar" rang out in the room. The doctor

raised his hand. "I'm aware of your operation, but I must tell you I have been informed that the window of opportunity to acquire the centrifuge-making technology is closing quickly. Dodge is screwing up and the U.S. government is close to taking over the operation. When that happens getting this technology will be like trying to pry a toddler out of the jaws of a pit bull."

The room exploded into an uproar of howls, curses and fulminations. The man with the well-known face again raised his hands for quiet. "The great doctor has given us some important information. Let us not blame the messenger. Of all the infidels in the world, Andy Dodge is the most unrepentant and depraved. We must do everything we can to exterminate Dodge from the face of the earth so we can march on a clear and certain path to victory in the Holy War. Let it be known, as God is my witness, I want to see the head of Andy Dodge mounted on the wall of our mosque."

The men sprang to their feet in a riotous cheer, pumping their fists in rhythm. The disparate shouts of fury grew more coherent, converging into the chant, "Allah Akbar", which spontaneously and seamlessly transformed into "Kill Andy Dodge! Kill Andy Dodge!" A.J. jumped up on the platform to lead the cheer, inspired by the spirit of camaraderie. It reminded him of American football pep rallies he had seen on the internet.

Marcia Riker, as she was now semi-officially calling herself, had been appointed director of the bank's Pretty-in-Paisley fund raiser and charity ball for Teenage Girl Eating and Skin Disorder awareness month. Purple and gold paisley banners inscribed with "A meal does not a pound make" and "Don't let a pimple pop her self-esteem" hung from the ceiling around the office. Employees had been issued paisley shirts printed with the campaign's motto, "Tell her she looks pretty, before and after each meal," and every day featured a new paisley give-away, from pens to coffee mugs to mouse pads. She enjoyed the work associated with the charity, in as much as it allowed her to use her organizational skills. She also would say, if cornered, that the cause was extraordinarily worthwhile. But meanwhile life and business—two areas in which she seemed to be getting further and further behind—chugged along inexorably. That the paisley campaign had come on the heels of the bank's brochure- and investor-prospectus recycling advocacy program didn't help. There were positions to fill, training to set up and performance reviews to schedule and every time she looked up there was another presentation to attend, coffee and cookie social or another employee-recognition award to bestow. Was it just she who thought the world was going ass-over-tea-kettle loony? Or maybe we had all just agreed to agree to fiddle while Rome burned.

Andrew's expulsion had put an added, unanticipated strain on her. Not that she missed him, perish the thought. But overnight her children had become latchkey kids, locking up the house in the morning before they set off to catch the school bus, and letting themselves in after school, there to play video games, eat junk food and God knows what else until she got home from work, usually well past 6 o'clock. Her husband, technically, still, until the divorce went through, had always had more flexibility in his work schedule and was often able to drive the kids to school, or nip home in the late afternoon, check in and make them a dinner, even if it was grilled cheese and a can of soup—that her children were getting a warm meal gave her peace of mind. While Andrew still saw the kids on weekends, she was now compelled to single-handedly keep tabs on their whereabouts, make lunches, plan dinners, buy groceries, put gas in the car, chauffeur them to and from practices and social events and run dozens of other errands which, while minor, had once seemed to take care of themselves. She was, in truth, astounded at how much Andrew apparently handled.

"What's the give-away today?"

Marcia, startled, suddenly aware she had been staring blankly at her computer screen.

"Oh, hi Justin," she said, turning in her chair and greeting one of the bank's financial analysts.

"Sorry to interrupt."

"No, no, it's fine. Just, you know, blue sky thinking, ha."

"Sure, gotta do that now and then."

"Yeppers, HA. Ah, how are you?"

"Good. I just thought I'd stop by. A few of us are going out for a glass of wine after work, wanted to know if you'd like to join us."

Marcia blanked for a second. "Oh, I'm sorry, I'd love to, but I have an appointment." She said, not wanting to mention it was with a counselor.

"No problem," Justin shrugged and smiled casually. "We'll make it a rain check."

"For sure. And BTW it's a key chain."

"I'm looking for some paisley socks."

She had started to visit Angelique because she needed to talk with someone, anyone. This wasn't just the generic female claptrap. She needed to get a read on her life from an impartial professional, with perspective. Friends such as Millie, her jogging partner, Tera, or even her sister, well-meaning though they might be, would feed her feel-good bullshit. Angelique, formally, was not a marriage counselor but a "life coach," a title that made Marcia wince. Yet, Angelique had come recommended by the bank's in-house staff person in charge of non-medical (addiction, crisis, nutbar) employee out-sources and benefits.

Angelique's office was in a tony strip mall, situated between a furrier on one side and a plastic surgeon's office on the other. Angelique, a tall, thin woman with long, frizzy straw-colored hair, greeted her effusively. Marcia had spent most of the first meeting filling out various "profiles," batteries of questions intended to provide insight into her values, goals and relationship needs. The sessions, Angelique explained, were not deliberately structured to delve into her marital issues, however, "in order to understand where she wanted to go with her life, she needed to understand where she had been." Marcia fidgeted, recognizing the catchy, euphemism-filled HR speak which usually meant, "brace yourself, I'm about to stick in the needle."

"What I find most interesting is the answers you gave under the compatibility section," Angelique said, sitting cross-legged on a divan opposite her. "In the responses that best describe you and your husband's tastes, you write that you like soft jazz and folk, while your husband prefers hip-hop and gonzo rock; you like a lean, organic, vegetable-rich diet, your husband is fond of pulled pork, corn dogs and fried mozzarella; your ideal night at home would consist of reading a book or watching a debate on C-Span, whereas your husband's idea of a perfect night would be shadow boxing an imaginary bout with Sugar Ray or repetitively viewing re-runs of NASCAR's 100 greatest crashes of all time … Marcia, be honest with me, are there anger issues here?"

"Oh, heck no, I have that out of my system. I'm resigned."

"Resigned to what?"

"To… to… to you know, the future. Fun, fun, fun."

Angelique shook her head. "I have trouble believing this."

"What?"

"You, your husband."

"Yeah, well like they say, you can't make this stuff up."

"My read on you is that you are not a self-destructive person."

"All I want is normal and all I get is wacko."

"Do you mind me asking why, then, did you marry someone so, so … different."

Marcia stared into space, trance-like for a minute. "I have this philosophy," she said, sighing. "Try to get out of your comfort zone. Variety is the spice of life. Andrew was different from anyone I ever knew growing up. He was funny, the life of the party, someone everyone liked to be around."

"So, you seek the exotic, the fruit that your family would forbid?"

"Oh, I got fruit all right."

"I see this all the time."

"What?"

"People say opposites attract, but over the long run it's the things you have in common that count the most."

Marcia thought about the statement. "It's true I find Andrew most appealing when he is organized, acts responsibly, goes to a play with me, sort of like myself."

"See what I mean?"

"But what about spice?"

"Say what?"

"You know, it don't mean a thing if it ain't got that swing."

Angelique gazed sternly at her. "I think you have some serious unresolved issues here, Marcia."

"I do, do I?"

"Yes, you can't go up a mountain and down at the same time. You can't have it all."

"'You can't have it all.' Wow. How much am I paying for these sessions?"

Ricky Santiago Mendez, the son of two migrant workers, grew up picking blueberries and fruit in bucolic Western Michigan long before white people driving along isolated county roads worried about eight-year-old Mexican kids working from dawn to dusk. Luckily, his parents, with the help of a distant cousin, naturalized when he was 16, which meant Ricky was free to pursue a real, dust- and perspiration-free American job. Unluckily, it also meant he was eligible for the draft. He survived boot camp and a deranged drill sergeant, who had a knack for innovative ethnic slurs, specialized in communications and electronics, and shipped out to Vietnam in the same platoon as Dick Gloss. They arrived shortly before the Tet offensive. Ricky was calling in for additional air cover when a rocket landed nearby, tossing him like a rag doll over 20 yards, and turning his left thigh into a facsimile of a raw shank of beef brisket. Unfortunately, his point of touchdown was in the very middle of the street in the village they were fighting, at inches per hour, to take. Whether the gooks didn't see him or decided not to bother wasting a bullet, he'll never know. They sure the hell took target practice on Dick Gloss, however, who ran into the middle of the street, grabbed him by the arm and dragged him to cover, rounds sputtering up chunks of cement on every side. Gloss was hit in the arm, yet, with his good arm, jury-rigged tourniquets for Ricky and himself, then hauled him on his shoulder, under fire, over a mile to the nearest platoon with a medic.

If prompted by the slightest reminder of that incident, Ricky would say, "I *geev* my *gonaads* to Gloss if he needed them." Around Christmas every year Ricky brought Gloss a couple of pounds of his favorite Kielbasa, laying the smelly, brown paper-wrapped bundle on his desk like Frankincense before the Manger of the Christ Child. With his code of Spanish *machismo,* Ricky carried a shame that in all the years since Nam, he had never really done anything to fully repay Gloss. The book was still open with a debt and that—no matter that it was a debt that no one held against him, no matter it was a debt that could never possibly be repaid in exact kind—was something that, as a man, he would never allow to be forgotten. He had thanked Gloss a million times in a million different ways. But thanking was not masculine. A great, perilous and brave deed could only be repaid with another great, dangerous and courageous deed—*muy grande.* And now that the call had come, the request made, Ricky moved with agile, urgent self-centered assuredness, channeling the persona of the hero he knew so well, having watched every action flick ever made.

With a solemn, stone-like expression, he walked without speaking past his wife and children having breakfast in the kitchen and out to the garage. He tossed a toolkit into the saddle bags of his Harley, kicked the starter, revved the engine to a sustained, ear-shattering decibel, and popped the clutch, catapulting out of the driveway as every eye in the neighborhood peered out their windows, transfixed by the spectacle of a reckless Mexican jackass barreling his hog between parked cars down the quiet residential side street at 80 miles an hour.

When he arrived at his store the only person to have reported to work was a materials handle who went by the name of Neo. "Bunch of goddamn *deedbeats,*" Ricky muttered, shoving open the side door to the office so forcefully it smashed into a coat closet, knocking the top-hung slide door off its rail, which came crashing to the floor. Ricky stepped over the door and paged Neo on the intercom: "Bring me a standard telemetry receiver, 40 giga hertz, type subminiature P, *muy rapido!*"

Ricky marched into his small office behind the main customer counter and grabbed a pile of faxes off the tray. He pitched a half of dozen pages onto the floor until he found the one from Gloss titled, "transmitter switch settings." He tramped back to the counter, untied the leather pouch containing his tools, rolled it out on the counter and laid the sheet containing the specifications beside it. Neo ran in with the device and gave it to Ricky.

"What's going on, boss?"

"Lock theee shop door and eef any fuck heads show up for work today, keep theem in theee back ahnteel I say."

Ricky plucked the tiniest Allen wrench from his set and unscrewed the back cover from the receiver, which looked like sleek black garage door opener with a tiny, round, grilled speaker in the middle. He pried off the cover and extracted a small, printed circuit board, connected at each corner to a wire. He snipped the four wires and flicked the board like a Frisbee into a trash bin at the far end of the counter. He unlocked a cabinet behind the counter and pulled open a dozen, narrow, felt-lined steel drawers until he found two micro coaxial connectors and a 2N 39 transistor inverter circuit board. He was a surgeon now, his hands moving by memory, cutting, splicing, soldering. Once he had the new board inserted and secured, he took the fax from Gloss and read the settings aloud, "transmitter switch 1, up; transmitter switch 2, down," until all 15 of the tiny switches in the middle of the circuit board had been synchronized. He snapped the back cover, screwed in the tiny screws and laid the device on the counter. Back in his office, he opened a secure website on his computer with a password Gloss had given him. He typed in several lines of code, hit the send button at the bottom of the page and leaned back in his chair, waiting. After a few seconds he heard an urgent-sounding, staccato "beep-beep-beep-beep," repeating in a four-second interval. He walked out, grabbed the receiver and pushed a button. The beeping stopped and he stuffed the device into his pocket.

Ricky walked back into his office and unlocked a drawer in his desk. He reached behind some hanging files and pulled out a 9mm Beretta automatic pistol, a shoulder holster and a box of shells. He popped the magazine out of the handle, loaded in ten shells, and then jammed the magazine back into the pistol, which locked in with a precise *click*. He took off his leather vest, put the holster under his arm and pulled it tight to his shoulder and chest. After putting his vest back on, Ricky dropped to his knees, made the sign of the cross, and said three Hail Mary's in Spanish.

"Dear Lord," he whispered trembling. "Please let something happen."

11 DEFLECTION SHIELDS

Imagine a cold, murky, dismal Tuesday afternoon, around 2:17 p.m. Lunch, the temporary reprise of the day, is over; and dinner, the next of the day's conscripted anticipations, is, at best, a stillborn idea. A steady rain—neither heavy, portending it might spend itself, nor light, a mildly cheering reprieve from a long winter evoking, with a bit of imagination, tulips and bikinis—beats down out of the amorphous gloom. The entire natural world outside the window is composed in a single hue of washed-out, nicotine-tinged gunmetal gray. A single sparrow, it too colorless and drab, perches on the ledge of an office window, flapping its wings in a futile attempt to fend off water. Somewhere a bus is idling in front of a concrete overhang while seniors dawdle down the steps into the bright tedium of a nearly empty casino and shuffle in the direction of the penny slots. Somewhere a mechanic is trudging through the slop in the back of a shop looking for a banged-up car that will again require countless hours of yanking, hammering, sawing, drilling and painting to repair. Somewhere an overweight nanny with a hangover is snoozing on a sofa dreaming of her Karaoke rendition of "If I were a Rich Man" as two preschoolers light matches in front of the television. Somewhere an owner of a metal-plating shop is sitting at his desk staring in stark meditation at the rain pattering the window, thinking he had never hired a hooker, shot up heroin or played Russian Roulette. He was also bemused at why someone appeared to be tramping around on the roof of the freshly vacated Eisner Industrial Lighting building across the street, but let it go, along with every other curiosity, hope and ambition, into the abyss of the permeating gloom. What the heck, he sighed. At least he'd been to a Super Bowl, played Pebble Beach and shook hands with three-time World Series of Poker-winner Caesar Chang. He'd done some things. It's not like he had a ton of re-grets. But what happens when one goes belly-up, down the tubes, leaving nothing behind but a 7-digit crater in a thing formerly known as your bank account? Now that's unexplored turf. Other than homelessness, or a facsimile thereof, what were the consequences of bankruptcy, poverty, penury, destitution? He had become acquainted with many new words to describe the condition of being bereft of cash. Did one just gradually and quietly fade from the consciousness of the family and friends, only to reappear years later as an owner-operator of a 7-minute car-window, rock-chip repair business in the parking lot of a Wal-Mart in Wheaton? "We heard from Dad. He's hanging in there, doing okay." The kids inevitably get to report, as word slowly gets around the neighborhood, causing more than one person to scratch their head and remark, "Andy Dodge? He's still alive?"

A new life. That is where this was all headed. Maybe a little flat over a tee-shirt shop in Cocoa Beach. Learn how to surf. Save up enough money to buy a moped. It wasn't unbearable; there were worse things one might endure—chamber music, the waiting area of a women's hair salon, two equally abject prospects that came to mind. What did Vince once say? You can't step twice into the same river. Change was a fact of life. Of course, it was one thing to choose change, and another to be bulldozed by it. He could accept that he had screwed up multiple shipments to Clancey, thus forfeiting tens of thousands of dollars. It was a learning curve and he was getting better at making the tiny tumblers. He understood he needed to hire a Sparky and an Al Gore, now delayed because he was compelled to jettison Melinda Chow from his life like a Tupperware container of rancid leftovers. Employee empowerment, he knew, would need time to take root, especially given the culture of drooling, thumb-sucking dependency he had inherited from Gloss. All this was, theoretically, under his control. What he couldn't figure out, however, was how he was losing customers, until now. Ian Hunt at Tartan had just called him to tell him Crossbow was undercutting him.

"It's a standard bloody predatory practice used by start-ups to pinch customers," Hunt said. "What's weird is that people don't usually jump ship for a few tuppence."

"So, how's Crossbow doing it?" Andy asked.

"They must have an angel."

"An angel?"

"One motherfucker of an angel covering their losses. It's the same principle as Chinese companies dumping steel with government backing. Bastards!"

Accelerating his descent into the realm of ignominy, OSHA inspector Darren Tilsdale was threatening to shut him down if he did not have fume control equipment installed by the end of the week. As the equipment would cost about $100,000 to install, this "new life" was becoming, minute-by-minute, less a figment of dark-humor conjecture, and more a certainty around which he felt compelled to start contingency planning. He was at this very minute searching apartment rental rates in Cocoa Beach.

He swung his feet off his desk, stiffened in his chair and shook his head violently, thinking if he jiggled his brain hard enough he could achieve the neurological equivalent of a reboot. Enough of this self-pity, he told himself. All was not lost—sure he was dangling by a thread over a pit of fire ants but he was still dangling. Even at $30,000, his take on the tiny tumblers after various late and penalty fees, he could still restore cash flow with a half dozen successive shipments to Clancey. That might buy him enough financial goodwill to secure the loan he'd need for the fume control shit, which in turn might buy him some leeway with Tilsdale, that snide, pompous prick of a bureaucrat-from-hell if there ever was one.

Then there was this astounding development: His new life, in a most unanticipated development, was already beginning, even without a move to Cocoa Beach. Banned entry to his man cave, denied access to his HD TV and home entertainment center, with no cash to spend, with none of the regular sources of diversion, he had picked up a library card, at first with the intention of borrowing DVDs. Then a foray through the joint led him to, wonder of wonders, shelves of books. He was happy to learn, upon browsing this section of the building, that there were some cool book titles, much better than the ones Marcia, no ill will intended, had given him. Books on golf, aviation, military history, break dancing and rock 'n roll. Rock 'n roll! There was even a book about the history of the chemical industry! There must be some value added in things that must be tortu-ously engaged, line-by-line, page-by-page, at a microscopic, granu-lar level, requiring one to sit for minutes, hours, days, years, with no other sensory input but letters, arranged in a sequence, and the se-quences arranged in lines spanning two dots, and the lines spread into arrays of blocks, on and on the pages accumulating, like time itself, into eons and eras, numbers too large to comprehend, com-prising knowledge too vast and detailed for the human brain to ever have more than a soupçon sliver intimation of its meaning or how to direct it to some purposeful end. Wait, did he just say 'soupçon'? Well there you go. Maybe words, and their meanings, were the meaning. Maybe words were an entry point into the hidden layers of the phys-ical world, also known as, a much brow-beaten concept, reality. He had loaded up a gym bag with books and piled them on the floor next to his apartment's lone reclining chair. By accident, he had found a perfect white noise-making machine, an air purifier in a back storage room of the factory, and the continuous, monotonous whirring sound it made was enough to neutralize most noises emanating through the wafer-thin sheetrock comprising the so-called walls of his apart-ment. At night he would pop a beer, sit in the chair, and escape into worlds of words. At first, he struggled to concentrate, his mind wan-dering down any alleyway of distraction—Marcia, his kids, bills; then swing to happier recollections—family vacations, the night he scored 26 against arch-rival Rockport High. Sometimes he would find half an hour had passed without having turned a page. Gradually he got the knack of focusing and losing himself in the story, and the words drew him away from his predicaments. He tore through a book on a moun-tain climbing disaster in four nights. He began to keep a note pad by his chair and wrote down new words and ideas. He learned that it had taken Edison many years and hundreds of attempts to invent a prac-tical light bulb (that's not the way they taught it in school, it occurred to him). He found out Henry Ford hadn't been the first to invent the car, that he had failed twice trying to start a company that made and sold automobiles, and he eventually succeeded because he had sev-eral talented, hard-working, right-hand men working for him (many lessons in this one). He was now reading a book about the men who had invented the computer chip, and the previous night, had written down two quotes by one of the scientists: "In order to succeed, I try to fail as fast as I can." (he had that covered) and "When faced with a big problem I try to break it down into a number of little ones." (Hmm).

Just as he was thinking about his new-found hobby he had an idea. He spent half an hour searching the internet, then punched the intercom—a leftover relic of the Gloss regime, but one Andy took to, viewing it as a more congenial version of the concept called "pushing a person's buttons." In this case you pushed a button and got a person—what's not to like about that? "Penny, will you page Mac to come to my office?"

A few minutes later Mac sauntered in. "Whassup, boss?"

"Sit down, Mac. Take a chair."

"Reckon it'd be nice to take a load off the dogs."

"How's it going out there today?"

"Ah'd say somewhere between yoootopia and the Armagadoon, as usual. Ja-Coby still can't cotton how to run which parts off the production sheet. Spends the better part of the morning figurin' it all out, then it's like trying to eat Jello with chopsticks the rest of the day."

"You helping him?"

"Best I can."

"Good. That's the best way to learn, doing it. Edison and Ford failed many times before they succeeded."

"No guff?"

"Yep. Trial and error my friend, that's what it takes."

Mac sat on the edge of the chair and pointed in the direction of the shop. "We's got to get parts out the door, boss."

"No. We's got to get good parts out the door."

"That's what I'm saying."

"Mac, we need to bring our costs down, reduce our scrap and improve our efficiency. And we don't have a lot of time."

"No shit, especially with China tryin' to muscle in on the iron ore market."

Andy gazed across the desk at his plant manager, dressed in

his perpetual plaid, button-down shirt, jeans, faded brown cowboy boots, and back pocket stuffed with a magazine.

"Mac, you're a bright guy."

"Ah, *sheet* no, I just have a knack for reetainin' useless infoomation, as Mr. Gloss used to say."

"Fuck Gloss. Listen, Mac, I need an electrician, but can't afford to hire one right now. I was wondering if you might be able to help me."

Mac smiled from ear to ear. "You mean do it on the cheap?"

"Exactly, well, not *just* cheap. I was looking online. There are some basic electronics courses out there. It's not going to get you your Journeyman's card but in a few weeks you should be able to tell a diode from a capacitor."

Mac shot Andy a guarded glance. "I gotta be honest, boss. What's in it for me?"

"Once we get our people empowered, you won't have to be eating Jello with chopsticks all day. I'll bump up your pay, you'll have fewer headaches."

"Now that's what I'm talkin' 'bout. All my ex-wives gonna be real geeked. Gonna help with some of the rehab for my daughter too —none of that shit is covered by insurance."

"In the meantime, we gotta get our employees empowered, Mac."

"I'm trying, boss. You can lead a damn donkey to the water, but you can't make the cuss drink."

"Mac, you have my permission to shove their heads under until they gag—if you need to, of course."

After Mac left his office, Andy walked down the hall to the small cafeteria and poured himself a coffee. Luann was sitting in her blue lab coat at a table reading the newspaper on her break. Luann, he had observed more than once, had mastered the art of transmitting vibes which, when received by the attuned passerby, translated unmistakably into the obverse of an SOS signal. Andy fought his way through the powerful force field, which was focused and magnified through the aura of her body language—her back arched catlike and turned toward the door, shoulders hunched, hands held along the sides of her face functioning as eye-contact deflection shields; if one were to walk around the table, crouch and catch a glimpse of her bowed face, the visage of a scowl, one corner of her mouth etched in a downward running crease that seemed to be a perpetual precursor to a smirk, snort or grunt.

Andy stood at the side of the table attempting to catch the attention of Luann. She had state-of-the-art deflecting shields, that much was apparent. "Need a fill-up," Andy finally said, pointing at her coffee mug.

"What?" Luann looked up. "Uh no, I'm fine," she said, re-deploying her shields and turning her face down.

"Mind if I sit down?"

"No matter to me," she said without gazing up.

Andy took a chair across from her and grabbed one of the sections of newspaper lying on the table.

"Geez, more budget cuts in Lansing. Maybe the governor will have to start brown bagging, ha"

Luann shifted slightly in her seat.

"Pistons lose again. You ever been to a Pistons game?"

Luann snorted, put down one of her shields and turned the page of the newspaper. After several minutes of silence Andy began to hum the notes to *Panama*.

Luann began to execute an intricate fidgeting maneuver suggesting imminent bailout from conversation, table and lunchroom.

"So … what's happening with you?" Andy asked just as she started to rise from her chair.

Luann turned sideways and looked at Andy in astonishment.

"Why would you want to know?"

Deflection shields temporarily removed Andy was able to gaze directly into her eyes. "Why wouldn't I be? You work here. The job you do is important."

Luann, starring at Andy as if he were a mannequin who just started talking, let out a derisive chuckle and shook her head. "Well, if you really want to know, I've got a car with a bad ignition, a house that needs a new furnace, a back that's still sore from slipping on ice because someone didn't shovel the sidewalk in front of the office, and a deadbeat ex who hasn't sent me a dime for child support in over two years. Glad you asked?"

"At least you have a house," Andy said casually, turning a page of the newspaper.

Luann, who had stood and took a step toward the shop door, paused. "You got a house."

"Apartment. Wife kicked me out."

Luann's scowl softened. "Sorry to hear ... welcome to the club."

"What club?" Andy gazed up at her with an air of bewilderment.

"I need to spell it out? The bad-luck club."

"Luann, has anyone ever called you on a negative attitude?"

"Uh-uh. And if they did, I'd smack them."

"Luann, you have a negative attitude."

"That's it, I'm out of here."

"No! Hold on," he said sternly, not really knowing what he intended to say to her.

Luann, in full scowl, folded her arms and gazed at the ceiling, breathing rapidly.

"I have ... to be ... frank, er honest," he stammered, "You're a black hole of negativity. You're the queen of doom and gloom. The witch of woe is me. The duchess of defeat.

"Whadaya want me to be boss, happy?" She flashed him a wide, fake smile.

Andy pondered her response for a few seconds, having never been in an employee-attitude shake down, a situation that had once seemed as remote as climbing the Hillary Step in one of the mountaineering books he was reading. "No— shit, no," he somehow summoned a few words that aligned with a budding train of logic. "You are as free to be as miserable as you want. Go ahead, be yourself. Don't worry, feel shitty."

Luann cast a sarcastic glance at him and turned to leave, and Andy saw her start to go limp. He jumped up as she fell forward into his arms.

"I'm ... sorry ... boss," she said through stifled sobs. "I'm ...

just … tired. I … sniff … try… but … nothing …. sniff … works."

Andy patted her gently on the back.

He held her awkwardly in his arms as she cried, finally thinking to hand her a paper towel to dry her eyes. "Luann, you know the schedule better than anyone. I'm going to make Mac maintenance manager. Do you think you can handle production?" Luann looked up at him with surprise suffusing her red, swollen eyes, and once she digested the proposal as real, nodded. "Good," Andy said. "There's a raise, eventually, but you have to demonstrate a better attitude and leadership skills. I'll book some human relations training for you with Ms. Stuart."

Having descended into the lion's den and come out alive, Andy felt invigorated; entertaining thoughts and feelings he couldn't describe and had never experienced. He wasn't off the plank just yet, but maybe, just maybe he could turn this drunken boat of a factory around before it hit the rocks. He walked back into his office thinking, "Break a big problem into little ones.' Okay, in that case, what else could he do? Bingo: Why not call the customers Crossbow stole from him, if for no other reason than to acquire some firm intelligence on the tactics of that dingleberry-encrusted dung beetle, Brad Jurasic

He reached voice mail for the first two customers, owners of small job shops, one a screw and fastener manufacturer, the other a maker of decorative ceiling fans. As both owners were in when he called (receptionist: "May I ask who's calling?") it was brush-off city. He was surprised, then, when his call to the head purchasing manager at his largest automotive customer, Vulcan Inc., went straight through.

"Mr. Birksdale, this is Andy Dodge over at Gloss Industries."

"Ah yes, Andy, I was expecting your call. I see you didn't *dodge* the bullet Crossbow fired, ha ha."

"No, that one got me square in the udder."

"Isn't capitalism great? What can I do for you, or rather what can you do for me?"

Gloss Industries had been nickel-plating 1000 pump-cover shafts a day for Vulcan for over a decade. The loss was no small chunk of change.

"Maybe you can tell me what Jurasic is charging you."

"Mmm, let me see, is that ethical? Oh, shit. in the interest of fair trade—a buck a part."

Andy nearly gagged. He had been getting almost two dollars a part.

"What the hell, it costs a buck and a half just for materials and labor."

"I know, I know, it's cold, cruel world, isn't it, my friend?"

Andy gulped. "Okay, here's what I'll do. I'll offer to do it for 90 cents," he said, figuring some money was better than none.

Birksdale laughed. "Oh, you don't have to do that, just match him, and I can rationalize a reason to my boss for sending the business back to good old Gloss Industries."

"Just match it?"

"Yep. See, I discovered Jurasic graduated from State, my alumni's scurrilous nemesis. Now normally I keep my personal feelings separate from my professional decisions, but after they cheated to win last year's game against us, reprisal in any form is justified, don't you think, Andy?"

"Yes sir. Those bastards have it coming."

Andy put the phone down and sprang onto a spontaneous dance vaguely resembling twerking. "Hell, yes!" He jumped spread-eagled, pumping his fist. Now that he had the business back, he might be able to squeeze a few pennies here and there from the cost to manufacture the damn part. At the very least, it would keep Crossbow from getting any more of a foothold than it already had. "Take arms against cruel misfortune!" Hmm, he wondered, where the hell did that come from?

Melinda Chow was pleased to find it dark and miserable when she woke that morning. She didn't have to wait around all day to recommence operation Cotton Candy. Since Eisner Industrial Lighting had been purchased by a third party to a third-party holding company, she had visited the factory several times and surveyed the view. Standing on the front edge of the building's roof, she had a direct line of sight into Dodge's office, which jutted out from the side on the main building and faced the street with a wall-to-wall window. The window either had no blinds or Dodge elected to never close them. She could not have custom designed a more perfect perch with which to carry out "Plan B."

Shortly after lunch, garbed in hooded, bulky rain gear that made her indistinguishable from a man or woman, she began to piece together a small box-like blind made of inter-connected tubular PVC and black canvas flaps at the end of the roof farthest away from the street and Dodge's office. If anyone were to gaze up at the building's roof, the contraption would look like a standard's workman's blind, which it was, used to protect workers from the elements. Shortly after dark, which still came early in March, she dragged the blind to the front edge of the building and crawled inside, holding a duffle bag in one hand and a case with a 7.62 x 51 mm M40, semi-automatic sniper rifle in the other.

She took a rectangular piece of thick foam out of the bag and laid it on the floor of the blind, so it ran lengthwise and out the front flap to the rim of the roof, which was elevated by a berm about three inches high. The roof was asphalt embedded with painfully hard pebble and she was glad she had thought of the foam. She reached into the bag in a moment of panic, grabbed a pin light, flicked it on and checked to see if she had remembered the floor plans with the locations of the laser motions sensors and master control panel. She had, of course, she chuckled. She was too damn good to pull a rookie mistake like that. Then, removing the first layer of rain garb, she rotated and lay prone on the foam, extending the binoculars through a slight crease in the flap, and gazed into his office.

Dodge was lying on the floor in his underwear doing sit-ups. She sharpened the focus and could see his head bobbing up and down, cheeks red, mouth puffing out the cadence to each crunch, "38 ....39 ..." He made it to 45 before he collapsed, lying on the floor with his arms behind his head, lungs pumping up and down, gasping for breath. He rested for several minutes, then stood, stretched, and began doing jumping jacks, counting until he reached 25. He fell into his office chair. She watched him talking or singing to himself; lip reading, at one point he seemed to be saying, "Let's get it done, come on," then, "Da lights are on, but you not home," then something to the effect of "Momma loseeta, papa eat meata."?? A few minutes later, he jumped out of his chair, and still in his underwear, loose flannel boxers printed, it appeared, with the blue gnomes of a cookie brand, began practice putting at a weighted flagstick placed at the far end of the office.

Melinda put down the binoculars and rolled to her side. "What a flipping wingnut."

The rain had slackened to a light drizzle. She had convinced Finch it wasn't a good idea to try to bribe Penny or anyone else for the pass codes into the building. These Midwesterners were all boxes of chocolates to her; one couldn't be sure that their honesty and loyalty to a cause, even a hopeless one, wouldn't trump their own self-interest—baffling and not worth the risk of tipping off the plan. As an alternative they had hired a computer whiz to hack into the company's computer system. Gloss had installed a state-of-the-art firewall, but because Dodge surfed dubious websites, the geek was able to send in a trojan and steal his password. They couldn't find any entry pass codes, but for a moment they thought they might have found the formula used to make the uranium enrichment tubes in a file called "big mother bazookas." The file, however, turned out to be a procedure, not a formula, just spelling out how much of each solution was used but not what the solutions were. Furthermore, the temperature settings had been redacted, all of which they could have expected: There was no way Gloss would have left a file vital to national security on a computer entrusted to the care of Dodge. Besides, the formula to plate the tubes was only one part of the puzzle; they also needed a sample of the blank, un-plated tube, as well as a model of the plating tank and fixtures. Luckily, the problem of securing the entry pass codes solved itself. In her first couple of nights on the roof she had discovered that Dodge kept the code on a card in the pocket of his jacket, pulling it out every time he entered the building. The simpleton couldn't remember a five-digit number and because of that they were about to pick the pocket of one of Uncle Sam's most valuable technologies. All that remained to be learned was the location of the bunker, and how he got into it.

Andy walked down the hall to the restroom, splashed some water on his face and underarms and toweled off. It was the night he had to make a batch of the tiny tumblers for delivery to Clancey the next day and he wouldn't be able to stop at the gym on the way home. The last employee had gone home several hours ago and, faced with the prospect of returning to his stark apartment, his euphoria about the earlier successes earlier had faded.

Back at his desk, his thoughts turned to Marcia, Dylan and Jessica. Surely, he could find some way to convince Marcia to take him back, but how? He had now accepted he had, at best, conflicted reasons for asking Melinda to the basketball game. That he could prove that he had not intended to take her (because he had called his parents volunteering to keep the kids for the weekend) meant nothing to Marcia. All that mattered is that he *had* taken her and that she *had* stayed at their house overnight. Women were sticklers for detail on these types of things. Millie's testimony added considerable weight to the rock that had him sinking to the cold, dark seabed of divorce. He had left his wife doleful, pleading messages 'swearing on a stack of bibles that he had never intended to do anything with that woman and that, in fact, didn't do anything,' again and again. Marcia, who in nearly 4 weeks had still not spoken to him directly, responded with a text message saying, "Of course you are going to lie about what happened and of course I'm not going to believe you." And there it remained; ball not even close to his court.

"Cocoa Beach, here I come."

In the interim there were intermittent, itinerant, noisome annoyances. Were those all words or was he becoming delusional staying up later and later each night with nothing to do but read … and think? Once he traveled nearly bagless; now … there was Gloss's security system. As he frequently stayed late, he had tripped the motion-detector alarm, which activated at 6 p.m., at least a dozen times in his tenure as apprentice CEO. He had to remember to manually de-activate it every evening. Then there was the paranoid pass-code entry system Gloss had devised, requiring not only a swipe of a card, but entry of a 5-digit number that randomly changed every week. Sheer freakin' overkill, as if his insignificant 15,000 sq. ft. Quonset hut of hazardous chemicals and clueless employees were the NORAD command center of the free world. Finally, there was the fob to get in and out of the bunker to make a handful of parts no one, other than an Afro-American on steroids and a few DoD geeks, knew were made here. Instead of a fob, which he had to keep track of, how about a simple in and out button? An implanted infrared transmitter at the end of his knob would be preferable.

He would have liked to reconfigure the building's security set-up but didn't know how, didn't have the time to learn how, and didn't have the money to hire someone. He had lost the first key fob Gloss had given him sometime around the night of the basketball game with Melinda Chow in tow. Luckily, Gloss had placed a spare key fob in the office safe. Andy now pulled the fob out of his pocket, clicked the button to open the floor panel, stepped onto the platform, clicked on another button to descend, all the while scatting "dum, da, da, da, dum, dum-dum-dum-dum, da, da dum," the Bond movie background melody. "Dodge here, James Dodge. Probably a beautiful young woman around here trying to kill me," he intoned, laughing at the absurdity of the idea.

At the suggestion of her boyfriend, who collected and indulged numerous erotic fetishes, one being women and guns, Melinda Chow had taken up trap shooting, and typically, mastered it. Within two years of entering the sport, she had won the Florida Trap Shooting State Championship, hitting 73 of 75 clay pigeons. She was so good at it, it bored her; and she had taken up Texas Holdem and the modern pentathlon as challenges more worthy. But she still liked the look and feel of a gun, as she affixed the tripod to the M-40 sniper rifle, running her hand along the barrel under the scope, then sliding the gun into position through the blind's front flap along the edge of the roof. She had watched Dodge, now wearing pants and a shirt, use the fob to open the bunker and lower himself into it. She stared through the binoculars into the office, watching for eons, it seemed, for him to finish and exit the bunker. Finally, she saw a panel in the floor move, and up through the floor he rose. When he reached the top, Dodge crouched holding an imaginary pistol and glanced to the left and right. He reached into his pocket, grabbed the fob, clicked it, then put the fob back in his pocket. "Perfect. Just fucking perfect."

Melinda Chow's heart began to race. She had never whacked any one on her own. Certainly, in principle, she had nothing against it. It was business. It was like firing someone—permanently. If you did it only when necessary, it wasn't like there was a shortage of people in the world. She could live with herself. Every philosopher from Augustine to Nietzsche had considered the problem of good versus evil. She didn't think much of Kant's categorical imperative with its universe populated by absolute rights and wrongs. There was a Kraut, if there ever was one, who was fucked up from his *Kopf* to his *Gesäß*. Truly the moral realm was incremental and fluid. She preferred the Manichean solution: Evil touched good. She believed in the material: cause and effect. For someone who wanted to transcend self, you needed to exercise will, and to exercise will you needed to tap into your whole being—good and evil, if that's what it was. Observation of the material world led to several simple deductions. The self-reflected consciousness of the reflected self is a form of living death. It's informing position: You are not unique, indispensable or, if truth be told, even you—or at least the one you think you are. How is absolute moral indoctrination possible in such a universe? Life eats life. Sartre hit the nail on the head: We're all unutterably alone in this glorious, but inveterately sleazy celestial pop-up. Then why was she nervous? It could easily be her in the crosshairs. She had been part of jobs which required offing someone. She'd seen blood, the carnage a bullet can do, imploding a chest or skull. Still, doing it, being the one who pulled the trigger, was, she suddenly realized, different. It'll be fun, she told herself. A new experience, something she'll be able to tell her grandchildren about. She watched as Dodge gathered his stuff and put on his coat, readying to leave. He's my clay pigeon, she told herself. My $4 million dollar clay pigeon.

He emerged from the office foyer into the shadow behind the outside glass door. She could see his darkened silhouette in the reflection of the glass. She edged forward on her stomach, arching her back and raising the gun so it nestled firmly against her shoulder. The crosshairs of the scope lay directly on the upper portion of the glass door. Dodge remained behind the door for several seconds then, casually pushed it open and walked directly toward his car, parked ten feet away. Melinda Chow leveled the scope hairs on his head and followed it as it moved. Through the scope she could see his mouth moving, singing, "*Who better than me, fall into be seen, draw fire and then pray quiet I'm too low, low, low,*" snarling and gyrating his hips. He paused at the car door and reached into his coat pocket for his keys. She tightened her finger on the trigger, gazing through the scope at the shaggy-haired, boyish-faced head of her former shooter-partner and date. Dodge kept digging into his pocket, finally retrieving his keys. The gun was shaking as she tried to steady the sight on a point just above his ear. Then, in a second, he opened the door, fell into the driver's seat, started the car and wheeled out and away up the street. He was gone. She lifted her head from the scope, blinked, and buried her face in the arm of her jacket in a torrent of sobs. It was the first time in her life she had been weak.

12 THE HANDLER
AND A HITMAN

The next afternoon, Calvin Coolidge Clancey was in the strip-mall parking lot of choice waiting on Dodge to deliver the 100 tiny tumblers. He was, as usual, on edge, antsy. He flew in every Tuesday evening on a military aircraft to make the pickup and any delay or hiccup messed with his hectic personal agenda filled, as it was, with extra-curricular activities and downlow romantic rendezvous. When he had graduated from a small, liberal arts college in Atlanta ten years earlier he had majored in voice, intending to follow in the footsteps of J-Slop-Jo, Do-Me and Up Yours, successful, local hip-hop/rap groups he venerated. His mama, however, had insisted he get a real job while pursuing his dream so when DoD came down to recruit, Clancey had cued up to listen to a bunch of white folk and a token brother or two pitch the merits of working for Uncle Sam. When Clancey told the recruiter, "I don't wanna work in no damn office," the recruiter responded he had just the job for him—special assignment, field work. His job kept him in a swank Georgetown loft, but it was his parallel life outside work that consumed his energy and attention. He was two tracks away from completing his second demo CD; his agent was telling him that people over at Mantra Records were anxious to hear it after his first demo picked up a respectable 5,000 downloads and "turned some motherfuckin' heads upstairs." Later that same night (he was already cursing Dodge for cutting the delivery time close) he was scheduled to DJ at a D.C. night club and the following evening he was going to sing at a slam-down in Baltimore, where it was rumored that platinum-record recording artist Bust Nuts would be making an appearance. Upkeep for dalli-ances with three ladies in three different cities took a considerable chunk of his time; he was also in charge of his church's Stuff-the-

Bus program, an ambitious "intervention crusade" sponsored by the president, encouraging parishioners to fill a bus with Saturday Night Specials, switchblades, needles and crack pipes confiscated from family, neighbors and friends.

At about the same time Clancey was fretting and fuming in his DoD-issued Land Rover waiting on Dodge, the 1000-meter-long aircraft carrier *USS Narwhal* was cruising in the Arabian Sea approximately 300 nautical miles off the coast of Somalia. The ship had just completed maneuvers in the Indian Ocean and was heading due north for a classified mission in the Persian Gulf. Captain Dirk Levenger was seated in the bridge sipping coffee and reviewing the mission briefing report. He had been unable to sleep, and rather than toss and turn, he had showered, dressed and ridden in the elevator up to the bridge for a peek in on the graveyard shift. There was nothing he enjoyed more than being at the helm of his ship, among his officers in the command center of this floating city. When mission-ready and cruising with more than 5,000 people on board, the ship literally hummed. The hum was the sum of all the mechanical, electrical and nuclear technology in operation. It was the sixty-cycle hum, the telltale sound of electrical sine waves bobbing up and down in sync with generators spinning at the same frequency. It was a steady, whirring hum, almost like that of a gnat on steroids, always positioned at the same distance from one's ear. Some people found the hum annoying, but for him it was the opposite—a pleasant; indeed, deeply soothing sound: His state-of-mind and entire well-being, was directly co-joined to that simple monotone melody; and any variation in its pitch, tone or timber caused an instant uptick in his pulse and blood pressure. Captain Levenger was about to turn a page of the report when just such an anomaly occurred. He lurched slightly forward in his chair and then the hum droned into a deep, fading silence, like an ordinary vacuum cleaner powering down from the off switch. Levenger froze in his chair, every muscle fiber flooding with calcium ions giving the command to a billion myosin filaments to contract and commence a variation of a physiological emergency fire drill—fight-or-flight.

"What the fuck is that?" He said to the helmsman.

"Lost power, sir."

"Lost power?!"

"Yes, sir."

The captain nearly ripped the phone off the control console.

"What the hell's going on down there?" he yelled at the ensign in charge of the engine room.

"Uranium fuel rods are depleted, sir."

"What about the fuel rod cache?'

"Empty, sir."

"Why wasn't I told about this?"

"Supposed to be a shipment in today, sir. Didn't arrive."

Commander Levenger immediately placed a call to Desron 34 headquarters in Kuwait, which placed a call to 5th Fleet headquarters in Virginia, which placed a call to the Pentagon, which placed a call to 1600 Pennsylvania Avenue. The president, who had just finished having a beer in the Rose Garden with a white teacher who had posted rude remarks on Facebook about a black principal's handling of a confrontation between Chinese and Thai students in a largely Latino school district of Los Angeles, tossed his planner on his desk, leaned back in his chair and sighed.

"Get me Calvin Clancey."

Andy opened the passenger door of the truck and saw Clancey holding his cell to his ear and gesturing frantically. "Wait … wait … wait a second, boss, here's the main man right here," he said, holding his hand over the mic and pushing the phone into Andy's stomach. "It's the prez."

Andy climbed into the car and gave Clancey a smirk. "Yeah right, and in a former life I was Quetzalcoatl."

"Take the motherfuckin' call, man," Clancey shouted in a whisper.

Andy, a sudden look of trepidation coming into his face, took the phone and slowly put it to his ear. "Dodge here."

"Hello, Andrew, it's the President of the United States. How are you today?"

"Ah, fine, I think, sir."

"Andrew, I have a little problem and I need your help."

"My help?"

"Yes. Got a little warship drifting in the Arabian Sea, out of fuel. Andrew, this ain't the S.S. Minnow were talking about, it's the real billion-dollar carrier, baby. You understand what I'm saying?"

"Yes, sir."

"Now I don't know if you know this, Andrew, but a drifting ship is an endangered ship, sort of like a wounded wildebeest in the middle of the Serengeti with the hyenas and vultures circling, you see what I mean?"

"Very vivid analogy sir."

"Thank you, Andrew. I got elected by speaking in pictures. At any rate, my people tell me our ship's got no pop in its poop because of miscues on your end, is that right?"

Andy gulped. "I think I have things straightened out now, sir."

"I understand about life's twists and turns, ups and downs—did I ever tell you about the time my grandmother needed emergency bunion removal surgery—terribly painful. Insurance didn't cover it—can you imagine that? At any rate, we're in a bind and we need more of the tiny tumblers."

"I'm just dropping off a delivery to Clancey now, sir."

"Not enough. What's your production schedule like?"

"One hundred a week."

"Up it to, say 300. I'll tell Clancey to adjust your pay."

"That's about max capacity, sir."

"That's called 100 percent efficiency—the businessman's holy grail."

"Yes, sir."

"By the way, you are a six-sigma company, right?"

"Oh … heck, yeah. We Six-Sigma our pencil sharpeners, sir."

"Good. We need high quality parts, none of this planned obsolescence bullshit we're used to seeing from the private sector."

"Yes, sir."

"How's your security?"

"Tighter than a nun's ass, if you'll pardon the expression, sir."

"Good. We can't spare any personnel to cover you. I've got

more plots and cells and Osama-bin-wannabes to keep track of than a Mormon has wives—don't tell anyone I said that."

"I won't, sir."

"Anything else?"

Andy, who was relieved the conversation seemed to be closing, was about to sign off when a thought occurred to him. "Actually sir, there is. I'm being hounded by an OSHA inspector, a Darren Tilsdale."

"Tilsdale? I've heard of him. Good man. He got a national service medal—set a record for shutting down the most businesses in a single year for safety violations."

"Yeah, well he wants me to install fume control equipment that I can't afford."

"Can't help you there. If the Sierra Club finds out I gave you a pass, I'm toast."

"Damn, I mean darn, sir."

"How much you need?"

"Hundred thousand."

"Installed?"

"Yes, sir."

"Tell you what I can do. I'll give Ben a call over at the Fed and we'll cut you a check check—a small business loan."

"Cool."

"Five percent, 20 years, no monthly rollovers—you good with those terms?"

"I think you're thinking of cell phone minutes, sir."

"Oh yeah, right. Solving every one of the world's problems makes it tough keeping the jargon straight. Now let me get your address."

Andy gave the president the address of his former home. "You know, Andrew, getting government money usually comes with some strings."

"Yes, sir, I was expecting that."

"You have any women or minorities in management positions?"

"I'm AM the management, sir."

"I'll look into that loophole. How about renewable energy? Got anything going there?"

"I buy off the grid, sir."

"Okay, now we're talking—think outside the bun, Andrew. I'm going to send you the name of a company that makes vertical-axis windmills. Put one on your roof and, bingo, free, emission-free energy—enough to power two or three coffeemakers *all day*."

"That'll pay for itself."

"Why can't businessmen figure this out? Andrew, it's been an eye-opener talking with you—really learned a lot. Keep those tiny tubes coming and who knows, maybe someday I'll be giving you a national service medal. Now put Clancey back on the line."

Andy held the phone out and Clancey began waving his hands and silently mouthing "I'm in the john." Andy shook his head and mouthed back, "It's the president—he knows everything."

Clancey angrily snatched the phone out of Andy's hand. "Sir, with all due respect, sir, gotta catch a flight, toot sweet."

"This won't take long. I've upped Dodge's production. You're going to have to make three pickups a week."

"Damn, brother, I can't do that!"

"Come again?"

"Shoot, Mr. President. This could ruin my chance at a major recording contract."

"I liked your first demo, especially the track, "Hangin' and Bangin'."

"Yaw, but y'all see ..."

"How many tracks you away from a wrap, my man."

"Two."

"Okay, here's what we do. I've got your tail covered over at the DoD—no face time required. You just make the pickups and spend every spare moment in the studio. Sound like a plan?"

"Hail to the chief. Hollywood, here I come."

"Not so quick, Clancey, we gotta job to do."

"Yes, sir, I'm on it like white on rice."

"Or black on Flack—Roberta."

"Ha ha ha ha—that's why you the main man, sir."

"You still handling the Stuff-the-Bus program at the church."

"Hell, yes.

"Good. Like to plan a photo op around that in the next few weeks."

Andy loaded five boxes into the back of the van. Clancey cranked the jams and floored it out of the parking lot heading in the direction of the Air Force base.

In advance of the windfall from his uber-deal and his purchase of the Woolcott estate, Eastman Finch decided he needed a handler—a person who could organize and run his day-to-day affairs, as well as someone who could gather intelligence on personal and professional opportunities and market him: part aide-de-camp, part agent, part Mary Poppins. He had hired a search firm which had hired a consultant to look for such a person, and Finch had interviewed several candidates, settling on a young man by the name of Stephen Congreve. Stephen had entered the cognoscente of dog walkers, personal fitness trainers and image consultants who inhabit Manhattan after graduating from Columbia with a fine arts degree, discovering he was unemployable and learning he could make more money working fewer hours as a "domestic entrepreneur" than he could waiting on tables. He was now officially pursuing a master's degree, unofficially writing a novel, and the work, he would tell family and friends, gave him the time, money and flexibility to do both while having some fun and not even coming close to breaking a sweat. Finch had flown him down to Sarasota for an orientation session, even though he didn't really know what the job was going to entail.

Finch picked him up at the airport Wednesday afternoon. He was on his cell parked along the curb in a Jaguar convertible as Stephen walked out of the terminal. Finch waved him into the car while talking.

"Marissa? How you doing, darling? Listen, I need my boat dropped. I'll be there in about 20 minutes; you handle that for me?

You're a sweetheart—wanna come out with us?"

Marissa, the marina manager, declined the invitation and Finch and Stephen headed out into Sarasota Bay on a perfectly cloudless day, the sun glistening on the turquoise water. Finch was apologetic about his modest 25-foot cabin cruiser.

"I'm getting rid of this tub. Looking at a 440 horsepower, 38-foot cigarette boat— tops out at 100 mph. I can just picture the terror in my wife's face when I crank that baby—ha ha."

Finch steered the boat into a slippage at Marina Skip's, an upscale, open-air restaurant and bar with a foothold on both the bay and downtown Sarasota. The place was lively, a happy-hour band playing covers of Bob Marley and Jimmy Buffet. They took a seat on the deck nearest the water. Scenery of any kind did not matter to Finch and he preferred to sit at the bar where the action was, but today he thought he might need a little more privacy to talk with his new handler. After taking the table, however, the prospect of sitting alone with another guy having a conversation bored him, and he stood and walked inside.

"Fuck this shit," he said, waving Stephen to follow him.

Finch greeted Jimmy the bartender and several waitresses as they took seats at the bar. He ordered a Bombay and tonic and Stephen asked for a beer after receiving a chiding from Finch for ordering an iced tea. The kid might be a domicile, but Finch desired someone he could buddy with, which meant someone with an attitude. He didn't really care what the angle of that attitude was, but one HAD to be an unrepentant snob about something—women in the win column, superior stylistic sensibility, immodest flaunting of money of course, or even—and this one piqued his fascination—the unabashed exercise of over-the-top snobbery for the sheer hell of it, on a whim, with or without anything to back it up. Now that was a ripping good show, as the Brits put it; and they should know, as they had invented a complete, self-referential caste system resting on nothing more substantial than how one muted certain crass vowels, such as the weak /i/ in *really* in favor of the more catching, sonorous *reeely!*, or, conversely, ramped up the hoity-toity leverage on banal consonant combinations in words such as *sshhedule*, even though the contemporary keepers of the Anglo-Saxon heritage, including the language, intoned the 'ske' syllable in *scholarship* and *schizo*, the reversal itself serving as an object lesson in the arbitrary nature, and appeal, of pure snobbishness indulged in without the slightest conveyance of self-consciousness of the actions they engaged to pull it off. Finch thought none of this, but he instinctively understood the principle. And on this front, Stephen, while he had the upbringing, the connections, a modestly natty wardrobe (he wore gabardine slacks, a Brooks Brother's dress shirt, and a tie with a proper Windsor knot to the interview) and the artsy-fartsy schooling, was showing to be a bit slow out of the gate. It was something Finch couldn't mentor, even he had wanted to, and he didn't. The New York Minute required you proved you had it, and proved you got it, right now, or there was no hope. It was still early, he allowed, and maybe the young man would overcome his deferential reticence and find his groove yet. For the moment, there were bigger balls to bust.

"When we move into Woolcott in a week, all hell is going to break loose," Finch said, drawing off his drink. "That's the first thing on your plate."

"That is so cool you got that place."

"Yeah, it is cool."

"You excited?"

Finch gave him a withering glare. "Oh, yeah, I'm going to squeal and jump up and down on my sofa in my Pooh-bear pajamas."

Stephen chuckled. "It's not exactly an everyday purchase. I heard Aaron McNutty was looking at buying it."

"You see, there's the problem with your thinking big guy. McNutty *works* for…?"

"Rothebys."

"He is therefore a…"

"Rich, internationally recognized art dealer?"

"Wrong! Do I have to dot the I's for you, dude? He's an employee. A salaryman."

"He's got his own TV reality show now."

"Yeah, the one on channel 1235? In ten years, he might be

able to make me an offer on my gardener's shed."

"Aren't you neighbors with Studebaker DeVries, the guy indicted in the Ponzi scheme?"

"I could see that coming. I worked with DeVries for a while at Cosgrove-Linch. My wife is still friends with Coco, his wife."

"He's toast now."

"Pshaw. In a few years he'll be out on parole, get on the talk show circuit, become a spokesman for Kittens for Kids or anti-bullying and get right back in the game, bigger and better. That's the great thing about this country. Nobody remembers anything."

Finch was giving him a talk on the importance of keeping all his professional and family matters confidential when his burner cell phone rang.

"Ms. Chow, are we on schedule, my sweet little Natasha?"

"Ah, that's a negative."

"What?"

"Couldn't do it."

"You have to do it."

"Can't."

"Why not?"

"I wish I knew myself. I'm still analyzing it."

"Son of a ... come to your senses, girl."

"I know, I know ..."

"The world will be a better place for offing this guy."

"Probably."

"You're out $2 million."

"One million— that's my charge for reconnoitering the location and the way into the bunker."

"That's the easy part."

"Maybe, but I have the information and you're short on time."

Finch went silent.

"Okay, sit tight, I'll be in touch."

Finch ended the call and downed the last of his drink. "Ever hire a hit man, Stephen?"

"Thought about it when I worked for that Lorna Holmsby bitch up on Park Avenue."

Finch laughed and drew his head back in admiration. "Now that's what I'm talking about," he said, hopping out of his stool. "Come on, you can find anything on the internet."

After his call from Clancey, Gloss was in a foul mood for several days. He had considered flying straight to Washington and demanding to speak with the Secretary of State, but then realized Clancey was right—he really didn't have the rock-solid evidence, a "smoking gun," to back up his claim that Terrorism Inc. was hatching a plot to steal his uranium enrichment technology *at this present time*, and that any request for back-up security would fall on deaf ears. The assertion rested on "chatter" the CIA picked up in routine surveillance. But in this instance, was it not imperative to err on the side of caution? The funding for which he was requesting was a pittance, especially on the scale the federal government printed and spent money it didn't have, given the potential stakes. Then it instantly occurred to him: He was being railroaded, flummoxed by the sleazy political maneuvers that flourished in one place and one place only—the Swamp. This feeling of impotence made him even more furious; resolved that no one, not even the President of the United States, fucked with him, he decided he had only one recourse. Playing one of his good-for-a-lifetime, pay-back chips his friend Ricky had granted him for saving his life in the jungle 40 years earlier.

As they had flown into Paris on short notice, and as a gathering of some sort made hotel rooms scarce, Angie had found them a room in a small hotel near the Palais Royal, on a rather non-descript street, Rue Sainte Anne. Their room in the hotel was clean, but spare and cramped, and Gloss did not like spare and cramped—he liked full and roomy. The elevator was another problem. It consisted of a glass tube and a locker-sized compartment so tiny that two people could barely fit into it. Given Gloss's girth, he and his wife had had to ride up to their floor separately. The ride was excruciatingly slow and Gloss, a closet claustrophobic, came close to panicking every time he rode it. Angie had begun the search for another hotel immediately and found an opening at the Ritz two days hence, which meant they were trapped at "Le Hotel" for the time being. On the evening of the second day, not wanting to walk far, they had strolled down Rue Saint Anne and stopped at a restaurant called La Marseillaise, where they were given a table near the lone diner, a man eating by himself. Once seated and studying their menus, they began to hear a strange noise, something like a dove or pigeon cooing. Gloss searched around the floor to see if a bird had gotten into the restaurant. After a few minutes he realized the noises were being emitted by the man sitting next to them. Gloss requested a new table, but the compact dimensions of the restaurant meant they could hear the man wherever they sat.

"This place is strange," he remarked on the walk back to the hotel.

"Dick, you find fruitcakes in New York, too."

"Exactly my point."

"We're moving in a day; chill."

Gloss cheered up once they absconded to the five-star. They were given a sixth-floor room with a view of the Eiffel Tower. It was the first time he had had an unobstructed view of the iconic structure and even from a distance it caught his imagination. "That, I've got to see."

Later that afternoon they rode the Metro to the Champs de Mars and walked the few hundred yards through a small commercial district to the plaza in front of the tower. As if hypnotized, Gloss continued walking while gazing up at the 1063-foot-tall spire, eventually coming to a stop directly below its base. Angie gently pulled him to get in line for the elevator. They rode it to the first level where Gloss spent the next half hour taking pictures and peering downward through the tower's arching beams and iron latticework trying to analyze its design and structure. Angie left him to ascend all the way to the top level. Gloss, no fan of heights, stayed behind.

"It is an amazing feat of engineering, is it not?" said a man who had come up to stand at the railing near Gloss.

The man was medium height, paunchy around the waist, and of Arabic descent. He wore a brown sport coat over a white shirt, open at the collar. Gloss, glancing over at him, mused aloud, "What I can't understand is not that the French built it, but that they built in the 19th century."

"Ah yes, the emotional, cowardly, child-like French. But it was a different time then, no?"

Gloss, who had meant the remark as a sort of joke, grasped the man's sarcasm. Typical, he mused, and turned, continuing to stare mesmerized by the massive web of curving, intricately inter-connected steel beams and latticework.

"The tower has over two million rivets, 120 antennas and gets painted every seven years. The four legs of the tower stand in a square that measure 125 meters on each side," the man said. "The foundations for each leg are 15 meters underground. It took five months for hundreds of workers just to build the foundation, using only ordinary spades."

Gloss nodded appreciatively. "The man-hour side of this thing is obvious. The engineering achievement boils down to the lifting and positioning of the beams."

"Ah, yes, you are correct. You see the difficulty in the assembly of the floor we are standing on. It lies in the point of departure at the base of the truss frame. The beams had to be positioned precisely, at a tricky, slanting angle, so they would meet the horizontal beams on the first floor."

"Calculation and execution, impressive."

"And hydraulic jacks."

"That was the breakthrough, hoists and scaffolding had been around since the time of the Romans."

"Yes, and by our standard the hydraulics were crude, but as you can see, they managed."

"Admirably."

"You would not believe today that monsieur Eiffel faced public ridicule and hostility for his plan—some called it the Tower of Babel."

Gloss laughed heartily. "No, that's the easiest thing in the world to believe. If the damn finger-waggers of the world had their way, we'd all still be painting watercolors in caves."

The man drew closer to Gloss. "You are an engineer by training, no?"

"Yes and no. Everything I know I've learned by doing. What about you?"

"I am like you, I train myself. I read and contemplate."

"I do then contemplate."

"Ah yes, Americans are a race on the go—men of action."

Gloss puffed out his lips and nodded. "No problem checking the box on that claim. French used to be."

The man was quiet for a moment as he considered the remark. "Yes, I will allow something has happened to sap the confidence and will of this country that once produced so many great men of vision. But you see, fortunately, I am not French." The man then bowed in Gloss's direction and walked away from the railing. "Bonjour, Monsieur. Enjoy your stay in Paris."

After he had departed, Gloss, continuing to examine the structure of the tower, had an epiphany. It was not, or should not have been, an epiphany, as anyone who had ever talked with him more than five minutes was aware of it, but it was an epiphany to him. He had traveled more than half-way around the world and it suddenly hit him that he didn't give a damn about the reason most people traveled—culture and it's spin offs. The universal laws of physics ran through this shit. He wasn't one for lying all day on some damn beach thinking every other minute, "Man, it doesn't get any better than this." He didn't give a shit about the bragging rights that came with drinking coffee made of beans defecated by civets, or surviving a twelve-hour ride in a Mexican bus driving up single-lane, dirt switchbacks to reach Chichan-nitwit in order to sit cross-legged at dawn and channel the aura of the mighty Izdak civilization, known for its invention of a Base-33 numbering system and how it staved off destruction from the comet-god by slitting the throats of ten virgins girls a day. But stuff—how it was conceived, tested, designed, made —that was the ticket. Stuff could be analyzed, critiqued and understood. Seeing stuff, good stuff, was the only logical reason for putting up with the nonsense and discomfort of travel. And Paris, it suddenly hit him, had a lot of good stuff.

And, so it was, Gloss set out on a more ambitious exploration of the city and found himself being slowly corralled and charmed by the Frenchman's embrace—long ago, admittedly—of the life of reason, science and engineering. Upbeat and inspired for perhaps the first time on a trip now nearing three months, he pored over his wife's Michelin Guide. He made a pilgrimage to Napoleon's Arc de Triomphe, studying the four relief sculptures at the base. He visited the Musée d'Orsay, overwhelmed, nearly tearing up, at the technical magnificence of Renoir's *Bal du moulin de la Galette*, van Gogh's *Starry Night* and the sculptures of Rodin and Claudel. He confessed to being "blown away" by the Notre Dame Cathedral, which he first saw at night, the church's massive western façade and twin towers emerging in a blaze of light as they walked along the Seine toward the Île de la Cité. Returning the next day, Gloss stalked the entire perimeter of the church, analyzing the design and placement of the flying buttresses, then taking up a position in front of the entrance where he stood staring at the gargoyles and demonic statuettes carved along the pediment above the door, quipping to his wife, "These old bastards had a sense of humor." He strolled down the Boulevard St. Germain, scrutinizing the stately four and five story apartments with their steep, hipped roofs, tall windows and small balconies with wrought-iron railings; at last taking a seat at the Café des Deux Magots where he could gaze up at the Romanesque tower of the Abbey of the Saint Germain de Pres, which, as the oldest church in Paris, he read, had been torched by the Normans four times. Then, sitting at the café while his wife shopped, something in the Michelin caught his eye. The weather was unseasonably pleasant, and after eating a *jambon et baguette*, he decided the several-block jaunt to the Pantheon would be good for his digestion.

Gloss was breathing heavily when he reached the top of Montagne Sainte-Genevieve, the small hill on which the domed edifice overlooks the city. He walked up the stairs, through the portico of massive Corinthian columns and into the building. In the middle of the open, cross-shaped nave he could see what he had come for: The pendulum experiment designed by Leon Foucault in 1851 to prove the rotation of the earth. A low, circular barricade in the middle of the marble-floored nave marked off the area in which the iron ball swung from a wire suspended from the top of the dome. Inscriptions of times on the floor indicated the movement of the ball as it changed its plane of rotation throughout the day. A crowd of people stood around the circle watching the pendulum swing. Gloss contemplated the experiment. He understood it perfectly. The pendulum is fixed at the top but the direction along which it swings is displaced by the rotation of the earth. The angular speed of the pendulum varied with latitude; the higher the latitude the greater the speed, all perfectly logical. He was considering the effect of air resistance on the pendulum when he let his eyes wander to the opposite side of the circle. There, standing alone in between several groups of people, he noticed someone vaguely familiar. Gloss carefully examined the man who was posed with his chin in his hand studying the moving sphere. It was the stocky Arabic man he had met at the Eiffel tower a few days earlier. The man, who wore the same brown sport coat and shirt, appeared lost in thought. Gloss chuckled and shook his head as he turned to leave. Why couldn't I routinely run into the inventor of the integrated circuit or a Swedish pinup model, he muttered to himself as he walked out of the Pantheon and down the hill.

The next afternoon Angie tried to talk Gloss into attending an organ recital at the Notre Dame Cathedral. He declined and took a seat in the lobby of the hotel after lunch, watching people come and go and flipping through the pages of the Michelin. He decided to pay a visit to Montmartre, once home to the Moulin Rouge and famous artists, which sounded like the next most interesting site in Paris he had yet to see. The concierge waved for a taxi and held the door as Gloss climbed into the backseat. The driver was talking on the phone in Arabic as he sped away from the hotel. Gloss placidly eyed the passing people and buildings as the driver maneuvered the car through the maze of streets. He turned down a narrow alleyway devoid of traffic. Probably a short cut, Gloss thought. Suddenly the driver slowed and stopped at a corner and a man quickly opened the far door and jumped into the backseat. It was the man from the Eiffel tower and Pantheon.

"Bonjour, monsieur Gloss," he said, lifting a pistol from his pocket and pushing it into Gloss's ribs. "Do you mind terribly if I take you for a tour of my neighborhood?"

13 FLYING, FINCH AND A
BRAVE NEW WORLD

If, for Andy, there had been one clincher in Gloss's pitch, it had been his dispatch that the joint ran itself like a player piano and that Andy, with even a modicum of managerial moxie, could be on the first tee by noon every day. Gloss had uttered the declaration in various forms repeatedly, and it had taken root in Andy's mind, paralyzing his powers of reasoning and skepticism. If it was a beautiful lie, it was one he bought into, believing a giant oak might conceivably be cultivated out of even a tiny seed of truth. A lie it had very definitely turned out to be, but Andy, partly in anticipation of rolling in enough dough to at least pull off an approachable bluff of an executive's lifestyle and ferry, to say, Hilton Head over a weekend, and partly to fulfill a life-long dream as a pilot, had enrolled in flight lessons.

In two months he had completed about half the flight hours required for his pilot's certification and had become adept at take-off, reasonably capable at navigation and instrument flying and a quick study at rules and regulations. Landing was a work in progress.

Marcia had pointedly registered her pique at the announce-ment he was going to lay down five-grand for flight lessons. "You're going to kill yourself, and probably others!" Andy, who had built up immunity to poor reviews and low expectations, was undeterred. He knew better than anyone that the world (which included Marcia) had one and only one definition of intelligence—an Einstein, or on a more modest pedestal, a lawyer or accountant. But Einstein and hosts of timid, klutzy accountants would never make good pilots. Flying did not require a cerebral arsenal capable of solving Schrödinger's equation or writing *War and Peace*, he debated, internally, with his wife. Flying, like many other aspects of life, was about a certain *type* of intelligence, of which researchers had identified many; this one involving touch, feel, a calm, level-headed personality, and an ability to complete a checklist—cards, as anyone could see, he had been dealt in abundance. Fortunately (or from a more practical point of view, unfortunately) he had prepaid for the lessons. He could have never foreseen sinking to a depth at which a quarter-pounder at Micky D's would be out of his budget most weeks. The lessons, however, provided solace from the trials of Job, a dude he had read about in a book about perseverance and a man (biblical though he may have been) with whom he now felt a strong affinity.

Torsten Zweiback, Andy's instructor, was waiting for him late Thursday afternoon at the Tri-County Airfield about four miles from his shop. Andy normally took his lessons on the weekend but Torsten had called to inform him of an opening due to a cancellation and Andy had jumped on it. He could only fly during the day and March's weather had been abysmal, forcing Torsten to scratch several of his lessons. This day was clear and almost windless as Andy taxied the Cessna single-engine *Skyhawk* onto the tarmac.

Torsten fed him the usual preflight drill: "Right foot on rudder before applying power;" "Ease on the throttle;" "Never give it full power;" "Pull back slowly and smoothly on the yoke at rotate speed."

Andy lifted the plane flawlessly into the air and vectored to the southeast over some wooded lots interspersed by subdivisions, leveling the plane off at an altitude of about 5,000 ft. He felt exhilarated, his worries and woes receding with every foot of elevation. "Controlled space to the south and northeast so let's just head easy east out over Lake St. Clair and double back," Torsten said through the headset.

They practiced some touch-and-goes on the runway. On one approach Andy came into too steep and another too low; Torsten took over control and aborted both. On the third attempt he came in like Little Red Riding Hood, bouncing the wheels onto the runway then taking it back up.

"Bingo," Torsten yelled ecstatically, fist-bumping him across the cockpit.

The successful landing put them both in a buoyant mood.

"You are getting the hang of it, my man," Torsten said. The

mix of a heavy Swedish accent and street lingo sounded funny to Andy, who had learned that Torsten had come to the U.S. on a transfer with a giant Swedish home-furnishing retailer, took up flying, and quit his day job to start his own flight school. It was a narrative Andy found appealing; and right then and there he vowed, for some reason obliquely related to Torsten's career change, to make a turkey for an upcoming dinner—he would call it *Thanksgiving in March.*

"You a golfer, Tort Suit?" Andy asked, using the American nickname he had given him, having to explain the meaning of the jest to him.

"Ya, I am picking it up. In Sweden we don't play so much."

"What do you play?"

"Long winters make for, how do you say, 'playing between the sheets'."

"I've forgotten how to play that game."

Torsten, who had discovered that his client was going through a divorce, and who was trying to learn to mimic the way Americans talked with cheerful, embarrassing intimacy about the most depressing and humiliating aspects of their lives, shook his head nonchalantly. "No problem. Let's make your first solo flight to Sweden. I hook you up with some go-go blonde Swedish bunny rabbits, ha ha."

"No thanks, Tort Suit, we're getting back together. It's all going to work out—I just have a feeling. Love will conquer."

Torsten was on uncharted ground with this remark. Supposing a real American would try to console him, he fumbled for some words. "Well … I guess … ya, that could happen," he finally said. "You are a good man," he said, slapping Andy on the shoulder and glancing at him with a rubber-stamp smile.

They made several more passes over the lake and back to the airport. On their final loop Torsten noticed a traffic helicopter below and to the south of them. He pointed it out to Andy. "A helicopter is not so much a flying machine as it is an unstable platform," he said, suddenly laughing uncontrollably and using his hand to make erratic, wobbly motions. "The … funniest thing … ha … I saw … ha … some yokel … phist, snarkkk … tried to bank a helicopter too sharply and lost lift. It went straight down … boom!"

"No survivors!?"

"No … ha … fucking … ha … survivors. Straight down—boom! It was … ha ha … hilarious."

After his lesson, Andy had to stop by the house to pick up his mail before returning to the shop to run another batch of tiny tumblers. As he pulled into the driveway of the colonial, red brick and siding two-story—a roomy, comfortable house, but one nonetheless built before kitchens became oversized, granite-imbued venues for entertaining—he became aware of how already, in little over a month, the house and neighborhood had taken on an alienating, semi-hostile presence. Strangely, all the windows on all houses on either side and across the street had their shades completely drawn, as if, it seemed, all the neighbors wanted to ensure no eye in *their* house catch sight of a wayward, foot-loose, soon-to-be-ex lest anyone begin to think he looked none the worse for the wear. He walked up the driveway gazing at the houses of the Carriers and Van Duesens, people with whom he had once been on the closest of neighborly terms, built over the years at backyard barbeques and Christmas cocktail parties; but now, he surmised, people he would perhaps never see or talk to again. Ah well, he chuckled darkly, at least there was one upside to being thrown out of the house. He noticed a new crack in the concrete steps leading up to the front porch and a patch of wash-out on the ground at the base of the garage, evidence of a blocked downspout—minor house-maintenance glitches he would have already fixed before they became major headaches. The garbage container and recycling bins had been moved to be closer to the back door, and Dylan had left various toy guns strewn around the garage floor, a no-no he enforced with zero tolerance.

He walked through the garage door which led through a narrow laundry room into the kitchen. Dylan was at baseball practice and he found Jessica upstairs doing homework in her room.

"Hi, Sweetie."

"Hi, Daddy!" Jessica bounced up from her chair and hugged him.

She would be 14 in a month, and by the week, a confident, composed young lady was, like a butterfly, emerging from the co-

coon of a giggly, jittery teeny bopper.

"How are your classes?"

"Got an A on my civics exam—that class is sooo boring."

"If it doesn't kill you …"

"I know, I know."

They talked, her telling him about their cat Archie's rumble with a raccoon and brush with the hereafter, and he telling her about his flight lessons and call from the president.

"No way!"

"Yeah, I'm still pinching myself."

"He really wants you to put a windmill on your building?"

"Yup. Also wants me to switch to a biodegradable toilet bowl cleaner and start eating more organic produce."

Jessica giggled joyously.

"Daddy, are you and Mommy going to get back together ever?"

Andy looked into his daughter's eyes, beginning to water. "Heck yeah, are you kidding?" He said, putting his arm around her. "We're going to get it all worked out. Your mom's just been a little mad at me about a misunderstanding. Sooner or later the truth will come out and I believe she will forgive me."

Andy walked down the hall to use the bathroom before leaving. A book titled "*A Thousand Places to See Before Dying,*" had been left on the countertop, and underneath that was a spiral-ringed craft book on making bracelets out of hemp. He opened one of the two glass-paneled cabinets above the sink looking for a bottle of rubbing alcohol he intended to take back to his apartment—his own bathroom being a bit short on medicine-cabinet basics. Every nook and cranny of every shelf was crammed with bottles, vials and tubes, just as he remembered: There was Sweet Pea Body Splash and Brazilian Watermelon Shower Gel. There was honey and oats face scrub, Vitak for dark circles under your eyes and glitter hair spray. There was Midol, Murine, melatonin and Metamucil. There was cod liver oil, calcium, folic acid, Stress-Plex, Gas-X and "total energy" vitamins. There was tea tree oil, vitamin E face mist, and oddly, a box of After-Eight dinner mints. He pulled out the box and popped one of the mints into his mouth. A green bottle on one of the cabinet shelves caught his eye. He opened the bottle of aspirin, poured some into his palm and stuffed them, along with a packet of Glide dental floss into his pocket. Finally, he found the rubbing alcohol in the cabinet below the sink and walked down the stairs, through the living room and into the kitchen.

The cat was scratching in its litter box in the laundry room. Marcia had set his mail in a neat pile on the kitchen counter in front of the toaster oven. On top of the pile was a plain white sealed envelope with his name written on it.

The note inside read: "Andrew, it has been nearly six weeks since we separated, and you have yet to respond to single letter from my lawyer. We have multiple things to discuss, among the most important being division of property, child custody and how you intend to buy out my half of Gloss Industries. It is not doing you any good to keep pretending this isn't happening. I would like to meet you at your office this Saturday, 1 p.m., if that works, so we can begin to sort this out. I'll expect this arrangement is satisfactory unless I hear otherwise. Also, I suggest you get a lawyer. This is, as you always say, the United States of Attorneys."

Andy held the letter in his hand and gazed up at the set of Time-Life cookbooks in the shelf above the microwave. Thinking, as he approached 40, he should adopt a healthier lifestyle, he reached up and grabbed the "Fish" volume to take back with him. As he grabbed it, he noticed other books, slightly hidden under a couple of unread newspapers, lying on the counter. Marcia was a voracious reader, and now that Andy had taken up the hobby, he was curious to see what she was perusing. He lifted the newspapers to the side and gazed at the title of the first book, *Silent Death.* "Very interesting," he said, in imitation of the German colonel in a long defunct television sitcom. He was intrigued enough to read the back cover: "Poisons and the art of killing with stealth are part of humanity's folklore and heritage, and in this homicidal manifesto, master chemist Uncle Fester has turned his attentions to the venomousness that Homo Sapiens hath wrought, and how these toxic substances are gathered, synthesized and put to use." Another, related volume, *The Poisoner's*

Handbook, lay beneath this compelling read. Dark period, obviously, Andy thought. Reader that he was, he now understood how mood could dictate what one sought to read. Just as there was a time and place for the blues in one's musical tastes, there was a moment in one's life when one might be intrigued by books on the topic of poisoning. Who was he to stand in judgment?

He walked to the pantry and shook open a plastic grocery bag, into which he deposited the mail, cookbook and rubbing alcohol, as well as two cans of French-cut string beans, and half a loaf of bread. As he reached the door, the cat was sitting, staring into the garage. Andy looked down at the brown and white tabby he had helped pick out at the humane society with the kids over five years ago. "Hey, Archie boy, what's up?" Andy said, reaching down to pet it. The cat hissed and swiped its paw, etching out a painful hairline of blood across the length of his knuckles. "Son of a ..." he yanked back as the cat scattered into the house. Andy stiff-armed the door and strode outside, licking the back of his hand.

Stephen Congreve was flipping through the Finch family photo album set on the serpentine-shaped, green glass coffee table in the living room of his boss's condo on Longboat Key. The album traced the tribe's (the word young, Manhattan-based singles employed derogatorily to refer to parents and kids with their usual noisome presence in restaurants, parks, museums) history in roughly chronological order with the children, of course, being the main thematic element of the timeline. Pictures of birthday parties, Christmas gatherings and other family events were interspersed with photos of family trips—shots with backdrops of the Rockies, the Tower of London, the church of *La Sagrada Familia* in Barcelona, the pyramids at Giza. Finch seemed to prefer big-ticket sightseeing, sort of like the type of person who only buys tickets for A-list bands, acts, shows. No incidental, throw-away moments here. There had to be something monumental about a travel photo for it to make it into this album. A B-side appreciation for out-of-the-way jaunts, hidden treasures or novelties—an impromptu visit to a field of plinth stones left by a pre-historic people, or a day spent putting around the English countryside, stopping in villages and pubs along the route, the way Stephen preferred to travel—was nowhere to be found. There were plenty of family group and kids' pictures taken on the beach, Stephen assumed, in front of their condo. But something else peculiar caught Stephen's eye: Everyone in the photos changed except Finch. Babies turned into toddlers turned into grade-schoolers turned into preteens. Beatrice, who with dark, wild hair and pale porcelain skin in her twenties bore a passable resemblance to Waterhouse's *Lady of Shallot*— even in one photo wearing a wreath of braided flowers in her hair—had become smart and conservative, her hair chopped short and her once voluptuous mouth often pinched into a coy, somewhat mirthless vertical line. Finch, however, was like the song that never ended. While one could detect a slight, very slight, thickening of his features with the passing years, there were yet no bags, sags or crags—even though, from Finch's commentary, Stephen had deduced his age to be late-40s, pushing 50. That alone, in many men, was not especially extraordinary. But Finch not only did not age, he didn't tick. Art major that he was, Stephen knew most people, even when posing formally, betrayed in their facial features the inner foible known as mood or personality, which could change from day to day, moment to moment. Abigail Menowitz's renowned photos of celebrities was perhaps the most pertinent case in point. But looking at the photos of Finch it seemed there was no inner in the working. In every photo, going back to the first pictures of Beatrice and him taken on the U-Mass campus, where they had apparently

met, up until near present and his son Sullivan's 16th birthday party, Finch's expression was the same: A vacant grin set into the middle of his preternaturally smooth, tan features. There was a mind-numbing uniformity to it, almost like those cloned, air-brushed pictures of Chairman Mao once popular as novelty posters in frat houses. And to think, he was only in the initial stages of getting to know the man behind that dazzlingly vacuous smile. Nice to be living in interesting times, Stephen thought.

Finch was streaming music on his phone, a mix of contemporary pop, hip-hop and dance. Finch informed Stephen that wife and kids had been down the previous week, coinciding with spring break, and returned to Connecticut, where his wife would be busy finalizing plans for the move to Woolcott, as it had now, Anglo-estate style, officially been deigned. On the way back from the marina Finch had stopped at a store and purchased over $3000 of wine, liquor and sundry supplies, including a bottle of Martell XO, a case of Chateau Brane-Contenac Margaux and a box of Cohiba Maduro 5's. A neighbor of Finch's was stopping by for drinks later. Stephen had downed three beers, already more than he usually drank in a week, and was feeling drowsy. He yawned as Finch strolled into the living room, just getting off a call.

"Whoa, whoa, whoa, Geronimo," Finch scolded. "Don't start fading on me yet, big guy. The night is young!"

The day had been hectic. After returning from the marina, Finch, with the help of his contact, Graham in London, had located an operative to take the place of Melinda Chow. Knocking off that bimbo Dodge was taking way too much of his time and money and cutting into his profit. It had pained him to have to buy the building across the street from Dodge's plating dive, but time and efficiency were of the essence. Graham had told him that the client would be demanding the return of the upfront $20 million should the operation fall apart, a bit of sticking point as the money had already been spent on the purchase of Woolcott. The hiring of a new operative would take a further cut of his take. Topping the day off, Brianna had delivered, via burner phone, her ultimatum: marry me or I'm having the baby. Finch deflected the demand with a chuckle, a Street tactic which, on face simple, took years to master—humans had evolved with a mouth designed to blab. The call had actually ended amicably, with little darlings and Finch promising a one-time lump sum payment that would allow her to buy a house and some vaguely imbibed in child support, disbursements which, even uttering, caused him to wince with the realization that he would have to pull off at least a few more uber-deals of the kind in the works to fund, now given the living standard, with its bar-raising expenses, to which he had graduated.

So be it—keep him at the top of his game. Besides, he finally had it wired: It had taken him 30 years, but he had figured out how the world works, how it had changed, and what it all meant.

This journey of "discovery" had its roots in an incident that occurred when Finch was still earning his financial knickers. After a particularly acrimonious meeting one day during which one of Finch's co-workers denounced him (in so many words) as a scoundrel and a liar, his boss had pulled him aside saying, "Don't sweat it. If someone in the world somewhere wouldn't mind seeing you dangling from a meat hook, you are doing something wrong, young man." This wasn't just the 'nice guys finish last,' bromide, Finch had realized. This was the logical imperative that there had to be a certain amount of odium and ill will in the universe to balance all the peace, love and understanding; the anti-matter, if you will, of matter. That odium was generated, not necessarily by evil, but by the simultaneous existence of humans with diametrically opposed needs, desires and psycho-logical wiring. Mindsets and behavior conditioned, not only by one's experience, but by the immediate moment, which would change in an instant, creating a new condition. It was like an algorithm that, once it started running, could not be mitigated; certainly not re-versed. Would a bad taste in Brianna's mouth smolder over time and compel her to channel Kill-Bill mode? Perhaps. Yet, in his long experience of provoking bad vibes and animosity, he knew the lust for pure revenge never lasted long. It was expensive, for one. You might get cat-scratched in the eyes or have a dead rat tossed at you occasionally, but vehement, personal dislike usually spent itself. The world ran according to the tenets of *dinero*, cash, not on emotional one-upmanship. Short of extortion or first-degree murder, it would forgive and forget a whole range of screw-ups and transgressions. Get caught sleeping with a guy's wife and you might endure a few months of menacing text messages. Under-tip a bartender and you'll be drinking diluted cocktails at that establishment forever. Short a tenant a few hundred bucks of his security deposit and you'll be hounded for life.

Cam Delacroix, a former colleague of Finch's who lived in an adjacent condo unit, loped in and, fueled by martinis, he and Finch launched into a pecuniary-infused rodomontade.

"Leveraged buyouts, junk bonds, credit default swaps are dead," Delacroix announced. "Today, a real estate investment trust is considered a sexy deal. That's how fucking far we've sunk."

"There's tons of cash out there looking for a home," said Finch. "Just not for conglomerates."

"But then what's to fucking leverage, pin dick."

Finch, apparently attempting to assume the veneer of another persona—a naïf?, a gay guy?—raised his eyebrows, but merely looked like himself with a goofier mien. "Dreams. Let us trip the light fantastic." He made a waving gesture with his arm as if spreading fairy dust.

"Whaahhhh?"

"Scooter, God fucking bless you, but you're still thinking in terms of earnings per share, short selling and raising equity as capital. The world has changed. Activist investors, tree huggers, indoctrination, canticles. Free speech my ass! Today a company's stock can drop 20 percent if someone posts an Instagram of the CEO eating non-free-range chicken. Shit, even asset managers are being told when to eat, shit and get off the stool."

"Schmuck. That's just fucking noise— yada, yada. Didn't you watch bloodbath at the Congressional Inquisitions over the last five years? And that's not my read. We got a government out to deep-six the entire fucking system."

"Exactly," Finch punctuated the retort by draining his martini.

"The pattern is always the same: some dumb fucks orchestrate a crash, everyone panics, government expands, all the loopholes get plugged, people begin stuffing their spare cash in socks, and guys like us have to fish … forget the bait. There's no voodoo to it. It is what it fucking is."

"You're wrong. The masses don't know what they want until you give it to them—the Forbidden Fruit dude said that."

Delacroix, tall, with a head of wavy blonde hair, balding in front and swept back from a high forehead, aped a look of stupefaction. "Am I missing something?" He asked, appealing to the young man sitting on the sofa. "You know, Stephen, I'm actually *not* a rube.

I made a seven-figure bonus last year."

"And paid taxes on it."

Delacroix fell into the sofa next to Stephen, stretched his long arms along the back of the cushions and crossed his legs, as if settling in for a performance. "Okay, Eastman Gecko, spill the beans. What's the scam?"

Finch, weaving a bit, swaggered over to the wet bar and returned with two more martinis and a glass of wine for Stephen. The sliding glass doors to the wrap-around balcony were open and a warm, ocean-scented breeze wafted into the brightly lit, plush, comfortable room. Stephen noticed two Miro prints hung on the wall opposite him, along with another painting (squiggly vertical lines intersecting a mesh of bright-colored cubist forms) vaguely reminiscent of an artist currently hot in New York art-buying circles.

Finch raised his glass. "Doesn't get any better than this, *mes amies.*"

"*Plus ça change, plus c'est la même chose,*" Delacroix replied. "Or does it, monsieur *Freixenet?*"

"It both does and doesn't, mademoiselles."

"So, fucking tell us how it doesn't."

Stephen's wine tasted slightly of onion. He stared at Finch holding his martini in front of his navy polo shirt and noticed two large pearl onions bobbing in the bottom of the glass.

Finch swigged at his drink and strolled stage-center, standing in front of the bank of sofas on which Stephen and Delacroix were seated. "Fifty years ago, gentlemen, the hot commodity was bricks-and-mortar businesses, companies that made shit like station wagons and paint and hula hoops and Mr. Clean—stuff the masses consumed by the fucking boat load that was either disposable, expendable, breakable or obsolete overnight. At that time, it is true, we made money by quaint concepts known as profits and efficiency. Then *Sesame Street* and Martha Bluenose ruined the great American compulsion for consumption. People began to seek 'value'; doing shit like recycling, making home-made chicken stock and investing in like one L.L. Bean down parka every fucking ten years. Just when it looked like our best option for sending our kids to boarding school in Switzerland boiled down to buy and hold, we were rescued by the revenge of the fucking nerds—software and hardware dick-coms. Here, we're talking mid-90s, we made money not on profits but on expectations of profits. After that nice little bubble, expectations were high for a return to the good old days. Cell phones became the new Rolexes; Play Stations and Xboxes an essential element in the normal upbringing of every 10-year old boy. There was an uptick in consumption, but all that shit was made in China, enough said? Alas, the lost decade when the market spun its wheels. At the same time, unbeknownst to us, our government had had enough of playing second fiddle to equity and markets and wanted its pound of flesh. It started giving money away, brought the whole chalupa down and now owns and operates the biggest chop shop this side of Encino. We are now all government employees."

Delacroix waved his hand. "Cut to the chase, Pericles. What's the scam?"

"You're asking the wrong question. You should be asking what's the new commodity? That one thing people covet more today than a Rolex or thy neighbor's wife."

"Drum fucking roll."

Finch leaned forward announcing in a whisper: "Power, and I don't mean kilowatts."

Delacroix gagged on his martini. "Oh shit, I knew it," he said, wiping booze that had splashed in his eyes. "You've finally gone off the deep end, Finch, and you've always been close to fucking edge to begin with. Next you're going to tell me you're reading Dabunk Chakka and using crystal suppositories."

Finch shrugged his shoulders. "I guess $40 million makes me a schlemiel. Go figure."

Delacroix shot upright. "What the fuck?"

Finch threw back the last of his martini as if he had just fleeced the house at the Bellagio. "You need another," he pointed casually at Delacroix's glass as he sauntered back to the wet bar, *en continuendo.*

"Hard to believe. Once power was the domain of countries or corporations. Now it's a black pearl, and a seductive one, fought for by *everyman.* Remember him? Struggle, fight to impress, rise up! Think about it—we pop out of the nappy hole wanting to get our way 24/7. The tantrum is the single most innate, instinctive human behavioral trait. We must be whipped to learn to cooperate; threatened with ostracization to be taught to tolerate not getting our way— "time out" is the first corporal punishment meted out to children and must be repeated ad nauseum until it clicks: *you just another brick in the wall little mofo.* The internet has changed all that. For the first time in history, human nature can be fully realized. No longer do the ignorant, lazy and talentless need to concede anything to the smart and ambitious. Anyone and everyone can be heard, make a claim, and on equal footing, strive to have it all. The age of greed has been replaced by the age of me. It's a rant a nanosecond out there. Vent, spleen, venom. Enter a new kind of science and with it, a new kind of fixer, middleman. The layman power broker. Et voilà! C'est moi.

"Forty fucking million?" Delacroix mumbled, taking the refill from Finch.

"Breaking it down, it is purely and simply a deal about power —who has it and who wants it."

"And who in the fuck wants it, if you don't mind me asking?"

"Why would I mind you asking? Some outfit out of the Orient, as it used to be called."

"What do they want?"

Finch, who was giddy with the alcoholic truth serum, screwed up his brow and looked at the ceiling. "I think the technical name is rum—the radioactive kind.

Delacroix pulled his drink away from his mouth and glared at Finch. "You've got to be fucking kidding me."

"No. Do I kid?"

"What are they planning on doing with radioactive rum?"

"One, client confidentiality, two, none of my business. But just between you, me and the loggerhead turtles, I'm sure for peaceful, humanitarian purposes—probably making electricity to power all the new schools they're building for girls in Islamabad and Aleppo."

Finch's laughter pealed out of the room into the balmy night air tinged with salt, where it mingled with the sound of waves washing up the beach, then hissing back into the ocean.

By the time Andy reached the shop after his lesson it was past eight o'clock. He had stopped at the grocery and bought the smallest turkey he could find, a ten-pounder, and had just enough money left over to buy potatoes, French-fried onion rings and a can of cream of mushroom soup. Not only, he decided, was his idea of Thanksgiving in March an affirmation, à la Torsten Zweiback, that man had control of his destiny and wasn't ruled by conventions or expectations of others, but it made good economic and fatherly sense. He'd invite the kids over for dinner this weekend and still live off the leftovers for the rest of the following week. A win-win-win.

Exhilarated by his flight, he had also spontaneously decided to stop for a beer at the Post-Up sports bar, a usually lively venue in which he had not set foot in since his days as a Tartan Chemical salesman. He had no cash, but after careful calculation, figured he was five, maybe ten dollars under the limit on his credit card, enough for at least one beer and maybe some chips and salsa.

The place was crowded and loud, big screens beamed March Madness from every nook and cranny. He sauntered around the elongated bar looking for a spare stool and spied one near the back, and next to it, a familiar, hunched figure nursing a beer.

"Sit down, mate," Ian Hunt said, greeting Andy. "You look to be wearing the mantle of a newly minted CEO well."

Andy confided he was broke, waiting on a $100,000 check from the president to avoid being shut down and going through a divorce.

"I'm buying," Ian announced.

Ian was good to drink with any day but especially good when shit was falling like rain in Seattle.

"Here's to life," Ian toasted when Andy's beer arrived. "One big fucking mess."

"I need a trip to Las Vegas."

"And I need a rocket launcher."

Ian described Sondra Cleaver's reign of terror, at Tartan. Sales targets had been raised 20 percent and webcams had been activated on all computers enabling her to monitor employees from her office. "Stop picking your nose," she had pinged Hunt one day. Joe Gemelli had been fired and half dozen others had resigned.

"The kids she's hired don't know jack shit. Luckily, I'm so insignificant I'm under her radar screen, except for my boogers."

One beer became two, and two became three, just as in the old days. Whether it was the beer or the creeping accumulation of stress, Andy was seized by a sudden anxiety.

"Ian, I think my wife may be trying to get rid of me."

"Well, yes, old bloke, she has filed for divorce."

"No, I mean do me in, like 'murder she wrote.'"

"Now what put that silly thought in your head."

"I found some books on how to silently poison people in the house today."

"Ah yes, the holy grail of murder—killing softly."

"It makes perfect sense. I'm nothing but a big fucking liability."

"Nonsense. Who would pick the kids up after school?"

"I die, she still collects on the insurance, sells the business and gets all the money, not just half."

"Poisons are a fascinating subject, really. There's nightshade, hemlock, strychnine, curare, oh … and don't forget arsenic."

"It's totally logical. Damn, I can't believe I didn't see this coming."

"Helium would work, but I doubt she could keep the mask over your face long enough."

"We're meeting Saturday. I bet she'll bring me some cookies as a peace offering."

"Oh yes, then there is death in a bottle: pentobarbital. You can buy it off the shelf in Mexico. Used to euthanize animals. Few drops in a drink and bam, lights out."

"Not touching them."

"Then there's my all-time favorite poison—water. More people have died swallowing water than of DDT or global warming, but you don't see any celebrities on TV preaching safe drinking."

Back at the shop, Andy hurried to put in a batch of tiny tumblers. He had to make a delivery to Clancey tomorrow afternoon, and with a 14-hour turn-around, had just enough time to get them in and out and over to the raving lunatic. The production increase ordered by the president had boosted his cash flow, but for the time at least, all the money was being diverted to pay over-due accounts, of which there were many. To keep operating he had secured lines of credit with all his suppliers, including Tartan Chemical, and was paying a hefty interest on the balances. No get-away weekends to Sin City on the horizon.

As the former Mr. Bobblehead, Andy still, on occasion, experienced a time delay between the occurrence of an event and a grasp of its meaning. He knew, upon reflection, that his suspicions of Marcia plotting to murder him were silly, absurd. Yet … Yet …? Why else would she have books in the house about how to poison a person? For light reading? As some comedian once said, you aren't paranoid if everyone really *IS* out to get you. The gravity of it had sunk in on the drive back from the bar. It was show-down at the OK corral in less than two days. But hey, in hopeless, we're-all-dead, imminent-impact-with-an-asteroid, opportunity, right? All that was needed was calm thinking. He would beg—it was that simple. He still loved her, couldn't live without her or the kids, and now with time spent in exile, fully recognized his need for spousal self-improvement. Besides, he was on firm moral ground: He hadn't done anything wrong. If that failed to move her, he would take out a gun, point it at his head and threaten to pull the trigger. Ya gotta do whatcha gotta do.

The tubes were in the tank. Exhausted, Andy pushed his arms into the sleeves of his windbreaker, flicked off the lights and walked out to his car. He stood a moment at the door of his car, looking up at the stars and breathing in the cool, fresh smell of spring thaw. KAW-WAP! A spasm of electric fear shot through his body, every muscle recoiling at the booming retort of an explosion. Still crouching, he heard a car squeal away in front and glanced up just in time to see the limp figure of a man falling from the roof of the old Eisner building into the hedges. Shaking, he yanked open the door of the car, crawled in, cranked the ignition, and leaning prone on seat, steered the car blindly out of the drive, pushing the accelerator to the floor once he hit the street, fishtailing down the road away from Gloss Industries.

14 LE BANLIEUE, GLOSS AND A VIDEO

"Refusnik. R-E-F-U-S-N-I-K. Double letter score on the F plus a triple word score, for a total of 57."

"Refuse what?"

"Refuse-NIK. It's a word from the Soviet era, dear. It means a Russian refused permission to emigrate."

"Pig Latin."

"Anything that found its way into the newspapers in English is kosher."

"Really? So, I suppose Smitty's Sunoco is a word … Have to put the tea on… oi, oi, oi," Martha Riker winced, grabbing her back as she stood up from the table.

Robert Riker was having grave misgivings about returning early from sun-drenched Naples. They had, once upon a time, stayed through May, but as she aged, his wife had grown less tolerant of being away from her nest and her kitchen, to the point where it had now become a ritual for him to threaten her to go down alone each winter. The weather in Massachusetts had been execrable; even now, the last days March, there were still patches of snow around the flower beds along the esplanade leading down to the lake, which was struggling to get warm enough to melt the remaining ugly mottled floes of ice. It made no sense to leave to escape the winter only to return in time to catch the last frigid act of the dreadful season. Things had to make sense! He would pack Martha in a crate and ship her overnight next year if need be to stay until May and outlast any of Jack Frost's shenanigans.

He had also been out of sorts since February with the news that Marcia was filing for divorce from Andrew. Now talk about something that didn't make sense! Sure, Andrew probably had shortcomings from a wife's perspective—all men did. But he could not fathom that this thoughtful, likeable, level-headed young man would deviously plot to cheat on his daughter. The notion, in fact, was preposterous. That was the realm of his other son-in-law, Eastman Finch, who could not be trusted with the proceeds from a little league weenie roast. Martha was on the other side on this one, arguing that one couldn't doubt the truthfulness of what their own daughter was reporting. But that, Robert Riker thought, wasn't his point exactly. It wasn't that he thought Marcia was making up a suspected affair, it was that there had to be a mix-up, a screw up of some sort that had gotten Andrew into hot water. It also affronted his sense of justice: Andrew, with his unpretentiousness, his new, legitimate business, his real-world knowledge of industry and manufacturing, was a better person than Finch with his freeze-dried facade, his shady deals, and ostentatious Bentleys, and it was Andrew who was getting thrown to the wolves. It wasn't right, and he hadn't been able to let go of the idea that there was something fishy about it. Suddenly, with the thought of Finch and the Bentley, it hit him—Finch was behind this!

He got up from the table and walked with his long, slightly tilted stride into the living room. Someone, probably Claire's boyfriend, Barrie, had left on the television. Mr. Riker attempted to locate the remote to switch it off, but unable, resigned himself to the blathering of a news commentator and sat down on the sofa next to the end table with the telephone. As it was Saturday, he reached Marcia at home.

"Father? Is everything okay?" Marcia's panic a reflex, as her father rarely, if ever, called her.

"Oh yes, do not worry, dear girl. I am still officially an old fart and your mother is in the kitchen right now in complete misery."

Damn television, Mr. Riker thought, as the volume was turned up and the broadcaster segued annoyingly into some sort of special report.

"Look here, dear, I've just had a revelation about your marital dispute with Andrew. Eastman Finch is to blame."

Marcia silently attempted to digest the statement.

"What?!"

"Don't you see—it's perfectly clear."

"Father, what is clear?"

"Finch set him up, duped him."

"Ah … okay," Marcia said after a moment. "And how did you reach this conclusion?"

"As Sherlock Holmes once said, when you have eliminated the impossible, whatever remains, however improbable, must be the truth. It's the only explanation that makes any sense. Finch hatched this plot as revenge for Andrew blowing up his Bentley, or should I say the conspiracy theory thereof."

"Plot?"

"A plot to have a beautiful woman seduce Andrew and destroy his marriage."

"What on earth are you talking about?"

"Marcia, every man is weak, but it is one thing to be tempted and quite another to succumb."

"He brought the woman home! She spent the night in MY house with MY husband!"

"Poppycock, dear girl. She probably drugged him to make it look like Andrew was at fault. I wouldn't put it past Finch."

"Father, I think it best we end this conversation. I was just going out the door to meet with Andrew at his office and finalize details of the divorce."

In the background noise coming from the television Mr. Riker heard a couple of words that caught his attention. "Marcia, will you please … wait a second," he said, pulling the phone away from his ear.

"Father? Father, are you there?"

Mr. Riker who, if it were up to him, wouldn't have had a television or computer in the house, suddenly became raptly attentive to the video-audio montage assaulting his senses. A woman in a trench coat stood holding a microphone in front of the glass Pyramid of the Louvre. "*Authorities in Paris are investigating the sudden, mysterious disappearance of American businessman and war hero, Dick Gloss. His wife, Angela Gloss, reported Mr. Gloss missing when he did not return from a planned trip to the popular Paris tourist attraction of*

Montmartre earlier this afternoon. Authorities say they have no leads at present but have narrowed down the investigation to two possible scenarios: that Mr. Gloss might have passed out on the street after eating food that disagreed with his digestion, or that he might have been attacked after making disparaging remarks about the character of the French people. Police are searching secluded Parisian streets and alleyways."

"Father! I have to leave."

"Wait a minute, wait a minute! What is the name of the man from whom Andrew acquired the company?"

"Dick Gloss ... Look, Father, I ..."

"He's missing ...been kidnapped ... in Paris."

"Who would do something like that?"

Robert Riker felt his heart begin to race as he gazed in a trance at the television. "Finch," he mumbled. "Eastman Finch."

They had driven him somewhere at least an hour from his hotel. Gloss, blindfolded and with hands bound, assailed his abductors with a barrage of curses and threats the entire way.

"Ah," said the man who had been following him and jumped in the cab. "So, you don't like it when you're not in control, when the foot is on your chest? Now you know how it feels."

"Fuck you and all your fucking cry-baby comrades. I can tell you this much right now—whatever you want, you're not going to get it. I've licked death's pussy. I've had 40 bonus years as it is."

"Yes, you were a big war hero. I respect you for that. But America lost the war. What a shame, and how you say, what a waste, no?"

"What would you know about combat, as opposed to slaughtering innocent civilians?"

The man laughed with loud insincerity. "Well, we will begin the process of re-education shortly."

Gloss was being interned in a windowless room with peeling,

plastered walls. A ceiling fan had fallen from its mount and dangled at an angle, hanging from two green and white wires. From the wires, which were not in code with modern international standards, and cinderblock brickwork visible through the patches of fallen plaster, Gloss estimated the building was at least 50 to 70 years old, perhaps even older. A faint smell of toluene, or methyl ethyl ketone, mixed with a lingering scent of epoxy, led Gloss to surmise he was in a plastics factory or warehouse. The French, it was well known, had a knack for making things such as canoes, paddle boats and storage tanks via a low-cost technique known as hand lay-up manufacturing. The process was also notorious for spewing out head-dizzying amounts of toxic emissions and had been virtually banned in the U.S. years ago.

"Welcome to my neck of the woods, Mr. Gloss— *le banlieue*," a lanky man wearing jeans and a polo shirt said, striding briskly through a door after Gloss had been deposited in the room and left alone with a sullen, Uzi-toting guard for about an hour. The man was much younger than his abductor, who strolled into the room a few seconds later, sipping coffee from a foam cup.

"Luh ban what?" Gloss asked, wondering if he could get an accurate gauge of his whereabouts. He had been intensively studying maps of Paris for weeks.

"You do not speak French?"

"No."

"What a surprise. So I will translate for you—"*quesque ces't en anglais*," he said, looking at the other man. "Le slum?"

The two men and the guard both laughed heartily.

"Excuse my humor. My name is Sadi and this is Farouk. The man with the gun goes by the name of Ochocinco, in honor of his favorite all-time American football player. Is there anything I can get you? A coffee, a magazine, something to eat?"

"Fuck you."

Sadi chuckled, lit a cigarette and sat down on top of a bare desk across from the battered Naugahyde sofa on which Gloss was sitting.

"We were so pleasantly surprised when we learned that a man of your stature and many accomplishments was paying an extended visit to our fair city, Mr. Gloss."

"Yada, yada."

"Do you watch *Seinfeld?* I am a big fan. You see we have something in common already."

"Yeah, I get hemorrhoids, too."

"You have a good sense of humor, Mr. Gloss. Perhaps if things work out this won't have to be too long or unpleasant a stay for you."

"What do want with me?"

Sadi took a drag from his cigarette. "To be totally honest with you, strictly as an insurance policy."

"You're trying to steal my uranium enrichment technology, I knew it."

"We don't want to steal it, Mr. Gloss. We just want to share it."

"You won't get it."

"Yes, we admit your anointed successor, Andrew Dodge, has proven to be a, how you say, a tougher nut to crack than we imagined, but with help from a big deal maker in New York, we are, even as we speak, about to come into possession of the secret to make lots of bomb-grade boom-boom in a short amount of time, God willing."

"They know about it. You'll get caught."

"Yes, and they knew about 9-11 too, and so, you see, we are not too worried. But if those twin formidable forces of Andrew Dodge and the U.S. government combine to thwart our plan, we have you, our insurance policy."

"Like I was telling Farouk here, you can go ahead and kill me. I'm not telling you a thing."

"Mr. Gloss, what makes you think we would do such a horrible thing. Besides, we aren't so unwordly to believe you'd give us the formula of your invention."

"That's true."

"But we imagine your wife might have a soft spot in her heart for you."

Gloss vaulted out of the sofa at the mention of his wife. "Leave her out of this," he yelled, moving menacingly toward Sadi before Ochocinco forced him back into his seat.

"Mr. Gloss, please calm down. As I said, this is strictly business, nothing personal, an investment; one we hopefully won't have to cash in. So, you see," he said, looking at his watch, "we will sit tight and see what happens and if all goes as planned perhaps you will be enjoying dinner with your wife on the Rue de Rivioli later tonight."

A jaunty ring tone bleated and Sadi deftly extracted his cell phone from his pocket.

"Oui?" His expression turned quickly to concern. "Je ne sais pas!" he pointed at the phone to Farouk, turned and scurried out of the room gesturing excitedly and switching to Arabic.

With Sadi's exit, Gloss spent most of rest of the afternoon in the company of Farouk and Ochocinco. Farouk was intent to engage Gloss in conversation, mostly, it appeared, to promote his credibility as an engineer and an entrepreneur. Gloss listened glumly as Farouk outlined all the courses he had taken at Umm Al-Qura University in Saudi Arabia, talked about a way to build a better shipping container and debated with himself about the possibility of constructing a space elevator. Gloss, despite his bravado and belligerency, was worried … and scarred. Those dumb fucks Clancey and the government! He could take some solace that he had been prescient enough to tip off Ricky to the possibility of trouble. But Ricky was a stagehand at this point, not a player, someone who could only react, not prevent. Without the surveillance and security he had explicitly requested from the U.S. government, it would be largely on Andy's shoulders to outwit and defeat an attack. Hopeless. But then again … Hopeless! Goddamn the incompetence in this world! It wasn't Andy's fault. He hadn't meant for it to turn out like this. Now it appeared something was going to go horribly wrong and he was ultimately to blame. Shit not ultimately—totally and fucking completely.

Gloss ruminated as Farouk rambled about a way to make a cheap, ultra-strong, quasi isotropic composite sandwich material from polyurethane, crushed seashells and camel dung. Farouk was right. He couldn't stomach the feeling of relinquishment; of being directed by the will of others, guided by unseen forces, like a leaf in the wind. If he let it, the thought of the next 24, 48 or however many hours, with the prospect of being sequestered, contained, imprisoned, would literally drive him over the brink of the friable precipice of sanity to which he was clinging by his nails. Death, to him, was preferable. He had spent his whole life in battle with the unruly and inane. And now, what could he do? Not a goddamn thing. Whatever would happen, would happen and he would in due time find out about it. Yet, as he listened to Farouk, there was, not so much in the tone of his voice but in the motivation for what he was saying, a message, a theme that, Gloss realized, might lend itself to a slight assertion of his will. It was the theme of respect, the need for it. It was something everyone was clamoring for and demanding. Understandably, Gloss mused, respect would be an even more valuable commodity to a person from a culture that perceived it was universally disrespected, or at least disrespected by the Great Satan it loathed, but also, at some deeper level, craved respect—America. Gloss *was* America to someone like Farouk. He knew Farouk viscerally loathed him and could be cajoled with a complimentary copy of *Le Monde* to play fiddle on his jugular with a scimitar. But it was also apparent he desperately wanted Gloss to consider him his peer, someone whose views were worthy of taking seriously.

"Hey, Farouk, back up there a minute on that space elevator idea. It won't work until the cost of carbon nanotubes comes down."

Farouk smiled broadly, revealing a gold-capped incisor. "But, monsieur Gloss, the cost has come down. Ten years ago a kilo of carbon nanotubes cost $1000, today its $100."

"Still too much for something that's gonna take, oh… a hundred billion tons of the stuff. Then there's the whole logistics of building a cable 150 miles long and dangling it from a counterweight in geosynchronous orbit. That's going to be a pretty expensive roller coaster ride."

"Yes, but as Konstantin Tsiolkovsky showed, it is theoretically possible. Nothing about it violates the laws of physics."

"Right now it violates the laws of economics and common sense."

"At one time so did the airplane."

"True enough, but DaVinci didn't try to build one before he could. He sold paintings instead. Don't go tiltin' at windmills, Farouk.

Concentrate on what you can do, that's my philosophy."

By four o'clock, an hour after he had expected to be back at the hotel from his excursion to Montmartre, Gloss felt his acid reflux begin to smolder like a volcanic caldera in his upper abdomen. Farouk left Gloss alone with Ochocinco and walked several blocks to a pharmacy to buy antacid. Gloss gobbled down five tablets with some water and began to instruct Farouk about how he could make his idea for a shipping container more commercial.

Farouk sketched out a design on a piece of paper. Gloss modified the design of the panels to be interlocking, saving space and material.

"Find out what the best, most-used shipping container in the world is," Gloss told Farouk, who listened attentively. "Then figure out how and why yours is an improvement. Then you get yourself one of those 3D printers and make a prototype. Take it out to some customers and explain how it can improve their efficiency and reduce their costs, and bingo, you're off to the races."

Another two hours passed and Sadi had still not returned. Farouk ordered Ochocinco to fetch some baguettes and coffee. When he had left, Farouk, cradling the Uzi in his lap, smiled warmly at Gloss.

"Monsieur, I will tell you something in secret, no?"

"Whatever you say, Farouk, is between you, me and the fence post."

Farouk bent forward and lowered his voice. "I only do this for the pay."

"Do what?"

"You know, kidnapping, coercion, blasphemy, that sort of thing."

"What do they pay you?"

"One meal a day, plus expenses."

Gloss sniggered, chuckled and began to laugh, leaning forward on the sofa. Farouk stood and pointed the Uzi at Gloss.

"Monsieur, do not mock me."

Gloss waved his hand and fell back against the ratty Naugahyde cushions. "Farouk, I'm sorry, relax, it's just …"

"You think of us as the scum of the earth."

"No, my friend, no. Let me tell you a little story."

And Gloss began to explain how in America, with a low-interest loan from the Small Business Administration, Farouk could be president of his own company and, in less than a year, be on the first tee by noon every day.

As he watched the sun slowly sink behind the brawny, gray shoulder of a mountain overlooking the Khyber pass to the west, A.J. felt a profound sense of peace and tranquility. Sitting cross-legged in front of his mud-walled house, he sipped tea and watched his son Naib milk his dromedary camel while the noble beast munched contentedly on his neighbor's thorny hedges. He reflected on how life very often had more twists and turns than a Coen brothers' movie. Only a year ago, he had heated the house by burning camel dung; now he had a wood-burning stove and a satellite dish which picked up all the famous American television shows—*Dysfunctional Family, Wives for Sale, Cruelest Nanny and* (his favorite) *Caught Naked.* God was great and now, after a year of grinding, back-breaking labor, everything was coming to fruition. Yet, only a day ago everything appeared on the verge of falling apart. The trouble had started on Friday, the Sabbath, when he received a text message while praying in the mosque. The message alert signal had sent the Mullah Baba Chaka Kahn into a rage and he had had to plead "special circumstances" to prevent him from smashing his phone against the mosque's marble floor. Nonetheless he was barred from reading the message until prayers had ended hours later. When prayers were finished, he discovered that operation Cotton Candy had been postponed. For the next three hours he frantically attempted to reach his contact in London. A.J. informed Graham to consider life without a scrotum if he ever failed to pick up his phone again. Graham, who began to sob, told A.J. he had been working to repair a malfunction with his scrambling encoder. Graham then told A.J. that the operative hired to replace the initial operative had gone missing and that at this point his deal maker in the U.S. did not have a clue as to how he was going to salvage the operation. It was then that A.J. gave the go-ahead to the Parisian cell to kidnap Gloss. A member who worked at the Ritz as a desk clerk had alerted headquarters that Gloss was vacationing in the city and A.J. had ordered him trailed. With Plan A on hold, Plan B would be to extract the information they needed from Gloss by hook, crook or machete. Then, an hour or so before the planned gathering of Gloss, A.J. learned operation Cotton Candy was on again. Fearful that the American media would make a big deal about Gloss's disappearance and raise red flags in Washington, A.J. had tried to reach the cell leader, Sadi, and cancel the kidnapping. By then, however, they had already abducted Gloss and were holding him hostage in Paris. Several hours of anxiety then ensued as Sadi, himself, and the Great Leader waited for any sign that Gloss's dematerialization had been discovered. But God had blessed them with the incoherence and lassitude of decadent Western society, and the numerous inefficiencies and delays in the reporting and investigation of a potential crime had apparently conspired to work in their favor and given them just enough time to initiate the mission to confiscate the most sophisticated uranium enrichment technology ever invented. With this way to make large amounts of fissile uranium rapidly, the Great Leader had told them, they would commence a turning point in history that would bring on a golden, 10,000-year rule of the Koran and the teachings of Mohammad—although A.J. secretly hoped small pockets of Western depravity would be allowed to survive. He, they, could be supremely confident in success. In less than 24 hours, the Great Leader would convene the brotherhood at the landing strip they had worked all year to build to receive the magical technology to make a nuclear bomb and, perhaps, the cherry on top of everything, also the head of the unwashed retrograde formerly known as Dodge—shipped free overnight via the monopolistic enterprise founded by the satanic capitalist Jeff Zobes (everyone knew he would ship anything). Already, Mullah Baba had given orders for a feast and celebration; in preparation, tents were being raised, lambs slaughtered, and a loudspeaker system and stage erected in the village square. A.J glanced at his son, who was still preoccupied milking the camel, deftly reached under his robe and pulled out a pint of Ron Rico 151 proof rum. He unscrewed the cap and took two quick swigs before returning the bottle to its hiding place. "Allah Akbar," he said, wincing as the slug of alcohol burned its way down his esophagus. He looked forward to the celebration and in preparation he had hidden two more bottles beneath the floor of his house. Still sitting, A.J. began to sway to-and-fro, humming a Def Leppard melody and play-ing air guitar. "We are going to rock," he said, throwing back his head and gazing up at stars appearing in the darkening sky.

15 DODGE BALLIN'

Andy screeched his car into a spot in front of Little John's Quicky-Mart, jumped out, strode into the store and slapped a lottery ticket on the counter.

"That's a winner," he said to the man seated behind the cash register watching a small television attached to the wall.

The man stood, strolled languidly to the counter and picked up the ticket. He inserted the ticket into the top of the machine.

"Not a winner," he said, tossing the ticket at Andy.

"I matched two out of six numbers—that's a free ticket."

The man rolled his eyes, sighed, put on his glasses and studied the ticket. "You need to play the kicker to win with two numbers."

Andy crumbled the ticket, threw it on the floor and stomped back to his car. He was running a bit late for his meeting with Marcia. Eddie, his neighbor in the apartment above him, had kept him up most of the night arguing with his wife. The apartment building's impeccable acoustics allowed Andy to discern that the dispute seemed to relate to Eddie's purchase of a set of four, 18-inch custom chrome wheels and Mickey Thompson mag tires for their Honda Civic. When, at 3 o'clock in the morning, the argument finally seemed to be winding down, the baby woke bawling with a severe case of colic. Andy ripped the bedspread off the bed and tried to fall asleep in the armchair in the living room. He gave up after an hour with a kink in his neck and shoulder. Baby finally pacified, he crawled back into bed and tossed and turned until nearly dawn, when he finally fell asleep, and he didn't wake up until noon. He hurriedly showered and dressed, rushed out the door and hopped in his car, but had to double back to his apartment when he remembered he had forgotten to take the turkey out of the freezer to thaw. He had no idea what to expect from the meeting with Marcia, and had had no time to think it through. The day before, the police had spent several hours at his office questioning him about the shooting he had reported seeing Thursday evening while leaving the building. A team of police officers searched the perimeter, offices and roof of the old Eisner building and returned to report they had found nothing. This caused amused consternation for the sergeant in charge. "So, you say you heard a shot and saw a body fall into the bushes in front of the building, correct?" Andy repeated his description of the incident, reiterating that he was certain that he had witnessed a murder or attempted murder that night. The sergeant raised one eye, "Well, I guess the guy took a flesh wound and walked away. We'll let you know if he comes in to talk to us, but I wouldn't count on it. People who hang out on roofs of buildings at night are usually not the types who like to go on record about what they do—go figure." To muddle up things further, Calvin Clancey had called and requested an additional "emergency" batch of tiny tumblers for delivery tonight. "Don't go screwing this up, Yankee Doodle," Clancey issued his usual demonic qualifier. "I got studio time booked Saturday night to record the last motherfuckin' cut on my soon-to-be platinum album."

When Andy arrived at the office, Marcia's car was already parked in front. He pulled up beside her and waved. Marcia got out of the car holding a large yellow envelope and stood in front of the building waiting for Andy, who was detained as he rifled through the pockets of several jackets strewn in the backseat for the paper with the pass code. He found it in his windbreaker in the same pocket as the key fob into the plating bunker.

"Hello, Andrew," Marcia said business-like. "How have you been?"

"Baby kept me up last night but other than that ..."

It was a warm, sunny first day of April. Marcia was wearing jeans and a white blouse. She had tinted her hair a shade of auburn and let it grow, with a wavy touch, almost shoulder length. Andy had never seen her more attractive.

They walked together toward the door of the building and Andy fumbled in his pocket for the pass code.

"I can never remember this damn thing," he said, gazing at the paper and punching in the numbers on the keypad. With the entry of the last number the door made a clicking sound and Andy yanked it open. The next instant he heard a rustling from the bushes in front of the foyer, and a lithe female wearing sunglasses and a hoodie vaulted nimbly into the doorway and stuck a pistol into his kidney.

"Let's keep it moving people," she said, making a motion with the tip of the gun for them go inside. It was Melinda Chow.

Melinda kept the gun on Andy as they walked ahead of her into the building.

"I'm so sorry we have to meet up this way, Andrew," she said, once the door had closed. "In an ideal world we would only have fond memories of people."

Marcia looked aghast. "You know her?"

Andy shifted his weight and exhaled deeply. "She's the reason we're meeting."

Marcia scrutinized Melinda. "So, you're not only a slut but a criminal?"

"I'm also pretty good with a gun too. Down the hall."

They moved in a line past the cafeteria, board room and into Andy's office. Melinda smiled and shook her long dark hair out of the hoodie. "Believe it or not I almost pulled out of this job because I like you, Mr. Dodge, I really do. This puzzled me though, because how can anyone like another a person enough to forfeit four million dollars? So I began to think about it and I remembered the line from *Macbeth*, "If chance may have me king, why, chance may crown me," and I realized it wasn't an affection that was holding me back, but an affliction, a fear of exploding blood and gore. Can you believe it?"

Marcia snickered sarcastically.

"But then all the world's a stage, isn't it? So, I came to my senses and realized there didn't really need to be any blood in this … well, yours anyway. Had to off the hit guy they had hired to J-F-K you —yuck. I never could watch that Zapruder film."

"Thursday night, in front of the Eisner building?"

"Ten-four, good buddy. Bull's eye, heart shot, very little mess in a hit like that remarkably. Dude was probably going to die of cir-rhosis in a year anyway."

"So, we should thank you?" Marcia intoned.

"You can donate to the Free Tibet Society in my name. Now, Andrew, I want you to reach into your pocket and hand me the key fob to the bunker."

Andy slowly fumbled through his pocket, pressing what he thought felt like the larger, oblong, red alarm button on the fob—whatever good it might do—before pulling it out and tossing it to Melinda.

"Nice little set up you have here, very spy-versus-spy retro." Melinda punched the top button on the fob and the panel in the floor opened. She put the fob in the pocket of her jacket and pulled a walkie-talkie out of her pocket. "Bring the van to the front."

"Now, Andrew, here's what I want you to do."

Andy located a pushcart on the shop floor. It took him five trips into the bunker to load the plating bath tank, two fixtures, 20 boxes of centrifuge blanks and a dozen crates of "solution A" and "solution B" into the back of the van. Melinda covered Andy from the door and a man wearing a ski mask in the back of the van covered Andy while he was loading. Marcia was left in the office, her arms and feet tied with duct tape. When he finished loading the equipment, Melinda led Andy back into the office.

"That's a good day's work," Melinda said, cutting the tape off Marcia's wrists and feet. "'Labor is its own reward,'" my parents used to say."

"Go to hell bitch," Marcia spat out.

"Watch it, honey. She's got a gun and she'll do anything," Andy said.

"Yes, I will. The world is just full of people behaving badly, isn't it? Fain were it otherwise—and I mean that."

"Aren't you going to tell her the truth?" Andy asked as they stood on the bunker lifting device.

"The truth?"

"Yes, the truth."

Melinda stared at Andy. "All right, in the interest of verity, or setting the record straight, or whatever ... I didn't sleep with your husband."

Marcia eyes darted between Andy and Melinda. "You were in my house."

"I was … and your husband passed out."

"Ha, that hardly gets him off the hook."

"Look, I'm clearly not an above-the-board person. On that alone you owe him a pass. Sort of like the Patty Hearst defense.

"Nuh-uh."

"Oh well, Mr. Mojito, I tried."

"She posed as a vendor," Andy protested. "It was a set up."

"And it worked," Marcia deadpanned. "I'm sure you wouldn't have been so accessible if she had a cleft palate."

"Marcia, be reasonable."

"Look what you've done… oh my God!!"

"Me?"

She began to cry hysterically. Andy tried to comfort her, but she jerked herself free.

"She's right," Melinda Chow chimed. "The conclusion to this play has an ending that's already been written. It's a powerful ending, but I'm afraid not a pleasant one."

"You're as phony as your tits."

"Perception is reality—especially when it comes to boobs," Melinda said, aiming the gun at them, and at the same time, pulling a plastic bag full of grayish granules from her pocket. "But just so you know, I do have a heart. I could make an extra 100 grand just for bringing back your noggin, Andrew. Someone wants Mr. Mojito for a wall decoration, but then there's the whole question of what do you pack it in, is it a hazardous waste, expedited or regular shipping? There's only so much multi-tasking a girl can handle.

"You won't get away with this," Marcia yelled.

"I already have."

Marcia took a step to charge, but Andy grabbed her arm.

"Yes, I have a gun and I will use it. At least this way you have, oh, about a one in ten million chance of surviving."

She pressed a button on the key fob and the platform began to lower Andy and Marcia into the bunker. "And now our revels are ended," she said, opening the bag as the two descended. "And these actors, as I foretold, were all spirits." The pellets began to fume.

Then, as she pictured Mr. Mojito break dancing, a fleeting pang of remorse, a sliver of the empathy she had once had and long lost, drifted into her conscience. "Marcia Riker Dodge, your husband is an honorable man, he never made a single pass or advance at me."

The platform descended, Marcia put a hand on Andy's shoulder and buried her head against his chest, "Oh no, no, no." Melinda Chow dumped the entire bag of cyanide pellets into the bunker as the platform reached the bottom and the latch made a creaking thud as it clamped shut and assumed the look of the carpeted floor. Chow took one step onto the hollow spot below the floor. "Were all spirits. Spirits! And are melted into air ... into thin air."

About 10 p.m. Paris time the same day, Farouk and Gloss were drinking coffee and debating who should be credited with the invention of algebra.

"The Arabs kept the teachings of the Greeks alive during the Middle Ages," Farouk said, his hand tracing a circular pattern with his cigarette as he talked. "The main learning centers were Baghdad and Andalusia."

"I understand that, Farouk, but it was Ptolemy and Archimedes who got the party started and Descartes, Fermat and Newton sealed the deal."

"The word 'algebra' is Arabic, taken from the title of a book written by the great mathematician Al Khwarizmi!" Farouk said excitedly. "He was born 700 years before Descartes."

"Okay, point taken—where can I get a copy of this book."

"I have one in my taxi."

Suddenly Sadi, who had been away all day, rushed into the room. "We have just heard from London. Operation Cotton Candy was a complete success."

Ochocinco, Farouk and Sadi whooped, high-fived each other and broke into a celebratory dance, passing around the Uzi and twirling it over their heads.

"Never again, monsieur Gloss, will we be under the thumb of America," Sadi, frothed in Gloss's face.

"Congratulations," Gloss said. "You can now murder millions of innocent people as payback for your sloth and stupidity. Now when can I leave?"

"I'll drive him back," Farouk said.

Sadi slapped Farouk hard on the chest. "Are you crazy man? We can't let him go and risk everything we've just won."

Sadi and Farouk, talking in Arabic, began to feud vehemently.

"It's not under discussion. The Leader has given the order."

Ochocinco pushed the tip of the Uzi against Gloss's temple. "Just say when, boss."

"No, we make video."

"Video?"

"Yes. Here," Sadi said, pulling out an 18-inch, saber-shaped, scimitar from under the desk and handing it to Farouk. "You get the honors, my brother."

Farouk looked at the knife in terror. "Why not just use a bullet?" He asked, glancing at Gloss who had now begun to shake and sweat, an expression of abject terror on his face.

"Good PR," Sadi said, as he casually began to set up a video camera on a tripod. "We will get 10,000 new mujahideen recruits when we post this."

"It is God's will. Kneel!" Ochocinco said, jabbing the barrel of the Uzi into Gloss's back and forcing him to the floor.

Farouk, trembling, tied a blindfold around Gloss's eyes. "Farouk, tell my wife I love her. Send her a message that these were my final words, please."

"I will, my friend. That I promise you."

"Do it quickly. Let's get it over." Gloss said, mustering a sense of calm from the thought that his life had been productive and much longer than it reasonably should have been.

"We all die, monsieur Gloss," Sadi said. "In many ways you will be better off than most of the miserable wretches alive, especially in the Gaza."

"Thanks for putting things in perspective."

"No problem," he said, positioning himself behind the tripod fitted with a digital Nikon camera. "Now, ready to cue, counting three, two, one—Farouk, it's your show."

Farouk positioned himself behind Gloss, lifted the saber above his head and began to wail an eerie Arabic chant, inflecting his voice up and down, drawing out certain syllables and words. After a minute or two he began chucking his neck and head back and forth in the manner of a wading shorebird, emitting a guttural clicking sound, then snapping his body into the ruler-straight posture of a soldier at attention, holding the saber at his side. Then, in a British accent, he began to discourse: "When in disgrace with fortune and men's eyes, I all alone beweep my outcast state, and trouble deaf heaven with my bootless cries, And look upon myself and curse my fate, wishing me like to one more rich in hope …"

"What the …?" Sadi remarked, looking from behind the camera.

A glazed, demented expression came into Farouk's face as he paused from the poetry recital, and in the next instant a mischievous, 'aren't-I-hot' smile came into his face, his eyes leered out into the middle distance and he began to wiggle his tush. "Ba-da-ba-da-ba-dum, dut, dut, dut." Raising and twirling the saber above his head he sang "*They Told Him Don't You Ever Come Around Here, Don't Wanna See Your Face, You Better Disappear, The Fire's In Their Eyes And Their Words Are Really Clear, So Beat It, Just Beat Itttttt.*"

"Farouk! Come to your senses!" Sadi shouted.

Farouk stopped singing, Sadi's rebuke seeming to register; he once again turned stern and stone-faced. Then, by degrees, his eyes widened into saucers and his mouth puckered into a perfectly oval, coquettish 'O'. He raised the palm of his free hand to touch his cheek, bent over and angled his buttocks upward and outward, aping the famous pose of an actress holding down her dress over a sidewalk air vent. "*I'm a Barbie girl, in a Barbie world, life in plastic, it's fantas-tic.*" He sang in falsetto, gyrating his hips, spinning and waving the curved saber in circles above his head.

"Farouk! Stop him!" Sadi yelled at Ochocinco.

Ochocinco took a lunging step toward him and Farouk pirouetted gracefully bringing the blade down and across his body, slicing off Ochocinco's hand cleanly at the wrist.

Ochocinco dropped the Uzi and fell writhing to the floor in shrieks of pain. "Oops, I'm sorry," Farouk said. "This damn thing didn't come with a label. Who can I sue?"

Sadi sprinted out from behind the camera and charged at Farouk, who was standing with his back toward him. He was just about to tackle him when Farouk quickly spun, whipped the saber around and up, in a technically perfect tennis back-hand, lopping off Sadi's head. The knees of the person formerly known as Sadi wobbled, and the noggin-less body collapsed, the coconut of the fledgling filmmaker bouncing and rolling to a stop near the base of the camera tripod, eyes open and gazing upward.

"Cut!" Farouk spat with a director's disgust.

Farouk took the blindfold off Gloss and helped him to his feet.

"Goddamn, Farouk, if you'll pardon the expression. You da man."

"They got on my nerves anyway."

"I hear ya. You know where we can get a good steak in this town? I'm buying."

Ricky Santiago Mendez was sitting in his living room watching *Rush Hour 2* with his son when the makeshift transmitter, which he had been carrying in the pocket of his leather vest for two weeks, beeped. The hair on the back of Ricky's neck began to tingle. He sprang to his feet, dashed upstairs to his bedroom, grabbed the 9mm Beretta automatic pistol from the nightstand drawer, stuffed the gun in the holster under his leather vest, bolted outside, hopped on his Harley and sped in the direction of Gloss Industries. Ricky ran every red light and by the time he turned down the street leading to Andy's shop, two cop cars were on his tail. Ricky turned sharply into the drive and spun out his hog, coming to a stop in front of the door of the building. He jumped off his bike just as the two cop cars squealed into the drive behind him with sirens wailing.

Ricky ran up to the cops, who had jumped out of their cars with pistols in the using position. "Emergency, national security, no time to explain, follow me."

Ricky pulled out the Beretta, blasted the door lock, kicked open the door and chugged his 260-pound frame down the hallway, two policemen in his wake. An acrid, stinging odor invaded his nostrils when he reached Andy's office. He grabbed the transmitter from his pocket, hit a button and the panel in the floor slid open. A white plume of noxious fumes wafted out of the shaft, causing Ricky and the policemen to retreat in gags and coughs.

"Cyanide," Ricky yelled. "Stand back—this is Nazi-certified shit."

Ricky ripped off his vest, threw it to the floor, pulled his tee shirt over his head, put the shirt to his face and rode the lift down into the bunker. Coughing and waving his hand, Ricky staggered through the thick fumes calling Andy's name. He heard a noise like a thud or banging and made his way in that direction. He came to a door, opened it and found Andy and Marcia huddled on the floor. Andy, who was lying over Marcia, waved his hand feebly. Ricky yanked Andy to his feet, bent over and in one motion tossed Marcia over his shoulder. The bundle of people collectively coughed their way through the fumes, which had begun to disperse through the opening above. Ricky punched the transmitter through his pocket and the lift rose up the shaft and out of the bunker. Ricky led the group away from the bunker shaft and laid Marica on the floor just as medics rushed into the room.

"Another minute and we wouldn't have made it," Andy said after a couple of breaths through an oxygen mask.

Marcia sat up and wiped her eyes with a cloth. "The ... uranium ...centrifuges."

Andy jumped to his feet. "We've got get to the Tri-County Airport."

"How do you know they're going there?" A police officer asked.

"The driver of the van asked me directions when I was loading up the equipment."

About a half mile away, Calvin Clancey was sitting in a Land Rover embossed with the insignia of the Department of Defense staring anxiously at the readout on the vehicle's clock: 2:03. The scheduled delivery time for the tiny tumblers was 2 p.m. Clancey smashed the top of the dashboard with his fist. "Dumb fuck! What the hell part of this shit don't he get? I'm gonna kick his white ass from here to motherfuckin' Beijing. Let the motherfuckin' goon squads deal with his shit."

Clancey jumped at the sound of his cell phone, quickly snatching it from the driver's side seat. "Where in hell you been? I told you I got motherfuckin' ...."

"Calvin, hey, hey, hey pipe it down now, you hear? This is the President."

"Say what? Heh heh, sorry, boss. I thought you was that fuckface, I mean nitwit Dodge."

"You have to clean up your language, Calvin. You are a United States employee."

"Yes, sir. Ah, I… I… I been thinking about that myself."

"We'll talk about that later. Listen, we got a situation. Dick Gloss has been kidnapped in Paris. We think this means Terrorism Inc. is launching a mission to appropriate the new uranium enrichment technology."

"Say what?"

"Steal, Calvin—you know as in armed robbery."

"Damn."

"Need you to get over to Dodge's factory pronto. Think there might be trouble."

"Ah, boss, can't you call in the feds, I gotta a flight ..."

"Calvin, listen up. My administration has made it a point of denouncing tactics like water boarding and other forms of torture, but I will personally fly you to Camp X-Ray if you don't stop dithering and get your ass in gear this second, y'all understand?"

"Yes, sir."

"And one other thing—do not, under any circumstances, give the police details or report anything to the media. I'm sending someone to help you on that."

"Got it. Goddamn heat ain't coming anywhere near this shit."

"Calvin?"

"Sorry, boss—gosh darn heat."

A convoy comprising Andy and Marcia, two police cars and Ricky on his Harley, sped toward Tri-County Airport. Just as they were leaving the industrial park complex, Clancey's Land Rover turned in front of the convoy. Clancey spotted Andy, who waved and pointed for Clancey to follow. Clancey made a quick U-turn and steered behind the police car at the rear. Andy, driving Marcia's van, followed the police car in front of him as it wove around traffic, raced through intersections and topped out at 100-plus miles an hour. As they drove into the small municipal airport's first parking lot, Andy spied a white Econoline van on the tarmac parked next to a helicopter. Andy waved his hand out the window to slow the convoy. A woman with long dark hair walked around from the side of the van, slammed the rear doors and climbed into the pilot's seat of the helicopter. "That's her, Melinda Chow," he yelled out the window to the cop in front of him.

Andy followed the police car to a nearby gate in the tall chain link fence bordering the tarmac. The helicopter was sitting about 200 yards from the gate with an unimpeded view of the convoy on the other side of the fence. The rotors on the helicopter slowly kicked to life as the policeman struggled with the gate padlock. "Sir, I think I have the key here," Ricky said, taking out his Beretta and vaporizing the lock with a single round.

Andy ran ahead as Melinda Chow gave the rotors full throttle and the copter began to lift off. "They're going to get away," he shouted, as he sprinted across the tarmac. Ricky and the three policemen opened fire on the copter. Andy heard one shot ping off the steel rotor blades. The helicopter shot straight up into the air, spun its tail and accelerated away from the group across the open space above the airfield.

Andy jogged to a stop, panting, and put his hands on his

knees to catch his breath. It was over. He had let Melinda Chow toy and play with him like a puppet. He had betrayed the trust that Dick Gloss, his wife and his country had put in him. He was the world's biggest, bonafide jackass. As he stood and gazed across the tarmac, queasy at the thought of having to return and face his wife, Ricky and Clancey, he noticed something familiar on the tarmac. It was Torsten Zweiback's blue and white Cessna Skyhawk. Andy began to hypnotically walk toward the plane, broke into a trot, then sped up into a flat-out dash. The door of the cockpit was open. Andy put his hand on the engine cover—it was warm. Torsten was probably between lessons. He hopped in the cockpit, turned on the fuel pump, flipped up the master switch, turned the ignition switch and opened the throttle. The engine quickly sputtered to life. Seeing he had about half a load of fuel, he released the brake and taxied out to the runway. He checked the flaps while taxiing but didn't have time for a complete flight check, or to wait for clearance for takeoff. Sometimes you had to bend the rules.

He opened the throttle to full and accelerated the plane down the runway. He reached V1 in less than half the runway, and shortly after lifted and banked the plane hard to the east. "Bird away," he announced to the tower, with an apology to Torsten and a recommendation to chat with the police on the tarmac before declaring a Code Red.

Melinda Chow was flying the helicopter on a route that would take her over Lake St. Clair into Canada. Her destination was a soybean farm field 20 miles from the nearest town. At the farm, owned by a cousin of the Mullah Baba Chaka Kahn, Hank, she was to rendezvous with a contact. The contact would transport the equipment to a regional airport and load it on a Lear jet modified to hold enough fuel to make a trans-Atlantic crossing. Melinda would proceed by separate transportation to a different private airport where her boyfriend was flying in from Miami to pick her up.

As she flew she patched into Eastman Finch's phone through the headset.

"Everything's on schedule," she informed Finch.

"My sweet little Natasha. You are the right person for the

right job. I'm glad you stuck it out."

"It was tough, but in the end I decided the world would be a better place with four million more dollars in my bank account."

"You'll teach the world to sing, I'm sure. Whack Dodge?"

"Affirmative."

"I'm starting the grieving process right now with a snifter of Martell XO."

"Save me…"

Melinda suddenly lost her connection to Finch. She looked over at her co-pilot, who shrugged.

"Chopper two zero four come back on your bearing," they heard through their headsets.

Melinda killed the speaker and glanced with alarm at her co-pilot. "Who the hell is that?" Melinda and co-pilot began to scan the airspace. A few seconds later the man nudged her and pointed below and slightly to the southwest of their helicopter. A blue and white, single-engine airplane was crowding into their air space.

"That's weird," Melinda said. "Probably some dumb fuck rookie. They let anyone fly these days."

The plane began to gain altitude. "It's coming up," the co-pilot said.

"What the fuck is this guy doing?"

After a few minutes the plane was level with the helicopter.

"He's getting way too close," Melinda said, gazing out the window nearest her co-pilot. The airplane's pilot was in clear view now, and as he pulled alongside them, shook his head in surprise, then smiled and waved. He had a boyish face and a mop of brown hair. Melinda blinked, and blinked again.

"Holy shit!" Melinda yelped. "It's Dodge."

They were beginning to fly out over the blue-green expanse of Lake St. Clair. Andy dropped the plane down below the helicopter and bounced it back up on the pilot side of the chopper. Andy chuckled in anticipation that it would now be he who toyed with her. He gazed at Melinda, her mouth gaping in stupefaction, then, leaning back in the pilot's seat, put his hands behind his head as if relaxing on his deck, the yoke nestled between his legs. Just then, Melinda veered the chopper in front of the airplane's nose, almost clipping off the propeller with the chopper's landing skid.

Andy lunged at the yoke, dropping the nose, then throttled up. "Okay, game on Chow."

They were going farther over the lake. Andy quickly caught up with the chopper and realized he really had no plan, and no idea what he was doing. He could follow her to wherever she was going, but what did it matter. She could land any place and he couldn't. Gas, or lack thereof, would soon become a factor. Once she landed, she could call her contact and spirit away the equipment, likely well before the cavalry could arrive to save the day. Then it hit him: He had to prevent her from landing, and he had to keep her close to shore—the American side.

Andy positioned the plane to the left, in front of the chopper and began to inch it closer, hoping to push her off her bearing. Melinda Chow, who was born with a hair-trigger hostility toward anyone trying to make her comply, steered the chopper south a few degrees to avoid colliding with plane, fuming and cursing as she did. Then, grasping the meaning of his tactic, she quickly jerked the helicopter up, over and around Andy, and resumed her course nearly directly east.

Andy sped the Cessna up to outflank her and attempted the same maneuver, drifting into her path, forcing her south and west toward the shore of the lake. Melinda Chow again whipped the craft up and over his plane, this time nearly shearing off the plane's tail fin.

"Shit, shit, shit." This was not going to work. He was getting close to the point of no return, traveling farther over the lake toward Canada. He had enough gas for about a half hour more of flying. He had to do something out of the ordinary. Hell no, he had to do something fucking insane.

It was a calculated risk: The probability of obliteration was high to approaching certainty. Yet, if he doubted everything, he could not doubt this: Melinda Chow, as ruthless and cunning as she was, wanted to live as much as he did. Short of an air-to-air, heat-seeking missile, nothing was going to deter her from her plan. But a game of double dare, if executed properly (and a big if it was) might not give her a choice.

Andy gave his plane full throttle and ascended in a tight arc a few thousand feet in front of her. He dipped the yoke, banking the plane in a direct line with the helicopter. He streaked at a slight downward angle toward the helicopter. At a quarter mile of separation, the helicopter pitched left, then right, uncertain which way to turn. At the last fraction of an instant, Andy lifted vertically, the belly of the plane clearing the side of the copter and the rotors by no more than half a dozen feet. The force of the concussion made the helicopter wobble violently.

"One point, Dodge," he noted, taking the plane up again steeply.

He banked the plane, staying above her by 500 feet, and opened the throttle, speeding ahead of the chopper. In less than 30 seconds, a half mile ahead of her, he swooped down again, this time approaching from the south and east at an angle of about 25 degrees to her. He bore down, surprised at how fast he was closing on the bird, which seemed to be suspended motionless in the sky. An instant before he was going to swerve his plane over her, Melinda lifted the tail of the copter up and free fell a couple of hundred feet. His plane swooshed through the vacuum which a millisecond before was occupied by a very identifiable flying object.

"At least she knows I mean business," he said, turning and accelerating ahead again. She was keeping enough of her composure to stay in control of the chopper, and worse, was still flying toward the Canadian shore. He had to force her hand. The time had come … He had to go extreme, loco, x-rated. What the hell, Andy thought, his whole life everyone had written him off as a knucklehead, party-boy, or, in the lexicon of Dick Gloss, pond scum. He too had adopted a persona of someone who happily let the world slip by and off him for the sanctity of being left alone, not realizing this was interpreted by the world to be a person who perpetually failed to live up to a standard he seemed incapable of grasping. He had never felt sorry for himself. He was who he was, damn the beef tornados. But who he was, wasn't how the world had come to tag him. Society, even the people you knew best—they fabricated a story. Why? Not because they were petty or mean, but because the facts were too unknowable and complex. And they didn't care anyway. The problem was, if you let it, you started to become that story. Screw it. He knew who he was, and he was better than bimbo material. And he sure in the hell was not a coward. Between the sale of the company and his life insurance, Marcia and the kids would not be unduly burdened financially. And for saving the world from nuclear blackmail, God might let him into heaven. He only hoped it had shallow bunkers, flat greens and wide, waterless fairways.

Feeling butterflies the size of pelicans, he checked his altitude —2,500 ft.—and banked the plane in a sweeping arc, leveling off and racing in a direct line toward the chopper, the size of a thumbtack hovering a mile in front of him. There was no turning back now. There was time for one last melancholic reflection about the transience of life: Damn he was going to miss these surly bonds. Not bad, not bad, he thought, taking aim at the helicopter as if gazing through a rifle scope, pointing his plane straight at the cockpit's pod. As he neared it, the helicopter took on the appearance of a giant, hideous gnat. He was going to kill that gnat. Hurtling forward at full throttle, the distance between him and the gnat diminished at an accelerating rate of fractions of fractions: half mile, quarter mile, 300 yards, 100 yards. At 50 yards, less a nanosecond before impact, Melinda Chow wrenched the helicopter violently upward. The aircraft made a gymnast-style twist and turn, flipping nose over tail, righted itself momentarily, then dovetailed in a spiral and started to flail, tail spinning around the axis of the cockpit like a whirlybird, down, down. Sensing the g-force of the plane and affirming he was still very much bound by surliness, Andy opened his eyes, his heart thumping against his sternum, and saw the chopper plunging toward the lake. Its flight direction reversed, it was falling south and west, toward the American shore. For a moment, the chopper's tail stopped spinning, and the craft veered first to the left, then the right. Melinda Chow was struggling to regain control. The helicopter continued to fall, rotors tilted nearly vertical one moment, then swaying back through the horizontal and coming up vertical again. At less than 1000 feet of altitude,

Melinda Chow put the nose down and appeared to accelerate. Her only chance, it seemed, to apply thrust in the direction of the lake. Tail whipping like an angry cat's, the chopper dove toward the water. At less than a hundred yards from surface, the helicopter seemed to buffet upward, like a bird catching a thermal. Less than 20 feet above the lake, she pointed the nose forward, gave the beast every bit of juice it had, and leveled off, skimming the craft mere feet over the choppy, turquoise water.

Andy was a quarter mile behind her when she brought the chopper out of the dive. He swooped the plane downward like a falcon on the tail of a titmouse. This was his only chance. He recalled Torsten comparing a helicopter to an unstable platform. It had taken her nearly all of two thousand feet to come out of a tailspin set off by an inadvertent roll. Now that she was much lower in altitude, all he had to do was direct a command repeat performance.

Melinda Chow appeared to be tentatively gaining her bearings. She was flying parallel to shore and was still only 20 to 30 feet above the water. Andy had closed stealthily behind the chopper to within 50 feet. He knew he had to make his move fast. Within seconds she could be taking the bird up and over the water again. He throttled the plane ahead and flew under the helicopter, aligning the aircraft's fuselage with the underbelly of the chopper. Before she could detect him, he lifted the plane, catching the copter's landing skid on the upper fuselage and wings. The chopper's skid clanged and rattled loudly against the fuselage above his head, the G-force of the lift acting like aeronautical glue, sticking the chopper to the top of plane. He now had to do something he had only watched Torsten execute. Closing his eyes, he jerked the yoke and rolled the plane. As the plane rolled on to its back, the rotors of the helicopter sucked the chopper downward. Andy completed the roll, leveled and turned back to look in time to see the helicopter drop straight into the drink with a glorious splash of white—the color of concussions and the hereafter. It was the most beautiful thing he had ever seen, the sweetest moment of his short life.

"Yes, yes, yes," Andy pumped his fist and banked the plane in a long arc over the glistening water. He radioed in the coordinates of the downed chopper. He had maybe three minutes of gas, barely enough to get him back to the airfield. He made one final pass over the helicopter, which was floating on its side in the water, turbid from the spring runoff. The air trapped in the cockpit capsule was keeping it afloat. Melinda Chow and her partner had climbed out and were hanging on to the tail section partly immersed in the lake. As he flew low over the water, Andy waved his wings, the pilots' universal gesture of peace and love. Melinda Chow, soaked and disheveled, raised her hand in the universal gesture denoting the opposite.

Minutes after the chopper crashed, a phalanx of police cars, fire trucks, ambulances and salvage vehicles arrived on the scene. Ricky Hernandez drove up on his Harley a few minutes later, followed by Calvin Clancey in his Land Rover. Clancey burst out of the vehicle waving his hands.

"Y'all stand back, hear? This is a government job. Move yo' asses out."

One of the police officers standing on the shore directing the rescue of Chow and retrieval of the chopper, ran up to him.

"Who in the hell are you?"

"Department of Defense."

"Got any I.D.?"

Clancey began patting his jacket and pants. He did not like carrying a wallet. "I got one it's just …"

"Yeah, and I'm the Lone Ranger," the officer turned away.

"Wait, wait, wait," Clancey said, grabbing the policeman by the sleeve. "I got someone y'all need to talk to." He took out his cell, hit a speed dial number and handed the phone to policeman.

Shortly after the president of the United States chatted with the officer, clarifying the situation, and inviting him and the entire precinct to the White House for an upcoming cribbage and gumbo cook-off night, three black limousines drove hastily up to the scene. A crew of men wearing suits and earpieces swarmed out of the cars pushing back police, emergency personnel and onlookers. "Everyone clear out," one of the men shouted, flashing a government badge.

The only outside people allowed to remain at the site were divers and a crane crew working to pluck the copter from the lake.

Two plainclothes men led a sodden, hand-cuffed Melinda Chow up the bank of the shore. An Asian female approximately the same age and height of Melinda Chow emerged from one of the limos as a helicopter descended on a grassy knoll near the shore. "We already have the flight plan from the chopper's GPS," one of the suits told her as the fresh helicopter landed. "Your job is to get to the next appointed rendezvous. The big guns will take over from there."

The men escorted Melinda Chow to one of the limos. "You the chick try stealing' that shit?" Clancey said as she walked by.

"Fuck off," Chow scowled.

"You one bad-ass bitch. But my man Dodge badder."

"Tell that clown he missed the best lay of his life."

Clancey scoffed. "I think that dirt ain't going nowhere. Besides, it is my understanding Mr. Dodge is a happily married man."

16 A GOOD DAY TO LIVE

Nearly a day after these events, early Sunday evening, Pakistani time, a dozen bearded, robed men piled into a couple of white Toyota Land Cruisers to begin an hour drive to a locale newly christened by the Mullah Baba Chaka Kahn, X-Ray International Airport. There was a festive spirit in the air. Earlier in the day The Great Leader had called a meeting to report he had received confirmation that operation Cotton Candy was a success and that the bomb-making equipment was in transit. After the riotous cheering had subsided, the world-renowned atomic physicist and national hero, Dr. Kubla Kahn, rose to speak. He told the men that 100,000 kilos of raw uranium ore had been shipped from Kyrgyzstan and that with the arrival of the titanium-niobium centrifuges, uranium enrichment operations could begin as early as next week. The men poured into the streets of the village after the meeting holding AK-47s and Uzis over their heads. A group, which included A.J., Malak and Zubair, convened at the village square where tents and games were erected for the celebration. One of the games, a George Bush "duck shooting" arcade, was in operation and a horde of boys and young men jostled one another for the chance of blasting the targets with an air gun. The targets, saucer-sized steel-plates painted with the head of a grinning George Bush, moved along on three tracks—slow, fast and faster. One youngster shooting was being mocked for missing all but the slowest of the targets. "You do like this," said Zubair, unstrapping his AK-47 from his shoulder and opening fire. The crowd gathered in the small tent hit the ground as Zubair mowed down the entire top row of Bush ducks.

"There. What's the prize?"

The joviality in the caravan was contagious. A.J. nudged Malak and handed him a pint of Ron Rico rum. Malak quickly took a hit and passed it to Zubair.

"Psst," A.J. whispered. "I mixed some INXS into the party tape."

"No Coltrane?" said Malak. "You suck."

They parked the trucks at the end of the runway, which workers had cleared of camouflage the night before. The Great Leader, standing on the hatch door of the truck, took a call on a satellite phone, raising his hand for attention. "The plane with the gift from God is approaching. Before we walk out to receive the gift, we should all give a round of applause to A.J. and his crew for building the airstrip on time. Allah Akbar."

The group of men sauntered a few hundred yards down the runway, shielding their eyes from the sun setting between craggy mountain crests. A faint speck of light began to glimmer on the horizon, flashing bursts of silver and orange. The flickering speck gradually became a steady white dot, growing in size and intensity until it took on the familiar shape of an airplane. The Great Leader smiled as he recognized the sleek private jet of his cousin, Sheik Afaz Abdul Faisal. The jet swooped down out of the sky, leaving a brown-black contrail of exhaust against the silvery sky. The nose of the jet raised slightly as it touched the ground, sending up a billow of dust as the wheels hit the freshly graded dirt strip. The jet safely on the ground, the men clapped and cheered. The jet coasted down the airstrip, slowed, and taxied toward the group. Murmurs of excitement spread among the men as the aircraft steadily moved toward them, the high-decibel whine of the engines piercing the air. The jet at last stopped and cut its engines. The men moved forward in unison, all eyes on the door at the front of the cabin. After a minute that seemed like an hour, the door rose upward and outward. As it reached the top, a man in a suit emerged in the doorway. The group of men emitted a loud, collective gasp and stood frozen to the ground in utter, traumatized stupefaction.

"Whatsa' matter, felllas, cat got your tongue?" said the man with the face they had last seen in the duck-shoot arcade. "Special envoy, George W. Bush, at your service."

A.J. began to blabber incoherently, Malak's teeth started to chatter, and a puddle formed in the scrabble beneath Zubair's robe.

Inch by inch the group sidled away from the jet, then turned and ran frantically with shrieks of terror toward their trucks. At that moment, a droning sound materialized into a thunderous vibration and an enormous C-130 transport plane glided around the side of the nearest peak, flying in a direction opposite to the running men. The men skidded to a halt as the gigantic, harrowing air machine swooped down toward them, not more than 50 feet above the ground. As they gazed up in dread, the belly of the plane opened, and a wide net of meshed hemp rope dropped down, suspended from the plane by long cables, dragging the ground as the plane hurtled forward. The men attempted to spread out but the plane overtook them in a flash, the netting tripping up their legs and scooping up the entire troop, arms, legs and turbans protruding through the mesh as it lofted them upward, like a big load of King Crab, into the hold of the plane. As the C-130 flew overhead George W. Bush saluted. "Sorry you couldn't stay longer. I was looking forward to trying some fa-lay-fil."

Eastman Finch was beside himself over the disappearance of his fledgling aide-de-camp, Stephen Congreve. His last recollection, a hazy one, was throwing an arm around his shoulder on the balcony of the condo and attempting to cajole out of him, with crescendos of bawdy cross-examination, Cam Delacroix as wing man, the tale of the best fuck of his life. He couldn't remember if tawdry paydirt was hit; waking groggily the next day he sloughed off his absence until, evening and unreturned calls spelling out, it couldn't be denied: the kid had split. "What the fuck," he said to Beatrice as they drove to the Woolcott Estate in the Hamptons on the day of the closing. "I pick the little shit up from dog-walking detail, take him under my wing, and he stiffs me like I'm hawking caramel corn on Rockaway Beach."

Outwardly, Finch was in his usual swaggering, unflappable mood, a grin of mild, perpetual amusement etched on his face. Inwardly he was slightly agitated. Something wasn't right. In the 24 hours since the heist, he had not heard from Melinda Chow, even though Graham in London had assured him all the transfer checkpoints in the plan had been confirmed and the equipment success-fully delivered to the client. He suspected Melinda was just lying low for a few days as a professional precaution. Another worry doll, slight but puzzling, was absence of second-hand discovery and news, he supposed would be delivered by his wife, of a dead Dodge. Granted, Marcia, as she had been trying to rid him from her life for the past two months, might be so preoccupied with celebrating, she might forget to inform her sister of the "tragedy." Joking aside, Finch ra-tionalized, the divorce proceedings had minimized contact between them; so it would not be inconceivable that no one would notice the absence of the vagabond for a few days. Ratcheting his anxiety up another notch, Graham had missed his promised call to him today, a call in which he was to provide details of the transfer of the final $20 million he was owed. He had unsuccessfully tried to reach him several times earlier this morning, and now Finch was beginning to wonder if he had botched the set-up of the deal. Perhaps he should have had the equipment detained for a period at a sort of waystation until his final payment was secured. He wasn't writing off the final installment of his invoice yet, not by any means. He'd fly to London and track this Graham guy down if he had to. But there were some teaching moments here. It was his first time putting together a type of deal like this. If he took the high hard one, all in all, $20 million wasn't a bad paycheck for what amounted to data usage on his cell phone.

The real estate agent, Chelsea, a stunningly blonde and tanned woman, greeted them at the side entrance to the main house and ushered them into their spacious, gleaming, 1000-square-foot open-concept kitchen. A domestic staff consisting of a house maid, cook and groundskeeper outfitted in crisp uniforms stood at smiling attention as the pair strolled through the door.

"This is Juanita, this is Philippe, and this is Oscar," Chelsea intoned cloyingly, as if introducing a group of third-grade children. After an exchange of pleasantries, Finch quizzed Philippe, the cook, on his plans for stocking the wine cellar. Philippe told Finch his cooking was best complemented by full-bodied Bordeaux wines, es-pecially from the regions of Medoc, Pomerol and Sauternes. He also had a fondness for certain vintages of Oregon Pinot Noir, as well as chardonnays and a few aromatic wines, such as Riesling, from New Zealand.

"You see, babe," Finch said, giving Beatrice a playful squeeze on the shoulder. "You spend $30 million on the house, you save $10 million on bar and restaurant tabs."

Everyone, with Chelsea leading the way, laughed extravagantly, as Finch, with an urge to explore his castle, strolled nonchalantly, hands in the pockets of his trousers, through the voluminous, sunken, Brazilian cherry-floored entertainment area adjacent to the kitchen, down a hallway with several different themed drawing rooms, past the mahogany-walled library and into the great room with its walkouts to a wrap-around redwood balcony, and finally down to a Leonard Aubrey-designed terrace and gardens fronting the ocean. Joy, giddiness—just thinking about those feelings made him squirm in embarrassment. He had purged those effete emotions from his system long, long ago. Now, surveying his domain, he instinctively summoned the one deportment and outlook that perfectly summed up the moment: A chuckle. A rolling, gratifying chuckle. A chuckle for everyone who had doubted him. A chuckle for everyone—Beatrice's father, Robert, came to mind—who patronized and secretly belittled him. A chuckle for all the less visionary, less enterprising, but nonetheless envious hypochondriacs of the world. A chuckle here, a chuckle there, a chuckle to the stratosphere.

He rubbed his hand over his eyes and face and shook his head, suppressing what was perilously approaching a sensation of unrestrained elation. He took a deep breath of the ocean-scented breeze; just then noticing a dull thudding in the distance. Helicopter. Looking west down the beach Finch noticed one, then two of the machines flying directly in line with the shore in his direction. Something he'd have to get used to. Probably the damn media and paparazzi. The helicopters approached, the air vibrating with the deafening 'thwack' of the blades through the air. As the choppers drew even with the Woolcott estate, they slowed, rotated toward the house, and floated in slowly, hovering about 100 yards above the beach. Damn, these assholes are aggressive, Finch thought. What the hell, he'd play along. Probably a spot on *Entertainment Today* or the prattle page of the *Daily.* Finch smiled caustically and gave a limp, bored wave, as if having his privacy invaded by reporters were a routine annoyance. The sooner he gave them what they wanted the sooner they'd leave.

"DO NOT MOVE!" Finch jumped at the sound of a bullhorn. "PUT YOUR HANDS ABOVE YOUR HEAD."

Finch slowly raised his hands noticing that two men in the open doors on each side of both helicopters had rifles trained directly on him. He then felt a sharp jab in the small of his back. It was Philippe.

"Monsieur Finch you are under arrest for aiding and abetting terrorist-related activities and threatening the national security of the United States," he said as he pulled Finch's arms behind his back for cuffing. "You have the right to remain silent ..."

As Philippe led a cuffed Finch to an FBI van, Beatrice sobbing by his side, Finch protested. "You have the wrong man. There's been a huge fucking mix-up."

"That will be for a court of law to decide, Monsieur."

"You ever hear of proof? You don't have it and won't get it. You don't know anything!" He shouted, his countenance, even under duress, still composed with an expression of mild amusement.

"Oh yes, I suppose we are all assholes. I do know, however, that they do not have a wine cellar at Attica."

At the evocation of the abject, vintage-less reality awaiting him, Finch shuddered, and for the first time in his physiognomy's corpuscular memory, the buffed color in his perpetually jocular visage faded to ash. His eyes bulged out like oval, glistening, freshly laid turtle eggs, and corkscrewing his upper torso into the air, he let out deep, bestial terrified bellow, jerked his arms wildly, broke free of Philippe and began running up the drive, bawling like a toddler with nappies full of ca-ca. Philippe fell backward awkwardly, twisting his ankle.

"Stop!" He yelled, struggling to get to his feet.

Finch ran frantically up the drive, then fearing he would be shot, plunged headlong into the thick hedges along the drive. He darted and ducked between the branches, diving instinctively to the ground at the loud pop of gunshot. He monkey-rolled to his feet and resumed running. Away, he had to get away. Sinewy limbs and vines clutched at his arms and whipped him across the face as he sprinted and lunged ahead. Suddenly he felt the ground go out beneath him and he fell forward, tumbling down a bank and into the cold water of Woolcott Creek. Finch bobbed to the surface; touching his feet to the bed of the creek, he began pushing himself with the direction of the current, seaward. In a second, he had regained his composure. There was no sound of helicopters. It was peaceful, the sun dappling golden patches of light through the overhanging branches. This was doable, he thought. He had his wallet and a water-proof cell phone in his trousers. The Hamptons were full of work crews. He'd make up a story and give some stiff a few hundred bucks to cut off his cuffs. Lie low for a while at Brianna's, change his identity. It was his next grand adventure. As he floated on his back he gazed up at the sky, wondering if he should pick up a white or red for dinner tonight.

About a week after the capture of the entire leadership of al Qaeda and ISIS, and the arrest of Eastman Finch and his counterpart in London, the U.S. government lifted the news blackout of the story and released information, selectively, to the news media. CSN was chosen to be the first to get the story and it broadcast a huge, prime-time, all-evening program featuring grainy film clips of the captured al Qaeda, live reports from the village in Pakistan used by the "insurgents" as a sanctuary, and multiple talking-head interviews with politicians and experts on terrorism around the world. All major broadcast and cable news networks followed suit, interrupting primetime programming with a stream of updates and special reports. As details were parceled out in deliberately sketchy measure, the reports focused almost entirely on the collaring of al Qaeda's "Great Leader," once presumed dead, as well as the Mullah Baba Chaka Kahn and other key members of the modern-day equivalent of the Nazi Death Squads or real-life Spectre. Especially riveting were the details of the spectacular sting and ruse operation, perfectly conceived and executed, used to bring the villains to justice, including the involvement of one poker-playing diplomatic envoy, George W. Bush. Commentators and reporters grilled White House officials repeatedly, wanting to know how the Department of Defense and National Security Agency had not only pinpointed the whereabouts of al Qaeda's senior leadership, but tricked them, were answered with stock twaddle, "key information came to light," and "this is something we had been piecing together for some time," and "there was a crucial element of timing on this thing that allowed us to be successful." This dissimulation was done in part to mislead and allay public fear should it become apparent how close Terrorism Inc. really was to acquiring the technology to make a nuclear bomb, but also to insinuate as much credit for the operation and aggrandize public esteem, and favorable poll numbers, for the White House and president.

The White House, in fact, had no intention of telling the whole story but its hand was forced by a teen with a YouTube identity of Joey Z. Using his cell phone, Joey had filmed the grand finale of Andy's pursuit of Melinda Chow, catching the plane as it flipped the chopper into the lake, as well as portions of the events afterward, including the arrival of the police, Calvin Clancey's fulminations, and the police sergeant's conversation with the president, in which he can be heard saying several times, "Yes, sir, Mister President, national security cannot be compromised." Joey, who had no clue or interest in the story behind the video he had filmed (he had told his friend, "Dude, this reminds me of one of the level-three chase games on my Q-box.") posted it the next day. In less than two days the video had a million hits; a week later it had reached 10 million, putting it on a par with the clip of the girl who had made her prom dress out of gum wrappers. In an interview with a local television station, Joey confessed to being "blown away" by the video going viral. He received an offer to act as a consultant for a movie about the making of the video, another offer to appear in a new reality television series about people who post the most popular YouTube videos, and still another offer from a local dive to flog its deep-fried pizza on Yahoo. He was going to blow off a request for an interview from a newspaper reporter, not really knowing what a newspaper was, but his agent told him to keep it. "It's still early days—you're two, maybe three weeks from the gold standard marketing platform—a person who's famous for being famous."

With the media drawing even more attention to a viral video that clearly showed a ranting Department of Defense employee and a police officer in conversation with the president (and with a considerable bump in approval ratings already in the bag), the White House concluded it was only a matter of time before the whole story came out and decided to go public.

Andy was sitting in his office with Mac and Luann discussing the recurrence of the perennial electrical problem that caused the heaters on half the plant's plating tanks to shut down when Penny came running into the room.

"Andy, … Mr. Dodge, it's … Lincoln … Copper, from CSN … on the phone. He … wants … to interview … you. Oh my God … He's such a hunk."

Later that day Andy drove to a Detroit television studio assigned to feed the interview to CSN. A woman applied makeup to his face, and he was escorted to a closet-sized room and directed to sit on a stool in front of a camera. They gave him an earpiece and Andy could hear Copper talking on his show. "After this break, we'll come back with the extraordinary story of a real-life action hero who saved the world from a possible nuclear Armageddon and made the capture of terrorist leaders possible. Don't go away."

Copper came on the earpiece. "Andy?"

"It is he."

"This is an amazing story. Just be yourself, you'll do fine."

"I've got ice water in my veins, except when I'm putting."

"We've got 30 million viewers for this."

"Just me, the camera and a closet on my end."

"You've got the right attitude. On in 30."

The camera went live and the first image of a smiling, 39-year old man with a bowl of brown, boyish hair flashed around the world. Andy's face was shown on split screen with the video of Andy's plane in pursuit of Melinda Chow's helicopter, while Copper set it up.

"Here you are, chasing the person who has stolen the uranium enrichment equipment … "

"And tried to kill me and my wife." Andy interjected.

"Oh yeah, there's that part of the story, too … The danger you're in at this point, what were you thinking?"

"That's a situation where you don't have much time to think. That's when I'm at my best."

"Okay, here you are catching up to the helicopter. Now folks, what you are about to see is one of the most amazing feats I've ever witnessed, something right out of a movie—watch as he comes up under the helicopter, catches it underneath, then ROLLS THE PLANE! What were you thinking?"

"I know, it was crazy."

"All this would be almost beyond belief even if you had been flying for years, but I understand you do not even have a pilot's license yet, is that right?"

Andy chuckled. "I'm going to take the 5th on that one."

"Given your inexperience as a pilot and the difficulty of pulling off an aerial maneuver like that, what were you thinking?"

Andy shrugged. "I had let down my wife, my family and my country. It was time to put up or shut up."

When Andy drove into the parking lot of his shop the next morning, three television crews were waiting. Andy obliged everyone with an interview and strolled into the office where he was greeted by hoops, hollers and huzzahs. Red, white and blue balloons adorned the front reception desk and a banner reading "Andy Rambo Dodge," was taped to the wall. The group broke into a chant: "You are the man! You are the man!" Luann, in tears, threw her arms around him and Duberg and Ja-Coby exchanged double-pump, forearm hugs.

"Boss," Penny ran up. "We're swamped with requests. "There's ABC, NBC, C-Span, Coneman, Flacon. You're famous!"

"Now hold on a minute," Andy said, raising his hand for quiet. "This is really cool of you to do this. I haven't had this much fun since we upset Saginaw Northwestern and the cheerleaders got to ride home with us on the bus. But we also have a job to do. Penny, I'm not taking any more interviews today until we figure out how to get the heat on in tanks 3, 4, 7 and 8. I also have a meeting with OSHA inspector Tilsdale about installing fume-control equipment, so he doesn't shut us down … We'll celebrate after work, mojitos on me."

Andy walked down the hall to his office and closed the door, relieved to be alone in this sanctuary of work. His March Madness bracket had blown up weeks ago. Back to earth.

"Your wife on line two," Penny said through the intercom.

"Hey, sweetie," Andy said, picking up the call.

"Saw your interview from the parking lot on the morning show," Marcia said. "You're a natural."

It had been a period of intense, often heated discussion, contrition and make-up between the couple, and Andy didn't emerge from the doghouse immediately. Having survived, together, an attempt on their lives had made the slights and irritations of the past seem trivial in comparison and awakened their bond. Marcia assured Andy she had no plan to secretly poison him—the books were research for a speaker at the Women's Tri-County Business Association —however she was still sufficiently pissed about her husband's fling or attempted fling with Melinda Chow, and Andy's many attempts at explaining that night never did completely wash. Ultimately Marcia, certainly aware of what the power of feminine wile and beauty (even she had to admit Melinda Chow was stunningly gorgeous) could do to a man, convinced herself that her husband had been gullible enough and stupid enough to succumb to the calculated flirtations of a much younger woman out to manipulate and destroy him. That, together with Melinda Chow's bunker-side testimony and credible evidence that Andy had been totally shit-faced, making any physical consummation of the evening impossible, even if she or he had wanted, which he forcefully and semi-convincingly disavowed, gradually softened her. There was also one other factor in her equation of forgiveness. Andy had, quite simply, been magnificent. She had watched the video many times and it was beyond her ability to comprehend. Where, how … who in the hell was this man she had been living with for 14 years? This was … a miracle? A work of art? She was a trained human resource professional. The existential essence of her job was an ability to assess the strengths and weaknesses of people. Most people believed they were more talented and harder working than they were in reality. It was human nature. Others, such as her husband, were modest, unassuming, and did not pretend, or barter to be, anything more than they were, warts and all. Had she come down heavier on the warts, at times, than she reasonably should have? Watching the video, coming to terms with what her husband had done, she was now prepared to admit that perhaps she had. For it was now obvious that whatever shortcomings Andrew had, and he did have a few, below the surface was a motherlode of an almost super-natural life force which, when harnessed, was capable of anything. Now, here he was giving live television interviews before tens of mil-lions of viewers like a pro. Who knew? Who knew jack shit about any-one? Inside that placidly friendly persona of her husband, the white-hot caldera of a volcano steamed, ready to erupt and gush, scorching anyone or thing that got in its way. It was all very dizzying to her and left her, quite frankly, completely turned on.

Andy had been allowed to return to his house and family that same night. All outstanding issues were put on hold as mother, father and children were simply relieved to be alive and reunited. The next day, Sunday, Andy, as planned, cooked his turkey, although thankfully not in a kitchen located below the one used by his endear-ing fellow tenant, Eddie of the thundering hoofs. He served it with mashed potatoes, dressing and the renowned green bean casserole, the surface delicately crusted with the dish's signature ingredient, canned French-fried onion rings. The theme of the dinner had also been changed from "Thanksgiving in April nee March" to "Turkey: A Gift from Me to Thee." Andy, who had lost nearly ten pounds in two months, ate heartily, and afterward hit fly balls to Dylan in the park until dark, blissfully content with hearing the thud of the bat against the ball and watching his son run frantically, catch some, miss some, but try his damned hardest.

"Andrew, I have something to tell you." Marcia said as Andy sat rocking in his office chair. "I think Beatrice is coming to live with us for a while."

"Ouch."

"She's a wreck and it looks like she may lose everything."

"I know how she feels."

"Mother is going to watch her kids at the house in Connecticut until school ends."

"So, their house on Long Island …"

"Up for sale. Eastman put all their available cash into the down payment so there's nothing to pay the outstanding mortgage."

"Any word on wench, I mean Finch?"

"Nothing. Beatrice seems to believe he's been taken in by a shaman who is leading him through a spiritual cleansing."

"That's what I call lifetime spiritual employment. What's she doing for cash?"

"She's selling her effects. The first thing to go is the Bentley Eastman bought to replace the one that blew up."

"I hear that is a car with great curb appeal."

"I also hear it's a blast to drive."

"I don't know what you are talking about, dear."

"Dick Gloss and guest are in the lobby."

"Shoot, I forgot about him. Gotta run, babe."

"And?"

"Love you, sweetie."

"Love you, too."

Gloss, like Andy, had lost weight during the past three months. "The bad cholesterol is down; the good cholesterol is up and triglycerides are about the same. I'm feeling pretty good."

Andy nodded and smiled at the requisite state-of-Gloss blood-work moment, assuming his acid reflux, hypoglycemia and restless leg syndrome were status quo. Since returning from his travels, Gloss had contacted him once, congratulating him on foiling the plot and giving him few details about his disappearance in Paris: "I didn't get punched out in an alley for making Frenchy-phobe comments, I'll tell you that much." Other than reporting he was released safely, the media had been derailed from digging into Gloss, first, by the Bush fly-in bust, and now by the revelation of Andy's role in it. The media had yet to connect the dots between Gloss and Andy, and that was fine by Gloss who was refusing to be de-briefed by reporters or the government, the latter for fear that they would leak it. "I put the media a notch below al Qaeda and ISIS," he told his wife. "We caught the bastards. That's the main thing."

"Andy, I'd like to you to meet Farouk," Gloss said, waving at the diminutive man seated to his right.

"It is huge honor to meet you," Farouk said extending his hand. "You have done great deed and in America's much-admired system of reward based on merit you will be justly compensated."

Andy chuckled. "Harassed."

"Farouk here saved my life. Enough said, except to say that Farouk could have a promising career at any Japanese steakhouse chain of his choosing. But he also has a good business idea and I've decided to invest in it. In fact, Farouk is going to be your neighbor. We've purchased the old Eisner building across the street, which for some reason was going cheap."

Gloss had taken Farouk with him to the American Embassy in Paris, where the Ambassador had told him it would be months, if not years, before Farouk could be granted a visa to enter the United States. Fortunately, Farouk had been a peon in the Parisian cell he had joined, as he chronicled, for the fringe benefits, and passed the background check with flying colors. He even had a commendation from a reputable mechanical engineering professor at the Sorbonne. Gloss fast-tracked the visa process with an implied exposure of the U.S. government's incompetence in the affair, and three days later Farouk was on the same trans-Atlantic flight as Gloss and his wife.

"You knew, didn't you?" Andy asked Gloss

Gloss squirmed in his chair uncomfortably. "Look, whenever you're involved in making sensitive technology for the U.S. ..."

"You knew."

"It wasn't supposed to play out this way," Gloss protested.

"Play out? Play out my ass. You nearly got my wife and me killed—dumb fuck."

Gloss gazed ashamedly at the floor. It was the first time Andy had ever seen Gloss humbled, yet instead of the anticipated sense of satisfaction, Andy felt a twinge of sympathy.

"Dick, has it ever occurred to you that there are other points of view, other ways of doing things?"

"Sure, all the other ways that don't work."

"And what about this place 'running itself,' as you once so charmingly sold it?"

"What, you got problems?"

Luann tapped at the open door and took two sideways steps into the office. "Slap it on the calendar—Mac got the heat on, boss. Guess those classes you sent him to are working."

"Mac's in charge of electrical maintenance?"

"It's called employee empowerment, Dick."

"Hey, if you want to roll the dice, be my guest."

"Then there's cash flow. Even with the bump in orders for the tiny tumblers, I'm barely breaking even."

"Yeah, I thought about that one after the fact," Gloss said, rubbing his hand over his chin. "Forgot to figure that my take of the royalty would cut into your profit margin."

"No shit."

"But I'm going to correct that. I'm transferring my rights on the patent to you and the company."

"Oh, for Christ's sake no, I don't need charity, Dick. Once I get my customers back from Crossbow ..."

"You can't stop me, it's in the contract. Besides, I need to be free and clear of Gloss Industries to avoid any conflict of interest when I begin helping Farouk in his new venture."

Andy pushed back in his swivel, swung his feet up on his desk and fixed his eyes on Gloss, sitting in the chair he had sat in so many times in the past. As they stared into one another's eyes an unspoken realization of the poignancy of the moment came to them. Andy raised his eyebrows and cocked his head to the side, as if conveying tacit recognition of this feeling to Gloss, and a sidelong, soupçon of a smile came slowly into Gloss's face.

"Remember what I said to you a long time ago," Gloss said, raising his hand. "Don't worry, I'm not going to go loopy. But if you *were* my son, Mr. Nickel, I'd ... be ...proud."

Interview and appearance requests streamed in, forcing Andy to hire a part-time assistant to handle his personal affairs so Penny could do her job. Over the course of several weeks, Andy made guest appearances on Good Morning US, Katy, Kelly, Kimbo, Donty Q, and Flacon shows. Andy beat Flacon in a cooked-up version of whack-a-mole in which turbaned terrorist's heads popped out of the holes in place of the furry rodents; then, to howls of delight from the audience, Andy played air guitar on the mallet as the band segued to a commercial break. *Tempo* ran a feature article titled "The Man Who Saved the World," giving the public its first, in-depth details of the crisis as it unfolded and taking the reader "inside the cockpit" as Andy pursued Melinda Chow's helicopter. The article included a sidebar on the heroics of Ricky Santiago Mendez who, under orders from Gloss, had refused to be interviewed for the story. *Persons* devoted a sprawling, eight-page cover story to Andy and his family, with a montage featuring photos of Andy and Dylan shooting baskets, Andy's parents, Andy and his fraternity brother Vince, Andy and teammates celebrating his high school's Class B district championship, Archie, the family cat, and a shot of the outside of Gloss Industries inset with a photo of the plating bunker in which Andy and Marcia had nearly perished. The article also dished the juicy, heretofore unknown details of Andy and Marcia's marital troubles, climaxing with a three-column-wide, half-page picture of Andy and Marcia happily embracing with a caption quoting Marcia: "I'm as awestruck as everyone, only this hero is my husband—Andrew David Dodge." The spread elicited the magazine tens of thousands of effusive, deliciously weepy emails.

As Andy became a national "everyman" celebrity, the president convened a special meeting of his closest advisors. Mass awareness of Andy's death-defying heroics, coupled with his likeability, was creating the perception that the administration was unjustly usurping all the credit for the capture of terrorism Inc., putting at jeopardy his party's hold on power, which up till then had been an assumed cinch. The full palette of D.C.'s underhanded, ignoble ways and means were all on the table. As the meeting wore on and the options failed to sort themselves out, the president's chief-of-staff exhaled a deep sigh of frustration. "Hey, I know this is counter-intuitive but why not just do the right thing and award him the Medal of Honor."

Heralding it as a brilliant example of politically-savvy, inverse poll-psychology, the president ordered his press secretary to contact Dodge and arrange a news conference immediately to announce the rare conferring of the nation's highest citation. Two weeks later, on a bright, warm May afternoon, Andy and his family stood beside the president on a dais in the Rose Garden facing a throng of reporters and television correspondents from around the world. Also in attendance were Andy's parents, Don and Joanne, Martha and Robert Riker and his buddy Vince Delray and his wife.

"This is a story as American as baseball and auto company bailouts," the president said, taking the podium. "How this young man rose, not only to become the president of a thriving, innovative small business, but rose to the moment, risking his life when his country needed him most."

As cameras clicked, Andy and the president clasped the Medal of Honor between them and held a smiling pose.

"Sir, I don't mean to be ungrateful," Andy said under his breath. "But I still haven't received that check for the fume control equipment."

"Hmm, yes, I've been meaning to talk to you about that. My check-writing privileges have been revoked."

"Uh-oh."

"You don't need the money now, do you?"

"It's all about cash flow, sir."

"Tell you what I'll do; I'll get Tilsdale off your back if you install some of those vertical-axis windmills I told you about."

"Deal."

"And we need to play it up—photo ops, the whole nine yards. I need to get the Sierra Club off my backside."

"Yes, sir."

Work became his refuge; he most looked forward to his cup of coffee and chat with Mac in his office each morning. According to the new-age parlance of his wife it "centered" him, trendy term for what he likened to sitting on the tail of a pickup truck listening to ruminations on the best recipe for barbequed armadillo accompanied by a moonshine-infused critique of the latest issue of *Hoover Digest*.

"Looks like you and the prez tight, boss."

"Mac, the extent of the president's fondness for me is a two point rise in his approval ratings."

Mac doubled over with a convulsive hack, a spasm that frequently came over him when the impulse to laugh got derailed by a two-pack-a-day habit.

"Ain't that the damn way of the world tho'," Mac said after an excruciating minute.

"It's the way of Washington."

"Yeah well, what goes around, comes back to slap you on the arse. Seems France is out to sell some *Meestrals* to *Roosha.* Now the Meestral is a two football-field long *foo* battleship with am*feeb*ious landing support capability. Could tilt the balance of power in the *Ballkoons.*

"That's been causing my dermatitis to flare up."

"Throw in the *Yoookaraine* and Eeboola outbreak and I'm bettin'' the prez is shittin' bricks."

"Oh hell, Mac, he's crepuscular."

"What the heck's that mean?"

"Can't remember, but It's my word of the week. Figure I'll keep using it till someone calls me on it."

"Word of the week?"

"New hobby—reading and journaling. Trying to emulate you, Mac."

"Well, I don't write stuff down."

"With a brain like yours, Mac, you don't need to."

"Guess … When you gettin' the windmills?"

"Next week."

"aha har, har, har."

"What?"

"That's what I call a red herring if ever there was."

"Yep."

"Why people so damn *gallible.*"

"It's the spin principle, same as the windmill."

 "Calvin Clancey line one."

"I'm on my Goddamn motherfuckin' knees right now."

"So, I finally get some respect."

"What you talkin' 'bout. I always been givin' you love."

"Yeah, English dungeon style."

"Some people needs that shit."

"Everybody in cell block C."

"Ja, sheeeee … When y'all get cool?"

"Yesterday. When's the next pick up?"

"That's why I'm dicing on my *i*-cing. I ain't workin' for that hybrid bro' of a prez no mo'. I'm deep nixin' my day job. Got a three-record deal. Goin' on tour with Baby Bling Boo."

"Man, I've got every one of her records. Who's my contact?"

"Some dude, Ted or Henry or sumpin'. He'll call y'all and set up a tee time."

"I'll miss all our discussions on great books."

"I'll call when I'm in yo' hood. Set my man up with a backstage pass—just don' be hittin' on the sisters."

"I'll be on my best behavior."

"Cool."

"Well. It's … been …real, man."

"Ja rah, ditta-dit-ding, ditta-dit-dang, ditta-dit-dong, y'all."

"Yeah … ya … ba … daba … doo."

"Say what?"

Andy had one last meeting that day, an after-business-hours' tête-à-tète with a representative from a talent marketing agency who had been pestering him for weeks. Andy was going to blow him off, but Marcia had Googled the company, a firm in Los Angeles, and learned it represented many actors and celebrities, some of whom were known for something other than being known. "What's the harm, honey?" She told him. "If nothing else you'll get a good story out of it."

Andy greeted Cody Carlyle in the lobby and led him back to his office. Carlyle, tall, slender, fastidiously dressed, walked with an exceedingly upright, almost impossibly perfect, posture. His dark, gelled hair was pulled back into a short ponytail. He settled in the chair across from Andy, crossed his long legs and removed his tiny, oval-framed sunglasses.

"Let me lay my cards on the table, Mr. Dodge. The sky's the limit. You've got a platform the size of the San Andreas fault, with just as much seismic potential—TV shows, movies, book deals, the inspirational speaking circuit, your own line of clothing—'Dodge Aviator Wear: Dress like the man who brought the terrorists to justice,'" he said, printing a line of imaginary copy in the air with his cupped hand.

"I've always wanted to tango."

Carlyle smiled and smoothed the lapel of his dark olive blazer, appreciative that this new potential client 'got it' and desired, however eccentrically, to be a player.

"I'm sure we could get you an audition for *Dancing with the Divas*."

"There's one catch—my partner has to be my wife."

Carlyle snapped bolt upright in the chair. "Oh, my God, that is perfect! After that cover story in *Persons* you two are America's favorite couple."

"Okay, work on that."

Carlyle extracted his cell from the inner pocket of his blazer and tapped the screen with his finger. "You have any causes?"

"Windmills."

"Fantastic! Fits right into the *métier* of the day. We might be able to get you some endorsement deals with big polluters who want to curry favor with the government."

"I only represent myself."

Carlyle blinked and gazed open-mouthed at Andy for a second. "And that's okay … you have that everyman persona that is *soo* hot today."

The discussion began to go south when it became apparent that Carlyle intended to foist some sort of hard sell, reminding Andy that his life had "changed forever" and how he should be "acutely aware and *muy agradecido*" that he had "freed himself from a life of ordinary nine-to-five toil."

Andy leaned forward across his desk. "Cody— may I call you Cody? I know this may be difficult for you to comprehend, but I'm actually fond of my tedious little existence."

"Mr. Dodge, I didn't …"

"You know what I think is tedious, the idea that you have to be a celebrity to register as a non-insect form of life," Andy said, slapping his desk and eliciting a look of horror on the face of Carlyle. "That the only people with talent, brains, ambition and ideals in this country are the bimbos who have sucked or fucked their way into the movies or television … That anyone with a quote "ordinary" job is to be pitied, patronized or pissed on!"

"Sir, I …"

"You and your ilk, Cody, wouldn't last five freakin' minutes out there," Andy said pointing in the direction of the factory floor.

"You know what else I think is tedious—having to drive down from Beverly Hills to Melrose Avenue and eat at *Chez Daniel's* or some other over-rated, over-priced, primped-up jizz-joint and be seen in the right car, wearing the right clothes, with the right people."

"Ahem, I think …"

"And forgive me for being such a consummate, incorrigible jackass that I fail to appreciate the glamour of a lifestyle consisting of a never-ending round of visits to your plastic surgeon, divorce lawyer, pimp, addiction counselor, junky and electro-shock therapist."

"Now, look here."

"No, I'm done looking. I do not want what you want me to want, Mr. Carlyle."

"What do you want, Mr. Dodge?"

"An ice-cold beer and a game of catch with my son, both of which you are keeping me from. This conversation is over."

After Carlyle had been shown to the door Andy returned to his office, flopped in his chair, closed his eyes and soaked in the silence. Guess one couldn't be a bobblehead forever, chuckling at the thought. People took a run at you. Not caring inevitably became not you. Words were the front line of defense. He was beginning to like words, much more than he once had. Still, there was only so much anyone could control. Even the president could have a hold put on his bank account. But there was something that stayed with you, regardless of how life might ambush you and force your hand. Perhaps he was naturally predisposed to carry on and be content regardless of his circumstances. Yet it was not so simple. Could he have started a new life in Cocoa Beach or Wheaton working as a human billboard, taken up surfing, perhaps even rallying for a comeback as a *bon vivant* insurance broker or Moose Lodge president? Perhaps. The will to survive was strong. But he would never, ever, be as happy as he was right now, at this moment. He stood up, tossed an operational manual on windmills into his briefcase, walked out the door, got into his car, pulled out of the parking lot and drove, steering in the direction of home.

EPILOGUE

The trawler *One If By Sea* plowed through choppy seas about 25 miles off the coast of southern Maine. It was the height of the soft-shell lobster season and skipper Tom Hardigan was out early to lay down a line of pots he hoped would outflank the other boats on the far edge of the shelf. The crew was preparing to pay out the traps and ground line when Captain Hardigan looked back from the wheelhouse and saw one of the crewmen waving from the main deck. "Come about, skip!" He heard the man shout, interpreting his hand signal to steer sharp to port. As the captain circled back, a group of men gathered along the gunnel, waving and shouting up directions to the wheelhouse. "Slow! Hold, HOLD!" The captain pulled back on the throttle to stall the boat and ordered the first mate to take the wheel. "This better be more entertaining than a piss break."

The men were leaning over the port side, making way for the crew chief who had fetched a gaffe hook. "Look at the fucking monster," one of the men said as the captain walked up and laid eyes on the largest great white shark he had ever seen bobbing belly-up in the swells slapping against the boat's hull.

"Holy mother of freakin' Mary," the captain said, gazing at the creature, its head alone the width of a brawny riding lawn mower.

"Pull on that thing, you old dick skinner!"

"It's too … fucking … big!"

"Bring the winch!" the captain yelled.

Two crewmen scampered up the catwalk to the winch platform. A signal man below snatched the hook and cable as it slackened, leading it toward the gunnel as the crane man extended the boom. A crewman attached an eighth-inch thick, double-loop steel lanyard to the hook and snapped a carabiner onto the loop at the other end. Four men yanked on the gaffe hook, pulling the shark close enough for the man to lean over, slit open a gash under its gills, ram the carabiner through its open mouth and out the incision, loop the lanyard back and attach the carabineer to the winch hook.

The winch pulled in the cable, straining against the rolling sea to lift the leviathan up and over the gunnel. The trawler began to list to port from the weight and the captain ordered the first mate to steer against the weight to keep the boat level. The winch had reeled in all the cable and at least five feet of shark was still in the water. Every man aboard pushed forward on the shark's huge sandpapery-like flank, as the crane man swung the beam of the hoist mid-stern. At last, the tail swung over the side, then whipped back as the tension on the cable released, scattering four crew men across the slick deck like bowling pins.

"Get the damn thing down!" the captain barked.

The creature took up a quarter the length of the trawler's main deck, over 25 feet. The boat's six crewmen stood on the shark's side as the captain snapped pictures with his cell. "Shouldn't we do an autopsy, skip?" One of the crewmen came up to the captain pulling out a 12-inch-long flensing knife from a sheath on his hip.

The man lanced the blade into the shark's belly just under the front dorsal fin and dragged it sternward as the animal's innards spilled across the deck like curdled crimson milk. The men gathered curiously around the carcass as their fellow crewman now nipped the tip of the blade into the shark's huge, distended stomach, turned his head, and ripped upward. The gray-green emulsified remains of past meals fairly exploded out of the punctured bladder, settling out in assorted-sized lumps and chunks. The men, repelled at first, now drew close to examine the mystery of the sea monster's dining pre-dilections. A foam shipping-channel buoy, a bottle of Old Grandad and a toy nerf gun were the least digested and most readily identi-fied items.

"Never heard of death by constipation, until now," the captain grunted.

"What the hell is this?" The man with the gaffe hook said, poking at a hefty, indistinguishable clump of matter on the deck. He wedged the hook under and flipped it and seven sailors recoiled and shrieked at the sight of a mangled, half-eaten human torso. Two crewmen ran to the gunnel holding their hands over their mouths.

"I'll radio the Coast Guard," the captain said after a minute.

"Hey, skipper, look here," one of the men said, reaching down into the slop. "A wallet!"

The captain took the faded leather wallet gingerly, wiped it with a rag one of the crew handed him, and pried it open.

"Lots of cash," he said, extracting a wad of soggy hundred-dollar bills. "Here's a card, let's see … and the winner of the all-in-clusive, swimming-with-the-sharks package for one, was …Eastman Finch … Dude," the captain said, looking down at the gnarled earthly remains. "You look more like Eastman Lunch."

The captain turned to walk back to the wheel.

"Hey, skip, what we do with that?" One of the men said, pointing to the shark's disemboweled carcass.

The captain turned and paused. "How long you think it's been dead, Jimmy?" He asked the crew chief.

"Not much bloating, no more than a few days."

The captain shrugged. "Butcher it and ice the meat. That's a goddamn delicacy to the Japs."

The 7th hole at Turnover Hills is a 122-yard par three made trickier by a green that is slightly elevated and sloped to the left toward the hole's only bunker. Marcia Riker-Dodge stood in the ladies' tee box, which shortened the hole to about 90 yards, lining up her shot.

"Do you think a five iron is enough club?" she asked her husband sitting in the cart.

It probably wasn't, Andy thought, but then it didn't really matter. His wife had only been playing the game about one month, since he had bought her a new set of Lady Wing-It golf clubs for their anniversary and hit every club about the same.

"Go ahead and hit it, honey," Andy said, adding, "Tee it up nice and high."

It was a balmy, brilliantly sunny late-September day and a

gentle breeze was tinged with a ripe, earthy aroma that signaled the approaching autumn. Andy smiled as he watched Marcia square up her shot, musing that, at one time, he would sooner have expected to come home and find their cat Archie smoking a Cohiba than to witness the day he'd be playing a game of golf with his wife. Marcia stared down in motionless concentration at the ball. She lifted the shaft of the club back and over her head, bringing it down in a quick, choppy stroke used by most beginners. The ball shot up in the air and Andy lost it in the bright sky.

"Where'd it go?

"Up the fairway a bit. I think you popped it up, honey."

"Damn it!" Marcia said slamming the iron into the ground and gazing up the fairway for a sign of her ball.

"Don't worry," Andy said. "Probably have a nice little six or seven iron to the green from there."

Andy had hit his ball in the bunker next to the green and they drove up the center of the fairway, expecting to catch sight of Marcia's ball in the first 30 or 40 yards. He slowed the cart, turning first to the left, then to the right. He drove up almost to the edge of the green, then circled back, crisscrossing the fairway several times.

"Must have gone into the trees to the right. Just hit a ball from here," Andy said, pointing to a spot about ten yards in front of the green.

Marcia dropped a ball, took out her wedge and swung, rolling onto the far fringe of the green.

"Good shot, honey." Andy said. "Meet you up there."

Andy parked the cart, grabbed his sand wedge and walked into the bunker. Marcia strolled across the green and put her hand on the flagstick waiting for Andy to shoot. Andy was just about to whack at his ball in the trap when Marcia shouted to him.

"Andrew, hold up. There's a ball already in the hole."

"Take it out, I'll catch up to the foursome in front of us and give it to them."

Marcia reached down and pulled the ball from the hole. "It's a Nike 3, with a pink logo."

It was the ball Marcia played. Andy stood up, blinked, exclaimed the holiness of shit, bounded out of the trap, heaved his wedge over his shoulder where it landed in the branches of an ash tree 100 feet away and ran toward his wife, who was standing on the green holding the ball with both hands in front of her mouth, open in shock.

"Oh my God, oh my God, OH my GOD!" Marcia began to jump up and down on the tips of her toes as Andy approached.

Andy spread his arms and Marcia, now bouncing as if on a pogo stick, hurled the golf ball in the air and ran, tossing herself into his arms. HOLE …IN …ONE …BABY!" Andy shouted, twirling her around as Marcia sent shrieks of joy into the air that could be heard all the way back to the clubhouse. Around and around they whirled, laughing and whooping, finally falling in a heap on the green, where Marcia crawled on top of Andy and began to kiss him.

"Thank you," Marcia said.

"What the heck for?"

"For expanding my horizons."

"I'll remind you of that on the next hole when you shoot a ten."

Marcia began to pummel him on the chest and shoulders with her fists as Andy, laughing hysterically, crossed his arms and curled his body into a fetal ball.

Back at the seventh tee, a retiree laboriously disembarked from his cart and shuffled a few paces down the cart path, peering with a puzzled expression in the direction of the hole.

"Is anyone on the green?" His wife asked.

"It appears as if someone is getting laid on the upslope side of the pin," the man said, his hand shielding his eyes against the sun.

"Will wonders never cease!" the woman said disgustedly, and with a groan extricated herself from the cart and stood to have a better look. "Isn't that against the rules?"

The man pulled on his cap, shrugged and turned to walk back to the cart. "Not if the stick isn't in the hole yet."

THE END